FRUITCAKE

The truth is out there

Beth Woffenden

Beth Woffenden
July 2018

Visit me on t'internet at:

https://www.facebook.com/WofferBooks/

https://twitter.com/WofferBooks

ACKNOWLEDGEMENTS and AUTHOR'S NOTE

So... welcome to round two and huge thanks for purchasing this second book and previously, I assume, the first in the trilogy (i.e. Nutjob). I hope you'll enjoy the read and come back for the final instalment (i.e. Crackers) in 2019.

Again, I'd like to thank numerous people who helped me to get Fruitcake into the public domain. As mentioned in Nutjob, my parents thoroughly enjoyed cat-sitting whilst I was roadtrippin' stateside (checking out roadside body dump sites, more like); SSA Joseph Lewis and Linda Watkins from the FBI continued to answer the questions Google couldn't; Claudia Tejeda brought the horchata, although I'm yet to bring the margaritas to my expert on all things Mexican (which is probably due to her actually being Mexican...); the good people of the Absolute Write Water Cooler forums continued to answer my downright weird questions with politeness and good grace; Victoria Melia at Hawkeye Proofreading dealt with my hyphen phobia; and too many unknown strangers filled in those little snippets that make all the difference.

New faces appeared in the form of three detectives from Lancashire Police's Cold Case unit, namely Dave Meadows, Lisa Baxter and Ian McVittie (a.k.a. Jaffa). Their insights and patience in explaining how they would investigate the Preston-based parts of the case were an immense help in adding authenticity to Boothroyd and his team's role in the story. Hope you enjoyed the "Serial Killer Cake", folks!

Hazel Stephenson at MEL Chemicals, Manchester carried out a workplace profiling assessment on *Mr Good Guy* and *Mr Bad Guy* (and yours truly!), which offered insights into their personalities and helped me to decide how both would react to some of the situations they experienced. Apparently I have a very *blue* personality, which roughly translates to being anally retentive and a stickler for detail. There's worse things to be, I suppose!

As in Nutjob, there are many instances in the storyline of combining fact and fiction; for example, certain FBI departments and where specific teams of detectives work from. Most of the locations mentioned do actually exist, although I may have fictionalised the finer details of some settings and, to varying degrees, fabricated the interior of almost every building that isn't fictitious. Names, characters, events and incidents are either the products of my imagination or used in a fictitious manner. Any resemblance to actual persons, living or dead, or actual events is purely coincidental.

Lastly, chapter 24 is dedicated to a very special group of people who survived the 2012-13 academic year and beyond. You know who you are.

And with *that* out of the way (again), all I now ask is that you please enjoy this next instalment of the Unholy Trilogy (its unofficial name continues to stick)...

Prologue – Saturday 22nd August 2009

9.17pm – EDT
Arrivals, JFK International Airport, New York

Maria Volonte unclasped her wrinkled hands and focussed on the procession of weary travellers leaving Immigration and Customs' air-conditioned comfort. Her fingers drummed against the railings, hinting at her frustration now that the last person had passed through a pair of sliding glass doors and into the anonymous humidity of a New York summer evening.

'Where's my boy, Vinnie?' she snapped. 'He texted to say he was waiting in line to board, but you remember what these kids are like. They're always getting themselves into mischief.'

Vincenzo Volonte's dark eyes rolled skyward as he patted his wife's tense shoulder. 'I'd hardly call him a kid, Bella. He's thirty-five and he's bringing his fiancée, and he's probably gotten stuck at the back of the line. We already discussed how Franco received Giuseppe's share of the timekeeping genes. It's a goddamn miracle he actually got his ass on that flight. That boy's too–'

Maria's squeal interrupted him, the high-pitched sound startling an elderly man behind her.

'My baby boy! Giuseppe!'

Vinnie's frown deepened when he took a second look at the black-haired man pulling a silver trolley case. 'That's not him, Maria. You should think about getting a sight check. Sears has some good offers this month.'

She met him with a quizzical expression and returned her attention to another small group of passengers who'd arrived after their long journey from London. 'It's not Giuseppe?'

'No, that guy's alone and he's wearing glasses, like you need to,' Vinnie replied as he scanned a larger wave of emerging people.

'You're really sure?' Maria asked. She fixed Vinnie in an iron stare and moved her hands to her hips. 'You ain't getting any younger either, smart ass, and don't you forget it.'

'He'll be out in a minute.' Vinnie's tone revealed his exasperation. 'You know what Carmela looks like, don't you?'

Maria shook her head. Perhaps old age really had sunk its evil claws into her, defying her best efforts to remain physically and mentally young? She continued to watch the familiar man she'd mistaken for her nephew, turning away only after he'd walked through the glass doors and into the darkness.

Chapter 1 – Wednesday 22nd July 2009

7.03pm – PDT
Los Angeles International Airport, California

Jesus wept! How much longer?

A steady procession of people filed onto the plane, repeatedly scanning the printed combinations of letters and numbers on their boarding passes and the corresponding symbols beneath the overhead baggage compartments. One by one they located their seats; those closest to the windows having no option other than to drop into the grey and red upholstered foam with ungainly relief.

Thank Christ they gave me an aisle seat.

Konrad Kratz closed his eyes and gritted his teeth. The extra Percocet he'd swallowed a couple of hours earlier had merely taken the edge off his throbbing gunshot wounds and a dull ache in his ribs. It was a damn shame the pounding in his head remained in the form of a compressive band now threatening to eject his eyes from their sockets.

He contemplated the more serious of the injuries he'd sustained five days earlier at the hands of the Fernandez brothers and their cousin, Carlito. The wound where the bullet exited his torso appeared to have developed an infection, in contrast to the slightly tender entrance wound that was already starting to heal. Hopefully the remaining antibiotics stowed in his hold luggage would be enough to treat the sepsis before it got worse – assuming the pills made it through customs. His chest felt noticeably sore every time he moved; its livid blue bruises a constant reminder of where Carlito Read acquainted him with a baseball bat more than once.

You shouldn't really think ill of the dead.

To the best of Konrad's knowledge, Read remained propped up behind a boulder in Death Valley, mummifying in the relentless desert sun. In the unlikely event someone walked behind that particular rock, he'd carefully planted enough evidence that night *and* over the past few weeks for Konrad Kratz to be confirmed dead.

The flight was due to land in Zürich the following afternoon, around four o'clock Swiss time. He recalled two family vacations spent at his mother's cousin's apartment in the city and anticipated a timely touchdown to conform to that age-old stereotype. Back in the eighties, Liesel, Chris and Peter Umpleby had been delighted to receive an invitation to stay in the spacious apartment owned by Gretel Baum in the city's Stadelhofen area. Used to the unpredictability of English life, the clean and efficient Swiss way of doing things and how easily they could be disrupted highly amused *Peter*. Another invite had never been forthcoming.

He planned to make his way to Stadelhofen on arrival and book into one of its many hotels, all situated conveniently close to the city centre and only a short train journey from the *Flughafen*. There was then the issue of obtaining a new supply of whatever the hell the Swiss called Percocet, or maybe something of a similar potency. This had to be his number one priority after exchanging some of the one hundred dollar bills he'd hidden between the pages of a bible for a supply of Swiss francs.

Konrad gazed at the finely crafted Rolex he'd purchased earlier that month in Phoenix. He'd keep possession of it, knowing that one day it would eventually justify its purchase.

'Excuse me, sir.'

His eyes met those of a dark-haired woman he vaguely recognised from the check-in line. 'That's my seat,' she continued, pointing to the empty space between Konrad and an elderly Swiss gentleman next to the window.

'Uh... yeah, sorry.' He pulled himself to his feet and stepped into the aisle. Why was it taking her so long to lift her hand baggage into the overhead locker and take her place? He noticed her watching him support his side and grit his teeth as he lowered himself into the seat again.

'Are you okay?' she asked when his complexion paled.

Konrad nodded and took a shuddering breath. 'Yeah, I'm fine.'

'Don't think I'm being rude, but you look sick,' she replied, remembering he'd displayed the same tension at check-in.

'I'm not the best flyer.'

Obvious concern replaced her curiosity. 'Does it always make you this nervous?'

'Only since a bad landing in London a few years ago,' Konrad said. He leaned his head against the headrest and closed his eyes. 'I'll be okay once we're up in the air. At least if anything goes wrong mid-flight and the pressure drops we'll all be unconscious in seconds, so we won't feel a thing.'

She raised her eyebrows and wondered if she needed to reassess her perspective of flying. 'If I can do anything for you, just ask,' she eventually said. 'I'm Freya, by the way.'

He turned to face her and opened a reddened eye. 'I'm Thomas. Pleased to meet you, although it would've been preferable under different circumstances.'

I'll say. We could've had some fun together. I'd have shown you the best time of your life.

She removed a well-worn copy of *The Shining* and a packet of mixed candies from her bag. 'So, what's a Brit doing on a flight from America to Switzerland?'

'Long story,' he muttered. One of his hands remained firmly pressed above his waist as if able to dispel the pain caused by getting up from his seat. 'I've lived in Palmdale for six years, since my job transferred from London. The firm's opening an office in Zürich and muggins here is spending the week there in an advisory capacity. You'd think the Swiss would already know enough about banking.'

Freya switched off her cell phone and smiled at his transparent attempt to lighten the atmosphere. 'Have you been to Switzerland before?'

'A couple of times as a kid. My great-grandparents were Swiss but they died when I was young.'

That's the first thing you've fed her that's not bullshit.

He coughed a couple of times and grimaced as the pounding in his head resumed. 'God, I really should get a grip; I've given myself a bloody migraine over it. So, why are *you* sitting next to me?'

'I work for a publishing house,' she replied. 'We're putting together a guide book about European city breaks. I'm in Switzerland for four weeks researching Zürich, Luzern, Geneva and Bern.'

'Nice work if you can get it.'

She shook her head. 'Folks think it's glamorous, but you need a vacation to get over these work trips. I'll race around for the whole month checking out locations without taking the time to properly enjoy them. I can't even relax properly in an evening because I need to type up my notes while everything's still fresh in my mind.'

'Yeah, I can imagine,' he replied. A sudden chill passed through him and he wondered why the heating hadn't come on.

Freya looked closely at his pallid face. 'Did we ever meet before?'

'Not that I recall, and I'd certainly recall such a meeting.'

She unconsciously twirled a section of hair around a carefully manicured finger. 'You're a real charmer, right?'

Butter her up… deflect the conversation onto another topic.

'Just honest. I'd never forget a beautiful woman like you.'

'You're kind of familiar, like I met you someplace else.' She thought for a couple of seconds. 'I live in Castaic. Did you ever go there, like for work?'

I've probably been to Castaic. Most likely as a photo on your television screen with a Fed giving you the lowdown.

He shook his head. 'Not since last summer. It's lovely there, isn't it?'

'Sure is, especially around the Lagoon. You must have a double,' Freya said. She offered him the bag of candy.

'No, thank you,' Konrad replied. The thought of eating anything enticed his previous nausea to return with a vengeance. 'He'll be pretty handsome if he's stuck in your mind for this long. All my relatives are in London and Kent, so it must be a coincidence.'

She sensed she'd missed something important and smiled at him, not wanting to press the issue. 'I guess so. Anyway, you should take a rest. Good to meet you, Thomas.'

'Likewise, Freya,' he replied, closed his eyes and swallowed hard. The pilot's pre-flight announcement commenced as the flight attendants took their positions for the on-board safety display.

'Maybe we'll see each other in Zürich over the weekend?' she added.

You'd better hope for your sake that we don't.

****

San Fernando Road, Los Angeles, California

LAPD detective Ronnie Mosley smoothed a hand over his neatly trimmed grey hair and stared vacantly at the laptop on his desk. 'Christ, someone hook me up to a caffeine IV.'

Fellow detectives Dave Hallberg and Emilio Muñoz rubbed their aching heads in unison, the latter twisting his neck to one side to produce a loud crack.

Mosley's sharp eyes looked daggers at Muñoz. 'Quit doing that!'

The men had worked as a trio prior to their team expanding by one when rookie cop Alex Gibson impressed the station's Commanding Officer. The slightly-built young man regularly called upon his knowledge of the neighbourhood he'd been raised in, and ably assisted Mosley in solving three high profile murders produced by a drug-related feud. He'd been immediately welcomed by Muñoz and Hallberg, who at that time were both relatively new to Mosley's team. Thirteen years later the four detectives were still a tight unit, keen to maintain their reputation as a formidable investigative force at LAPD's Northeast Division.

Gibson stared at the left half of his desk, which remained piled high with case files after the revelations of three weeks earlier. Since then, he'd put in fourteen-hour shifts on all but two days and the resulting chronic sleep deprivation, a junk food diet and chain-drinking anything caffeinated had already taken a physical and mental toll. The team's steady review of any unsolved homicides possibly pertaining to Konrad Kratz soon became all-consuming, able to produce a fresh groan of despair whenever another case file landed on Mosley's equally cluttered desk.

The heels of Gibson's hands pressed against his tightly-closed eyes. 'Man, I don't know how much longer I can keep this up. Seriously guys, we can't be effective in this state. The alarm went off this morning and it was like I'd woken up dead. We *all* need a break. Even one day would make a difference.'

'I totally hear you,' Mosley said. He sucked stale air through his teeth and felt a nerve in his left eyelid twitch into life. 'Until we catch this bastard a normal existence goes straight out of the window.'

'Those hooker murders may be swamping Robbery-Homicide, but the Chief said their Cold Case Special Section will try to investigate any local unsolved cases with new leads we bring to their attention,' Gibson added. 'At least we don't have to take on that side of things.'

Hallberg carefully spread peanut butter and grape jelly onto a pile of crackers. 'Is the DNA back on Kratz's body, assuming it's really his?' he asked in a tone veering between hopeful and desperate.

'You'll be lucky,' Mosley replied, eyeing the plate enviously. 'We sent the sample on Monday and there's one hell of a backlog. They said it'll be over a week, even though we paid megabucks for the express service. Tony Pell's trying to pull some strings, but if nothing happens over the weekend I'll head on over to the labs and refuse to leave without it.'

Muñoz distributed four large cups of station house coffee. 'Are you buying that this body is actually Kratz's?' he asked. 'It's strange for the killer to take the time to cut off his fingers and leave a driver's licence in his pocket.'

'It's like whoever dumped the body wants to convince us it belongs to Kratz,' Gibson mused. He sipped his drink and winced. 'This stuff gets nastier by the day!'

Mosley accepted the anaemic-looking concoction, reached into his top drawer and pulled out an unopened packet of chocolate cookies to mask the coffee's surprising level of bitterness. 'The evidence fits, although I agree it's almost too convenient. Call me a cynical old bastard, but if something seems too good to be true, it usually is. My alimony payments are proof of that.'

Chapter 2 – Thursday 23rd July 2009

7.15am – PDT
Eagle Rock, Los Angeles, California

Joel Hattersley placed a crate of beer into the trunk of his 1957 Chevy and, after quickly checking he'd stowed everything he intended to, carefully closed the lid. The red soft top Bel Air had proved to be an enjoyable restoration project; a welcome distraction from the acrimonious divorce digging its poisonous tentacles further into his sanity each day. Satisfied he'd securely locked his neatly maintained home, Joel admired the car from a short distance before climbing behind the wheel.

His gaze alternated between two CDs he'd picked up and Joel took a few seconds to ruminate over whether Bruce Springsteen or Van Halen would accompany his journey. The next five nights at the Chula Vista home of his old college buddy Kenny, also newly single, were filled with the promise of reliving old times. He slid a disc into the CD player and stretched a grin across his tanned face when the first riffs blasted out of his new speakers.

I'm sure as hell bet good ol' Bruce approves.

Joel accelerated onto the street, oblivious to a small, black puddle on his driveway.

****

4.28pm – CEST
Zürich Airport, Switzerland

As predicted, the flight landed close to its expected arrival time and disembarkation passed swiftly and without incident. A slow walk across the tarmac took the passengers into the terminal building, where Konrad locked himself in a toilet cubicle to tend his wounds. Much to his relief, there had been no obvious deterioration since an inspection in the aeroplane toilet's cramped surroundings five hours earlier; a possibility he'd dreaded.

The entrance wound continued to heal cleanly, although its evil twin throbbed to an infected rhythm where the bullet exited his body. He'd carefully used a tissue to dab away a small amount of thick, yellow pus, wrinkled his nose and dropped the flimsy paper into the toilet. Konrad exited the stall and made his way to where a group of businessmen he recognised from the flight and a Japanese school party now waited for the *Skymetro* to arrive.

The crowded train, reminiscent of a cattle truck's interior, sped through a brightly lit tunnel towards passport control; the freedom promised beyond its checkpoint tantalisingly close. Assorted sounds of mooing cows and alpine horns piped into the carriage did nothing to alleviate Konrad's physical or mental discomfort, his additional irritation the result of a couple of the businessmen imitating the cow with monotonous regularity for the trip's duration. A multi-language information bulletin ended and the train slowed to a halt, before its doors slid open to release the passengers from their glass cocoon.

Konrad's already heavy heart sunk further when he reached the escalators and saw the crowds in front of the gates. He already felt decidedly strange, thanks to a full day without proper sleep, minimal food intake, a minor concussion and an infected gunshot wound conspiring against him. The recent decline in the amount of Percocet in his system probably wasn't helping matters either.

He retrieved the passport from his backpack, headed for the smaller EU and Swiss Nationals queue and breathed deeply to alleviate a sudden unpleasant combination of trepidation and nausea. Konrad maintained his faith in another successful quest for freedom. If the fake passport had managed to fool fastidious US-based officials, he couldn't think of any reason why their equally anally-retentive Swiss counterparts wouldn't accept it unquestioningly.

Proven correct and painfully aware of the stinging in his side, he found the baggage reclaim area and waited for a haphazard assortment of luggage to appear on the carousel. Sod's Law dictated his must be the last to emerge, but it was a pleasant surprise to see the silver case near the front – intact after another long journey and two sets of baggage handlers.

To his relief, everything was plain sailing from that point: through the *Nothing to Declare* customs channel, across a crowded arrival hall, through a pair of double doors and into the cool, damp air. The taxi rank's surface suggested the light rain had fallen steadily for hours, seemingly confirmed by the constant procession of vehicles sending a constant fine spray into the air. Konrad aimed a longing stare at a row of taxis, almost overwhelmed by the urge to sink into the leather upholstery of the nearest Mercedes.

Instead, he reluctantly adjusted his backpack and dragged the trolley case to the adjacent *Bahnhof*. The escalator's descent into the ticket office provided an opportunity to check the lower level for *die Bullen*, or whoever else might be waiting for him. A nearby Bureau de Change caught his attention where, for the first time in his life, Konrad experienced a small degree of gratitude for his late mother's insistence on regularly speaking German at home.

Another survey of the concourse yielded no visible threats and, after a greedy self-service ticket machine snatched the twenty franc note he'd fed it, Konrad approached another group of escalators. He descended further underground, relieved to see *Hauptbahnhof* in electronic yellow letters on the front of a two-level S-bahn train approaching the subterranean platform.

****

7.52am – PDT
Glendale Freeway, Los Angeles, California

'Too fuckin' early, man!' Esteban Fernandez scowled at his failed attempt to recline the Dodge pick-up's front passenger seat. 'I need my bed so, so bad.'

Paco cuffed the side of his eldest son's shaved head. 'Don't be such a goddamn pussy. You know we've been told to get to Silvia's place fast, before the old lady meets her maker. Cousin Alejandro says the end is close.'

19

'Mom says she'll enjoy the heat downstairs,' Milagros added from her cramped back seat position between their younger brothers, Luis and Rico. 'Don't blame her refusing to come. Did you hear what Silvia said when Abuelo was murdered?'

The grey hair around Paco's temples caught the early morning sunlight as he nodded. 'Your mom bought it?' he asked, steering across to the lane on their right.

'What the hell didn't you tell her?' she snapped, confused by Paco's comment.

Her father checked the rear-view mirror and grinned. 'Silvia ain't the main reason we're going to Tijuana. Got some other business to attend to, right?'

Luis and Rico smiled eagerly as their dark heads nodded in unison.

Milagros pushed her sunglasses to the top of her head and squinted at her father. 'You can leave me in San Diego today, because *I'm* now going shopping. Don't want none of your hinky shit,' she added. 'There's been enough of all that already.'

The pick-up left the freeway and kept right as Paco followed a series of signs for I-5. Esteban looked at her over his shoulder. 'That's your choice, Mila, but we're still going to Silvia's place once we're over the border. First stop. Just sayin'.'

She shook her head and thought she detected something more sinister in his expression. 'No, you take me to cousin Raquel's place in Paradise Hills. She don't work on a Thur–'

Esteban noticed a vintage soft top passing the group of palm trees ahead of them. 'Hey, cool car!' he exclaimed. 'Always wanted to get me a Chevy like that. Man, think of all the ladies wanting a piece of my dick if I was behind the wheel.'

The road curved to the right and all four men stared admiringly at the sleek red car approaching a series of overpasses. 'That is one *sweet* set of wheels,' Luis agreed. 'Damn shame that old Mustang didn't make it past–'

The Bel Air's brake lights unexpectedly lit up. 'What's he doing?' Panic thickened Rico's voice. The smaller car decelerated, its warning lights flashing. 'Slow the fuck down, man!' he screamed as the distance between the two vehicles rapidly closed.

Esteban's eyes were wide open, all thoughts of his comfortable bed forgotten. 'What the hell's on the road?'

The Dodge skidded on the asphalt and Paco's muscular arms frantically attempted to correct its steering. 'Fuck! Won't stop"

Before its occupants could comprehend what was happening, the vehicle slammed into a concrete wall and instantly deflected into a pirouette. It spun across both lanes, coming to a sharp stop when a supporting pillar ploughed through its hood and into the mangled interior; the scene watched by horrified commuters who, until seconds earlier, were following their own usual weekday routines.

Inside the Dodge silence reigned over the carnage for a split second, until a deafening explosion reverberated around the area.

Chapter 3 – Friday 24th July 2009

8.27am – PDT
San Fernando Road, Los Angeles, California

Hallberg dragged his gaze away from the large bottle of champagne on Mosley's desk to check a large clock on the opposite wall. 'I always said he's a goddamn alcoholic,' he commented, his flat voice not conveying the attempt at humour as well as he'd intended.

Gibson's bloodshot eyes reopened and stared across the homicide incident room to where Muñoz had slumped lower and lower in his seat since his arrival. Mosley's unconventional choice of early morning beverage would usually pique their curiosity, but the more immediate concern was to replenish their caffeine levels now a new day had ended another night of fractured sleep.

Mosley grinned, his uncharacteristic happiness unnerving the other detectives. 'This bad boy's been sitting in my locker for over fifteen years.' He took a deep breath and watched them wrinkle their noses. 'Today, the cork pops. The big dude in the sky has gotten around to answering my prayers.' He paused again and narrowed his eyes this time. 'Even if he did take his fucking time over it.'

Hallberg raised an eyebrow and tried to ignore his rumbling stomach. 'Your ex-wife got hit by a Mack truck?'

Mosley shook his head and rubbed his hands together. 'Better!'

'We give up, boss.' Muñoz shrugged, too tired to humour him.

'Remember that fatal MVA on the freeway yesterday morning?' Mosley teased, lovingly caressing the bottle's curved exterior.

Gibson continued spooning instant coffee granules into a plastic cup of dishwater-coloured liquid from the vending machine. 'The pick-up truck that carved itself in half?'

Mosley nodded. 'That's the one. Some old Bel Air's oil pan gave out and dropped a load on the surface. The pick-up directly behind skidded on it, slammed into the wall, slid across the road and crashed into those pillars supporting the Glendale Freeway overpass.'

'Still ain't getting it, boss,' Muñoz muttered whilst thumbing through a new case file he'd found on his desk.

'Four birds killed by one stone,' Mosley continued. He popped the tab on a can of Red Bull instead of the champagne's cork and took a swig. 'Okay, so the girl was collateral damage; some things can't be helped.'

Gibson exchanged the coffee granules for sugar and a confused expression. 'Four birds? I thought five died.'

'Paco Fernandez and his asswipe sons are partying in the morgue.' Mosley reclined his chair and stretched his arms out to each side. 'It's like Christmas come early.'

'No shit! It was their vehicle? They're *all* dead?' Hallberg spluttered, his idea of suggesting they go out for breakfast now forgotten.

Mosley nodded and punched the air in jubilation. 'They sure are! Don't it feel awesome?'

Muñoz glanced sideways at Mosley and sipped his drink. 'It went up in a fireball, yeah?'

'Oh yeah,' he replied. 'Crispy around the edges, if you know what I'm saying. Who needs a KFC when you can have CFF?'

'CFF?' Muñoz echoed, not entirely sure he wanted clarification.

The older man snorted with laughter. 'California Fried Fernandez. Anyway, I feel an early finish coming on today.' His grin widened as he surveyed their astounded faces. 'And, I may even shout you all a beer.'

****

9.29am – PDT
Libby Drive, Las Vegas, Nevada

Sarah Greenwood stood in front of her bedroom window, resting her hands on her ample hips as she stared across the quiet street she'd called home for the past eleven years. 'I'm calling them. Should have done it days ago,' she repeated, her posture reflecting her present bad mood.

'How do you know it don't belong to one of the neighbours?' her husband asked. His unease increased when her frown deepened, certain of the outcome if he failed to agree.

She pursed her thin lips, causing Darren to blink nervously. 'A hunk of junk with a California plate? It's been abandoned, I tell you,' she replied, exasperated he continued to stall about phoning the local police.

'Awww, do you think there's a body in the trunk?' he said. The mocking inflection in his tone wasn't lost on Sarah.

'You wanna be that body?' she retorted as she fixed him in a withering gaze.

Fourteen years of marriage meant Darren knew when the time had come to backtrack. 'Call the cops, if you seriously believe they'll come out for *that*.'

Sarah grabbed her cell phone from the dresser and scrolled through her contacts. 'I'd like to see those douchebags refuse.'

****

10.03am – PDT
San Fernando Road, Los Angeles, California

An olive-skinned couple in their early fifties waited second in line at the police station's front desk, wishing the elderly man ahead of them would hurry up and finish his complaint about an upsurge in dog fouling around the neighbourhood. Miguel Read placed a thin arm around his wife's shoulders and gave her a reassuring squeeze. 'C'mon sweetheart, I'm sure we don't need to do this. You know what Carlito's like, he'll be running with his boys somewhere.'

Ella sniffed and dabbed a faded cotton handkerchief under her nose. 'That's what worries me. I know exactly what he's like. He tries to be a badass but really he's just Momma's sweet baby. You know they all take advantage of him, especially Paco's boys.'

Miguel nodded. 'This time I think they're telling the truth. I saw Esteban on Tuesday in the 7-Eleven on South Glendale. He said he ain't seen *El Güero* for over a week.'

'El Güero,' she echoed, fresh tears streaming down her pinched cheeks. 'Why couldn't he have hung out with those nice kids on the block Sasha knows?'

Miguel's thoughts turned to their daughter, an attractive brunette fourteen months older than her brother who easily passed for a full-blooded Latina. 'I guess she don't feel she has to prove herself,' he replied. 'Can't have been easy for Carlito, looking so different.'

More tears filled her large hazel eyes. 'What if something bad happened to him this time?' she whispered.

'The worst that'll happen is that I'll kick his sorry ass for putting you through this crap as soon as he comes home,' Miguel replied, his tone tense.

The elderly man shuffled to the exit as the officer on duty turned away from her computer and rubbed a tanned hand over her forehead. 'Good morning, sir. How can I assist you today?' she asked, sounding more cheerful than she appeared.

Miguel mirrored her strained smile. 'Good morning, ma'am. My wife and I are here to report our son missing.'

****

1.46pm – PDT
LVPD, Las Vegas, Nevada

Crime Scene Investigator Elliot Lloyd reared his sandy-coloured head seconds after a tow-truck pulled up in the Crime Lab's parking lot, an elderly Mercedes strapped to its flatbed.

'What the hell is that?' he asked through a mouthful of the triple cheeseburger he'd craved all morning, after waking up too late to grab breakfast. 'There's plenty of scrap yards in Nellis; that thing needs rerouting.' He glared at the nearby motorbike he'd been dusting for fingerprints. 'As does this piece of crap.'

Helen Kinski set down a double shot latte and Bavarian cream doughnut she'd bought minutes earlier from the new branch of Holey Heaven Donut Shack half a block away. 'Castro phoned it through while I was out getting lunch,' she replied. 'Some snotty bitch called it in to the cops this morning. They were going to tow it straight to the lot and

25

decided to pop the trunk. You know, see if there's any evidence to identify the owner.'

'Who does it belong to?' Lloyd asked. He narrowed his eyes to bring the vehicle's rear end into sharper focus. 'Looks like a Cali plate.'

A nod of her head made her thick, black curls bob up and down. 'Yeah, according to the DMV it's owned by some guy from La La Land who goes by the name of Carlito Read.'

'Another out of town prick who's lost his ride?' He rolled his eyes. 'So, call him up and tell him to get his fat, lazy ass around here to collect it.'

'Let me finish; it ain't that simple. Cops put his details through CODIS to see if he has any prior convictions suggesting why the car's been dumped in Vegas for nearly a week. This morning his parents filed a missing person's report on him.'

'The dude obviously ain't in the trunk.' Lloyd sniffed the air in an exaggerated manner.

'Yeah, but a dried up blood pool is,' she replied. 'We've been told to go over the whole car with a fine toothcomb and see what else turns up. Kareem wants the blood samples and anything else we find in the lab by six, so finish your burger and get suited up.'

****

6.21pm – PDT
San Fernando Road, Los Angeles, California

'Man, give me a couple of beers and I'll sleep like the dead tonight,' Gibson said. He massaged his aching neck whilst his laptop initiated its *shut down* procedure. 'I feel like shit.'

Muñoz and Hallberg nodded their agreement, even though the homicide incident room's atmosphere was the lightest they remembered in months. The Fernandez family's decimation guaranteed a short period of respite for the detectives – until another criminal clan stepped into their newly vacated spot.

Hallberg stared at the door. 'Where's the boss?' he asked. 'I told my wife I'd be working late again, so I need a beer and a nice big plate of nachos before I head home.' He frowned, imagining the plateful of *green stuff* in the refrigerator ready and waiting for him.

'It's for your own benefit, big guy.' Gibson eyed the other man's midriff. 'Think of all the good you're doing for your ticker.'

'It's going to stop from a lack of food,' he grumbled. 'I still say she's trying to kill me. Can't you guys investigate her? You can't leave my kids without a father, right?'

Muñoz's chuckle died when the door rebounded off the wall and Mosley strode into the room. Immediate silence descended at the sight of his apoplectic expression.

'No goddamn beers for us this evening, or for the foreseeable future,' he raged, thrusting wads of printed paper at the three detectives. 'CSI went over Paco Fernandez's pick-up again this morning and found all its brake lines had been punctured. Luckily, even if it doesn't feel that way at this exact moment, the fire crews arrived in time to save enough of the vehicle's underside. They then went to the family home and examined the family's other cars. All the vehicles were sabotaged in the same way.'

'Punctured brake lines?' Hallberg repeated, aware of the sinking sensation that had replaced the hollow one in his gut.

Mosley nodded and realised by Hallberg's frown he'd also reached the same conclusion.

'You know it's probably a coincidence?' Gibson's feigned optimism failed to convince anyone. He looked at a box of barely touched case files on his desk and felt his heart rate speed up.

Mosley nodded. 'If you ask me it's way too much of a coincidence. Looks like we're duty-bound to investigate the possibility that piece of shit Konrad Kratz ain't really dead.'

Chapter 4 – Saturday 25th July 2009

'Gentlemen,' Mosley said, his resumed jovial manner disconcerting as he pinned a photo onto the incident room's main notice board. 'I'd like to introduce you to Carlito Read.'

Gibson sipped his coffee and squinted at the image of a fair-haired man in his early thirties. 'Is that the guy whose parents filed a missing person report yesterday?'

'Yeah, that's him,' Mosley replied. 'I've gotten news of recent developments which may make this more than a missing person's case. After his parents reported Read missing from home for over a week, I assumed he'd gone somewhere with those Fernandez cousins of his.'

'He's a relative of Paco's?' Gibson asked, trying to recall the family tree Mosley had shown to him around the time he'd joined the team.

Muñoz nodded and stirred creamer into a large cup of coffee. 'Great-nephew once removed or something similar, although he's never really drifted across the radar. We theorised the Three Amigos only ran with him because Carlito looks like a gringo so, using their logic, it'd be less likely he'd get stopped by the cops.'

Mosley laughed. 'Who are you calling a goddamn gringo?'

'Best of both, so I can take either side in an argument.' Muñoz grinned and eased an oatmeal breakfast muffin from a paper bag. 'This guy is half-Mexican, half-British on both sides. I guess the recessive genes got together for a tea party.'

Hallberg cast a wistful eye at the muffin. 'So why's his face gracing the board?' he asked, momentarily sad for the man smiling down on their breakfast briefing.

'I took a call from the Las Vegas Crime Lab last night, soon after you guys left,' Mosley replied. 'Yesterday morning, some broad called in a California-registered Merc abandoned on her street for days. The cops decided to check out the trunk for anything they could use to identify the owner before it got towed and found a blood pool and little else. The plates were run through DMV records and the owner confirmed as one Carlito Read of Atwater Village.'

'So they suspect foul play?' Hallberg asked, sipping the fruit smoothie his wife had thrust into his hand on their way out of the house.

Mosley shrugged. 'That's the line of inquiry they're following, unless they uncover evidence to prove otherwise. The blood was sent for urgent DNA analysis and they're trying to trace the car's last movements in Vegas. Read's not in CODIS, so we asked his father to bring in a toothbrush and hairbrush for the lab to extract a reference sample from.'

Muñoz failed to suppress a yawn. 'How long before the results come through?' he asked, hoping he wouldn't rack up another late finish.

'I told them it's urgent and they gave their usual line about trying to get it to us in less than a week,' Mosley replied. 'I know we don't need this shit but, assuming the blood matches Read's DNA and someone locates his body, this should be a relatively easy case.'

****

7.41pm – CEST
Kreuzplatz, Zürich, Switzerland

A pair of flies buzzed lazy circles around Konrad's head, infuriating him with their resistance to his attempts to swat them towards a different area of the coffee house. The barista cast him a cursory glance and then returned to her task of preparing a latte for the smartly dressed woman who'd perched herself on a high stool. Konrad surveyed his surroundings from a sofa directly opposite the door, his senses sharpened by the caffeine from his second cappuccino.

He broke off another piece of muffin and realised – for the first time in over a week – the taste of food didn't generate disgust, now his injuries no longer dictated every action and reaction. The more-than-likely cracked ribs had definitely undergone a slight improvement and he noted that, despite some residual tenderness, the exit wound felt considerably better than when he'd arrived in Zürich two days earlier.

Konrad picked up his cup, swallowed the last of its contents and thought back to his first day in the city. By the time he'd negotiated his route to Stadelhofen and emerged from its underground shopping area into daylight, he'd barely been able to muster enough energy to drag his case to his destination. The hotel, modest by Swiss standards, was chosen years ago; his earlier research compiling a helpful itinerary of where to go if he ever needed to make good on his escape plans.

Because you just never know when it'll all go tits-up.

The Percocet he'd discarded in an airport trashcan before check-in had taunted him from afar; the hot waves of burning pain in his flank impossible to ignore. The lure of collapsing onto the large bed and sleeping for days became a temptation almost too great to resist, but he somehow found the strength to leave the hotel. He'd soon returned to his room for a couple of hours, stretched out on the bed and fell into a fitful doze; the generic painkillers purchased at an *Apotheke* visible from his current position barely scratching the surface.

The main (if not only) advantage of strongly resembling a walking corpse meant it had been easier, albeit more expensive than anticipated, to obtain a week's supply of Oxycodone. Within minutes of finding a seat in the seediest – again, by Swiss standards – bar he could find he'd been approached by a small, thin man, who'd wasted no time in asking exactly what he was *interested* in.

The guy, probably only in his mid-twenties, readily swallowed Konrad's story about a recent relocation from Germany. They'd reconvened an hour later on Münsterbrücke and walked along the narrow cobbled streets to Stadelhofen, where a wad of colourful banknotes disappeared into one of Reto Meier's trouser pockets as he'd simultaneously pulled an innocuous plastic bottle of pills from the other.

Konrad placed his empty cup and plate on the counter, nodded a farewell to the barista and emerged onto the pavement. His surroundings continued to bustle with trams and pedestrians as he walked along leafy streets past rows of neat apartment blocks, then turned onto a narrow road. It didn't take long to cover the last stretch to Seefeldquai, where he squeezed through a line of parked cars and approached a wooden bench overlooking Lake Zürich.

The evening air's humidity increased closer to the water, carrying the threat of thunderstorms for the following day. Seconds later, a prickling sensation announced another mosquito bite to add to the substantial collection he'd already acquired. Konrad scowled and slapped his arm. The little bastards were certainly quite partial to foreign food. He repeatedly looked in both directions along the wide, tree-lined path running parallel to the lakeside until Meier appeared, nodded a silent acknowledgement to Konrad and lowered himself onto the bench.

A whispered conversation soon concluded and Meier's hand disappeared into his jacket pocket. Konrad smiled, accepted the small paper bag and inspected its contents, then slipped them into one of his own pockets. They sat in silence, their eyes darting between diverging ripples made by sparse raindrops hitting the lake's surface. Konrad blinked and turned his head, unsurprised that Meier had already disappeared into their darkened surroundings.

Now safely ensconced in his nearby hotel room, Konrad inspected the German *Reisepass*. A steady fingertip traced the gold emblem of an eagle set against a burgundy background, ready for Andreas Baum's decision to leave the country.

****

7.06pm – PDT
Stellar Avenue, Atwater Village, Los Angeles, California

The rich smell of fresh coffee filled an unmarked police car parked halfway along the block from the Fernandez house. Mosley and Muñoz sipped from Styrofoam cups and watched a sickly-looking brown cat meander across the deceptively tranquil street, flop onto the sidewalk and lift its aged, scrawny face upwards to savour the evening sun's warm glow.

Muñoz peered at their destination through the windshield. 'Her husband and sons might have been scumbags, but I feel sorry for Marisol.

Apparently the daughter never posed a problem. Such a goddamn shame they pulled her into their shit and she paid with her life.'

'You can't tell me she didn't realise what the men were doing,' Mosley replied in a scathing tone. He swirled the last of his drink around the bottom of his cup. 'Surely she's not that dumb?'

'Maybe, maybe not.' Muñoz countered. 'She could have gotten an idea. You just don't know to what degree they kept her in the dark.'

'When did they release her from the hospital?'

'Late this morning,' Muñoz confirmed. 'Tony Pell called to say he's in town today. He'll be at the house while we speak to her, if she's up to it.'

Mosley nodded and pictured the English forensics guy they'd worked alongside from time to time over the years. 'How's he dealing with it?'

'I think he feels more sorry for his aunt, rather than for the deaths of his uncle and cousins. Apparently there wasn't much love lost between them. That's one of the reasons he transferred to Barstow, to get away from the Fernandez side of the family.' Muñoz took another sip of his coffee. 'Tony said his mom's surprisingly cut up, even after barely speaking to Paco in the forty years since she moved to the UK.'

'We need to trace their movements over the past week.' Mosley placed his empty cup in a holder between the car's front seats. 'See if anything unusual occurred that may have led to their cars being vandalised.'

Muñoz arched a dark brow. 'What if they didn't tell her?'

'Even if she doesn't know the details, she'll hopefully know where they've been and make it easier for us to fill in the rest. Apparently she's dosed up on horse pills, so we'll have to pull her down from the ceiling before attempting to get anything useful out of her.'

'Ever the sympathiser...' Muñoz noted.

Mosley pointed to the younger man's cup. 'You finished?'

Muñoz nodded and opened the car door, the surrounding air unpleasantly warm away from their vehicle's comfortable air-conditioned interior. 'I guess we'd better do this.'

They soon reached the house and noticed its drapes were drawn. Mosley squinted up and down the street, knocked on the door and tutted when flakes of faded green paint fluttered to the ground. He raised his hand to knock for a second time, the movement halted by the creak of a bolt sliding back. A tall, tanned man pulled the door open and offered them a tense smile.

'She's through there,' Tony said in a low voice. His head jerked to one side to direct them into the house's dingy interior. A large crucifix adorned the wall beside the front door and both detectives wrinkled their noses at the unidentifiable odour surrounding them. Tony pushed a recently painted door open to reveal a large kitchen, its heart filled by an old-fashioned wooden dining table surrounded by six matching chairs. Two middle-aged women were seated close together, the nearest of whom Mosley recognised as Marisol Fernandez.

Tony approached his aunt and laid a gentle hand on her arm. 'Marisol, these are the two detectives who'd like to speak to you.'

Her swollen red eyes stared at the newcomers. 'Like they care.'

'We do care, Señora Fernandez,' Muñoz said in what he hoped was a soothing tone. 'We're making every effort to catch those responsible for the deaths of your family.'

She gazed at where her wrinkled hands rested on the table's faded wood. 'All you did was give them shit when they were alive. Why start caring now they're in the morgue?'

The plump woman to Marisol's left patted the distraught woman's hand and then turned to the detectives. 'I'm Pilar Gomez, Marisol's sister. Is this necessary right now?'

Mosley nodded as sympathetically as he could muster. 'We're sorry to visit so soon. Anything your sister can tell us about Francisco and their children may enable us to catch whoever killed them.'

Pilar looked thoughtful for a moment. 'You're definitely calling it a homicide?'

'Yes ma'am,' Mosley replied. 'The evidence suggests a deliberate act. All your vehicles were sabotaged in the same manner and this gives us two angles to work from.'

Marisol pointed to the three battered chairs across from where she was seated. 'Please, sit. Pilar will get you a drink.'

'Just a glass of water for both of us, thanks,' Muñoz said. He pulled out a chair and lowered himself onto wood unintentionally polished by years of daily use.

Marisol took a deep shuddering breath. 'How is your investigation coming along?'

'Ma'am, we need you to tell us everything you know of your family's movements over the last week,' Mosley asked, aware of the sweat trickling down his neck.

She rubbed her eyes. 'What good will that do?'

'It may help us discover whether the perpetrator or perpetrators targeted your whole family, or just one individual,' he continued. 'At the moment all we have is theories, and to start a full investigation would be like looking for a needle in a haystack.'

'And your husband?' Muñoz prompted. 'Tell me about his routine over the past week.'

'Nothing different. Got up and went out, mostly locally and mostly on foot. Always came home to me at night.'

Muñoz nodded. 'Did his *behaviour* seem different in any way?'

She frowned. 'What are you saying?'

'Edgy, evasive, secretive...'

'No.' She offered him a sad smile. 'I can honestly say he was still the same old Paco. He may have done bad things from time to time, but he was my first and only love.'

'Any change of routine for your sons?' Mosley asked.

Marisol twisted her wedding ring. 'Yeah, I guess so.'

'Can you elaborate?'

'They went away on the weekend. I'm not sure where. They said they'd planned a surprise for their sister's birthday. Milagros turned thirty just last month.' She choked back a sob.

'Milagros went with them?'

She nodded. 'Esteban swore the others to secrecy.'

Mosley scratched his neck. 'Did anyone else go?'

'No idea. They all came back mighty happy late Sunday night so I guess they had a great time, wherever they went.'

Pilar smiled at her sister's words and listened to Mosley's continued questions. 'And during the week?'

'Life carried on pretty normal,' she said. 'I'd gotten a call about Aunt Silvia down in Tijuana on Wednesday afternoon. Cousin Alejandro said she didn't have long, the cancer was claiming her. Paco and the kids wanted to see her one last time.'

Mosley saw Pilar shake her head. 'Why didn't you go?'

Marisol narrowed her eyes. 'She's an evil bitch. When my father died she said some terrible things. I swore the next time I'd have contact would be to dance on her grave.'

'Your father being?' Muñoz asked, already knowing the answer.

'Jesus Gonzalez. You may have known him as Baby. He was killed in the same way, so you can't tell me there ain't someone out there targeting my family. Is it that Konrad Kratz guy? You've only just gotten around to telling us he's suspected of murdering my father.'

Mosley stared at Muñoz, his loaded expression a warning not to reveal any of the recent developments in the Kratz case. 'Ma'am, that's what we're trying to establish.'

Muñoz reached into his jacket pocket. 'Señora Fernandez, contrary to what you think, we're going to do all we can to solve this case.' He passed a small piece of paper to her. 'Here's my card and, if you think of anything which might help, no matter how small or insignificant it seems, I'd be grateful if you call me anytime. Day or night.'

'Thank you,' Pilar said. She reached across the table to give Muñoz's hand a grateful pat and returned his sympathetic smile.

'You must be tired. Unless you'd like us to stay we'll leave you to rest.'

Marisol nodded. 'I appreciate your concern. Pilar will give me strength.'

Tony watched the detectives make their way to the door. 'Aunt Marisol, I need to head off home now, but I'll be back in a few days.' He bent down to kiss her damp cheek. 'Take care of yourself.'

She grabbed his hand and squeezed it. 'Paco got it wrong about you, Antonio. You're a good boy and never forget it.'

The three men breathed sighs of relief as they left the house's claustrophobic interior and stepped out into the mellow evening light.

'Antonio?' Mosley echoed.

Tony shrugged. 'That's what she's always called me, even though it's not my real name. You still think Kratz is behind this?' He narrowed his eyes at the idea of the man he'd called *Peter Umpleby* during their Preston schooldays being responsible for these latest deaths. Tony glanced at his watch and his thoughts turned to the long drive up I-15 to his wife and young son at their Helendale home.

'My head says the fucker's chilling out in the morgue,' Mosley replied. He looked back at the house and new tension knotted his jaw. 'My gut says we can't rule it out

Chapter 5 – Sunday 26th July 2009

9.17pm – CEST
Stadelhofen, Zürich, Switzerland

Konrad admired the restaurant's elegant interior, sipped his drink and reproached himself for combining Oxycodone and an Eichhof. The beer buzz clouding his thoughts was not altogether unpleasant, but disconcerting enough for him to resolve to switch to water once he'd finished his beer. A steady stream of people passed the window to his left, oblivious to the man whose gaze had settled on the Bahnhof's modern architecture across the road. Konrad found it easy to maintain this latest identity, his mousey brown hair and ghost-like complexion the antithesis of the blond, tanned former hero who'd become instantly recognisable back in the States – and pretty much everywhere else.

'Thomas?' An enquiring American voice jolted him from his thoughts.

'Uh, hi! Freya, isn't it?' He stared at the familiar face surrounded by shoulder-length dark hair. 'Small world.'

She nodded, unsure how to continue.

He wracked his memory and recalled part of their transatlantic conversation. 'The research is progressing nicely?'

'Yeah, if I'm lucky I may have a half day to myself next week.' Her gaze seemed to penetrate him. 'I must say you look one hell of a lot better than you did above the Pond.'

'Indeed, and I have to say I feel one hell of a lot better too,' Konrad replied. 'Although when the return flight is imminent I'm sure I'll regress back to a gibbering wreck.' He smiled at her and forced the skin around his eyes to crinkle. 'Why don't you join me?'

'I wouldn't be intruding?' she asked, her tone hesitant.

He nodded at the vacant chair opposite his. 'Certainly not. Your company would be a pleasure.'

Freya smiled coyly and indicated her change of table to the waiter. 'Hopefully this'll numb my feet,' she added as she sipped a glass of Merlot. 'I'm exhausted after schlepping all over the city today.'

A police car screeched past the window and Konrad jumped again. 'Where did you visit?'

'Retail therapy research today so I hit the shops,' she replied, then winced. 'It was pretty good, even though everything's so damn expensive here.'

He gave an emphatic nod. 'I'll say. You leave the hotel with a wad of banknotes and return at the end of the day with nothing to show, other than an empty wallet.'

Freya giggled. 'I know! Ridiculous isn't it? Anyway, what about you? How's the new banking team?'

'Perfectly fine, so it appears,' he said smoothly. 'I met them on Friday and the hard graft starts tomorrow. It's been good to have a weekend chilling out somewhere different.'

Hook, line and sinker...

They compared their respective weekends and a ready flow of conversation across the table gave a relieved Konrad an excuse to eat more slowly. 'Did it taste as good as it looked?' he eventually asked, eyeing Freya's empty plate after she'd swallowed the last piece of her cordon bleu.

'Yeah, it sure did.' She caught a glimpse of her watch and her face flushed. 'It's not gotten too late yet. Care to join me for another glass of wine?'

'I've already had a couple of beers.' He hesitated, the faint fuzziness still discernible around his temples. 'Okay, one glass and then I should really head back. I've got the first of many early starts in the morning.'

Freya beckoned the waiter over and ordered two more glasses of Merlot, her eager attention hitting Konrad with a sudden realisation he needed to draw their evening to a close. Something about how she repeatedly stared at his face made him feel uncomfortable, not to mention the prospect of drinking something that tasted akin to piss-laced vinegar.

She sipped the deep red liquid and scrutinised him again. 'Don't get me wrong, Thomas. I noticed something familiar the first time I saw you at LAX.'

Konrad laughed more nervously than he'd intended. 'Perhaps I've got a doppelganger?'

'Yeah,' she agreed. 'I bet you look like someone I've met before, which doesn't narrow it down because I meet so many people through work.'

He set down his glass, half its contents already consumed in defiance of his loathing for any type of red wine. 'What was the last project you worked on?'

Freya caressed the stem of her glass. 'I usually work on travel books and wanted to extend my repertoire, so I recently finished co-editing a book analysing the last decade's most successful TV shows.'

'Which one won?' he asked, his voice low as he mirrored her subconscious hand movement.

She winked at him. 'That's classified information. I'll tell you we sure had some heated arguments over *CSI* and *H.O.S.T.A.G.E.*'

'Can't say I've seen either of them.'

'For real?' The incredulity in her voice caused it to rise an octave. 'It's a good job we haven't sent it to the printer yet.'

He arched his eyebrows. 'Why's that?'

'*H.O.S.T.A.G.E.* is on hiatus because the lead actor's gone missing.' She took another sip of her drink. 'You wouldn't believe the current speculation, especially now the FBI has released a statement saying they want to speak with him but they won't say why. My contact at Wolf says if he doesn't return in the next week they're casting for a new role.'

The hair on the back of Konrad's neck prickled. 'Who is this chap?'

'You're telling me you never heard of Konrad Kratz?'

'I don't watch a lot of telly these days.'

I suppose that's true.

'Can't believe you never heard of the guy,' she said, obviously surprised. 'A few years ago one of the shows he starred in filmed some scenes near Castaic. He's seriously hot.' Freya saw him raise his eyebrows, and giggled again. 'Sorry, that's the wine talking.'

'It must be strong stuff,' Konrad commented, keen to deflect the conversation. 'Like I said on the plane, you're a very attractive lady. I like that when it's combined with intelligence and a wicked sense of humour.'

38

Colour spread rapidly across her cheeks and he reached across the table until their fingers touched, causing another flush of heat to travel over her neck and chest within seconds.

'My hotel's only a short walk from here,' she whispered, moistening her lips in time to her foot rubbing the inside of his calf.

Konrad settled the bill and an unsteady Freya leaned against him as they left the restaurant. They strolled past shops and eateries catering for all tastes and budgets beneath a star-studded sky, from where the Großmünster's towers watched over the dark maze of narrow streets; nearly a millennium of righteousness unable to provide protection against the most dishonourable of intentions.

****

1.01pm – PDT
Walmart, Duarte, California

Mosley carefully read the nutritional information on a packet of hotdogs, rolled his eyes and returned the processed sausages to a promotional stand. He scowled and recalled his doctor's advice to lay off fatty foods in favour of a more balanced diet.

You should try it yourself sometime, you goddamn tub of lard.

Anyone would think he went out of his way to exist on a junk food diet but, after fifteen hour days at the station, the last thing he wanted to do was chop vegetables and sauté chicken. Today was his first day off in what felt like weeks and here he was, living life on the edge at the grocery store – with even more excitement to come when he returned home to thoroughly clean the modest Altadena property he'd owned since his divorce. To Mosley's further irritation, his thoughts drifted away from the last of the items on his list and returned to the Carlito Read case.

What the hell was the guy doing in Vegas?

The crime lab's discovery of a total absence of prints on the steering wheel and door handles escalated the team's suspicions, suggesting someone had wiped the Mercedes clean prior to dumping it. Unless the kid planned to go off the grid, Mosley assumed whoever could claim responsibility for Read's disappearance was also responsible for the clean-up. None of the residents of Libby Drive had seen anything; the car appeared on their quiet suburban street early one morning and hadn't moved since then.

A new idea raced through his mind whilst Mosley waited in line to pay. He'd take the groceries home and return to the station, even though this entailed the prospect of losing what little remained of his day off... again.

****

10.12pm – CEST
Zürich, Switzerland

Freya heard the heavy hotel room door swing shut and automatically lock behind her. 'Here we are...' She pressed herself closer to Konrad and stroked his cheek in an uncoordinated display of desire. 'What do you want to do first?'

He took in the room's minimalist décor and pointed to a dark wooden desk near the window. 'That's one bloody huge bar of chocolate.'

'My niece is twelve and loves Toblerone, so I couldn't resist buying that four-and-a-half kilo monster this afternoon.' Her hands slid into the back pockets of his chinos. 'It's her birthday in four weeks and I thought it might help cushion the blow for my sister when her daughter turns into a hormonal teenager.'

'Have you got any children?' he asked, inwardly cursing the residual tenderness around the exit wound. Usually he never declined the opportunity to screw an attractive woman, especially if she'd pretty much thrown herself at him.

Don't put bromide in the prisoners' tea – just shoot the bastards instead.

'No,' she replied. Sadness tinged her voice. 'Never met the right guy.'

Konrad felt her push his jacket over his shoulders and heard it fall to the polished wood floor. 'That's a shame.'

Remember what happened last time you thought you were on a promise?

Freya nodded, her smile forced. 'You do remind me of someone.'

Konrad mimicked her expression. 'I'm intrigued to know who, so I can apologise to the poor bloke for being dealt such a crap hand.'

'Hey silly,' she cooed. A clumsy hand reached for his belt buckle and he wondered if he'd be up for it, so to speak. 'Minus the glasses and in these different clothes, you're pretty cute. I thought about it on the way back here. You actually remind me of that Kratz guy, apart from you're not blond.'

He ignored the surge of adrenalin and managed to keep his tone neutral. 'And I assume he's not English?'

'You write like him. At the airport I noticed you hold your pen weird. So did Kratz when he signed autographs that time they filmed in Castaic.'

Konrad frowned. 'You're probably mistaken.'

'Yeah, you're a sexy Brit, not a movie star,' Freya slurred. Her arms encircled his waist and she pulled back seconds later when he hissed in pain. 'What's the matter?'

'I think I've, uh, bruised a couple of ribs.' He rubbed the tender area and stepped away from her. 'I slipped in the shower this morning and fell against the mixer tap.'

Freya swayed unsteadily now she didn't have Konrad to lean against. 'You want me to kiss it better?'

'Maybe in a short while, once it's stopped throbbing.'

She gazed at him through long, dark lashes. 'And your ribs?'

His sharp blue eyes scanned the room. 'Yeah, those too,' he muttered.

'I have some Tylenol in my washbag. I'll go get some for you, and a glass of water.'

Konrad perched on the edge of the bed and looked at the nearby desk again. 'Please, that would probably help.' He watched her slow, deliberate gait as she entered the bathroom and switched on its stark fluorescent light. A series of clicks soon followed the clunk of a glass being placed on the porcelain shelf above the sink, telling him she'd managed to open the Tylenol's plastic container.

'I dropped some,' she called. 'Won't be long, I promise.'

'Don't worry about it.' He jumped to his feet, used both hands to grab the Toblerone from the desk and listened to her scrabble for pills on the bathroom floor, her muttered curses interspersed by giggles. Konrad heard the toilet gurgle and silently crept to the other side of the doorway, where he raised his improvised weapon and waited for her to emerge.

'I flushed them down the *loo*,' she said, carefully carrying the glass and three small round white tablets. 'See, I can speak like a–'

Freya's words abruptly ceased when the triangular box swung through the air and smashed into her temple. She swayed back and forth, oblivious to the rivulet of blood flowing over a sharply defined cheekbone until it reached her nose and changed course. Her eyelids fluttered as she dropped to the floor, groaning faintly as she crashed into the polished wood.

He brought the oversized chocolate bar down for a second time and a sickening crunch filled the room, followed by silence so heavy it threatened to crush anyone in the vicinity. Konrad dropped the Toblerone and studied the saliva bubbling at the side of Freya's mouth in time with her shallow erratic breaths. He crouched beside her and draped the facecloth he'd grabbed from the bathroom over her neck. His hands squeezed tightly and she bucked beneath him, her weakening efforts to escape from him futile. Time became inconsequential, her death only confirmed when Konrad thought to loosen his grip and press a finger to her reddened neck.

The injuries he'd incurred a little over a week earlier screamed for mercy and he slumped against the bed and pushed the facecloth into a pocket to dispose of later. Across the room, a depressed area to the right side of Freya's forehead and the additional damage inflicted on her nose and cheekbone now marred her previously alluring features. Blood smeared the Toblerone's packaging, its numerous invisible fingerprints threatening to expose what he'd done, unless he could eradicate all tangible traces of his presence.

A pair of neatly folded carrier bags lay on the desk where Freya had displayed the giant chocolate bar. Konrad staggered to his feet, shook them open and was relieved to discover the murder weapon fitted inside without showing any of its glossy yellow exterior. The bathroom mirror confirmed his shirt and trousers had avoided all traces of blood spatter and he returned to the bedroom, where he picked up his jacket and cast a final glance towards the prone body.

Konrad tucked the *evidence* under his arm, opened the door and slipped out onto the corridor. He leisurely descended two flights of stairs, strolled through the hotel's small reception area and turned his head away from its solitary security camera to nod and smile at an elderly couple. The day's warmth had dissipated, coaxing a shiver as he blended amongst the few remaining locals and tourists strolling along Kirchgasse's cobbles.

'My good lady sure did,' Gibson replied. He reached into the box and grabbed a Bavarian cream. 'Hope there's plenty of these babies? I need to top up my depleted energy reserves.'

Mosley chuckled for a couple of seconds. 'I guess you all enjoyed your day off?' The other three detectives nodded in unison. 'I had a revelation in Walmart yesterday,' he added.

Muñoz pulled the Holey Heaven box closer. 'About the case?'

'Yeah,' he replied, wrinkling his nose when he noticed an inch of yesterday's coffee in his favourite mug. 'I figured Carlito Read might have been in Vegas for more than a fleeting visit, so I contacted Vegas PD and asked them to run his name past all hotels on the Strip for the two weeks leading up his vehicle being found.'

Hallberg inspected a chunk of kiwi fruit. 'And?'

'I received the results by email this morning, and our guy ain't on any lists. So he either went for the day or maybe he stayed further afield. There's a tech geek in Vegas repeating the search for all hotels inside a ten mile radius of the Strip.'

Gibson whistled. 'He'll be busy. That's one hell of a lot of hotels.'

Mosley emptied the coffee pot and nodded. 'Said he'd get back to me by the weekend, so we stick with the Fernandez case and keep our fingers crossed nothing urgent comes in.'

'Do you think there's any link between Read's disappearance and what happened to the Fernandez family?' Muñoz asked.

Mosley shrugged. 'Nothing would surprise me.'

****

8.27pm – CEST
Munich, Germany

Konrad gazed around the cavernous main hall as he half-listened to an oom-pah band's music merge into the low babble of nearby conversation. The Hofbräuhaus seemed much busier than he'd expected on a week night; its large wooden tables packed with holidaymakers and locals enjoying traditional Bavarian fare served by men and women in regional dress. The beer he'd ordered on arrival tasted good enough to make him consider ordering a second but, keen to avoid the fuzziness produced by the combination of painkiller and alcohol in his bloodstream, he quickly decided against it.

A young French couple opposite him studied the menu. Their echoed body language and proximity hinted at the newness of their relationship and, for the first time, Konrad wondered what it would be like to be half of a loving partnership, to desire a woman on more than a purely physical level. He'd never felt anything more than emptiness around other people; always seeing them merely as objects to use to his advantage.

A smiling waitress set down a large bowl of goulash and a side order of bread dumplings in front of him. Konrad thanked the young woman in her native tongue and noticed her plaited blonde hair and the corset enhancing her hourglass figure. She urged him to enjoy his meal and sashayed away, accustomed to admiring glances during her three years of employment there that had helped to pay her way through university.

He chewed the richly-spiced meat and pondered the day's events. After a timely arrival at Munich's Hauptbahnhof, Konrad left the station via a side entrance and made his way along a busy street past the colourful greengrocers' shops and kebab takeaways serving the local Turkish community. He'd soon reached a neat anonymous hotel and paid the full amount in cash, its receptionist delighted to welcome an Englishman of German parentage to their family-run establishment for the next week.

That'll cover my less-than-perfect Deutsch.

Since checking into the hotel, Konrad had only unpacked the bare essentials – including a wad of dollars he intended to exchange for more Euros over the next two days. From here there was one more Bavarian city to visit; part of his plan to keep the cops, FBI, MI5, Interpol and whoever else wanted to crawl up his arse far beyond reach.

Only then would he travel north to his final European destination.

****

7.32pm – MDT
Denver International Airport, Colorado

FBI Supervisory Special Agent Samuel Bury raised a hand to his mouth, pulled on a piece of skin next to his thumbnail and winced when a droplet of blood appeared. He repeatedly glared at an arrivals board, his eyes

46

drawn to the screen taunting him with its knowledge that the British Airways flight from Heathrow had touched down forty minutes earlier. Crowds of people thronged Jeppesen Terminal's Level 5, many waiting for passengers to clear immigration and customs, then emerge against the bustling backdrop of one of the world's busiest airports.

Sam returned his attention to the arrival gates and noticed a steady trickle of weary travellers increase in number. He'd arrived at the airport shortly before six o'clock to stare at the blue screens, waiting for the news he'd longed for since his wife and two young children walked through the departure gates three weeks earlier. Sam had decided there'd been no other option than to send them to stay at his parents' home in England, now the evidence strongly suggested his former childhood nemesis *Peter Umpleby* had tried to kill him.

Twice.

Everything now pointed to the international television and movie star Konrad Kratz, whom *Peter Umpleby* had so successfully reinvented himself as, being dead. Although the body's identification had not been one hundred percent conclusive, Sam quickly pushed this weighty issue to the back of his usually rational mind.

The information about BA219 updated and an unexpected tension spread throughout Sam's body. Would John remember him? Had Angela's distress faded, or did she still blame him? He sighed and pictured her small angry face demanding the answers he'd been unable to supply. For those minutes after Anna dragged their daughter away from him he'd remained rooted to the spot, feeling like a shredder had ripped him apart from the inside.

The day had passed in a state of anticipation: his morning occupied by a trip to the Target superstore at Colorado Mills and an uncharacteristically enthusiastic approach to long-overdue housework. He'd tracked the flight during an afternoon visit to the FBI's Denver field office and bid farewell to his teammates when the plane flew over the state line from North Dakota to South Dakota. By the time Sam arrived at the airport the early evening sun had disappeared behind the western mountains, their grey clouds promising one of the evening thunderstorms commonplace at this time of year. He'd left the family's car on the uppermost level of a short-term parking garage and made his way straight to the arrivals area, where the past ninety minutes had felt more like ninety hours.

Sam peered beyond two men holding placards aloft and picked at the small area of damage he'd caused to his thumb. His family rounded the corner and came into view, followed by a small, wiry porter pushing their cases on a trolley. Announcements faded, the babble of expectant voices fell silent and Sam's peripheral vision blurred as Anna met his eye and said something to Angela, whilst an oblivious John lay back in his stroller and gazed in wonder at the fibreglass roof's internal peaks.

He saw Angela pull her hand from her mother's and dropped to his knees. A blonde-haired tornado in a red cotton dress rushed towards him, her favourite rag doll flapping in her wake, her arms wide.

Sam's ears honed in on one word: 'Daaaaaddy!'

Chapter 7 – Tuesday 28th July 2009

6.22am – MDT
Golden, Colorado

Crisp morning sunlight partially permeated the window's heavy drapes, gradually lightening the bedroom. Sam became aware of the warmth radiating from beside him and rolled over to leisurely contemplate his sleeping wife's peaceful features and how she'd wedged their red and white checked comforter beneath her arm. Anna's eyes opened slowly, as if aware of his gaze; the room blurred until Sam's smiling face came into focus.

'Hi there, Sleeping Beauty,' he whispered as he leaned over to kiss her on the cheek. 'Go back to sleep, you must be exhausted after all that travelling.'

Anna released a contented sigh and, secure in the bedroom's familiar comfort, closed her eyes and lapsed back into a light doze. Moments later she turned onto her side, raised her head and caught a glimpse of the alarm clock's glowing red digits over Sam's shoulder. 'Are the kids still asleep?' she asked.

He nodded. 'They're usually pretty quick on the draw telling us if they're not.'

'I'll say,' she replied, stifling a yawn. 'The whole neighbourhood would have lodged a noise complaint by now.'

Sam gently pushed away the strands of hair which had fallen across her face. 'I didn't realise they could stay quiet for this long.'

'I guess they were tired after such a long day.'

'I've never known Angela be so compliant when we've mentioned bedtime.' He swallowed when he felt Anna lightly stroke his bare stomach. 'I suggest we leave them 'til they wake, whatever time that ends up.'

She smiled and turned her attention to his chest, already aware of the effect she was having on him. 'She didn't sleep on the flight; she was too excited about seeing her daddy.'

A finger followed the strap of her tank top and then moved to the soft skin on her shoulder. 'How excited were *you* about seeing her daddy?'

'Three long weeks...' She raised a suggestive eyebrow.

'Yeah?' he replied, their faces now only inches apart.

She lazily caressed the back of Sam's neck and detected an involuntarily shiver. 'I was so excited I fell asleep soon as my head hit the pillow.'

'You certainly know how to boost a guy's self-esteem.' He closed the distance between them and allowed their lips to brush. 'You've got a lot of making up to do.'

'I agree, and I apologise unreservedly for–'

Sam pressed his mouth against Anna's, her words stolen. He savoured the sensation of her body moulding into his and hesitated for a split-second, wondering whether the feelings rushing through his body and mind would prove to be nothing more than a product of his imagination when he awoke, alone again.

'I can't believe you're here, it's...'

Sam's voice faded, his grin wide when Anna pushed him onto his back. She straddled his waist and mirrored his smile as he pulled the tank top over her head.

'I don't think it'll take much to convince you I'm real.'

Sam's hands moved to her hips. 'Christ, you're beautiful,' he murmured. His eyes roved over her body until she leaned forward and pressed herself against him, both unaware of the comforter slithering off the bed. Hands moved over hyper-sensitive skin, their resumed kisses increasingly intense.

Anna rolled onto her side. 'Seems like there's an uneven balance of power here,' she whispered and looped an arm around his neck to bring him closer.

Sam exhaled audibly and felt her ease his waistband downwards. 'I missed you so much.'

'I can tell,' she retorted, stifling a giggle. 'Can you think of anything else I can do to make it up to you?'

He closed his eyes and shook his head, his mind fixated on the teasing motion of her fingers as memories of the past month melted into welcome oblivion.

****

8.06am – PDT
San Fernando Road, Los Angeles, California

Mosley read the last paragraph of the bulletin that had landed in his email inbox sometime overnight, pressed a palm against his aching forehead and wondered if this new information would further increase their workload. Deep in thought about whether the message's content held any relevance, the crash of Gibson's briefcase hitting the floor between their desks startled him back to reality.

'Fuck! You trying to give this old guy a heart attack?' he snapped and jumped again at the clatter of an empty cola can falling to the floor.

'Sorry boss,' Gibson said. He set down a cardboard tray of Holey Heaven coffee and noted the older man's scowl. 'Is it bad news?'

'Swiss cops found some travel writer chick murdered in her Zürich hotel room.'

'Since when did the LAPD cover Switzerland?' Gibson stroked his jaw in contemplation. 'I'd sure be happy to take one for the team and visit the crime scene. My wife's half-Swiss so we'd save on police expenses by staying at her grandparents' chalet in Engelberg, if that helps my case. They're a sweet old couple and I've only met them once. We'd like to see them again before they... you know.'

Mosley shook his head and grinned. 'Nice try, shit for brains.'

'What's the story?'

'Freya Burdett was thirty-six and found strangled to death after suffering blunt force trauma to the head. She lived in Castaic and worked for a Los Angeles publishing house. Swiss police are liaising with the Los Angeles County Sheriff's Department, so for now we've only been asked to keep our ears to the ground.'

Gibson frowned and reached for his coffee. 'What's that going to achieve?'

'The Swiss are keeping their options open,' Mosley replied. He took a sip of double shot and gave the large paper cup a nod of approval. 'They assume someone local committed the crime but they're not ruling out someone following her from California.'

'Isn't that a little far-fetched?' Gibson listened to his stomach growl, aware he'd missed breakfast. 'Surely it would be easier to kill her on this side of the Atlantic?'

Mosley shrugged. 'Let's humour them. Keep your eyes and ears open, but not at the detriment of our other investigations.' He opened the uppermost brown file on his desk. 'Let's recap what we already know about the Fernandez case.'

****

10.19am – MDT
Golden, Colorado

'Daddy...' Angela diverted her attention from a plate of waffles. 'Did you and Mommy wake up late?'

Sam and Anna shared a knowing look that went unnoticed by their three-year-old daughter. 'Yes, sweetheart,' he replied. 'I think it was your brother's demands for Weetabix that woke us up.'

'And probably anyone else on the street still trying to sleep,' Anna said. She saw John drop a spoonful of brown mush onto the kitchen floor and recalled their abrupt awakening twenty minutes earlier – and the resulting scramble to find their clothes – whilst Angela banged on the bedroom door. 'Try your mouth next time, sonny.'

John chuckled at her despairing expression, oblivious to the cereal he'd smeared across his chubby cheeks.

Angela's large blue eyes, almost identical to her mother's, returned to the cut-up food on her plate. 'Will Daddy come with us when we go on vacation again?'

Sam stroked her arm from across the table. 'We're all going on vacation, and all four of us are going to–'

'Are we going Disneyland?' she exclaimed.

He shook his head. 'Not this time. We'll go there when John's a little bit older.'

Her disappointment was obvious. 'Where are we going?'

'To the mountains to live in a little wooden house for a few days.'

'Neat!' She clapped her hands in excitement. 'Are we going on an airplane again?'

He stirred peach slices into his muesli. 'Not this time; it's just a short ride in the car.'

'Daddy...'

'Yes, sweetie?' he replied, deciding to leave the cereal to soften.

Angela narrowed her eyes. 'Why are babies so messy?'

Sam watched Anna help their son spoon the soft mixture into his mouth. 'I think I'd better help Mommy, so you be a good girl and finish those waffles,' he said as he made a detour past the drainer to pick up a cloth.

Anna smiled at Sam. 'Thanks, I can't quite manage getting the food into his mouth and wiping it off the floor at the same time.'

He gazed at the shadows beneath her eyes. 'You still look tired.'

'Whose fault is that, mister?' she replied, raising an eyebrow at the Broncos pyjama shorts she'd bought for him the previous Christmas.

'Entirely yours. If you weren't so damn beautiful I wouldn't have needed to let you–'

'Three.' She shook her head. 'Can't remember the last time.'

Angela narrowed her eyes. 'Three what, Mommy?'

Sam coughed and felt heat flush across his cheeks. 'Uh, just how many times Mommy searched through the closet to decide which clothes to pack after John finishes making a mess.'

'Babies are horrible,' she announced solemnly and pushed her finger through a puddle of maple syrup.

Anna smiled, relieved Sam found it so easy to neutralise Angela's insatiable curiosity. 'You really are incorrigible.'

He slipped an arm around her waist. 'Just wait 'til we're at the cabin; you must remember what that mountain air does to me.'

****

1.22pm – PDT
Holey Heaven Donut Shack, Atwater Village, Los Angeles, California

'How much longer?' Gibson squinted through the intense sunlight streaming in through a nearby window. 'He sure looked pissed when that call came in.'

Hallberg shrugged and swallowed a large bite of his bear claw. 'Could relate to the Fernandez case,' he suggested. 'I guess this means another late night?'

The others nodded, resigned to Hallberg's speculation becoming reality. A shadow passed across the window, followed seconds later by the beep of a sensor above the door.

'We ordered your usual,' Muñoz said. 'One double shot and these two beauties.'

Mosley nodded his appreciation at the pair of Bavarian creams waiting for him and slid into the booth. 'Thanks man, it's damn hot out there,' he replied gruffly. 'That call gave us another angle to investigate on the Fernandez killings.'

Hallberg set down a triple espresso. 'What's new?'

'Anonymous tip-off, saying our buddy Paco seriously pissed off Arturo Lopez recently.' Mosley saw three mouths hang open in stunned silence. 'Yeah, *the* Arty Lopez. Paco owes... owed him a shitload of cash for some crystal he'd been peddling around the Village, but the Bank of Fernandez had been operating erratic opening hours. Word on the street is Lopez planned to *rectify* the situation.'

'Surely killing Paco means not getting his cash?' Hallberg said, frowning deeply.

Mosley nodded and stirred a sachet of sugar into his drink. 'Lopez certainly had beef with Paco. Unless we can prove Kratz is still alive and in town, *and* that he had motive against the Fernandez family, we focus on the Lopez angle for now.'

Muñoz rubbed his eyes and then looked at his teammates. 'Say it *was* Kratz, could it have been a random killing?' he asked, intently hoping Wolf TV network's fallen angel would soon become a problem for another law enforcement agency, preferably one on a different continent.

'Probably not.' A mouthful of doughnut muffled Mosley's words. 'In all the cases we've identified as potentially committed by Kratz, there's always been an identifiable motive.' He picked up his drink and took a long swallow of the sweet liquid. 'Unless we uncover concrete evidence against Kratz, the big chief will expect us to investigate gang involvement first.'

Hallberg leaned back and stretched his legs under the table. 'So we forget the Kratz angle?'

'I wouldn't say *forget*.' Mosley wiped the froth from his moustache. 'Let's keep the piece of shit on the backburner, unless we get evidence to the contrary.'

Chapter 8 – Wednesday 29th July 2009

8.06am – PDT
San Fernando Road, Los Angeles, California

Muñoz pushed a printed sheet of paper under Mosley's nose. 'DNA came back on the Death Valley body and there's a problem,' he announced. 'One hell of a problem.'

Mosley diverted his attention from a map of Atwater Village and scanned the new information, his frown deepening. 'The body's DNA profile doesn't match any of the three profiles from those hair samples found at Kratz's two homes.'

'Are they in CODIS?' Gibson asked as he met Muñoz's gaze.

He shook his head. 'No, but Kratz's DNA isn't in the system either.'

Gibson sighed, his mind struggling to formulate coherent speech after another late night. 'Thanks to the fingers being removed, we don't have any prints to compare to those found at Chateau Kratz, which is a serious pain in the ass.'

'I've asked that *those* prints get added to AFIS,' Hallberg said. 'You never know when some chance arrest could provide a match.'

Mosley folded the map and tucked it into a case file. 'The most obvious explanation is the stiff in the desert ain't Kratz. We can pretty much say one of the DNA profiles taken from the hair found at both houses belongs to Kratz. The other two probably come from so-called donors, most likely not consenting. If that's the case, the body's DNA would be a match to one of the three hair samples.'

'So Kratz either didn't shed a single hair at either house…'

'Impossible!'

'...or that body's not him,' Hallberg continued. 'If it isn't Kratz, who's the victim and how did they get there?'

Muñoz shrugged. 'Kratz's driver's licence in a pocket tells us the body in the morgue had contact with Kratz at some point.'

'You think Kratz planted the body to stage his own death?' Gibson asked.

'Seems possible, and explains the missing fingers coupled with a too-easy-to-find driver's licence.' Muñoz eased back the tab on a can of Mountain Dew. 'And, if we consider the method used to kill the Fernandez family – it's one hell of a coincidence.'

Hallberg sipped his own can of soda. 'You think he's killed another three people?'

'Three?' Gibson echoed and looked across to Mosley, who'd listened to their exchange.

'Yeah, three.' Muñoz slotted the limited evidence together and organised his thoughts. 'The body recovered from Badwater and two others whose hair was found at each house. The DNA from the hair says three different men and we already know they were blond, like Kratz. An officer from Glendale interviewed residents on Kratz's street and no one recalls any blond men besides Kratz visiting the premises. Apparently plenty of blonde females were escorted back, but definitely no males.' He paused when the others grinned. 'The body dumped in Death Valley was similar in stature to Kratz, based on the physical data already held on him. Could Kratz have deliberately chosen a decoy? The fact the guy got his face shot off doesn't aid identifying him by mugshot.'

The four men didn't move from their positions around Mosley's desk, their minds working overtime as the implications of what they'd just learned began to sink in.

Mosley was the first to break the silence. 'What the hell is going on?'

****

6.27pm – CEST
Augsburg, Bavaria, Germany

Little had changed since Konrad's last visit to the city. The Hauptbahnhof's buff-coloured frontage still dominated a cobbled bus terminus and, if he walked for ten minutes, he knew he'd be surrounded by the city centre's historic charm and period buildings. Even though he hadn't visited his mother's birthplace since childhood, it still made him feel cold inside.

*This is half of you. Is **this** place responsible for everything that's happened?*

He pulled the trolley case behind him, negotiated a break in the traffic and turned onto Bahnhofstraße as if on autopilot. Augsburg was apparently so proud when he'd mentioned his paternal origins in that interview, unaware he'd constructed a complex web of lies which had recently disintegrated in an angry whirlwind of truth. He wondered how the townsfolk now regarded him – whether intense hatred bubbled at the surface, as in his adopted homeland.

Shop windows lined his route into the city centre, and he perused the clothes stores nestled between high-class confectioners and the bakery he remembered his mother taking him to all those years ago. The road soon widened where Fuggerstraße's straight expanse ran perpendicular, its tram lines slicing through both widths of tarmac. From his vantage point at a pedestrian crossing he spotted the hotel he'd reserved from a Munich internet café that morning. He planned to pay for another week although, as had become a habit, he'd leave the country days before he was due to check out.

The electronic figure on the crossing's display turned to green and *Andreas Baum* considered the long overdue business he needed to sort out at his next destination: a business transaction now owing him a substantial return.

He had plenty to organise during his stay.

****

2.32pm – MDT
Giberson Bay, near Frisco, Colorado

Anna proudly watched Angela frown in concentration as she scrutinised the mountains towering above Dillon Reservoir's opposite shoreline. 'How's my clever girl doing?' she called across from the adjacent picnic table, noticing Angela had selected a blue crayon.

'I'm gonna draw the sky,' the little girl replied, her heart-shaped face earnest. She turned back to the sketch pad bought by Sam in a Breckenridge art shop earlier that morning and resumed her masterpiece, oblivious to the light breeze ruffling her hair.

Anna nodded her head in approval. 'I think we have a budding Monet in the family,' she said, smiling as Sam reached across the wooden table to link fingers. 'She's sure gotten into her art this summer. Your dad took her to Tarn Hows one day in England and they did some painting. He said she's pretty good for a three-year-old.'

'It's certainly keeping her quiet,' Sam said. He glanced at the stroller where John slept soundly; the baby's plump hands grasped tight around a plush blue rabbit's neck. 'This one doesn't seem too impressed by his big sister's new hobby. As long as he's got a full belly and somewhere comfortable to lounge, he's a happy little chap.'

She narrowed her eyes. 'The apple doesn't fall far from the tree.'

He gave her a reproachful stare and shook his head. 'That's harsh.'

'You didn't seem in a rush to get up this morning.' Anna's eyes crinkled at the corners.

Sam's index finger traced indolent circles on the palm of her hand. 'That's nothing to do with laziness. I'd already warned you about the restorative powers of clean mountain air.'

She cast her mind back and giggled. 'Yeah, I couldn't miss it.'

'Which, coupled with you, is a combination this man can't resist.'

'I'd never have guessed the bumbling FBI agent who called to apologise a couple of days after literally bumping into me, and then needed to *call back* when he remembered to suggest dinner, was so smooth.'

Sam leaned in for a fleeting kiss. 'Still waters run deep.'

'Yeah, yeah. I only love you for your mom's fruitcake,' Anna replied. She reached for an airtight container on the table, carefully cut two large slices of sticky dark cake and saw Sam's eyes widen when its moist surface glistened in the sun.

He licked his lips in anticipation. 'I can't believe she sent back one of these beauties. On your way through customs did you declare the full bottle of brandy she usually feeds it with?'

Anna laughed and sniffed a waft of escaped alcohol. 'I noticed she didn't skimp on the stuff last week; she said at least a half bottle is specified in your grandmother's recipe.'

Sam picked up his portion of cake and admired it from arm's length. 'Isn't this great? I mean, see how happy the kids are, not to mention their mom and dad. It's like the past year never happened.'

Anna's gaze fell to the faded scarring above his left wrist. She nodded, squeezed Sam's hand and wished his optimism hinged on fact, rather than hope.

Chapter 9 – Thursday 30th July 2009

10.27am – PDT
San Fernando Road, Los Angeles, California

Mosley yawned, pinched the bridge of his nose and handed two sheets of paper to Hallberg. 'I really don't need no more of this shit.'

Muñoz glanced up from another new case file he'd been reading. 'What's up?' he asked, not yet sure whether to be grateful for the distraction.

'First the Swiss, now the goddamn Austrians,' Mosley replied and nodded his thanks to Gibson as the younger man handed out large disposable cups of bought-in coffee. 'Two missing backpackers from Vienna were supposed to arrive home two weeks ago. Their families reported them missing around a week later and a lab in Austria is now sequencing their DNA, which they'll send to us when the results come in.'

Muñoz picked up the email Mosley printed out minutes earlier and registered the similar shades of blond hair and blue eyes shared by the pair. 'Are they related?'

'Contrary to appearances, no,' Mosley confirmed. 'Herman Schmidt and Jürgen Moser, both aged twenty-five, were backpacking around Oregon and California for three months between finishing their doctorates and starting work back home in Europe.'

Muñoz read the small print on the sheets. 'Last heard from near Solvang on Sunday, June 7th. They told their parents they planned to travel south along the coast to San Diego, then maybe stay a week in Vegas. Their British Airways flight from LAX to Vienna via London Heathrow departed without them on Wednesday, July 22nd.'

'What do they expect us to do? Keep an eye open for Carlito Read's Austrian doppelgangers?' The irritation in Gibson's tone wasn't lost on the others. 'We're trying to locate Carlito Read, there's the Kratz case *and* there's the five Fernandez deaths. Seriously boss, we can't maintain this many cases and all these hours.'

Mosley nodded. 'If it's any consolation, all police and sheriff's departments in California and Oregon were emailed about Schmidt and Moser. Keep our eyes and ears open, like the Burdett murder.' He narrowed his eyes. 'You think Read looks like those Austrian guys?'

Gibson shrugged. 'Maybe. I guess it's their colouring.'

'Could the disappearances be connected?' Hallberg asked, deep in thought.

'You think there's a serial killer targeting tall, blond-haired, blue-eyed guys?' Muñoz asked. He frowned and imagined the extra work involved if this theory proved to be true.

'Could be worth checking out if there's other recent homicide victims or missing persons fitting that description,' Mosley suggested.

'I'll run it through ViCAP today,' Gibson said. He watched Mosley set down his empty coffee cup and smile his approval. 'See if there's any similar cases here or in neighbouring states.'

Hallberg drained his second double shot of the morning. 'What's today's plan of action?' he asked. 'Until that tech guy from Vegas sends the hotel information, the Read case can't move forward.'

'We're staying local today,' Mosley replied. 'Gibson has his cyber-mission and Muñoz is paying Marisol Fernandez a visit to see if she's remembered anything new.' He grinned at Hallberg's apprehensive expression. 'You and I are taking a trip to catch up with Glendale PD, but before that there's a little conversation me and Arturo Lopez need to have.'

****

7.35pm – BST
Preston, England

Another busy day passed swiftly at the Edward II which, since its grand opening nearly fourteen years earlier, had become one of Preston's most popular pubs; its scarlet paintwork a familiar beacon for those heading into town. The Garner brothers maintained its status as a firm favourite amongst a wide section of the town's community and the place was well known for, according to the *Preston Evening Chronicle*, '*good beer, good food and a good night out.*'

Although Michael 'Mikey' Garner's name adorned the licencing plate above the door, his older brother Steve and Steve's wife, Charlotte, mostly took care of the place behind the scenes. In the kitchen, Steve's old school friend Franco Volonte, now a highly regarded local chef, had produced a menu able to draw customers from all over the county to eagerly sample the food and drink on offer.

Steve filled the dimpled pint glass his father-in-law insisted on keeping behind the bar and noticed Roger Mortimer staring intently at a nearby beer mat. The older man's family-owned brewery proudly carried the Mortimer name and supplied ale to both the pub and their town centre restaurant, the aptly named Son of Edward. Roger Mortimer had silently invested in both ventures over the years, trusting the Garner brothers to use the money wisely in return for an annual cash pay-out – and his lack of interference in the running of either.

'You all right, old man?' Steve called across the bar. 'Penny for your thoughts.'

'You'll want a ha'penny change,' Roger replied. He winked when Steve sent over a pint of *Isabella's Revenge*. 'Nice job, lad. I need this tonight.'

Steve slid onto a stool beside Roger and watched Mikey return to his usual position behind the bar. 'We've been back nearly a week and you've not recovered yet? I can't tell you how much I appreciated you running the restaurant while we were in the States, not to mention checking Mikey hadn't burnt *this* place to the ground.'

Roger nodded and took his first sip of beer. 'No bother, he looked after me too well. Her indoors is nagging me about this extra weight I've put on. It's them bloody chips, you know.'

'I'll pass on your latest compliments to Franco. He's certainly trained those new chefs well, they did him proud while we were away,' Steve said. 'It was great to catch up with Sam and Tony, not to mention the glorious weather.' He raised his eyebrows. 'Anyway, what's been mithering you this week?'

'It's nothing, son.' Roger released a drawn-out sigh. 'I'd hoped for a week off. The missus wants a week on the Isle of Man, but some business associate phoned a couple of days ago and wants to meet up to discuss our... er, arrangement.'

Steve checked nobody was within earshot and leaned closer. 'I assume it's all kosher?'

'Negative, son.' Roger rubbed a hand over his thinning hairline. 'This chump phoned out of the blue. I've heard nowt from him for six years, since we set it all up. Said he's flying in this week, wants to meet and he'll contact me again when he's in town.'

Steve nodded. 'Where's he from?'

'Some bloody Yank,' Roger muttered in a derisory tone.

'In this backwater?'

'Got family connections here apparently; Grandad or similar. He wants to reconnect with his roots.' Roger took another gulp of his beer and pointed at the door that led to the kitchens. 'Any chance of a few of them chips before I head back to the old ball and chain, son?'

Chapter 10 – Friday 31st July 2009

Muñoz gazed at the incident room's clock and blinked repeatedly to clear his blurred vision. He'd arrived at work nearly three hours earlier, intending to clear his backlog of paperwork and return home as early as possible. Mindful he'd seen little of his wife over the past month, Muñoz called in a favour and reserved a table for two at Los Feliz's most popular restaurant, keen to surprise Katharine on their ninth wedding anniversary. One of the job's bittersweet perks, he mused, was how the restaurant owner's immense gratitude hadn't diminished in the six years since the prompt apprehension of his youngest brother's killer.

At the next desk, Mosley let out a frustrated groan and continued to proofread his report documenting an unproductive conversation at Arty Lopez's home. The middle-aged man had proved less than compliant and, as he'd swaggered away, threatened to report Mosley for police harassment. This time things seemed different and, after three decades in law enforcement, Mosley's unvoiced suspicion was that for once Lopez was being honest with them.

A squeal of hinges desperate for oil shattered the room's silence and diverted Hallberg's attention from the chaotic evidence board. 'What's he doing here?' he whispered.

Commanding Officer Iain Jones smiled at them from the door and Gibson shrugged. 'Perhaps he's come to tell us we're getting three weeks off on double pay?'

'Like hell,' Hallberg snapped. He pursed his lips and watched Mosley approach Jones to shake his hand. 'The slave-driver probably found more shit to add to the shit pile.'

They watched the two men confer. Jones frequently referred to a file he'd brought and, judging by the expression on Mosley's face, Jones' revelation wasn't sitting comfortably. The younger trio of detectives returned to their desks and followed Muñoz's example of catching up on overdue paperwork, whilst waiting for fresh information on their active cases.

The door hinges' protest against the lack of maintenance for a second time announced Mosley's return to his seat, where he slumped onto its worn fabric. Gibson was the first to stand and cautiously approach Mosley, whose long fingers now attempted to displace the pressure tightening its hold around his temples.

'You okay, boss? What did Jones say?'

Mosley tipped his head back and stared at the ceiling tiles, many of which were discoloured by age. He gave a long drawn-out sigh and wondered whether he could lay his hands on something stronger than Tylenol without leaving the building. 'Last night, the FBI's Vienna legat sent DNA profiles obtained from the missing Austrians' toothbrushes to the Los Angeles field office, who ran the profiles through CODIS. They've gotten two hits.'

Hallberg frowned. 'That means they've committed a crime here, or–'

Mosley leaned forward. 'They're both dead,' he said, his voice devoid of emotion.

Muñoz picked up a printed copy of the email received by all law enforcement personnel in California and Oregon the previous day. 'I thought the bodies haven't been found yet?'

'No, but samples of their hair have.'

'Hair samples?' Muñoz echoed, silently praying his plans for the evening wouldn't suddenly fly out of the window.

Mosley nodded and again wished for something considerably stronger than the coffee he'd poured minutes before Jones' visit. 'Schmidt and Moser's DNA is a perfect match to the profiles extracted from two of the three hair samples at Kratz's homes.'

Hallberg shook his head in disbelief. 'Kratz is responsible?'

'Looks that way,' Mosley said. 'I guess you better find more space on that board.'

****

11.37am – MDT
FBI Field Office, Denver, Colorado

Special Agent in Charge Colin Milne carefully carried two mugs of coffee towards the pair of leather armchairs occupying one corner of his office. 'These should keep us going for a while,' he commented to Assistant Special Agent in Charge Jared Pearson, his teammate of over fifteen years.

Pearson thanked Milne, accepted the mug and took a cautious sip of his drink. 'When did your contact at the Los Angeles field office send that email?'

'It was waiting for me this morning.'

'Don't you think they should have gotten in contact sooner?' Pearson asked. 'Kratz could still be running around out there. He may be in Colorado, and we all were oblivious to it.'

'LAPD only brought it to the Bureau's attention yesterday. They didn't pass it on until their evidence fitted together and was sufficiently conclusive,' Milne replied. 'Agent Baxter at the Los Angeles field office asked if we'd look over what's been discovered and see if we can add anything new. I've already passed everything to Niall Demaine with the hope he'll discover some additional information.'

Pearson reclined and took a short opportunity to reflect. 'Demaine's the best technical analyst I've ever worked with. He claims his brain's wired incorrectly, hence his so-called genius.' He laughed at memories of their first conversation after Demaine's appointment. 'This is one hell of a situation. Kratz appears to have faked his own death, killed five members of one family he'd already targeted back in the nineties, their cousin's disappeared and now two missing Austrians have been linked to him.'

'Where do you think he is?'

'No idea,' Pearson replied. 'Airports and road borders are on high alert, but if he fled the country already that's an almost impossible situation.'

'There's an additional issue.' Milne set down his mug. 'Do we tell Sam?'

'He's in Breckenridge with his family for another week.'

'They're back next Friday and he's supposed to return to work on the tenth.'

Pearson loosened his tie. 'Do you think he's in danger?'

'We can't discount it, although he didn't mention anything out of the ordinary occurring during his family's stay in the UK.' Milne crossed to the window and stared into the clear blue sky above distant mountains. 'If Kratz hasn't been apprehended by Wednesday, I see putting Sam and his family into a form of protective custody as the safest option. The Director immediately approved the idea and I've phoned an old contact who said I only need to give the word and it can be arranged in a couple of days.' He swallowed a mouthful of coffee. 'We won't mention it for now; let the family enjoy their vacation. I know relocation is usually permanent; however, this time I hope if it has to happen it'll only be for a matter of weeks at the most.'

A gentle knock on the door halted their exchange.

'Come in,' Milne called.

Demaine's freckled face wore a jubilant expression. 'You can tell me I'm awesome now, but I can wait for after my revelation. It's your choice, guys.'

Pearson smiled. 'What did you find?'

'Hold onto your hats, as this gets good real fast. A long conversation with a tech guy at Vegas PD told me Carlito Read didn't make a hotel reservation anywhere in the city on that weekend. I then took a look at the Fernandez case because those guys were Read's cousins. According to their mom, they headed off for the weekend and didn't say where. I wondered if there was a connection, accessed hotel databases on the Strip and hit the jackpot.'

Milne held out his hand to accept the sheet of paper from Demaine. 'Caesars Palace.'

Demaine nodded and grinned. 'What happens in Vegas doesn't always stay in Vegas. Friday, July 17th saw two rooms reserved for two nights in the name of Esteban Fernandez. Based on her date of birth, I'll guess it was a thirtieth birthday treat for his sister Milagros. However, they checked out one night into their stay and yes, I've sent the information to Detective Mosley at LAPD.'

'Good work,' Milne said, his admiration obvious. 'Did you discover anything else?'

'Not yet, but if Kratz is out there I'll find him eventually.' Demaine cracked his knuckles and caused Pearson to wince. 'These fingers and this brain,' he said, pointing to his head, 'are unbeatable.'

****

3.16pm – PDT
Las Vegas, Nevada

Elliot Lloyd walked into the Crime Lab's air-conditioned break room and sighed in relief. A relentless desert sun had followed Lloyd and his partner Helen Kinski as they'd processed a body dump site near Blue Diamond, the angry red shade of Lloyd's nose telling of his failure to learn from previous painful experiences of forgetting his sunblock.

'Man, it's hot out there,' he said. 'Next time remind me to check I brought up everything from the car.'

'You're over four months early.'

'Four months?'

'Yeah, *Rudolph.*'

'Rub it in that you got a superior deal on the melanin,' he grumbled as he grabbed a can of Red Bull from a small refrigerator. 'Has anything happened since I visited the cop shop?'

She nodded. 'DNA came back from the blood pool in the back of that old Mercedes.'

Lloyd whistled in amazement. 'Man, that's fast. You give them a rocket up the ass?'

'I think they had a call from one of those detectives in LA' she said, recalling a phone call to Mosley two days earlier. 'He don't mince his words.'

'Did it belong to that Read guy?'

'Nope, and I've been to see Kareem,' she said. 'He says we keep this one locked down.'

Lloyd frowned at the mention of their supervisor and lifted the can to his lips. 'I don't follow.'

'LAPD is still waiting on Read's DNA reference profile. This blood got a hit in CODIS–'

'But it's not this Read dude?' Lloyd interrupted. He absentmindedly rubbed his nose and winced when the tender skin objected.

'Jeez, let me finish.' Kinski opened a cupboard and scanned its contents for anything sugary. 'No it isn't. It matched a profile obtained from hair samples found at two different houses in Glendale, California and Golden, Colorado. It's a small place near Denver.'

'That's one hell of a coincidence. Who does it match?'

'Who's been all over the news for going AWOL?'

Lloyd grinned. 'Bin Laden?'

'Christ, you're a douche.' Kinski rolled her eyes. 'Does *H.O.S.T.A.G.E.* mean anything to you?'

His jaw hung slack now his brain had made the connection. 'No goddamn way! Konrad Kratz?'

She punched his bicep and hushed him. 'This is strictly confidential. Kareem's spoken to the FBI and LAPD already. No one outside this lab hears of this until the big guys investigate further.'

Lloyd nodded. 'Is the blood Kratz's?'

'Maybe,' Kinski replied. 'They don't have a confirmed DNA profile for Kratz to compare this to yet. Nobody can work out how what some folk think *could* be Kratz's blood has gotten into the trunk of Read's car.'

'Don't tell me this is all they know,' he said, casting his mind back over the celebrity magazines his girlfriend habitually left in their bathroom. 'The FBI went on national television appealing for information about the guy's location. They must have some heavy-duty shit on him.'

She lifted the cookie barrel's lid. 'That's what I thought. Seriously though, Elliot, you can't tell anyone outside. Not even Wendy. If that blood turns out to be Kratz's there's the issue of finding him *and* Carlito Read.'

'The desert's a huge place.' He offered the can to Kinski, who shook her head. 'Do you watch that show he stars in?'

'Yeah, it's awesome. He's a great actor.'

Lloyd got to his feet and walked back to the doorway. 'So it seems.'

Chapter 11 – Saturday 1st August 2009

7.42am – PDT
Alisal Road, near Solvang, California

Kayla Olsen listened to her husband's grey station wagon accelerate into the distance; inhaling deep lungfuls of fresh morning air as she quickly worked through a routine of stretches in preparation for her five mile pre-breakfast run. This route would take her past the fields and small wooded areas rarely visited by locals, then back to their home on the south side of town. Her springer spaniel tilted his head and gazed expectantly at his beloved owner, his tail thumping on the ground with excitement.

If she had to be truthful, Kayla enjoyed the solitude offered by these weekend early morning runs. She needed to be awake early on weekdays, and getting a reluctant seventh-grader out of bed and to school on time each morning – in addition to working part-time at a local bookstore – left little time for her fitness routine. However, things were different during these two precious days. Her husband was happy to entertain Davey for an hour each morning after he returned from leaving Kayla miles from home. The pair had soon fallen into the routine of enjoying a leisurely father-and-son breakfast, their time together limited during the week due to Trevor's travelling salesman job.

Satisfied her muscles were adequately stretched, Kayla broke into a steady jog and looked down to where the eager dog ran beside her in time to the faint *slap-slap* of her rubber soles on the blacktop. The landscape sloped gently up from the narrow road and a curve to the left marked where the density of the tree cover increased. Kayla glanced at Bobby and smiled at the sight of his pink tongue lolling out of the side of his mouth, which she swore he'd pulled back into a grin.

'You enjoying this, boy?' she called down to him, relieved the puppy obedience classes he'd attended last year had paid off and she could run without needing to keep him on a leash. His large brown eyes met hers, the contact broken off as quickly as it was instigated when he veered to the road's left verge and stood motionless.

'Bobby?'

The dog stared down into the trees and undergrowth below the road, oblivious to her exasperated tone. 'What you seen? Don't you be going anywhere; I ain't coming down there to drag your hairy ass back up here.' He continued to ignore Kayla and her irritation grew now he'd cocked his head to one side. 'Come on, I ain't getting back to soggy pancakes just because you sniffed out a dead rabbit.'

She started to jog away at a slow pace and assumed Bobby would lose interest in whatever had gained his attention and follow her. Kayla didn't hear the tell-tale tapping of claws on the road surface and her temper began to fray. She stopped and turned abruptly to see what the dog was doing.

Where the hell are you?

Her unease built as she jogged back to where she'd seen Bobby less than a minute earlier. She was relieved to hear the cracking of twigs from below as her eyes strained to catch a glimpse of brown and white fur through the trees and long grass. Kayla scowled, wondering why the hell her dog had suddenly chosen to behave in such a disobedient manner.

'Bobby, get back up here… NOW!' she shouted and reached into the small backpack containing two hand weights and her cell phone. 'I'll put you on this leash. This'll be the last time you come running, you hear me?'

The rustling sounds from below became louder and the undergrowth parted. Bobby emerged from between green fronds and Kayla stared at her pet through narrowed eyes. 'What you got there?' She crouched as he approached and saw he carried something in his mouth. 'You better not be eating dead rabbits again. Puking all over my nice clean kitchen floor, you dirty critter!'

The dog proudly dropped the item, sat down with a grunt and watched Kayla move closer. His feathery tail swayed from side to side over the road's dusty surface as Kayla recognised the object and recoiled in horror.

****

72

12.04pm – PDT
San Fernando Road, Los Angeles, California

Ronnie Mosley startled to attention when the shrill ring of the telephone on his cluttered desk shattered the incident room's unusual silence. Although he'd ordered the other members of his team to take a well-deserved day off, the call of a pile of case files on his desk proved too great for the veteran detective to resist, especially after the phone call he'd received the previous day from LVPD's crime lab. News that the blood pool in the Mercedes's trunk exactly matched a hair sample found at both Kratz's homes had as good as confirmed Kratz had murdered Read in an attempt to fake his own death. It took seconds for Mosley to decide to honour his agreement and allow them to enjoy a well-earned weekend rest day with their families. What else could they do unless they found something concrete to advance the case?

'Make the most of it, guys; you just don't know when that big ol' pile of shit will land.'

Mosley had awoken at his usual hour and, for the first time in weeks, took enough time to enjoy breakfast before the drive from his Altadena home to Atwater Village's familiar surroundings. He'd hoped to be finished by noon, giving him time to drive to Santa Monica and catch up over a couple of cold beers with an old college buddy, who now worked homicide in South Central.

Crazy bastard.

Mosley confirmed his name and listened to a Deputy from the Santa Barbara County Sheriff's Office explain how a woman out for an early morning jog near Solvang had been confronted by a particularly grisly sight. Less than an hour after her dog deposited part of a rotted human arm at her feet, a forensic team sealed off the area and commenced a search that would eventually fill the best part of two days. The two badly decayed bodies had already been recovered and were currently being examined at a morgue in Santa Barbara, according to Dennis Fellini.

'They didn't die in some bizarre camping accident?' Mosley asked, somewhat facetious in his irritation about being interrupted minutes from his intended departure time.

'No sir, the nature of the injuries sustained by both men makes it almost certain we have a homicide.'

He shook his head, grateful the other man was unable to see his impatience. 'No disrespect, but how is a double homicide in the boonies relevant to the Northeast Division?'

Mosley continued to listen to the case's additional details and a large weight descended on his chest. The bodies appeared to have been in situ for at least six weeks, and two backpacks displaying a little-known European brand were also located nearby. Fellini shredded Mosley's last thread of hope that he'd dialled the wrong number by announcing the local police were almost certain the remains were those of Herman Schmidt and Jürgen Moser. DNA samples labelled *urgent* were already on their way to the lab for processing.

Mosley returned the handset to its cradle and rested his elbows on each side of the case file he'd perused before the call came in. He knew he'd eventually need to devise a timeline of Kratz's known movements and relate them to the forensic data, whenever he received it. The only problem posed by this plan was – regardless of their evidence board groaning under the weight of the information it carried – other than a quick foray into Death Valley, Konrad Kratz's movements over the past two months were still a complete mystery.

****

11.02pm – MDT
Breckenridge, Colorado

Near darkness filled the cabin's lounge area, unable to penetrate the furthest corner where a television cast flickering shadows onto the walls. A cool breeze gained entry to the room through a partially opened window and made the nearby drapes sway, their slight movement enough to ramp up the movie's tension.

Sam stopped the DVD when its credits rolled. 'You reckon it lived up to the hype?'

'That ending was pretty scary, but the other parts were tamer than I'd expected,' Anna replied. She moved her head until it rested on Sam's shoulder. 'Let's hope we haven't gotten ourselves a poltergeist.'

He kissed her cheek, looped an arm around her shoulder and felt her relax against him. 'This is nice.'

'Yeah,' she murmured. 'The past few days have been wonderful.'

Sam nodded. 'Apart from Angela and John asleep upstairs, it's like we turned the clock back five years.'

Anna smiled and remembered their first weekend mini-break in Aspen, five weeks after their chance meeting. 'Yeah, we had some amazing weekends away, didn't we?'

'And now things have returned to normal there's nothing to stop us doing this more often.' He hugged Anna and she nestled closer against his chest. 'Maybe your folks could have the kids for an occasional long weekend? You can join me in New York or we'll fly to another city for a couple of nights.'

'Sounds great.'

Sam picked up on the hesitancy in her voice. 'You don't think we should leave them?'

Anna lifted her head. 'You know how much my parents love minding the kids, but are you really sure all this is behind us?'

'This?' he echoed.

She sighed. 'Konrad Kratz. You act like he's been confirmed dead.'

'They're certain as they can be.'

'Would the current evidence stand up in court?' She turned to face him and noticed his jaw clench in the low light.

An uncomfortable silence filled the room. Sam leaned forward, rested his elbows on his knees and rubbed his forehead. 'Anna, we can't think like that.'

'We have to while there's a chance the body isn't his.' She grasped his hand and squeezed. 'Kratz may still be out there.'

The breeze returned and the drapes resumed their movement. 'He can't be alive,' Sam whispered.

'Sam, if you were working this case, what would you advise the victim?'

Behind his mask of determination Anna saw the fear she knew he'd hidden all week. 'He can't be alive,' Sam repeated. He abruptly got to his feet, walked to the open window and surveyed the darkness beyond, the moon obscured by a blanket of cloud.

She watched him lock the window and pull the drapes together until they overlapped. 'He might be alive. We have to accept that.'

'I don't know about you, but I'm tired. That hike today didn't just exhaust the kids.' He pointed at the wooden stairs. 'Let's go up, I'm ready to drop.'

Anna padded across the polished wooden floor to rejoin him. 'We have to face facts, Sam. We may not be safe yet.'

He wrapped his arms around her. 'Look, even if he *is* still out there he'll be caught quickly. I have every faith in the FBI and the police.'

She nodded, reciprocated the hug and detected the returning tension strung across his back. 'Unless we hear otherwise, we assume he's dead. But you need to prepare yourself in case we receive news to the contrary.'

Sam kissed the top of her head. 'Yeah, that's what's scaring me.'

Chapter 12 – Sunday 2nd August 2009

His long-overdue return to Augsburg maintained its surreal feeling long after it should have abated; the idea he might actually miss the city amusing in its absurdity. Some shops had definitely exchanged hands and more traffic filled the streets these days, but he almost expected his grandparents to emerge from the café they used to insist on taking him to.

Konrad wondered whether he'd recognise the couple if he encountered them. Of course, for all he knew they were dead. He'd last seen them in November 1993, during his release from hospital for the afternoon to attend his parents' funeral. By then his grandparents were well into their seventies; physically and emotionally drained by the long journey they'd undertaken to attend the burial of their only daughter. His uncle had accompanied them, briefly reuniting the family in the face of tragedy.

You couldn't really call it an accident.

They'd returned to Bavaria days later, their parting gift the promise of a home for *Peter Umpleby* should he ever need it. Peter never harboured any intention of relocating to Germany and instead chose to *Go West* with a new identity. Even he'd been surprised at the fame Konrad Kratz had enjoyed and how he'd become a household name for his roles in numerous TV shows and movies. *H.O.S.T.A.G.E.* was what had really catapulted him onto the world stage; a combination of raw acting talent and good looks ensuring his unparalleled success.

And it had taken just one spiked drink to unravel the complex web of lies he'd so carefully woven over the years.

Konrad swallowed the last of the Almdudler he'd been pleasantly surprised to find in the Hauptbahnhof's shop. His thoughts shifted away from his imminent journey and returned to his fall from grace. Within days of the drink-spiking incident in an LA nightclub and mouthing off to the waiting paparazzi, a worldwide media frenzy unleashed itself. Naturally, the English instantly pounced on his venomous diatribe against their nation and a Channel 5 investigation soon uncovered the inconsistencies in his story. It was this that ultimately led to the FBI's involvement in the case.

Now they wanted him for at least sixteen counts of first degree murder and two of attempted murder, although that little detail hadn't been released to the press.

Yet.

****

9.23am – MDT
Breckenridge, Colorado

A delighted Angela broke off a piece of her chocolate muffin and held it aloft. 'Can we always have this for breakfast, Daddy?'

Anna picked up her coffee cup and watched her daughter push the dark sticky cake into her mouth. 'Only on vacation,' she said tersely, raising her eyebrows at Sam.

'Can we go on vacation every day?' Angela gazed in wonder around the small busy coffee shop, her voice muffled.

Sam smiled and placed a straw in her glass of milk. 'That would be lovely, but sadly Daddy doesn't earn enough money for that to happen.'

'You can get another job,' she replied, wrinkling her nose when Sam cut his bacon and Swiss cheese sandwich in half. 'Then you and Mommy can have muffins too.'

He laughed at her logic. 'Sweetheart, my job is so busy I don't have time to do two jobs.'

Angela inspected her chocolate-covered fingers. 'Mommy says you help the police catch bad guys.'

'That's right,' Sam said, watching Anna feed John his second bottle of milk of the morning. 'That's how I met Mommy. I helped her police friends catch a bad guy.'

'Is that why we went away on the airplane?' she asked between sips. 'So you catched bad guys?'

'Sort of.' He noticed Anna's shoulders tense and his voice faded. 'I was meant to go to England with you, but then a *very* bad guy needed catching and I had to stay here to help.'

Angela nodded without breaking eye contact. 'Did you catch him?'

Sam evaded Anna's pointed stare and focussed on a hanging basket outside the window, its bright flowers spilling over the sides to add to the sidewalk's colourful display. 'Yeah, I guess we did.'

'Next time can we all go, Daddy?'

He patted her knee. 'If there's ever a next time the four of us will all go, together.'

'And John?' she asked disdainfully, horrified to see the gurgling baby spit a piece of Anna's croissant onto her lap.

Sam nodded and smiled. 'That's right, we can't leave your baby brother behind.' He met Anna's inscrutable gaze and offered an apologetic smile. 'Let's finish breakfast and take a little walk before we go to the Recreation Center.'

Angela climbed down from the deep armchair she'd commandeered and held out her hands. Anna looked across the table; the sadness flourishing around her eyes unmissable.

'You realise you may not be able to keep that promise?' she whispered.

'I *will* keep it,' he replied, whilst using a baby wipe to remove smears of chocolate from Angela's cheeks and fingers. 'If you need to go anywhere, then I'm coming too. Whatever happens, he'll never separate any of us again.'

****

9.56am – PDT
San Fernando Road, Los Angeles, California

Day of rest, my ass.

Mosley finished his third coffee since arriving at the police station an hour earlier and grimaced as he set down his cup. The previous night had been a late one after an impromptu post-lunch visit to his law enforcement counterparts in Santa Barbara, then indulging in a couple of hastily rearranged evening drinks with his Santa Monica-based buddy after arriving back in the city. He shook his head at the not-so-new realisation he was now way, way too old for such shenanigans.

Although there'd been no official forms of identification inside the backpacks or what was left of the partially rotted clothing, other evidence found on and near the bodies strongly suggested these were indeed the remains of the missing Austrian backpackers. The DNA results due back in a matter of days were now, according to the Sheriff, likely to be little more than a formality. Deputy Sheriff Dennis Fellini had been almost apologetic for requesting Mosley's attendance at the scene, after mentioning the FBI's disclosure that the detective's LAPD team was also investigating Kratz's suspected role in more homicides than they could count on their fingers.

Due to increased rates of decomposition over the warm summer months, the Medical Examiner was unable to provide an exact date of death and surmised it likely occurred around the time the men were last seen alive, nearly two months earlier. Both had suffered extensive cranial trauma which would have proved fatal, the poor state of the bodies proving a hindrance to the detection of any additional injuries. Mosley cast his eye over the skeletons, whose darkened skin and mummified abdominal organs remained only where scavengers were unable to gain access.

He'd wondered aloud how one man managed to overpower both Schmidt and Moser. Photographs emailed by the Vienna police showed two muscular guys well above six feet in height and, according to their families, in peak physical fitness courtesy of an intensive and varied sporting regimen. Could they have been incapacitated by sedatives? The Medical Examiner returned the bodies to cold storage, removed his gloves and informed Mosley the outcome of a preliminary toxicology screen was due back in two weeks, with an option to carry out additional, more sophisticated tests if the results proved inconclusive.

His return journey south-east on the 101 had offered late-afternoon majestic ocean views on its approach to Los Angeles' urban sprawl.

Mosley ignored these, preferring to ruminate upon theories to explain how the Austrians were lured to their deaths. Both were well-educated, highly intelligent university postgraduate students – not to mention being built like tanks.

How the hell did Kratz reel them in?

Mosley knew from information provided by the English authorities that *Peter Konrad Umpleby* had been born in Preston to an English father and German mother, her maiden name *Kratz*. Without delving deeper into the continental family tree, Mosley guessed *Konrad* to be a tribute to a maternal ancestor. He'd also learned Kratz spoke German, albeit not fluently, based on interviews the snake had given to the media. Did the bastard pretend to be German and lull the Austrians into a false sense of security, before drugging them and taking them to a remote spot near Solvang to kill them? Had he intentionally harvested hair samples and then coldly dumped the bodies like pieces of worthless trash?

Mosley jumped back to the present day when Gibson perched himself on the desk's edge.

'I swear you bastards are trying to give me a coronary!' he snapped as both Muñoz and Hallberg stifle a grin. 'Which one of you has gotten a sudden hankering for my job?'

'Not me, man. I've seen how grouchy it makes you,' Gibson said. He ignored Mosley's withering expression, theatrically smoothed his collar and took a deep breath. 'I went through ViCAP for a second time. Nothing leaps off the screen about a bunch of blond-haired, blue-eyed men in their twenties flagging up missing or murdered, so I guess we can rule out that theory. Kratz is a smart guy, so he'll probably change his MO if he kills again. The random pattern shown by current victimology means he'll have to really fuck up to get me a hit.'

Mosley flicked a cookie crumb from his desk and sensed Gibson hadn't finished. 'Good work. What else do you have?'

'I also came to bring you up to speed on the Caesars Palace side of things. We know Esteban Fernandez reserved two rooms there on the weekend before the family ended up on slabs with corks up their asses. Couple of days ago I spoke to the assistant manager who's a nice guy and real helpful. Said he'd get security to compile video footage for the whole hotel from Esteban and the family's arrival to when they checked out. He's also going to access guest records and appeal to any staff who worked shifts at the relevant times for information. And, because he's in LA on business tomorrow evening, he said he'll personally deliver it all to save time.'

Mosley narrowed his eyes. 'Why's he being so helpful?'

'You're getting too cynical for your own good,' a grinning Gibson replied. 'Like I said, he's a nice guy. I figure he doesn't want any negative publicity either.'

'Yeah, I guessed as much,' Mosley said. 'I've been thinking about how it looks like it's Kratz's blood in Read's trunk. Read's missing, Paco Fernandez and his family are dead... Kratz *must* be the common denominator, but I can't work out how and it's pissing me off.'

The three younger men nodded, understanding his obvious frustration.

'The Vegas crime lab said whoever's blood is in the trunk had been injured severely enough to lose at least a quart,' Hallberg said. 'Have you contacted any hospitals?'

Mosley nodded. 'No firm leads have come in yet from Pahrump, Vegas or Barstow. I specified knife or gunshot wounds, but there hasn't been anyone matching Kratz's description admitted suffering those types of injury.'

'Which means he's probably not sought medical attention,' Muñoz said.

Hallberg raised his eyebrows. 'So either he's not too badly injured, or he's being treated elsewhere.'

'Or he's self-medicating,' Mosley countered. 'Treating himself to avoid awkward questions in the ER.'

'He might have burglarised a drugstore?' Hallberg suggested. 'We could check recent crime reports.'

Mosley grabbed a set of car keys from a bowl on his desk. 'You can buy any type of drug on the street if you know where to go and who to ask.'

Gibson eyed the jangling keys. 'You going on a mission, boss?'

Mosley grinned back at him. 'Just going to call in a few favours.'

Chapter 13 – Monday 3rd August 2009

Roger Mortimer stopped in his lounge's expansive bay window to briefly admire the Jaguar parked on the house's long sloping driveway and how its pristine silver paintwork reflected bright beams of sunlight. He'd purchased the new car three months earlier, hoping to advertise to prospective partners exactly how successful his businesses had become.

Unknown to Sheila Mortimer, his wife of nearly forty years, Roger was also mentally beating himself up over an uncharacteristic lapse of judgement. The man he'd viewed as a sound investor and who'd fallen silent since their initial business six years ago unexpectedly reared his ugly head six days earlier, in the form of a telephone call.

The transatlantic drawl caused him to upend an almost full mug of tea and send its contents streaming across the cream carpet Sheila recently insisted would look *lovely* in their hallway. The outrageously expensive wool carpet had quickly proved to be beyond impractical, but if he remembered to leave his shoes in the porch peace reigned over the Mortimer household – until Oliver Stamford phoned.

A dose of earache from his wife swelled the coffers of a North Shore professional carpet cleaning company and a further financial outlay to a local florist enabled Roger's thoughts to return to *that bloody Septic,* now on his way to the land of his forefathers. At their only meeting, Stamford agreed to invest a cool half-million in his father's hometown – an investment based on the promise of doubling his return. Roger had stipulated pounds rather than dollars and the two men shook on a deal which saw Stamford's money wired into Roger's bank account two days later from the small Nevadan city of Reno.

Roger listened to an ice cream van roll past, its tinny rendition of *Greensleeves* doing nothing to soothe his frazzled nerves. He'd invested the money wisely and could guarantee Stamford his doubled return, if he'd wait a few months for him to lay his hands on the cash. When he'd bought both South Shore homes during a booming property market, both sellers had eagerly accepted a full offer in the form of cash. However, the current national recession meant house sales were usually protracted affairs, and this turn of fortune wasn't conducive to Stamford promptly receiving of his share of the bounty – assuming the bugger wanted his money back.

Of course, the remainder of Stamford's cash had also been used to fund the less than legal aspects of the Edward II. That would remain Roger's little secret, hence the worry he'd have to sell both properties to pay off the guy. There should still be a few thousand in it for him once the properties were off his hands, judging by a couple of recent house sales in the area. His eyes moved to the phone which, at Sheila's insistence, occupied a prominent position atop a sleek mahogany chest of drawers. It stared back in defiant silence, ramping up Roger's tension at the prospect of a reunion with Oliver Stamford.

****

8.32pm – PDT
San Fernando Road, Los Angeles, California

Mosley eased the unmarked Chevy Impala into park and sighed in relief now he'd pulled the key from the ignition and stretched his aching back.

'You okay, boss?' Hallberg asked. He took a deep breath, hoisted himself out of the passenger seat and slammed the door closed. 'Traffic sure was a bitch on Ventura,' he added as he noticed a pair of uniformed officers unlock a cruiser on the next row.

'Traffic's always a bitch on Ventura,' Mosley muttered. 'I thought we left late enough to avoid the worst of it. Four goddamn hours!'

They walked across the enclosed parking lot to the police station's rear entrance. 'Solvang's a cute little place,' Hallberg said in an attempt to lighten the atmosphere. 'It's my wife's birthday next month. I might think about taking her up there for a weekend, if my in-laws will babysit the kids for a couple of nights.'

Mosley's narrowed eyes watched a lowrider carrying four teenagers drive past on Treadwell Street, the base beat emanating from their vehicle enough to make his eardrums vibrate. 'At this rate, you'll be able to combine it with this investigation.'

'I thought we wouldn't need to go there again, now we've briefed that team of detectives they deployed from Santa Barbara,' Hallberg said. He hoped nothing new had come in and he'd be able to return home immediately after collecting his belongings. 'They'll inform us of any new developments.'

Mosley nodded and walked through the door Hallberg held open. 'Thanks, man. This place is quiet for once, so let's collect our stuff and get the hell out of here.' He pushed open the incident room's door and made no effort to hide his surprise when he saw Muñoz and Gibson huddled over Muñoz's desk.

Muñoz looked up. 'Ventura?'

Mosley nodded. 'Bitch is a total understatement.'

'We heard the traffic bulletins,' Gibson said. 'Some douche rammed another guy for changing lanes in front of him and caused a twenty vehicle pile-up. No serious injuries. Damn miracle.'

'If I ever meet the prick he'll be drinking through a straw for a month.' Mosley grabbed a Bavarian cream from the almost empty Holey Heaven box and spotted a sheaf of papers on Muñoz's desk. 'Anything useful develop while we were in Viking country??'

Muñoz offered the last sweet treat to a grateful Hallberg. 'You could say that,' he replied. 'Carlito Read's DNA profile came in a couple of hours ago *and* we got a hit in CODIS.'

Mosley raised his eyebrows and took a large bite out of his doughnut, his empty stomach grateful for anything now the memories of their early lunch at a Solvang café had faded.

'Perfect match to the body recovered from Death Valley.'

'We've gotten ourselves a partial theory,' Gibson added.

Mosley swallowed and nodded. 'Go on.'

Muñoz cleared his throat. 'We already said we think Kratz killed the Austrians and planted their hair samples, in case his background got checked out after his little outburst. The third hair sample is almost certainly his, although we need a definite reference sample from Kratz to be one hundred percent sure. Gibson suggested Kratz was in Las Vegas that weekend, *somehow* encountered Carlito Read and this started out badly for Kratz, judging by the blood in the trunk. He soon realised how similar he looked to Read, killed the guy, obliterated his facial features, dumped the body in the desert *and* cut off his fingers. He'd gone to those lengths to impede identification, but a quick search found an obvious driver's licence in the pocket, like there'd be no other option other than to declare Konrad Kratz dead. We all said it appeared too good to be true, that something seemed shady.'

Mosley nodded again and realised the extent of his exhaustion. 'Good thinking,' he said. 'It's like we've found the four corners of the puzzle and we just need to organise the middle pieces, locate any that are missing...'

'And piece them all together,' Hallberg finished with a grimace, directly quoting Commanding Officer Iain Jones' infuriating favourite mantra.

Chapter 14 – Tuesday 4th August 2009

The eighties throwback greasy spoon blended seamlessly into its run-down surroundings; its green and white checked plastic table cloths adding a certain *je ne sais quoi* to the experience. Konrad didn't know whether to be pleased or surprised his favourite childhood café's cholesterol-rich menu continued to defy the so-called city's economic hard times. He dipped a chunk of black pudding into congealing egg yolk and peered through a grime-clad window. The town (as he'd always think of it) was destined to be a shithole forever, but he'd always missed the food. Years earlier, much to his delight, a stereotypical northern English café opened in Golden, a mere fifteen-minute drive from his Paradise Hills home. The scran was always spot on, although the ambience lacked... maybe *hostility* wasn't quite the correct word, but it would have to do.

Fred's Café had provided the venue for an encounter with the man who'd eventually become his nemesis: fellow ex-Crettington County Primary School pupil and now *Supervisory Special Agent Extraordinaire* Samuel Bury. Konrad wondered if he'd started hallucinating on that fateful day their paths crossed for the first time since their schooldays. An immediate attempt to protect his identity once and for all failed, although Sam's FBI partner Angelo Garcia met a nasty end when the tampered brakes of his SUV gave out on I-70 – a fate which should have befallen Sam.

The combined police and FBI investigation proved fruitless, much to Konrad's relief, and a second murderous opportunity presented itself years later when Sam began working every alternate week in New York.

87

In addition to co-ordinating the FBI's elite Critical Situation Research Unit, Sam's remit as one of Wolf television network's FBI consultants for *H.O.S.T.A.G.E.* led to them meeting formally on at least a monthly basis.

Konrad correctly assumed only a matter of time remained until Sam saw past the carefully constructed Hollywood façade, and soon took an opportunity to repeat history by puncturing the Federal SUV's brake lines during one of Sam's visits to the *H.O.S.T.A.G.E.* set. This seemingly infallible plan failed for a second time and Sam defied the odds to survive a catalogue of serious injuries, only to return to work months later branded by the physical and mental scars of his ordeal.

And then there was the drink-spiking incident that fucked up everything.

At least his own physical scars appeared to be healing. A slight residual tenderness persisted around the two wounds where a lone bullet had sped through his body, and the bruises on his chest continued to fade to a bilious yellow. Thanks to an effective selection of illegally obtained painkillers and antibiotics, he'd avoided an awkward hospital visit and preserved his anonymity.

But for how much longer?

Konrad wiped the last slice of thickly buttered bread across his plate, drained his mug of tea and glanced at a clock above the counter. He stopped at the door to nod his thanks at the café's elderly owner before stepping onto the litter-strewn street and setting off towards the town centre.

It was time to make another phone call.

****

4.23pm – PDT
San Fernando Road, Los Angeles, California

Gibson leaned back in his seat and squeezed his eyes closed, as if the action would dispel the grittiness from their corners. Mosley's swift exit to spend the day in Atwater Village locating new sources of information on the Fernandez family's activities had been partially copied by Muñoz and Hallberg, who'd departed to revisit Carlito Read's Death Valley body dump site. Hallberg's vociferous complaints about the impending desert heat were still audible after the door closed, much to Gibson's amusement. He grabbed himself another cup of coffee and psyched himself up to examine the surveillance footage and guest data from Caesars Palace, delivered by the hotel's assistant manager the previous evening.

Gibson returned to his desk feeling neither bright-eyed nor bushy-tailed, loosened his tie and started his analysis of the footage. A surprising degree of clarity enabled him to match names on the guest list to people on the screen and he easily managed to identify Esteban Fernandez and his companions, before following their movements during their stay.

Time passed quickly now he'd become engrossed in his task. Between viewings, Gibson paused to type his report and embed sequences of footage, oblivious to morning giving way to afternoon. A faint headache blossomed around his temples and he'd forced himself to leave the building for a late lunch, enjoying the bright sunlight whilst he walked two blocks to a conveniently located Denny's. Determined to take a proper lunch break, Gibson declined his burger's *to go* offer and found an empty booth in which to refamiliarise himself with the timeline he'd compiled so far.

Back in the incident room, Gibson's mind now buzzed as he spooned coffee granules into a cup and waited for his teammates. He felt especially proud that his completion of the onerous task included a condensed version of the file, ready and able to be emailed to any law enforcement agency in the world. The familiar squeal of door hinges cut across the silence and his spirits took a dive when a scowling Mosley entered the incident room.

'Christ! I hope you had a more productive day than mine. It's like the bastards are deliberately withholding information,' Mosley grumbled. He noticed a Holey Heaven box and two cardboard coffee cups in the overflowing trash can beside Gibson's desk. 'So you overdosed on caffeine, fat and sugar while I was out hitting brick walls all over town?'

'The key ingredients to fuel my genius,' Gibson replied. He pulled a seat closer and indicated for Mosley to sit down. 'I'm going home after you've seen this; I think you'll agree I deserve the evening off.'

Mosley sipped the coffee he'd returned with. 'Prove it.'

Gibson moved the cursor across the screen and clicked on one of four tabs at the bottom. 'This is shortly before nine on the evening of Friday, July 17th. You can see Esteban and his two brothers Rico and Luis waiting with their sister Milagros. They're soon joined by another man who'd been parking his car in the garage.'

Mosley stared at the screen. 'Isn't that...'

'Carlito Read,' Gibson confirmed proudly. 'Guess we have our answer why he was in Vegas. They join the line, check in and then it's soon gotten real interesting. Milagros gets upset and, after the guy ahead of them completes check-in, Luis follows him from a distance to the Centurion Tower elevators, waits at the bar for the guy to come back down and follows him again. He makes a phone call and a minute later Milagros leaves the room they've congregated in and heads on down to the casino.'

Mosley whistled appreciatively. 'If only I was twenty years younger. Why's she dressed like that? From what I know, Paco would go nuts about his only daughter going out dressed like a hooker.'

Gibson nodded. 'She had plans, or rather her brothers and cousin had plans.' He winked at Mosley and clicked on another video. 'See her prowling the gaming floor? She spots the guy Luis followed, the one who checked in ahead of them. There's a short conversation, they make out and then leave together.'

'Looks like he sealed the deal.' Footage from the elevator filled the screen and Mosley's eyes widened. 'Who *is* this guy?'

'We'll get to that little detail soon.' Gibson grinned at Mosley's reaction to how Milagros pulled the man into the bedroom she'd emerged from less than twenty minutes earlier. 'She didn't leave the room again until morning, unlike the men.' He continued to guide Mosley through the events of the next half hour. For once, Mosley had been rendered speechless and could do nothing more than inwardly speculate over what occurred in the hotel room before the Three Amigos half-carried, half-dragged their semiconscious victim to the drop-off point. He saw the men exchange words with a pair of teenage bellhops, then bundle the body into the Mercedes' trunk and speed away from the hotel.

Mosley flopped back in his seat and exhaled loudly. 'Jesus Christ! We need to interview those bellhops and that has to be Read's ride. How the hell did it wind up dumped in the 'burbs? And, who the fuck is the dude in the trunk?'

'One at a time,' Gibson said, amused by Mosley's failure to hide his excitement. 'Muñoz is heading to Vegas tomorrow and I've arranged for the manager to get the bellhops to come in. And, it's definitely Read's vehicle. I enhanced the plate and ran it through DMV records. Lastly, and I'm pretty much certain, the guy who checked in under the name André Wood is actually Konrad Kratz.'

Mosley's eyes looked ready to pop out on stalks. 'You're sure?'

'Physically they're very similar, although there's the brown hair. I ran facial recognition software on a close-up enhanced image isolated from security footage and on a photo of Kratz, and it came back with a positive identification. According to the first batch of staff statements, the chick at the desk said the guy spoke with an English accent. We know he's a Limey originally, so it figures he's still able to do the accent.'

Mosley rubbed his hands together when Gibson opened more footage on the screen. 'So what happened next?'

'The Three Amigos returned three hours later, in a cab. No sign of their cousin or Kratz. I put a call through to LVPD's traffic division and asked them to follow the Mercedes' route through town. I also called the cab company. They're checking which driver took the fare and promised to get back to me.'

'Man, this is better than Christmas!' Mosley said. His fingers tapped on the desk in his impatience to see the last part of Gibson's analysis. 'Then they left the hotel?'

'They checked out six hours later and so did the sister, but there's no Carlito Read. I'll contact the company tomorrow but I'm guessing they took the Greyhound back to LA. This is where it gets good.' Gibson took a deep breath and located the final video. 'Man, you'll just have to see it yourself.'

The lobby appeared, captured by a camera opposite the front desk. Mosley watched the Fernandez family approach the exit and set down their bags.

'What am I supposed to look at?'

'See that guy carrying the Walgreens bag?' Gibson pointed at a man wearing dark clothes limping towards the elevators. 'Konrad Kratz. I thought he looked familiar so I accessed the footage for the corridor outside his room and it's the same guy who goes in. Less than an hour later he left. Took his bags and didn't check out. I found him in the parking garage directly opposite a camera, so I got an awesome view of the licence plate.'

Mosley's nose almost touched the screen. 'It has the Arches on it. Utah?'

'Ten out of ten,' he replied. 'I put it through the DMV again. The Ford Taurus was bought in Midvale to the south of Salt Lake City on Monday, June 29th. A guy named André Wood paid cash for it.'

'So Kratz fled to Utah?' Mosley grinned at memories of a family vacation to the state many years ago. 'I bet it was right up his alley.'

'I spoke to that Demaine technical analyst guy at Denver's FBI field office. He said he'd run checks on the name André Wood, especially between Friday June 29th and Wednesday July 22nd.'

'The 22nd,' Mosley echoed. 'Why then?'

'Because five days after being dumped at LAX, that exact same car got towed to the pound.'

Chapter 15 – Wednesday 5th August 2009

3.00pm – PDT
San Fernando Road, Los Angeles, California

An air conditioning unit above a trio of filing cabinets shuddered into life, its low hum amplified by the quietness only a day allocated to catching up on paperwork could bring. Mosley and Hallberg occupied their respective desks for much of this time; the former analysing the limited intelligence gathered on the Fernandez family, whilst the latter constructed a timeline following the Austrian backpackers' movements.

Muñoz's dislike of flying got the better of him and he'd left home early that morning to drive I-15's dusty path north-east to Las Vegas, arriving around noon to interview the two teenage bellhops. Two hours and a sizeable lunch later he'd phoned Mosley to share the information he'd obtained, and confirm his readiness to commence the return journey.

Mosley's Los Angeles-based instructions to Gibson centred on collating all current evidence to provide a condensed sequence of events. An early morning phone call from Niall Demaine aided his task, thanks to the Denver-based analyst's search for André Wood proving more fruitful than anyone anticipated, given the short time frame. The search parameters made locating an uncommon name inside a relatively small geographical area easier than Demaine expected, and a series of warrants and his persuasive telephone manner circumvented privacy restrictions wherever necessary. Satisfied he'd uncovered everything available, Demaine compiled a timeline backed up by evidence to substantiate each part, then sent the information and an offer of unlimited further assistance directly to Gibson.

Mosley stared at the computer screen. 'What's new?'

'Man, this is better than my first time,' Gibson muttered when a nearby printer whirred into action.

Mosley patted him on the back, his previous foul mood forgotten. 'The unfortunate lady would no doubt agree.'

Gibson grabbed the papers. 'Wednesday, June 3rd. André Wood booked into a hotel in Solvang for a week, then no further activity occurred until the month's end. We know the neighbours spotted Kratz at his Glendale home before he disappeared.'

An impatient Mosley nodded. 'And then?'

'He took the Greyhound from LA via Vegas to Salt Lake City on Monday, June 29th, bought the Taurus at a used car dealership in Midvale and made a reservation at a nearby hotel for a week. He checked out early, reappeared in Cortez in the Four Corners area for one night on Friday 3rd. He then–'

'Did he visit his vacation home?' Hallberg interrupted between sips of the coffee he'd grabbed on his return from a bathroom break.

'Can't say for sure,' Gibson replied. 'A forensics team from the Denver area processed the Paradise Hills house and said someone gained access recently. No signs of forced entry and it looked like someone accessed the safe.'

Mosley narrowed his eyes. 'I'm guessing he kept a stash of cash and other fake ID there.'

'That's what they think too,' Gibson agreed. 'The next day he crossed into Arizona and stayed at two different Phoenix hotels between Saturday 4th and Friday 17th. He arrived in Las Vegas and checked into a room at Caesars for seven nights, but didn't spend a full night there before leaving without checking out. Let's hope what happened to Kratz in Vegas won't stay in Vegas for much longer.'

'You heard from the LVPD video surveillance guys?' Mosley asked as he skimmed through the information.

'Not yet, I'll follow up on it tomorrow. André Wood arrived at a motel in Burbank on Saturday 18th and stayed four nights. He checked out on Wednesday 22nd and the Taurus appeared in an airport parking lot later that day.'

'He could have fled the country,' Mosley said. 'Or maybe it's a ruse to throw us off the scent and the bastard's still in town?'

Gibson picked up his cup and swirled its contents as if waiting for the answer to reveal itself. 'Demaine said no passengers named André Wood flew out of LAX that week. If he did fly out he'll have used another fake identity.'

Hallberg nodded and finished his drink. 'What method will you use to prove he took a flight out of town?'

'Photogrammetric engineering. It uses known dimensions in a specific location to calculate the height of people in that location.' Gibson went on to mention two phone calls he'd made during Mosley's lunch run: the first to LAX's management, who'd offered unlimited access to all their security footage; the second after he'd recalled Tony Pell recently mention completing an updated course on the technique. Still keen to honour his offer of assistance in the hunt for Kratz, Tony agreed to negotiate a mix of agreed consultancy and vacation time, and make the return journey to the city the next day.

A smiling Mosley cracked his knuckles, patted Gibson on the shoulder and reached for his now tepid coffee.

****

5.22pm – PDT
FBI Field Office, Denver, Colorado

Assistant Special Agent in Charge Jared Pearson looked up from a thin file he'd been given minutes earlier by his immediate superior Colin Milne.

'Is Sam aware of this?'

Milne shook his head, his greying hair lighter than usual where it reflected the late afternoon sun streaming into the room. 'Everything's in place, according to the Director. I called Stateline's resident agency yesterday and discussed the situation with Jed Masters, the agent who's going to oversee Sam. The routine of work and his family's presence means I have every confidence Sam will cope well.'

Pearson sighed and tried to imagine Sam's reaction 'When will you tell him?'

'They return from Breckenridge this Friday afternoon, and I see no point in ruining their vacation before then,' Milne replied. He looked past the window to where thickening clouds had begun to congregate above the familiar mountains. 'I suggest we visit later that evening when the children will be asleep.'

'There's definitely no progress in locating Kratz?'

'I spoke to Detective Mosley from LAPD two hours ago and nothing specific was mentioned. Niall Demaine's helping them trace Kratz's movements, but it's a painstaking process. He said if you go by the *Den of Iniquity*, he's happy to show you what he's found.'

'Don't you mean the Bat Cave?' an amused Pearson countered.

Milne smiled. 'Hey, if it helps him get the job done. Seriously, we need to offer our assistance in whatever way we can. Demaine's working directly with them and the LA field office in addition to his duties here, and I've said if there's any indication Kratz has returned to Colorado we'll also investigate that aspect. To say Mosley sounds stressed is an understatement; his team's gotten one hell of a job dumped on them.'

Pearson nodded his agreement and both men descended into an uncomfortable silence, contemplating the news they dreaded having to break forty-eight hours later.

Chapter 16 – Thursday 6th August 2009

11.56am – PDT
Los Angeles International Airport, California

Against the bustling departure hall's brightly-lit backdrop, a steady stream of travellers and those bidding them farewell appeared surprisingly ambivalent about the LAPD forensic team carrying out their duties. Gibson, sporting a POLICE jacket emblazoned with fluorescent yellow letters, received little attention on his return from meeting the airport's Head of Security. He offered a thumbs up to Tony, confirmation he'd obtained surveillance footage covering the last ten days of July and an offer of later recordings, if required.

Gibson planned to carry out his analysis back at the police station, now he'd compiled a visual profile of Kratz from photographs and costume department data supplied by the Wolf TV network. After downloading these measurements and the surveillance footage they'd just obtained into a specialised computer programme, Gibson and Tony could then compare Kratz's recorded physical dimensions against those of departing passengers.

At the same time as Paco Fernandez made the move from Mexico to Los Angeles in the late Sixties, his sister – an ambitious young woman who'd always wanted to travel – applied to study in England. Sara Fernandez embraced the educational and employment opportunities this move provided, choosing to remain in Preston following her graduation. Weeks later, a protracted and violent robbery occurred at the bank she'd recently started working for, and two detectives interviewed Sara in the immediate aftermath. She'd encountered Eddie Pell again around a month later, this time during an unforgettable night out at the Top Rank.

Their son, Tony, made the opposing transatlantic journey over two decades later to study forensic science at UCLA, where he'd met Susie Read. The newly-married couple soon discovered they were both distant cousins of the now-deceased Carlito Read and, keen to increase the distance between their growing family and the Fernandez clan, Tony and Susie transferred their jobs to Barstow's safer surroundings in 2006.

'Man, you don't know how much we appreciate you helping us out,' Gibson said, pocketing a digital camera. 'If Mosley hasn't pissed off the Big Guy upstairs more than usual, we might have a result by the end of today.'

Tony nodded. 'No problem,' he replied. 'Glad I can help, especially if it locates Kratz.' He measured the height of the nearest check-in desk and ignored the bemused stares from a Chinese family nearby. 'Anyway, I'd asked for a week off and we'd planned to spend four days in Glendale at Susie's parents' place.'

'You and Sam went to school together? That must mean you also knew Peter Umpleby?'

Tony nodded again. 'Yeah, unfortunately. The guy was an arsehole right from day one, and by that I mean when we all started primary school at the age of four. He hated Sam pretty much from the beginning, for reasons still unknown to us. There's a group of us, five altogether, who stay in contact across the Pond. Obviously I see more of Sam, but the others visit regularly. They're quite insistent they're happy to travel.'

Gibson chuckled at Tony's last remark. 'Your hometown's that bad?'

'It's not the nicest place,' he replied, smiling wryly. 'I've been back a few times to see my parents and to go to weddings. Apart from family and friends I don't miss it.'

'Have you heard anything from Sam recently?'

'He returns from a family vacation tomorrow. From what Mosley told me, the FBI boss man at his field office is going to break it to him when they get home.' Tony shook his head. 'That's not a task I'd want. If Sam thinks his wife and kids are in danger he'll be devastated.'

Gibson scanned the departure hall. 'Surely the Bureau will make arrangements?'

'Yeah, I suppose. It's just–' The tape measure snapped back into its plastic casing and Tony jumped in surprise. 'Sam had pretty much recovered from his ordeal last summer and got his life back to normal.

He's invited my family to Colorado for a long weekend in the fall and we were all looking forward to it.'

'Yeah, I've heard the colours are beautiful at that time of year.'

'So Sam's always said,' Tony replied. 'Also, my wife's pretty cut up about her cousin. They didn't see each other often, but she always kept a soft spot for Carlito. Susie's got blonde hair and blue eyes even though she has a Mexican grandma, so she used to say her and Carlito needed to stick together.' He pushed the tape measure into his back pocket. 'Kratz also killed her grandma's brother, that Baby Gonzalez character, so it's hit a little too close to home. That's why we arranged a week away from work to come back to the city.'

Gibson tried to picture the extensive family tree neatly folded into one of the case files he'd sifted through over the past weeks. 'I thought Carlito was *your* cousin?' he asked.

'Shared relatives way, way back.' Tony's grin faded. 'So, what's the latest on Kratz?'

Gibson took a couple of minutes to update him on the early morning update he'd received from LVPD, now a network of surveillance cameras had tracked Read's Mercedes heading west out of town and presumably towards Death Valley. Speculation over its first destination endured, until later footage showed the Three Amigos getting out of a cab at Caesars Palace early on Saturday morning. At the request of local detectives, the cab company immediately located the driver who'd collected the fare. José Tejeda admitted to being apprehensive about the three passengers he'd picked up near Nellis although, to his surprise, they'd maintained a dignified silence for the journey *and* added a substantial tip at their destination.

'Shouldn't be too much longer,' Tony commented as two young male CSIs pulled a tape measure across a walkway and their older female teammate annotated a diagram of the departure hall. 'Then we can get back to the station.'

Gibson nodded. 'You're keen.'

Tony folded his arms across his chest. 'Bloody right I'm keen; I want that bastard caught!'

****

Mosley poured coffee into three mismatched mugs and, as Gibson and Tony conferred in low voices, waited impatiently for the photogrammetric software installed on Tony's laptop to run Kratz's data against all adult males in the departure hall on Wednesday, July 22nd. Gibson's main role was to match passenger check-in data against the times Tony flagged and record the personal details of those scoring a possible hit, ready for additional scrutiny.

Mosley picked up two of the mugs and crossed the room. 'The food shouldn't take much longer,' he said, referring to Muñoz and Hallberg's dash to a Glendale pizzeria the team often frequented when they worked late.

Gibson rubbed his eyes. 'Man, this is hardcore. We've reached late afternoon, ruled out five so far and just gotten a hit on a sixth. The check-in data says this one's a British guy named Thomas Moulson. I'll run him against the databases Demaine's authorised us to access, but it can wait until I've got a belly full of deep pan.'

'You guys are doing an awesome job,' Mosley replied. He clapped them both on the back and turned his full attention to Tony. 'We can't thank you enough.'

'No problem. I'll do anything for pizza if you lot are paying.'

'Where was this Moulson dude heading off to?' Mosley squinted at a tall brown-haired man on the screen. 'Looks like one of those physics geeks you see around Caltech *and* he looks like he needs a doctor. See how he's clutching his side?'

Tony peered at the check-in desk's emblem. 'That's Swissair. According to the departure list there was a direct flight to Zürich at seven-thirty.'

'Zürich?' Mosley repeated. His forehead creased into a pronounced frown. 'That's one hell of a coincidence. Didn't Freya Burdett fly out on that flight?' He noticed Tony's puzzled expression. 'American chick from Castaic working for an LA publishing house. Found murdered in her Zürich hotel room ten days ago. We were asked to keep our eyes and ears open because the Swiss police speculated someone followed her from here.'

'Seems like the pizza's going to take a while,' Gibson grumbled, painfully aware of the hollow feeling in his stomach. 'I'll take my mind off imminent starvation and see what comes back on Moulson.' His fingers moved over the laptop's keyboard and hit the *enter* key with a flamboyant tap.

Mosley coughed violently when a mouthful of hot coffee attempted to flow down his windpipe. 'What the fuck?' he eventually managed to choke out.

They stared at the photograph of an overweight man whose black hair fell in tight ringlets around his shoulders. Gibson skimmed Moulson's particulars. 'States his height as five-eight,' he said. 'He ain't the guy on the screen.'

'Check for workplace records,' Tony suggested, his own hunger forgotten. An icy feeling spread throughout his chest. 'This doesn't add up.'

Mosley leaned closer to the screen. 'He works for a computer consultancy firm in Santa Clarita and lives in Palmdale. Their personnel photo matches the one registered to the DMV.'

'So the guy checking in, that's Kratz?' Tony asked, incredulous they appeared to have achieved a successful result so soon.

'Find the footage from Caesars.' Urgency crept into Mosley's tone. 'The Saturday morning section where the Fernandez kids check out and that André Wood guy returns.'

Gibson clicked on an icon on the computer's desktop and brought up a sequence of film. 'Wood, otherwise known as Kratz, is holding his right side just above his waist. That's the exact same place as the guy pretending to be Thomas Moulson at the airport,' he said. 'I'll get the images enhanced so we can do a direct facial comparison, but if they're not the same guy I'll run naked down the Walk of Fame.'

Mosley grinned, a rarely displayed expression which completely changed his features. 'That's two reasons to hope we get a positive identification.'

****

7.58pm – MDT
Breckenridge, Colorado

Sam carried the last suitcase through from the cabin's unused fourth bedroom and took care to avoid a mound of shoes he'd nearly tripped over minutes earlier. 'These ten days have certainly gone fast,' he said. 'I suppose it's back to the daily grind next week, unless we win the state lottery this weekend.'

Anna reached into the closet to lift two pairs of shorts from their hangers. 'Have you bought a ticket?' she asked.

'Have *you* bought one?'

She carried the clothes to a suitcase lying open on the floor. 'I guess your alarm clock's ending its vacation at the same time you do on Monday morning.'

Sam groaned. 'Don't remind me.'

Anna picked up a pile of dirty hiking clothes. 'I always thought you loved your job?'

'I do, but I love my family more,' Sam replied, crouching to open another suitcase.

A warm smile spread across her face. 'For a big badass agent, you're kind of soft underneath.'

'You finally realised then?' He wrapped his arms around her waist and pulled her closer. 'I do wish we could stay here longer.'

She returned the hug and then reluctantly pointed to their belongings. 'While it's tempting to leave the packing, it won't do itself. The faster we get it done, the faster we can make the most of two sleeping children. They sure were ready for bed early.' She saw Sam wink, and rolled her eyes in response. 'And my mom thinks you're such a gentleman.'

'And she'd be correct,' he shot back and smoothed an eyebrow in an exaggerated manner. 'I'm glad I'm not back in New York for a couple of weeks. It'll be good to get back into the old routine, catch up with the Denver team and – most importantly for our family – enjoy a normal life.'

Chapter 17 – Friday 7th August 2009

5.23pm – PDT
Glendale, California

'Your night off starts here, gentlemen.' Mosley raised a glass of iced tea aloft and waited for his four companions to mirror the action. 'Shame it ain't beer, but we don't want DUIs on the way home, right?' The clink of glasses caused a middle-aged couple at a nearby table to smile and wonder what had led to such high spirits at this early hour.

'To the imminent capture of Konrad Kratz,' Tony added, gaining emphatic nods of approval from the detectives as they sipped their drinks.

'You think we'll get him soon?' Hallberg asked.

Mosley looked up from the laminated menu 'There's one hell of a lot more to go on than at the start of the week,' he replied. 'I sent all the evidence and video footage to the lead detective investigating the Zürich case. He immediately arranged to pull security footage from the airport and train stations, and he also accessed hotel databases in the city. Thomas Moulson paid for a week at a Stadelhofen hotel, disappeared four days later on Monday July 27th *and* Swissair's records show Freya Burdett occupied the seat next to Thomas Moulson.'

Muñoz nodded thoughtfully. 'So they're now hunting Kratz in Europe?'

'Yeah. Beate Gessler – that's the Swiss detective – said they'd focus on their country and asked for anything new we uncover.' Mosley passed the menu to Hallberg. 'His team pulled footage from near Freya Burdett's hotel on the evening she was murdered. She's seen walking beside a guy who matches both our images of Kratz at LAX and those obtained elsewhere in Zürich. They entered the hotel together and he left alone thirty minutes later, carrying a large bag.'

'The murder weapon?' Tony said, thinking aloud.

'Maybe,' Mosley replied, unable to wipe the amused expression from his face. 'Gessler found a receipt from an upmarket city centre store named Globus. All the items listed were soon accounted for, apart from a four-and-a-half kilogram Toblerone.'

Hallberg raised his eyebrows. 'As in the European chocolate you can buy at the airport?'

Mosley's grin widened. 'Based on her injuries and the missing candy bar, Gessler and his team theorise she suffered death by chocolate.'

'That's harsh,' Muñoz said. He shook his head and tried to keep his face straight. 'You really think he used a giant candy bar to kill her?'

'What's the likelihood of Kratz eating the evidence?' Mosley continued, enjoying the reaction he'd generated. 'I'm being serious here, guys. If he whacked her around the head and then took it, all he needs to do is eat the chocolate and dispose of the packaging. It's the perfect murder weapon.'

Tony nodded and felt himself start to relax after a stressful couple of days. 'It's certainly different.'

'Kratz travelled to Switzerland on a fake passport,' Mosley added. He cracked his knuckles and chuckled at Hallberg's wince. 'I went to the real Thomas Moulson's workplace this morning, that's why I was late. The poor guy's mortified and assured me he's not been out of the country since flying back to the UK at Easter to see his parents. He said he's especially particular about shredding documents and doesn't have a clue how his identity was stolen. I didn't tell him Kratz used it – just said it's part of an ongoing investigation into the production of fake passports in the Greater Los Angeles area.'

Gibson swallowed the last of his drink. 'We all know you can get anything you want in this city if you have the cash and the contacts.'

'I'd considered that,' Mosley replied. 'I could put one of you undercover and see if you can obtain a fake UK passport.'

Tony's mouth fell open when four pairs of eyes stared directly at him. 'Don't look at me, I'm not a cop.'

'Yeah, but you're a Limey.' Mosley turned his head to smile at the approaching waitress and then winked at Tony. 'I'll square you a few extra days away from the Barstow crime lab if we need you for any longer. Let's call it an extra assignment.'

****

8.30pm MDT
Golden, Colorado

Anna entered the kitchen and adjusted the straps on her sundress. 'That's what every woman should have,' she commented as Sam carried a pile of dirty plates across the room.

'A dishwasher?' he asked, pulling its door open with a flourish.

She laughed, the two margaritas she'd consumed on an empty stomach enough to make her feel pleasantly tipsy. 'Yeah, and a husband packin' a cute ass who ain't afraid to load it.'

He watched her retrieve a bottle of Chardonnay she'd placed in the refrigerator soon after they arrived home three hours earlier. 'I also put some clothes in the washing machine.'

'Man, you're just too good.'

'So you keep telling me.' Sam jumped to his feet and grabbed Anna around the waist. 'It's no use wriggling; you won't escape,' he whispered, listening to her laughter as he lifted her onto the countertop. 'What's so funny?'

Anna draped her arms over his shoulders. 'The other night, I was thinking back to our first weekend away together.' She leaned back and used both hands to massage his neck. 'Seems like yesterday.'

Sam let out a contented sigh and the flood of carefully stored memories stretched a wide smile across his face. He peeled the thin straps away from her shoulders. 'Aspen?'

'Yeah.' She was interrupted by Sam pulling her closer. 'Didn't see much of the place and behaved like a pair of horny teenagers most of the time. Much like now.'

'I keep telling you,' he whispered in her ear, reminiscent of someone sharing an unpatented secret. 'Fresh mountain air really does it for me.'

She realised he'd pushed up her dress and instant heat spread across her chest. 'What's your excuse now we're back at lower altitude?'

Sam tugged on his belt buckle with his other hand. 'All the extra oxygen flowing to where it shouldn't.'

Anna surveyed the pristine kitchen and blushed. 'Here?'

105

He ignored the sound of car doors slamming nearby. 'Why not? It's not like we never–'

The doorbell's piercing chime caused Sam to startle and step back. 'Who the hell?' he exclaimed, checking the wall clock.

Anna jumped to the floor and smoothed down her dress, then quickly moved to the lounge window overlooking the front of the house and pulled back one of its drapes. 'There's another car on the driveway,' she said, failing to hide her surprise. 'Looks like Milne and Pearson.'

Sam stared at his co-workers against the darkness enveloping the foothills, now daylight had faded. 'What the hell's going on?' he muttered, all previous intentions forgotten. He flung open the front door and immediately realised by the two men's demeanour that this wasn't any kind of *welcome home* visit.

Milne peered over Sam's shoulder and took in the house's light and airy first floor. 'Are the children in bed?' he asked. Sam picked up on the quiet tension in his tone and followed Anna's confused gaze from one man to the next.

He nodded and stepped aside, enabling them to enter. 'Why are you here?'

Pearson pointed at two large sofas nearby. 'Can we sit?'

'What's happened?' Sam demanded, his voice raised.

'It's Kratz, isn't it?' Anna closed the lounge door behind them to minimise the chance of awakening Angela and John.

'Sam, you need to sit down,' Pearson continued. 'Please.'

Milne tore his eyes from a recent family photograph on the mantelpiece. 'I hate to break it to you, but we're certain he's still alive. However, before you panic, the evidence suggests he's fled to Europe.'

Sam shook his head, slumped onto the nearest sofa and tried to comprehend Milne's bombshell.

'He could've come back,' he said, not specifically to anyone.

'Possible, but unlikely in the circumstances,' Milne replied.

Anna lowered herself onto the seat beside Sam and reached for his hand. 'Where is he?'

Pearson pulled a case file from his briefcase. 'Our last positive sighting of him occurred in Zürich eleven days ago.'

'So he might be anywhere by now.' Sam crossed to the drinks cabinet and grabbed an almost full bottle of single malt.

'Is that wise?' Milne asked when he spotted the pronounced tremble in Sam's hands.

Sam half-filled a tumbler and downed the whisky in two gulps. 'Probably not,' he replied, refilled the glass and returned to his seat. 'How long have you known?'

'For definite?' Pearson opened the file and placed it on a low coffee table in front of the couple. 'Two days.'

'You let me carry on like everything's normal while that psycho could be out there hunting my family?' Sam struggled to articulate the words, barely able to suppress his growing rage.

Milne allowed them to process the information. 'Only a handful of people knew where you were, so we deemed you to be safe. We also mistakenly hoped he'd be caught before your return.'

Sam and Anna listened to Pearson explain how both LAPD's and the FBI's investigations had uncovered Kratz's recent movements, both too stunned to speak as the news sunk in.

'I wish you'd told me sooner,' Sam muttered, unable to tear his eyes from a grainy image of Kratz riding an escalator at Zürich Flughafen.

Pearson retrieved a second file. 'We needed the time to get things in place.'

Anna swallowed and locked eyes with Pearson. 'You mean like protective custody?'

'Not quite.' He paused and considered his next words. 'We're unsure if you or your family is definitely in danger but, until Kratz is captured, we're not prepared to take the risk. There's a resident agency in South Lake Tahoe from where you'll be able to work. I've spoken to the SSA who oversees the place and you can reprise your CSRU role in New York from an office he's already prepared for you. All the secure connections will be in place by next week.'

Sam bit off a piece of thumb nail without realising. 'Have you told this guy everything?' he asked.

'Yes,' Milne replied. 'His other agents have also been informed. You'll be expected to accompany them in the field if necessary, although he assures me this would be minimal at most.'

Sam placed a protective arm around Anna's tense shoulders. 'And my family?'

Pearson handed what resembled a real estate brochure to Sam. 'Jed Masters, the agent who'll keep a close watch on you all, owns a family-sized cabin near Lake Tahoe. The place recently became vacant after the family leasing it moved to Reno. The Bureau will fund your relocation indefinitely, although be warned you may be moved further afield on a permanent basis if it's proved Kratz has returned to the US and then isn't promptly apprehended.'

'There's a car waiting for you in one of the airport lots and the house has been stocked with provisions,' Milne added. He noticed the tremor resume when Sam reached for the almost empty glass he'd placed on the coffee table. 'The four of you will take a flight from Denver to Reno tomorrow morning. Pack enough clothing for you all and ensure the children have familiar items. There's also an allowance for purchasing anything else you need to make life more comfortable. Remember that it gets cold at night, even at this time of the year.'

Anna stared at the ceiling separating them from the children's bedrooms. 'Are we safe here?'

'Jared will stay here tonight while you pack,' Milne replied. 'I'll return at six tomorrow morning to drive you to the airport. John isn't an issue, but what will you tell Angela?'

Sam glanced at Anna, his mind suddenly blank. 'I can't think.'

Anna swallowed to clear the lump in her throat. 'She knows Daddy helps the police catch bad guys. Tell her you need to work away for a while and we're going with you this time.'

Sam stared at the photo of their new home. 'At least it's a wood cabin,' he said. 'Angela should be fine. She loved the Breckenridge cabin and asked if we could live there forever.'

Milne shook his head. 'I'm sorry it's come to this. It goes without saying you tell no one.'

'What about our parents?' Anna asked, aware of the tears pricking her eyelids.

Milne nodded at Pearson, who extracted a Government Issue cell phone from his pocket and placed it on the table. 'It's not the usual protocol, but we can allow you both to make one short phone call. From then, all outside contact must be through the Bureau. You can contact me by email and I'll act as a go-between for your families.'

The two senior agents rose to their feet in unison. 'This won't be easy, but we know you'll both get through it,' Milne said, wondering whether the young couple would cope with this latest setback when he looked at their blanched faces.

Chapter 18 – Saturday 8th August 2009

7.31am – MDT
Denver International Airport, Colorado

Sam watched Anna approach the row of seating where they'd tucked themselves away from a constant stream of passers-by and carefully set down a cardboard tray carrying a breakfast he had no appetite for. The airport's bustling departure area was busier than they'd expected, especially this early *and* at the weekend. Angela heard Anna position the tray opposite Sam and eagerly turned her attention away from a distant take-off.

'Let's not make a habit of this,' Anna muttered at the sight of their daughter's growing smile.

The little girl studied a chocolate muffin nestled within some napkins. 'Is that mine?'

Sam nodded and forced himself to smile back at his daughter. 'That's right, sweetheart. Hold it in both hands.' Angela's face lit up and her small hands reached out to him. 'Eat it nicely and don't drop any crumbs,' he added after twisting the cap off a bottle of apple juice and inserting a straw.

'I got coffee and croissants for us,' Anna said. 'Figured you wouldn't feel like eating.'

Sam nodded and reached for one of the cups. 'Cheers,' he replied, forcing a smile when Angela pushed a large piece of muffin into her mouth. 'I'll have mine quickly, then I can feed John before we have to board,' Sam said. He picked up a jar of puréed apple and bottle of milk they'd brought from home. 'Take your time.'

Anna's gaze settled on their son sleeping soundly in his stroller, the image of contentment despite an earlier than usual wake-up call that morning. Thankfully, within minutes of being fed and dressed he'd returned to a deep sleep, although Angela hadn't been as easy to pacify. Sam had knelt beside her bed, wiped away the tears trickling down her cheeks and held her small hands in his as he told her he'd been asked to help the police catch a bad guy far, far away. He'd hugged his sobbing daughter and gently explained how it may take a very long time to catch the bad guy, so the whole family would go with him this time. Angela's eyes widened when she saw a photograph of the carved wooden animals on the cabin's porch; her smile finally returning due to Sam's promise of an extra special breakfast at the airport.

As night relinquished its temporary grasp, Milne had arrived at the family home and helped Sam load an assortment of trolley cases and bags into the trunk. Still reeling from two tense phone calls to their terrified parents and three hours of fitful sleep, Sam and Anna – both running on pure adrenaline – climbed into the vehicle. Anna wistfully stared at their home from the middle of the back seat, unsure whether they'd ever be able to return. An almost empty I-70 granted them a speedy journey to the airport, the car's motion lulling Angela into a light sleep against Anna's arm. Sam closed his eyes against the city rushing past, unable to process the images blurred by one scene merging into the next nor comprehend the magnitude of the journey on which they were about to embark.

****

4.56pm – BST
Blackpool, England

A quartet of middle-aged men congregated around the bar fell silent and gazed forlornly into their pints, as if expecting a reason for the town's decline in footballing fortunes to emerge from someone's glass. Roger Mortimer looked around the disconcertingly quiet pub, picked another strand of shredded lettuce from the BLT he'd ordered twenty minutes earlier and rued how its greasy, cheap bacon did nothing to settle his churning stomach. A young blonde woman behind the bar nodded at his raised glass and flashed him the briefest of smiles, then pulled him a second pint of the *piss* produced by another local brewery.

He returned to his seat and saw the heavy wooden doors open, revealing a dark figure silhouetted against bright sunlight. Roger shivered when an unexpected draught swirled around his table. He set down his beer and realised this must be the man who'd phoned him on Tuesday morning, the caller simply stating the time and venue before he'd hung up.

Oliver Stamford scanned the room, nodded in Roger's direction and strolled to the bar, where he ordered a bottle of imported lager. Time had done little to change the casually dressed man, Roger decided; his almost black hair a striking contrast against lightly tanned skin and vivid blue eyes, as it had been six years earlier. Tall and muscular, although not overtly, he carried a disconcerting air Roger hadn't picked up on the last time they met.

'Hey Roger, my man! Long time, no see,' Stamford said in a cordial tone. He carefully placed his drink on the scratched wooden table and reached across to shake Roger's hand. 'We shouldn't let it go so long next time, right?'

Something in the younger man's eyes instantly put him on his guard. Roger nodded and felt the hair on the back of his neck prickle. 'Are you here on hol– vacation?' he asked, relieved to see Stamford position his stool on the opposite side of the table.

'Kind of,' he replied and opened the small tub of Pringles he'd also bought. 'It's always good to come back, especially now I've gotten some business I need to take care of,'

'Anything I can help you with?' Roger asked, shaking his head to decline the offer of a crisp. 'I know of a great little restaurant in Preston, that's a town about half an hour from here, which wants to expand. We could always use some investment. If the original pub's anything to go by you'll reap a healthy return.'

Stamford shook his head. 'Sorry, man. That's just not possible. One of my ventures back home is in schtuck after I made a mistake with the guy I appointed to run the place. Goddamn waste of space. Place is up shit creek and if I don't lay my hands on some capital soon, it'll lose its paddle.'

Roger frowned. 'So how can I help you?'

'You said you'd double my money.' He raised his eyebrows expectantly. 'Did you?'

'Well, yeah. But...'

'Awesome! How soon can you transfer it to my account?'

'It may be a few months,' Roger replied, aware his mouth had become uncomfortably dry.

'Months?' The American's eyes widened. 'What the fuck do you mean *months*?'

A droplet of sweat trickled down Roger's forehead. 'I invested it in property. Prices have skyrocketed since, but legally I've got to give the tenants two months' notice before I can even think about selling the houses.' He gulped and picked up his pint. 'That'll probably take a while. There's a recession going on over here, if you've not heard.'

The sound made by Stamford's bottle slamming onto the table caused two of the men at the bar to stare daggers over their shoulders. 'I need my money,' he hissed.

Roger leaned closer and lowered his voice. 'And I'll get it to you, but I can't lay my hands on it immediately. Surely you understand, being a businessman yourself?'

He nodded. 'Okay, I hear you. Sorry to get... pissed. The situation's causing me a whole world of grief. I'll leave you my cell number and you can call me when you're ready to transfer the cash.'

Roger sighed in relief. 'I'm glad we've sorted things out. Perhaps in the future we can work together again?'

Stamford nodded again, swallowed the last of his lager and walked to the door.

/////

The same vivid blue eyes tracked Roger's Jaguar as it moved away from the kerb and accelerated to the end of the street.

Konrad steered his rented Vauxhall Astra into a gap in the steady procession of traffic and, at a safe distance, followed the Jaguar towards the town's northern suburbs.

****

'Man, I slept like a baby last night,' Muñoz commented to Hallberg and Gibson as they walked into the incident room. 'It's like I'm drunk on sleep, and it's an awesome feeling.'

'Don't get used to it,' Mosley interrupted. He picked up one of four blueberry muffins he'd purchased from a bakery two blocks down from his home and broke off a large chunk. 'You and Hallberg won't have time to breathe next week.' His eyes darted from one man to the other. 'The great American road trip,' he added, then chuckled at the confusion spreading across their faces.

'Us?' Muñoz asked.

'Yeah, I'm staying here with Gibson while you guys hit the open road. You'll be following the Konrad Kratz trail through five states. It's a special tour missing from all the guidebooks.'

Hallberg glared at Gibson, 'Why's he staying?' he asked, distinctly unenamored at the prospect of leaving his home comforts behind.

'I'm apparently the resident computer geek, so there's no road trip for me,' Gibson said. He thought back to his honeymoon and experienced a pang of longing for those carefree days following the Pacific Coast Highway south from Washington state. 'I did offer.'

'Jones said he'd rent a car for you,' Mosley added. He passed two box files of information to Muñoz and Hallberg. 'You'll drive from each of Kratz's destinations to the next and you'll need to stop at all manned rest areas between to show staff the photos.' He pointed to the files. 'You have images of the Taurus, and of Kratz disguised as André Wood taken from the cameras at Caesars Palace. If people ask for more information, and it's likely they will, tell them he's an escaped bank robber.'

Mosley bit off a large section of muffin and waited for Muñoz and Hallberg to read their itinerary. 'The hotels are all reserved,' he added in a muffled voice. 'I figured you could stay where Kratz did. It'll speed things along for you.'

'Speed things along?' Muñoz echoed. He raised his dark brows at Hallberg.

Hallberg sighed heavily. 'Seven nights? My wife won't be happy about this. Can't the local cops investigate?'

114

Mosley shook his head and explained what they already knew he'd say: that it would take too much time to bring all local divisions up to speed. He shared news that Commanding Officer Iain Jones agreed they'd both take the next day off, and at least the same had been granted upon their return, with no effect on their annual leave entitlement. The finer details of their assignment filled the next five minutes, followed by Mosley's promise he'd go through any new developments later that afternoon.

'What's happening here while we're away?' Muñoz asked. He closed the file and helped himself to breakfast. 'Won't you be short-staffed?'

'In addition to liaising with detectives from Kratz's hometown in England, an FBI agent from New York arrives next Monday,' Mosley replied. 'He's a member of Sam Bury's Critical Situation Research Unit, and is thought to be one of the best behavioural analysts in the business. We hope he can use the evidence gathered so far to suggest where Kratz could be, where he may travel next and the aliases he'll possibly use. We already know he isn't averse to ID theft.'

Hallberg picked up the last muffin and, to his surprise, detected an uncharacteristic lack of appetite. 'We'll do our best, boss,' he said. 'It's time I reclaimed my life.'

****

1.21pm – PDT
Kingsbury, Nevada

The Reno-bound flight boarded and departed on time; their two children sleeping soundly for most of the ninety-minute journey meaning Sam and Anna's morning was considerably less traumatic than anticipated. Sam collected their loan vehicle from a long-stay parking lot and chose to follow a longer route than their satnav suggested, making good time on the journey to Kingsbury after leaving the hot, semi-arid lower elevations behind them. Miles of switchbacks looped through wooded mountains as they ascended, before straightening out to skirt the edge of Lake Tahoe's startlingly blue waters. The breathtaking views captivated Anna and Angela, until the Saab turned off Kingsbury Grade Road and commenced the last part of the climb to the family's home for the foreseeable future.

Angela remained unaware of her parents' trepidation as they'd entered the cabin, preferring to inspect the wooden animals on the porch away from John's loud demands for the jar of puréed vegetables he'd seen Sam grab from a bag in the trunk. Anna fed the hungry baby and smiled at the sight of Sam carrying his daughter's suitcase downstairs to the cosy bedroom they'd identified on the floorplan the previous night.

'They sure thought of everything,' Anna said, now a contented John had allowed his parents to explore the property. She grabbed a large bottle of orange juice from the refrigerator and pointed to two packets of burgers and some bread rolls. 'If you don't want to go downtown, there's actually very little we need to go out and buy today.'

Sam lifted three glasses down from a wall cupboard. 'Unless we have to stay longer than we think.' He eyeballed the open plan living space, its modern décor at odds with the cabin's wooden exterior. 'So, what are we going to do here?'

'Make the best of it,' she replied, keen not to dwell on their situation so soon. 'There's two cases of dirty laundry to wash and dry, and there's not enough fresh fruit and vegetables for more than a day or two. Why don't you take Angela to the lake and pick up some groceries on your way back? It would be good for you to spend some time together and reassure her you're not going anywhere.'

He nodded and admired their view of distant mountains beyond the lake's opposite shoreline. 'Where is she?'

Anna smiled at the thud of footsteps echoing on the stairs. 'She *was* in her bedroom, arranging her teddies and books.'

'Do you like your bedroom, sweetie?' Sam asked.

'I've got a big girl bed,' Angela announced, her pride evident.

'That's because you're a big girl,' he replied, his heart lifting when she broke into a huge smile. 'In fact, you were such a good big girl today how would you like to go to the beach, eat lots of ice cream and help me buy some groceries for Mommy?'

Angela clapped her hands. 'Is *he* coming?' she asked, glaring at the baby.

'No, he's not,' Anna said. She scooped John from the playpen and tickled his cheek. 'This little guy's my boss this afternoon. You and Daddy are going to have fun and John's going to make sure I unpack everything neatly and finish the laundry.' She turned back to Sam. 'You two go enjoy yourselves, and stay safe.'

Chapter 19 – Sunday 9th August 2009

3.27pm BST
Hutton, Preston, England

Lancashire's Constabulary's headquarters and its associated training school occupied a large site on the town's southwestern side, situated between a long stretch of dual carriageway, scattered fields and a modern housing development. A grassy area easily large enough to double as a football pitch separated the main HQ from a group of utilitarian brick buildings, built in the seventies to provide extra room for the Force's expanding operations.

On the top floor of one of these newer buildings, nestled amongst the trees, the Cold Case Unit reopened and investigated unsolved cases, some of which stretched back four decades. Cold case detectives Martin Boothroyd, Paula Phelan and Dave Sanderson had been brought together four years earlier, having topped their game in the former SIO Team, Organised Crime and Drugs Support respectively. Assisted by advances in forensic technology and new investigative techniques, the team had recently clocked up more additional hours than they could recall during the reinvestigation of two local murders, both of which were now responsible for a great deal of interest five thousand miles away.

Boothroyd, the eldest of the group and still smarting after his recent well-publicised fiftieth birthday, sighed and reclined in the swivel chair he'd occupied almost constantly since arriving at police HQ seven hours earlier. A neatly dressed man standing a shade below six feet tall, Boothroyd's apparent mild disposition could change in a flash, which had proved an effective interrogation technique over the years. He'd transferred from West Yorkshire to Preston in 1992, shortly before his marriage to a young female officer he'd met during their respective teams' liaison on a fraud case. Boothroyd's flair for investigative work had drawn accolades from all strata of the organisation and rapidly catapulted him through the ranks, making him an obvious choice to lead the cold case team.

'Who wants a brew?' Boothroyd called across the office. He massaged his aching neck and tutted impatiently when two arms instantly rose into the air.

Phelan's steel-grey eyes glanced up from her computer screen. She grabbed a wad of recently expelled sheets from a laser printer on her desk and chuckled. 'Real Yorkshire men make the best tea.' she replied. 'So crack on, lad.'

Boothroyd winced on the short walk to the kettle. 'Age discrimination, that's what this is,' he grumbled.

'Bloody hell, Martin! What happened?' Sanderson grinned and held out a large yellow mug. 'Grim Reaper still chasing you?'

'The missus wanted the garden fences painting, so guess what I spent nine hours doing yesterday?' He rubbed his lumbar region to relieve the tension knotting its muscles. 'I'm knackered, and the bloody kids refused to help their poor old Dad.'

Sanderson set the mug down on the desk and looked at him in amusement. 'You did offer to pay them?'

'Like hell I did. I feed the buggers and put a roof over their heads.' Boothroyd saw Sanderson roll his eyes. 'They should be grateful,' he added.

'I've picked up a couple of emails about the Umpleby... Kratz case, whatever the hell he's called,' Phelan said. She held the sheets aloft and shook her head. 'I loved *H.O.S.T.A.G.E.* Can't believe the lead actor's probably a serial killer.'

'You realise this is strictly confidential?' Boothroyd added. A sudden sternness infiltrated his expression. 'Even the other teams here haven't been told we're working on this case.'

Phelan nodded. 'Oh yeah, I've fended off a fair few questions from friends. I mentioned those rape cases in Crettington Park ten years ago and that seemed to satisfy their curiosity.' She skimmed one of the emails she'd printed. 'That FBI legal attaché in London sends her thanks to Sanderson for passing on the latest information we've uncovered and says she'll be back in touch soon. We've also received a reply from the current head teacher at Crettington County Primary School. Sanderson emailed him a couple of days after the summer holidays started. He apologises for not replying sooner; he'd been in Bermuda for nearly three weeks.'

'Bunch of lazy bastards,' Sanderson muttered. 'They get more holiday than they know what to do with.'

'My hubby gets proper pissed off every time you say that to him,' a grinning Phelan said. 'Can't resist baiting him at this time of year, and we can't afford to go on holiday this summer so I've left him a list of jobs to do as long as his arm. Anyway, Kenneth Yates spent yesterday going through school records and sending out letters to staff from that time. He said he'd checked their addresses the best he could. There's also a pair of teachers from back then who still work there now; he said he'd contact them directly.'

Boothroyd nodded his approval. 'Did he say anything else?'

'That he's willing to come in sometime this week to assist.' Phelan's gaze returned to the papers. 'He also said he'd pass on anything he hears from his staff.'

'What have we got so far on the cases?' Boothroyd asked. He nodded at Sanderson, who picked up one of the files on his desk.

'Monday, sixth of January, 1986. Around 5.00pm Grace Winterburn drove her VW Golf southbound on the M6 between junctions thirty-two and thirty-one, having left Crettington Primary approximately half an hour earlier.' Sanderson flicked through the slim file and picked out the key findings from the police investigation over two decades earlier. 'On her way to the motorway, she called off at Hall's Butchers on Brown Cow Lane and purchased a large meat and potato pie, the remains of which were later found in the car's boot. The late Henry Hall was interviewed during the original investigation. He said Grace parked directly outside the shop for only a couple of minutes, and she seemed in good spirits.'

'So, how did Umpleby gain access to her vehicle?' Phelan's frown deepened. 'Surely the teachers' car park was out of bounds? And, would a kid just shy of his tenth birthday know how to fix the brakes?'

Sanderson's bony hands grabbed a ham sandwich from the towering pile his wife had sent him to work with that morning. 'We accessed DVLA records for that time. Peter's mother also drove the same make and model of car. Perhaps the kid read a repair manual and worked out what to do?'

'That's more than a bit out of the ordinary,' Boothroyd said. He frowned when his colleague picked up another sandwich and took a large bite. 'Do you ever stop shovelling food into that Mersey Tunnel gob of yours?'

'The missus is still trying to fatten me up. You'd think she'd realise it's a lost cause by now.' He studied a publicity shot from the last season of *H.O.S.T.A.G.E.* showing Kratz at the helm of his on-screen team. 'If his adult personality is anything to go by, he must have been barking bloody mad as a kid.'

The others listened to Boothroyd summarise the current facts: 'There's nowt in this ridiculously skinny file to suggest the school car park got tested for brake fluid or that Umpleby held a specific grudge against Grace. Unfortunately, those were the days before schools installed CCTV and used computerised data systems. Unless we get to talk to those teachers who worked there in the mid-eighties, we can only speculate Grace had a run-in with the little shit.'

Phelan, who'd allocated most of her time to the Stavros Pallis part of the investigation, reluctantly filled the kettle to its maximum level. 'The forensic report indicates the Golf's brake lines failed when applied at speed, in much the same manner as those on Pallis' Escort,' she said. 'Circumstantially, this also matches some of the cases linked to Kratz across the Pond. I've been in contact with an LAPD detective called Ronnie Mosley, and there's also an FBI technical analyst based in Denver called Niall Demaine. They've both been helpful in sending information through.'

'What's the Pallis connection?' Sanderson asked. He smiled at fond memories of his time at the town's university and its associated drunken nights out. 'It's such a shame,' he added. 'Malaka's always made the best kebabs in town, especially after half a dozen beers and a boogie at Jokes.'

'If you say so.' Phelan grimaced and shook her head. 'I only have memories of food poisoning.'

Sanderson patted his stomach and winked at her. 'Concrete innards.'

Phelan dropped teabags into the mugs and continued to recount details of the Pallis case. 'There's no obvious connection. Pallis' pal said he planned to go to the police station to report an attempted robbery on the Friday night, and met an unpleasant end on the way there. Apparently a young lad broke in, but if Pallis got a decent gander at him he didn't have chance to pass it on. This case only flagged up because it fitted the MO and the timeline Demaine gave us.'

'Bit of a coincidence it happened the weekend before the Umpleby family emigrated to Colorado, don't you think?' Boothroyd commented. He reached for a packet of custard creams. 'Again, is a child really capable of this?'

Phelan nodded. 'If it *was* Peter, why did he target Pallis?'

'Place was a money pit. The guy did an outrageous amount of business at a weekend,' Sanderson replied. 'We'd often be queuing back onto Great Shaw Street. It wasn't a good night out unless it ended with a spicy chicken donner.'

Phelan grimaced when she felt her stomach turn. 'So, there's nothing concrete on Pallis but it looks like Umpleby might be responsible. Perhaps he thought if he didn't get caught he had nothing to lose because of moving to the States a couple of days later?'

'Why did he want English money in America?' Boothroyd asked as he picked up the first of three biscuits he'd placed on his desk. 'I suppose he could occasionally change small amounts of it and say he'd just returned from visiting family back here. Many adults would hang onto the cash, ready for the next visit. Kids are different though. It's all about instant gratification, especially the teenagers.' He paused and chewed slowly. 'I have three of them at home, I more than know. Anyway, if he grabbed a couple of grand, depending on how often he changed it and the amount tendered at each go, I reckon he'd have been set up for a couple of years, at least.'

'Until we speak to those two teachers,' Phelan poured boiling water into the mugs and then checked her copy of the case file, 'Rob Armitage and Mandy Hall, there's not much we can do. It's not like we can ask his family, is it?'

Sanderson lifted a carton of milk from the mini fridge 'Perhaps that's one reason he killed his parents, to keep them permanently quiet?' he suggested. 'The grandparents on both sides are dead. Are there any aunts, uncles or cousins on his father's side who knew him and can tell us more about his childhood?'

Boothroyd considered the idea and nodded. 'That's something for you to research. Where was his dad from?'

'Somewhere in Yorkshire, if I recall correctly,' Sanderson replied. 'All that madness must be in the genes, eh?'

Boothroyd shot him a withering look. 'That Demaine character in Denver said he'd research anything we needed. I wasn't convinced at first, then he told me what I ate for breakfast.'

Phelan's eyes widened. 'How the hell did he know that?'

Boothroyd grinned. 'Cheeky sod accessed my Tesco Clubcard records. Told me All Bran was the only adult cereal purchased and I didn't come across as a Cocoa Pops kind of guy.'

'You want me to get onto that?' Sanderson asked.

'Yeah, send a request to Demaine based on what we've learnt so far.' Boothroyd reached for another biscuit. 'And, if we do need to meet the family, I quite fancy a trip back to the Fatherland.'

****

4.02pm – PDT
San Fernando Road, Los Angeles, California

'Some bastard can go right ahead and shoot me now.' Mosley groaned and closed his eyes, the remark directed more to himself than his nearby teammate.

'So much for a day of rest,' Gibson replied as he looked away from the laptop in front of him to crack his neck. 'My wife's getting pissed about the whole deal. She said if I'm not home for dinner by seven she'd call her sister over for the evening, log onto the Tiffany website and spend money we don't have.'

'She's one tough cookie,' Mosley said, unable to hide his grin.

Gibson sighed and sent a case report to the printer. 'We want to start a family, but these long hours... Let's just say they ain't helping, in more ways than one. Four months and nothing's happened.'

'You'll be home on time.'

Gibson tilted his head and frowned. 'I'm glad you're so confident.'

'I'll see to anything that isn't finished. Don't want to see you asking for the name of my divorce lawyer.'

'She's not *that* pissed.'

'She will be if this continues. Go home, have a nice meal, wash it down with a nice cold bottle of something expensive, get busy and give me an excuse to buy something cute in nine months.'

'You're quite the old sentimental type underneath, ain't you?' the younger man commented, relieved he'd beat the worst of the evening's rush hour.

Mosley pressed his index finger against his lips. 'Don't tell everyone,' he whispered and added a conspiratorial wink when Gibson's face broke into a relieved smile. 'And, quit it with the *old*.'

'Thanks, she'll really appreciate it.' He watched the senior detective raise one greying brow. 'So, what's the plan of action while Thelma and Louise are on the road?'

Mosley pointed to a pile of papers on his desk. 'First thing I do is finish collating everything, ready for Joe Studdert's arrival tomorrow.'

'Is Sam working the case?'

Mosley shook his head. 'He's too personally connected.'

'You also have Tony Pell assigned from Barstow. He's involved too.'

'Not to the same degree,' Mosley ignored Gibson's suspicious expression.

'Tony said he's been unable to contact Sam for the past couple of days. Is he okay?'

'I'm sure he's fine.' Mosley skimmed through a recent email. 'Lab report's come back on the car Kratz dumped at LAX.'

Gibson frowned and folded his arms. 'Something's going on. You involved Sam when we thought Kratz was dead, but since the asshole's miraculous resurrection he's disappeared.'

'I'll tell Studdert his profiling services won't be needed,' Mosley replied, a hint of tension audible. 'All I heard is the FBI decided to put Sam and his family into a precautionary form of protective custody until Kratz is captured.'

'Does Tony know?'

'I'll tell him when Studdert arrives tomorrow afternoon.' Mosley leaned across the desk, surprised by Gibson's apparent unease. 'You understand this situation is confidential?' He registered Gibson's nod and then narrowed his eyes. 'You okay with that?'

'Yeah, I guess I'm shocked how much of a shitstorm Kratz has stirred up.' Gibson reached for his coffee, which had long since cooled to room temperature. 'Sam's a decent guy and I hate to think of him or his family in trouble.' He laughed and shook his head. 'Anyway, listen to me going all mushy; I've gotten as bad as you. What did that lab report tell us?'

Mosley plucked a sheet from the pile of papers closest to him. 'Even though he tried to clean up, traces of blood were found on the driver's seat. Samples were sent off for priority DNA analysis and should be back in a day or two. They also found numerous fingerprints from inside the trunk to run through AFIS. He must have forgotten to wipe it down in there.'

'Any hits?'

'I'll say. The most frequently recorded recent prints match those found at both Kratz's properties, so we can almost certainly say they're his.'

'At least if the DNA matches the profile we suspect to be Kratz's, that's going to help provide almost concrete evidence it belongs to him,' Gibson said. 'It's a pain in the ass we can't get a definite sample.'

'We might have to consider the familial DNA route. Obviously the parents are dead.'

Gibson remembered a reopened case from two years earlier and wrinkled his nose. 'There's always exhumation.'

'If they were buried rather than cremated, it's a possibility. Another option is to see if Kratz has any maternal or paternal uncles and aunts who are still alive. They'd share a certain number of markers in common and there's also the Y chromosome if his dad has a brother.'

'How did you become such an expert?'

Mosley smoothed his brows. 'I like to keep up-to-date on technological advances.'

'And there's me thinking you went home and couched all night.'

'With our current caseload?' Mosley chuckled and shook his head. 'I wish!'

'Does Kratz have any kids?'

'Not that I'm aware of.'

Gibson unplugged the lead from his laptop. 'That's a real shame.'

'We could certainly investigate the possibility.' Mosley shook his head when Gibson groaned. 'Not us! I'd ask Demaine to locate any evidence of Kratz's little swimmers achieving their mission.'

Gibson recalled the furore in the aftermath of the actor's outburst outside legendary nightclub The Snake Pit. 'If he'd fathered any kids, the media would have crawled all over the story.'

'Not necessarily. Leave the father's name off the birth certificate and pay money into a woman's bank account on a fixed date.'

'Demaine did say he'd research anything we needed.' Gibson closed the laptop's lid. 'That means *anything.*'

'That's right,' Mosley agreed. 'It's something to chew over while I'm here at stupid o'clock preparing for Studdert's arrival. You and your good lady go increase the world's population.'

Gibson sensed a blush creeping across his cheeks. 'Well, if you put it like that.'

Mosley grinned and pointed at the door. 'I'll finish up here. And,' he continued, meeting Gibson's high-five as he passed the desk, 'I don't need you here until you've met Studdert at LAX. His flight arrives at midday so, if anyone asks where you are tomorrow morning, I'll say you're serving your public duty.'

****

4.45pm – PDT
Safeway, South Lake Tahoe, California

Angela repeatedly tugged her father's hand, pointed to a colourful display stand and gazed up at Sam through thick lashes. 'Daddy, *please* can I have some candy?' she begged.

Sam turned his attention away from the lengthening lines at the checkouts. 'Okay, okay. Just one item and you'll have to save it for dessert.' He shrugged when the beseeching blue eyes continued to stare up at him. 'I'm sorry, sweetheart. You know Mommy will get cross if you don't eat up at dinnertime.'

Her small hand hovered over a Kit Kat. 'Grandad had these at his house.' Angela looked at Sam again and frowned. 'Is he really *your* daddy?'

He crouched beside her and reached an arm around her waist. 'Yes he is, and he used to buy them for me, Aunty Hannah and Aunty Olivia when we were kids. Get one if you want.'

'Thank you, Daddy.' She picked up the chocolate and carefully placed it in their basket. 'Can we go home now?'

Sam immediately thought of their family home one thousand miles to the east, although he realised Angela was referring to the cabin as they joined the shortest line. 'Yeah, I just need to pay for this food and then we'll head back.'

She pulled on his hand. 'What happens if you don't pay?'

He pointed to the parking lot beyond a window directly ahead. 'You see that car?'

Angela's wide eyes settled on an empty police cruiser. 'Do they take you to prison?' she whispered, oblivious to the toothy smile from the elderly man in front of them. He continued packing his groceries into a large cloth bag, his tanned face creased in amusement.

Sam ruffled her hair. 'That's right, sweetheart. They take bad people to prison and look after good people. So, we always pay for things in shops because it's the law.'

Angela watched him place their items onto the conveyor. She silently processed the implications of what could happen if they left the store without paying and bit her lip when two burly male police officers returned to the cruiser and slowly drove out of the lot. Sam put the last jar of baby food into one of three carriers, pulled his wallet from his pocket and handed a credit card to the sales clerk.

'You won't get taken by the police today, Daddy,' she commented loudly.

He raised his eyebrows. 'No, not this time.'

Sam's dubious expression produced muffled laughter from the middle-aged couple behind and the woman smiled at Angela. 'She's a little cutie.'

'Most of the time,' Sam replied. He noticed his daughter sneak a glance in his direction and reach into the bag. 'Leave it for dessert, sweetheart. You don't want it to melt.'

'Sir...'

'How old is your little one?' she continued. 'Ronald, ain't she just the sweetest thing?' Her husband looked up from unloading their cart and nodded his agreement.

Sam stopped Angela from trying to lift the heaviest bag. 'Just turned three,' he replied.

'Dr Bury?'

The man Sam knew to be Ronald nodded towards the clerk. 'I think there's a problem.'

He saw the teenager stare intently at him, a puzzled expression on her face.

'What's happened?' he asked, his panic obvious now he'd realised she'd stated his name loud enough for those nearby to hear, and that he'd drawn attention to himself by failing to respond immediately.

'I'm real sorry, we've had some intermittent technical problems with the card readers today.' She attempted another swipe of the card and smiled at him apologetically. 'It may work again in a few minutes, or if you have the cash that may be faster for you.'

'Yeah, I should have enough to cover it,' Sam replied. He pulled a fifty-dollar bill from his wallet and thrust it at her.

He felt tugging on his jeans. 'Daddy, why did–'

Sam scanned the store for any familiar faces. 'In a minute,' he said, his voice sharper than intended.

She scooped a ten-dollar bill and a selection of coins from the cash register. 'Ten dollars and eighty-two cents change, sir. Enjoy the rest of your day.'

Sam stuffed the money into his pocket and grabbed their bags, unable to quash his need to escape. 'Yeah, thanks,' he replied as Angela bid farewell to the couple behind them. 'Come on,' he added, jerking his head at the exit. Angela fell into step beside him and they walked in silence to the Saab, Sam still deep in thought. He placed the bags in the trunk, opened the rear door and bent down, horrified to see a solitary tear trickle down Angela's cheek.

He knelt on the asphalt. 'What's wrong, darling?'

She flung her arms around his shoulders. 'Why are you mad at me, Daddy?'

Sam licked his lips. 'Whatever makes you think I'm mad at you?' he asked, relief softening his tone when a tall, blond-haired man nearby turned and an unfamiliar face revealed itself.

Another tear followed the track left by first one. 'You got mad at me in the store,' she replied, loosening her hold.

'Did I?' He watched her nod, recalling his sudden snappiness during the transaction. The thought sent a flood of guilt through him and he kissed her cheek. 'I promise I'm not mad at you. I was worried something had gone wrong with my card and we'd have to go home without our food.'

Sam lifted Angela onto the child seat and fastened the belts over her shoulders. 'Why did that lady shout at you?'

He frowned. 'She didn't shout at me. She needed to tell me about the problem.'

'You didn't hear her and she got mad.' Her small hands wiped another tear away from her cheek. 'It was scary, Daddy!'

Sam smiled at his daughter, determined to ignore his pounding heart and the shame over being short-tempered whilst Kratz's whereabouts occupied his mind. 'I think there's something wrong with the computer hidden in the till, and it makes it hard for her to do her job,' he said. He brushed wispy strands of hair from Angela's eyes and she nodded, readily accepting his explanation. 'It sometimes happens and I promise it's nothing bad.'

Angela nodded. 'Okay, Daddy,' she said quietly as Sam closed the door and walked around to the driver's side, the little girl oblivious to the weight settling in her father's gut.

Chapter 20 – Monday 10th August 2009

3.39am – PDT
Kingsbury, Nevada

In defiance of the warmth provided by Anna's arm draped across his stomach, sleep continued to elude Sam for the second consecutive night. He stared into the ceiling's infinite blackness; his wife's silhouette hidden by the clouds obscuring the moon's anaemic glow. Sam's eyes were unbearably heavy, yet still refused to close in the hope of seeing dawn's faint light edge past the drapes and into their bedroom.

Still too early.

Conscious not to disturb Anna, Sam eased himself from the bed and shivered when cool air collided against his skin. He pulled the sweater he'd grabbed from the back of a chair over his head and slipped out of the room, thankful he'd chosen pyjama pants over his usual summer shorts. A plug-in nightlight emitted enough energy to illuminate the base of the staircase and he cautiously ascended to the living area, where he took a couple of seconds to reorient himself to his surroundings.

Although an enduring source of fascination for Angela, her parents found the cabin's reversed layout had taken some acclimatising to. The hillside sloped away from the back of their new home, meaning entry to the property was gained via the upper floor's living area and the four bedrooms occupied the floor below. A spacious kitchen opened out from a wide archway on the lounge's opposite side, and the transition to its tiled floor caused Sam to ponder the need to invest in a pair of slippers. He switched on a lamp above the hob and watched weak light diffuse into the lounge, where the barely discernible hands of a nearby wall clock moved in a mocking jerk. Their message to Sam was a simple one: that he'd be

Chapter 20 – Monday 10th August 2009

lucky to get three hours of sleep, if the children maintained their usual routine.

His parents had sworn by the soporific qualities of hot milk throughout his childhood, despite Sam's enduring scepticism. He opened the refrigerator and, realising he'd reached the point of being prepared to try anything, retrieved an almost full gallon bottle of milk. The microwave's gentle hum followed Sam across the room to where a pair of doors opened onto the balcony. He pushed his fingers between the blinds and stared at South Lake Tahoe's twinkling lights only a few miles away.

It might as well have been in another country.

A sharp *ping* returned him to the present. Sam padded back to the kitchen and winced at the chill seeping into the soles of his feet again. His thoughts turned to the bottle of whisky Anna insisted he buy when they'd last gone grocery shopping. He stared at it for an indeterminate period of time, nestled between boxes of cereal in one of the wall cupboards, then poured an inch of single malt into his mug.

Sam seated himself at the breakfast bar and blew onto the drink, hoping the generous measure of spirits would enable a swift return to the bed's inviting warmth. He closed his eyes, inhaled the subtle scent of heather and recalled a family holiday in northern Scotland during the early nineties. One evening, his father had poured an extra glass of locally distilled Speyside malt and offered it to Sam whilst they watched the sun set behind the Cairngorms. Since then it had become a savoured indulgence, something to mark a special occasion...

...or to cushion the blow when life drops a massive pile of shit on you.

A light touch on his arm startled Sam back into the present.

'I woke up and you'd gone.'

He sighed. 'Yeah, I can't sleep and didn't want it to rub off on you.'

Anna eyed the cup and sniffed. 'Sleeping potion?'

Sam observed faint wisps of steam escaping into the gloom. 'I hope so. Getting three hours will easily beat last night's tally.' He nodded at the refrigerator. 'Would you like one?'

Anna shook her head and squeezed his hand. 'I'll give it a miss, thank you. Hot milk gives me stomach ache for some strange reason.' She slid onto the adjacent stool and covertly observed how the two-day-old stubble covering Sam's cheeks enhanced the heavy dark circles beneath his eyes. The coolness of their surroundings registered and she pulled the robe tighter around her upper body. 'I feel safer when you're next to me,' Anna added, giving his hand another squeeze.

He gingerly sipped the drink and then laughed, a hollow sound which took her aback. 'If you'd never met me you wouldn't be going through this, or need to feel protected. You'd be living a normal life in Boulder, rather than nearly ending up a widow and then being dragged here, there and everywhere in case the psycho who's been trying to kill me decides to come for you and the kids.'

'You mean you wish you'd never met me?' she asked. Her hurt expression forced Sam's gaze to drop into the mug. 'That Angela and John never existed?'

'Of course not. I'm nothing without the three of you,' Sam replied. He met her frown and traced his index finger across her cheek. 'But you didn't sign up for all this shit, did you?'

Anna shook her head. 'No, I didn't. I signed up for *you*. For better, for worse.' She swallowed down the emotions threatening to bubble to the surface. 'I meant every word of those vows four years ago. Our better is beyond amazing and, if this is our worse and we can get through this, we can get through anything.'

His eyes darted between the interlocked biotite and plagioclase crystals below the breakfast bar's polished surface. 'I don't deserve you.'

Anna rested her hands on Sam's shoulders and kneaded dense knots beneath their surface. 'I know. You've definitely gotten the better side of the deal.'

He sighed. 'What's going to happen if they never catch him, Anna? We can't run forever.'

'We won't be running forever,' she replied when his shoulders started to relax. 'They'll catch him. He's too arrogant. Mark my words; he'll slip up sooner rather than later.'

Sam nodded. He had to admit the rhythmic sensation of her slender yet strong fingers pressing into his muscles always managed to calm him. 'You sound very sure.'

'I've been a detective for eight years and I've met plenty of scumbags during that time. A lot of them think they're invincible, that they can do what the hell they want and never get caught. Trust me, he'll put himself back in the spotlight.'

Sam nodded and took a gulp of his cooling drink. 'Yeah, I know. It's the waiting game we have to play that's pissing me off. This has hung over our lives for nearly a year.' He cracked his knuckles and winced at his right hand's quiet reminder of the wall he'd punched in Niall Demaine's office five weeks earlier, on the day Demaine uncovered Kratz's real identity.

Anna observed him swallow the last of the milk and place the empty mug in the sink. 'Come on,' she said. 'We need to get some sleep before the monsters wake up.'

He reached for her hand and contemplated what he'd done to deserve having Anna in his life, the immediately wondered what she'd done to deserve being in his.

****

3.58pm – BST
Preston, England

Fucking rain...
It had been incessant for the past day. A steady deluge of water falling from dark grey clouds; their weight pulling them lower and lower until they threatened to smother the town's grey buildings, swirling litter and dirty streets. The antithesis of the American Dream he used to enjoy. He understood the need to bide his time, to select the right moment to *approach* Roger again. The old man's lack of compliance in returning Oliver Stamford's investment was unacceptable. Granted, he'd have been surprised if Roger was able to lay his hands on the cash immediately, but waiting for months was *not* an option.

He'd been aware of an increased nervousness over recent days, something he struggled to comprehend. Usually he found it to be the polar opposite, and that people felt uncomfortable around him. He wasn't sure what stirred this... could he call it an *emotion*? It wasn't like there were **WANTED!** posters plastered over all available advertising hoardings, or that millions of people had seen an appeal for information on the BBC's *Crimewatch*.

Twelve minutes had passed since he'd stopped his hire car outside the modest semi-detached house in Ashton, a respectable suburb two miles north-east of Preston's town centre. The house had changed markedly over the past nineteen years and now boasted modern uPVC windows and doors, a newly landscaped front garden and a block-paved driveway. His scrutiny settled on the window above the oak effect front door and he imagined its décor from two decades earlier.

When it was my bedroom.

He sighed as fat droplets trickled down the glass and wondered about the life he'd be living if he'd been allowed to take the alternate fork in the path – to stay in Preston rather than emigrating to Denver at the age of fourteen. Would he have found fame and fortune here, or would his destiny have been to spend his days stuck in a dead-end job in this dead-end town?

The door below the window opened and jolted Konrad from his thoughts. From behind an Ordinance Survey map he'd unfolded shortly after pulling up to the kerb he spied a small blond-haired boy, probably no older than five years, cautiously edge over the bottom of the door frame as if scared of tripping. The child smiled now he'd safely reached the top step, then jumped onto the driveway's herringbone brickwork.

A slim blonde woman who appeared to be in her early thirties followed him, their remarkable resemblance leaving Konrad in no doubt she was the boy's mother. She pointed a remote key at a VW Golf and smiled at the sight of her son opening its nearest rear passenger door. A downwards push on the front door handle confirmed she'd locked their home and Konrad watched her run to the driver's door. She flung herself into the car's dry interior and checked her reflection in the rear-view mirror, then leaned over to secure the child's seatbelt.

Seconds later she carefully reversed out of the driveway, too engrossed in her manoeuvre to notice the dark blue Astra parked only metres away. Konrad's sharp eyes followed the car along the quiet tree-lined street and wondered where they were going, and whether they'd return home in time to greet the boy's father.

Did he have a father?

Since his return to Preston, memories of his own family encroached further and further into his mind with increasing regularity. Konrad berated himself and contemplated the trigger behind all this sentimental bullshit. He certainly didn't miss his parents: getting rid of them and his subsequent move to the West Coast provided the opportunities and a lifestyle he'd never considered attainable prior to their deaths.

Konrad shook his head, more in irritation at himself than anything else, and returned the folded map to the glovebox. With a flick of his wrist he turned the key in the ignition and the car's underpowered engine came to life. After one last look at his former home, he glanced over his shoulder and pulled out onto the road.

****

12.25pm – PDT
Primm, Nevada

Primm's small community, if it could be considered as such, proved busier than Muñoz and Hallberg expected. Although it barely registered on their map, the random assortment of casinos, gas stations and fast food outlets straddling I-15 as it carved its way through the parched desert provided a welcome break – and the opportunity of a spot of gambling for weary travellers. An early start and the approaching Nevada state line energised the detectives' hunger pangs and Hallberg took little convincing to leave their anonymous dark green station wagon in an empty corner of McDonald's parking lot.

A breakfast-time visit to Los Angeles' Greyhound terminus had verified the time André Wood boarded the Las Vegas-bound coach, and offered an unexpected bonus when they learned the journey's driver had completed a night shift minutes earlier. Muñoz produced a modified photograph of Kratz to refresh Gianni Russo's hazy memory of specific passengers, the middle-aged man chuckling as he recalled the other passengers' reluctance to sit too close to the quiet, brown-haired man. He'd also mentioned the large bible the man carried not sitting too well with a large group of college students, and added that the guy's sombre-suited attire made him unnerving to some and conspicuous to many. Russo had been unable to provide any additional information; his present concern being the two cups of coffee and three cigarettes he'd enjoy now all his passengers had disembarked at the coach's final destination.

Thirty minutes after crossing the Nevada state line and a Big Mac each later, the detectives returned to their car, where Hallberg handed his almost empty water bottle to Muñoz and opened the doors to release an intense blast of heat. Grateful their destination lay around forty minutes away, Hallberg turned the air conditioning to its maximum output and, ignoring the sweat that continued to soak into his shirt, set off towards the Las Vegas-bound Interstate.

****

4.34pm – PDT
San Fernando Road, Los Angeles, California

Regardless of telling Gibson his presence wasn't required at the police station before he collected Joe Studdert from the airport, Mosley showed up at his usual time. He spent the first hour making a considerable dent in two cups of coffee, a pair of Danish pastries and the pile of case files proliferating on his desk until a mid-morning phone call from Hallberg forced him to break from his task. To his unexpected delight at such a promising start, he learned the coach driver had recognised Kratz *and* confirmed the disguise used by their fugitive.

Mosley took another break two hours later; this time to purchase a selection of sandwiches and a box of carb-rich treats from Holey Heaven, ready for a refreshed and smiling Gibson to usher Studdert into the incident room. They'd discussed the case over a leisurely lunch and, determined to take full advantage of one of the FBI's most respected brains aiding them for the next four days, Mosley had invited Studdert to stay at his Altadena home, rather than the Pasadena hotel used for visiting consultants.

Silence descended over the incident room when Gibson and Studdert departed to meet Glendale-based detective Paul Whitehead at Kratz's Brockmont home. Mosley returned his attention to the ever-growing pile of case files and devoured details of the Fernandez family's last moments; glad a significant thorn in his side had met a fiery end, yet resenting their paper-generating legacy. He set down the uppermost file, poured himself a refill of coffee and sipped it until the newest email in his inbox gained his undivided attention. A fist punched the air and Mosley carefully re-read the information forwarded by LAPD's crime lab, his grin widening further when he picked up his cell phone and scrolled through his contacts.

'Gibson? Mosley here... Studdert working his magic yet?... Yeah, we've just received the DNA results from that hunk of junk Kratz dumped at the airport... Matches the blood found in the trunk of Carlito Read's Mercedes and the other hair sample found with those two Austrians.' He permitted himself a smug smirk and listened to Gibson's excited response. 'Yeah, looks like we've gotten ourselves a real live DNA profile for the fucker.'

****

8.34pm – PDT
Las Vegas, Nevada

Hallberg lifted a glass of beer to his lips and took a long swallow. 'Man, I'm beat,' he said. 'Twenty years ago I'd be getting ready for an all-nighter on the gaming floor, and then I got old, fat and married.'

Muñoz grinned. 'In that order?'

'Dunno, guess it all crept up on me. One day I was a handsome guy who partied all night, the next day my wife's rationing me to rabbit food and soya smoothies. She says I'll be getting a Fat Man Letter at this rate.' A worried expression crossed his face. 'You want to go out partying? For real?'

'Calm your ass, grandad. I'm beyond tired, and we're working.'

Hallberg sighed, relieved he wouldn't have to forgo the full night of uninterrupted sleep he'd looked forward to all day. 'We had ourselves a pretty productive first day,' he said, ruing how quickly he'd consumed his beer.

'Yeah, that surveillance footage at the Greyhound terminus was a bonus,' Muñoz agreed. His dark eyes observed two new groups of customers entering the restaurant. 'We now know he travelled with a silver trolley case, but it's not like that's a rarity these days.'

Hallberg tried to ignore another rumble from his stomach. 'Ask Mosley to see if Demaine can enhance the images and pick out a brand to help narrow it down.'

'Sounds like a plan,' Muñoz agreed. A large group of women dressed as ballerinas reached the adjacent table, their squeals of excitement when a plump brunette also wearing a veil took her seat readily gaining the detectives' attention.

136

Hallberg smiled at the young woman and loosened his belt in readiness for the burrito he'd ordered ten minutes earlier. 'Damn shame there's no relevant security footage from later on in the evening. We know they dumped Kratz in the trunk of Read's Mercedes and drove out of town, probably to Nellis. I guess we'll have to theorise what happened before the Three Amigos took that cab back to Caesars. Where they went is anyone's guess.'

'There's no way Esteban and his brothers would leave their cousin alone with a psycho who'd already killed a member of their family.' Muñoz frowned and considered what he'd do in the same situation. 'Unless that psycho was already dead.'

'Which he obviously wasn't.'

'If they thought he was, they most likely headed back into town and told Read to go dump the body. One white guy is less conspicuous than three Hispanics driving around an area like Nellis late at night.' Muñoz smiled in response to Hallberg's obvious surprise at his candid remark. 'That's what some cousins on my dad's side told me. It ain't right, but that's how it happens in some places.'

'Did you get any shit?' Hallberg asked, suddenly realising he knew little about his teammate's early life, even though they'd worked together for over a decade. 'You know, when you were growing up?'

Muñoz shook his head. 'Not really; guess I got lucky. Some people *like me* don't get accepted as being white or Latino. My parents settled in a pretty diverse neighbourhood and any background seemed to be accepted. If there was any tension I stayed oblivious to it.'

Hallberg's gaze followed a server carrying two heaped plates of nachos past their table 'That's how it should be,' he said. 'So, Kratz faked being dead, and when Read took the so-called corpse into the boonies Kratz came back to life and killed Read?'

Muñoz nodded and held up his almost empty beer glass and two fingers to catch the eye of another server nearby. 'Judging by the blood in the trunk, Kratz had to be seriously injured.'

'Maybe a non-fatal gunshot or stab wound?' Hallberg replied. 'He could lose a quart of blood and still be able to function with little difficulty.'

'We've seen images of him clutching his right side and carrying a Walgreens bag, which I'm guessing contained medical supplies. We'll learn more at the store on Tropicana tomorrow morning. Like all store managers within the city, this guy received the time parameters a couple of days ago. He's trawled through the store's surveillance and isolated some footage for us.'

'How do we know it's Kratz?' Hallberg asked.

'Mosley got Gibson to run some images though the software that analyses faces, height and all that stuff. He's pretty sure it's our guy.'

'Read was shot at least a dozen times. If there was a gun in the trunk and, let's face it, dead bodies don't shoot back, Kratz could have turned it on Read when he opened the lid. All he'd need to do is hide Read's body and get the hell out of there.'

Muñoz shifted in his seat and twisted to one side to ease the day's tension from his back. 'He'd need to return to Vegas to collect his shit.'

'The silver case,' Hallberg said. 'My guess is it contains his escape stash, and that made it worth risking a return visit.' He nodded, more to himself than to Muñoz. 'Golden PD said Kratz's home in Paradise Hills was entered sometime after he'd left LA. The timeline fits and that night between him leaving Salt Lake and arriving in Cortez is unaccounted for. He picked up whatever was in the case and fled the area.'

'Cash?' Muñoz suggested. 'Wasn't there a safe at the house?'

'Yeah, and they're pretty much certain its contents were accessed. Perhaps he's travelling with valuable items he's exchanging for cash?'

'That's certainly possible. What did Mosley say earlier?'

'Joe Studdert arrived this afternoon,' Hallberg said. He turned his attention to the two new beers on their table and pushed Muñoz's towards him. 'He's been visiting locations, familiarising himself with the case file and, in the next couple of days, hopes to deliver a psychological profile of Kratz.'

Muñoz traced a finger through the rivulets of condensation on his glass. 'Do you really buy into all that psychology stuff?'

Hallberg cast his mind back three years. 'Mosley sending me to FBI headquarters for that criminal profiling course helped dispel a lot of misconceptions I held. People see all kinds of stuff on TV shows and think it's an exact science; that they're all mind-readers and the profile generated is definitive. It ain't. A lot of it is based on analysing evidence left behind by the criminal you're hunting.' He slowly exhaled. 'And that's putting it simply.'

'Yeah, I get that,' Muñoz countered. 'But, there's never been a previous version of Konrad Kratz.'

Hallberg leaned forward and a sudden enthusiasm shone in his eyes. 'He'll show certain patterns of behaviour. Even if they're not immediately obvious, especially to people like us, Studdert's an expert. He'll be able to identify them and from that he'll attempt to predict what Kratz may or may not do in the future. Then we hopefully nail the...' The words faded when he noticed their server, a slim man in his early twenties, carrying two enormous burritos towards their table.

Muñoz nodded. 'Let's hope you're right.'

Chapter 21 – Tuesday 11th August 2009

Gibson approached the desk allocated to Studdert and set down a large cup of coffee. 'How's it going?'

'Interesting,' Studdert replied, rubbing the back of his head. 'Kratz obviously has a preferred MO, which he deviates from if he perceives the need. He also uses aliases–'

'But he's changing his killing method and his name all the time!' Gibson interrupted, his obvious surprise causing a wide smile to appear on the older man's tanned face.

Studdert nodded, used to seeing similar reactions from the most seasoned of detectives. 'He'll still display consistent behaviours and habits, though he'll think he's done enough to evade us. It's darn near impossible to totally reinvent yourself. Our worry is the missing pieces of the jigsaw which could hold the key.' He smiled at Gibson and lifted the drink to his lips. 'The other problem is folks expect us to be psychic, to predict where he'll be and what he'll be doing with total accuracy. Behavioural sciences don't work like that. I can give you pointers and suggestions, but sometimes we get it wrong. I need you to understand that.'

Gibson reached for his own drink. 'We appreciate any help you can offer.'

'Believe me, I want to see this son of a bitch fry as much as you do.' A sudden flash of anger appeared on Studdert's face and he narrowed his eyes. 'My buddy's life got turned upside down because of this.'

'Sam Bury?'

'Yeah, he co-ordinates my unit in New York and is one of the best guys I've known in thirty years with the Bureau. I witnessed how Kratz screwed him over last year. If I can have any input into the bastard's capture it'll make everything I do worthwhile. Can't begin–'

They were distracted by the sound of Mosley slapping a printed email onto the desk. 'Gentlemen, we have lift-off.'

Gibson recognised Mosley's smile to be an indication of progress, however small. 'What's new?' he asked.

'I received an email from Beate Gessler, the lead detective from the Zürich team,' he announced, swilling the last of his coffee around its cup. 'Kratz, or should that be *Andreas Baum*, was identified on camera at Zürich's main train station the morning after Freya Burdett's murder. Using a time stamp on the footage, records of the ticket he bought tell us he boarded a train to Innsbruck and then transferred to the Munich service. The German police are already on the case.'

'If that name links into his family, there's always a chance he's rearranging old family names to create aliases.' Studdert's sharp gaze followed the lines of dark print. 'I'll need a family tree.'

'Niall Demaine at Denver's field office is the man for that job,' Mosley said. He saw Studdert nod and raised an eyebrow at him. 'You know the guy?'

'Sam always speaks highly of him. Apparently he can find out the brand of tightie-whities you wear, or so he claims. What else did Gessler say?'

Mosley exhaled loudly and wrinkled his nose. 'Not much. He's passed on our details to his counterpart in Munich, who'll get in contact when he knows more.'

'You realise he's probably long gone?' Gibson said. 'He's moving from one place to another every few days already.'

Studdert glanced at the cluttered incident board almost groaning under the amount of information pinned to it. 'If those places hold some degree of personal significance for him, he'll feel safer there. Does he have any connection to Munich?'

Gibson thought back to a conversation he'd had with Sam. 'His mom was German.'

'How does Zürich fit in?' Studdert asked, his mind already churning various possibilities.

'That's where a family tree would come in useful.' Mosley tossed his cell phone to Gibson. 'Demaine's in my contact list, and don't forget to ask nicely.'

****

10.14am – PDT
Walgreens, West Tropicana Avenue, Las Vegas, Nevada

Store manager Terry Sisask offered an effusive greeting to Hallberg and Muñoz within seconds of them walking into his store's air-conditioned interior and, following a convoluted walk through the shop floor, led them to a flight of stairs at the building's rear. They ascended to a suite of offices and a communal staff area, where Muñoz voiced their appreciation of the store's assistance in the ongoing investigation whilst revealing very little of what they were actually investigating.

Sisask directed them into the furthest and largest office, loosened his tie and patted the top of a small refrigerator. 'Can I get you guys a drink?' he asked. 'There's a coffee machine down the hall, but I figured you'd prefer something chilled in his heat.' He pulled the door open to display a varied selection of cans. 'What'll it be?'

'Gotta be the Mountain Dew,' Hallberg replied. 'Caffeine and sugar is always a welcome combination these days.'

'Make that two.'

Sisask reached into the refrigerator. 'I left some cups on my desk, so help yourselves.'

Muñoz passed a large red plastic cup to Hallberg. 'Thanks, man; we sure appreciate this.'

'Seconded,' Hallberg added. 'It's great of you to compile this at such short notice.'

'Always a pleasure to help catch a scumbag.' Sisask lowered his voice, as if the world's media had made camp outside the office door. 'What's he done?'

Hallberg and Muñoz exchanged a knowing look. 'It's more a question of what he hasn't done,' the former replied whilst pouring the soda into his cup.

Sisask's sandy-coloured brows rose. 'That bad, huh?'

'Well, maybe not that bad. He's a piece of crap we need to catch sooner rather than later. I'm sorry, I can't tell you more.'

'No bother, man. I understand the need for confidentiality and all that stuff.'

Hallberg squinted at a clock above the window. 'Where's the girl who served him?'

'I asked her to wait in the break room.' Sisask picked up the phone on his desk, pressed three digits in rapid succession and tapped his foot on the floor until it connected. 'Jen? Yeah, it's Terry. We're ready, so come on in.' He placed the phone back in its cradle. 'She's a good worker. Does all the hours she can to pay her way through college.'

Hallberg nodded, his next question concerning witness reliability already answered. 'Is she a local girl?'

'Born and bred. Her folks live out at Summerlin.'

They were interrupted when a young woman wearing a royal blue polo shirt poked her head around the office door. Sisask pointed to the remaining armchair. 'Come in, Jen,' he said as he opened the refrigerator for her. 'Grab a soda.'

She sunk into the chair's faux leather and deftly pulled back the tab on a can of root beer. 'Thanks, man. And, I guess you guys must be the cops?'

Muñoz nodded. 'That's us. I'm Emilio Muñoz and the ugly guy is Dave Hallberg.'

Jen Demetriou stifled a snort of laughter and waited for Hallberg to angle the computer's screen so she could see it properly. 'We're detectives based in Los Angeles and apparently you served the guy we're trying to locate,' he explained. 'Your manager has isolated this clip from the security recording. We want you to watch carefully and see if it triggers anything.'

Jen's deep brown eyes focussed intently on the footage showing the store's only cash desk. A date stamp glowed in the screen's bottom right corner, a reminder of her weekly early morning shift. 'This the guy?' she asked.

'Do you remember serving him?'

She nodded. 'Sure do. I even mentioned him to my boyfriend that evening. He was kind of weird.'

'In what way?' Hallberg asked. His eyes left the screen and he carefully observed Jen watching herself serve Kratz. Her tongue piercing tapped rhythmically against the inside of her incisors, a sound that always made Hallberg cringe.

'He was obviously injured,' she replied, her tone thoughtful. 'Not sure how bad. He sure seemed in a lot of pain. Dude was pale and sweaty and kept wincing. Claimed the stuff was for one of his buddies who'd been injured in some bachelor party prank gone wrong.'

Muñoz took over the questioning, as previously agreed. 'Did you ask him about his injuries?'

'Yeah, I suggested he go to Desert Springs and get himself checked out at the ER.'

'What did he say?'

'Brushed me off and said he dove into a fountain. He wasn't rude, but he wasn't willing to make conversation. He bought a whole bunch of stuff.'

'Is this the first time you served him?'

'Not that I can remember.' She narrowed her eyes. 'That's a weird question. If he isn't from Vegas I ain't gonna recognise him, right?'

'He might have called in before. Some people vacation here regularly.'

'I ain't got one of those eidetic memories.' She leaned against the back of the chair and folded her arms. 'I think you've come here knowing more than you're saying.'

Muñoz noticed her manager's eyes widen in embarrassment. 'You've every right to be suspicious,' he continued. 'This guy ain't Mr Nice Guy and he's wanted for questioning over a number of offences. You'll understand I'm not at liberty to discuss the details, so any additional information you give us will be real useful.'

Her narrow shoulders rose and fell quickly in a shrug and she looked past the window into the clear Nevadan sky. 'That's all I remember. Soon as he'd gotten his change he couldn't leave the store fast enough. I'm sorry I can't be more helpful.'

Hallberg nodded and froze the footage. 'You've both been extremely helpful and we sure do appreciate your time.'

Jen pushed herself out of the chair and shook hands with the detectives. 'No sweat, guys,' she replied. 'Just let me know if Tarantino wants me to appear in the movie.'

****

Tony Pell returned to the incident room and flopped into the nearest chair. 'I really shouldn't drink so much cola. Anyway, when did Mosley say he'd return?'

Studdert shook his head and pushed the laptop away. 'Not sure. He got called out five minutes before you arrived to interview a potential witness to a suspicious death.' He grinned at Tony and pulled a crisp twenty-dollar bill from his wallet. 'My brain's fried. What do you say we head out for a snack?'

'Sounds like a plan,' Tony replied. He returned a wad of paper to a sturdy box file. 'It's been suggested how I could go about locating the source of Kratz's fake passports. I hope that'll be the end of my involvement.'

Studdert pushed his chair under the desk. 'It's good of you to assist.'

'It's kind of by default. I first ended up coming back to town after my uncle and cousins were wiped out on the freeway. Then we discovered the body Susie was called out to in Death Valley was actually Carlito Read's. We're both distantly related to him.'

'You have American connections?'

Tony nodded. 'Mum's family originally came from a small town called Rosarito; it's around half an hour's drive from Tijuana. She moved to the UK to study, met my dad and never went back. Her brother, Paco, relocated to LA in the early seventies.'

'So you knew Kratz well, or Peter Umpleby as he was then?' Studdert held open the door and followed Tony onto a long corridor.

'Yeah, we were at the same two schools back in England and he's always been a nasty piece of shit. We weren't sad to see him emigrate.'

Studdert raised his eyebrows and chose to leave his next question unspoken. They walked through the lobby where three young men supported their semi-conscious companion, a bloodied bandage swathed around the injured man's head. 'You and Sam also went to the same schools?'

'Two for two,' Tony confirmed. He pushed open the double doors, stopped on the dusty sidewalk and squinted into the distance where buildings and roads appeared bleached by the harsh sunlight. 'Well, only up to age eleven, then he got a scholarship to some posh secondary school,' he added as an afterthought.

'He's a smart guy.'

'That's an understatement.'

They walked in silence until Studdert resumed their conversation. 'Sometimes he's too smart.'

'What do you mean?'

'He thinks about things very deeply,' Studdert replied. 'That's obviously beneficial in our line of work if you don't take it to a personal level. Sam sets extremely high standards for himself and sometimes maintaining them isn't possible. He gives himself a hard time if he doesn't think he's achieved his absolute best.'

Tony mirrored Studdert's smile. 'Sam's always been a perfectionist.'

'He hasn't said much, but he'll beat himself up over his family being dragged into this.'

'Don't you have a rule about not profiling your teammates?' Tony asked as they reached Holey Heaven's pink and blue frontage and found the place almost deserted.

'That's correct,' Studdert replied. 'However, in this case profiling Sam to a degree could help profile Kratz and his motives.'

'Do you think he still wants to hurt Sam?' Tony asked after they'd paid for their coffee and pastries and slid into a booth.

'It can't be ruled out,' Studdert said as two giggling teenage girls exited the adjacent booth. 'Hence the modified form of protective custody the family's been placed into.'

'Do you know where they are?'

Studdert shook his head. 'You know no more than I do. It's safer that way, for everyone.'

'Have you finished Kratz's profile?'

'I'd call it a work in progress. By establishing the type of criminal he is, I can use that alongside the evidence gathered to theorise how he'll behave in the future. I can't read the guy's mind though.'

Tony set down his cup and eyed his plate . 'Have you always done stuff like this?'

Studdert shook his head again. 'Only for the past sixteen years. Before that I started as a field agent and then transferred to white collar crime. Many cases the Bureau investigates have an element of psychology. I

146

attended lectures and seminars, then took the classes. Eventually an opening arose in *Behavioral Analysis* and I never looked back.'

'It must be fascinating stuff?' Tony asked as Studdert took a bite from a large bear claw.

Studdert raised an eyebrow and chewed with obvious enjoyment. 'Yeah, although it has its drawbacks,' he eventually replied, the statement surprising Tony. 'We've dealt with some horrendous cases over the years, stuff straight out of a horror movie. You close your eyes at night and it doesn't always go away. Sam started showing an interest, although I'd say that's changed over the past year. He no longer seems to want to understand how their minds work, and he's definitely shied away from anything like that since the accident. It's hard to see how it can affect your teammates at the best of times, but we all have people you come to care for like they're members of your own family.'

Tony stirred his drink, not sure how much he should say. 'He's been through such a lot. I tried to help by phoning regularly and offering to visit. He was flat, completely emotionless, for months.'

Studdert swallowed a mouthful of coffee. 'How much has he told you since?'

'I don't think he likes to dwell on it,' Tony replied, deciding not to mention what Susie told him on one occasion after she'd phoned Anna. 'I know things got worse before they got better.'

'That's another reason we're so desperate to get Kratz into custody. Whether or not Sam's being targeted, for his sake we need this case closed.'

'Not to mention the likely fate befalling anyone who gets in his way,' Tony continued. 'I reckon if Kratz doesn't get caught soon, this'll also be something that gets worse before it gets better.'

Chapter 22 – Wednesday 12th August 2009

Clive Porter waved a neatly typed letter inches from his wife's face 'What in the name of fucking hell is this?' he bellowed, his round face florid.

After fifteen years of marriage, Eileen didn't need a sixth sense to know when trouble was brewing. She wrapped her arms around her waist, as if subconsciously trying to protect herself. 'Who's it from?' she whispered.

Clive's biceps twitched as he clenched and unclenched his fists. 'It's that bastard Mortimer. He's giving us 'til the middle of October to get out.'

'We're being evicted?'

He leaned against the kitchen worktop, stared at the floor and attempted to bring his anger under control. 'Bloody wanker! I'll knock his fucking block off.'

'Let me see!' Eileen grabbed the letter and scanned its brief content. 'At least he's apologetic,' she added. 'He says due to circumstances beyond his control he needs to sell the place. It's not like he's kicking us out to be nasty, is it?'

'That'll be a bloody comfort when we're sleeping under the pier.' Clive stared through the window to the back garden where their nine-year-old twins were kicking a football around. 'The boys will be ecstatic.'

'We'll find somewhere.' She cautiously reached out to stroke his arm. 'We've enough in the bank for a deposit, so perhaps this is the push we need to actually buy a place?'

'I'll give him a proper fucking push,' Clive muttered. He stomped out of the kitchen and grabbed his car keys from a bowl near the front door. 'Right off the end of the bloody pier.'

She ran down the hallway and watched him pull on a pair of new white trainers without undoing the laces. 'Where are you going?'

The door slammed and rattled in its frame.

****

2.34pm – PDT
San Fernando Road, Los Angeles, California

'Do you have everything you need?' Mosley asked through a stifled yawn.

Studdert nodded. 'Enough for me to work with until Demaine sends that family tree.'

'He hopes to finish it tonight and email the information through in the morning. As for Kratz, surely he'd go off the beaten track?'

'Not necessarily. People are drawn to familiarity – it's comforting.'

Mosley frowned in surprise. 'You're saying a nutjob like Kratz actually forms attachments, if only to a geographic area?'

'If you know an area well, there's less to consider.' Studdert's eyes flicked over a map of Europe. 'Where things are, useful places to go, places to avoid. Hiding in plain sight is the ultimate double bluff.'

Mosley processed this latest theory. 'He'd have to be in disguise,' he countered.

'We've seen him change his appearance and he can change his accent. Whatever you say, he's a damn fine actor,' Studdert said. He noticed Mosley grimace. 'My daughters love *H.O.S.T.A.G.E.* and they only started watching because of Kratz. Even my wife got hooked.'

'So, based on his personality and places he's familiar with, you're telling me you can accurately predict his next moves?'

'I'll be able to suggest likely scenarios. Like I've said before, this isn't an exact science. It's more like a game of chess with many pieces to consider and often more than one possible outcome. We work with what we have while trying to anticipate his next move. Sometimes we're correct, sometimes we're way off the mark.'

Mosley exhaled loudly, unable to hide his frustration. 'How far have you gotten with it?'

'We're at an advantage because we know who he is. The more we learn about his past, the more we refine the profile. He's also highly intelligent, but school records suggest he didn't reach his academic potential.'

'You think that's relevant?'

Studdert reached for an open packet of cinnamon candies. 'It could be a factor,' he replied. 'He feels a need to prove his true worth, if only to himself. He also needs to feel in total control of a situation and anyone obstructing what he perceives to be his rightful path is brushed aside, permanently.'

'Could that signify some degree of insecurity?' Mosley's voice became muffled as he rolled the confectionery around his mouth. 'Surely someone confident in their abilities would strive to overcome any challenges and earn their success fair and square?'

'Not bad, for a cynic,' Studdert replied. He grinned when Mosley shot a trademark withering stare in his direction. 'Ultimately, he needs to preserve this new persona he's adopted, and at any cost.'

'There's a difference between going off the grid with a new identity, even if it's fake, and turning into a serial killer. Christ, the guy probably killed his teacher while young enough to be in middle school, he murdered his parents in cold blood, and the others who'd just gotten in the way put us too far into double figures. Do you think he'd kill again?'

'Based on the evidence?' Studdert pursed his lips and nodded. 'Yeah, I do. Although we've seen he can and will change his MO to avoid detection, his preferred method is to locate his victim's vehicle and sabotage its brake lines. Kratz has the intelligence to realise this generates a distinct signature, making it easier for his crimes to be traced. He'll now vary his technique to avoid leaving a path for us to follow.'

Mosley uncrossed his legs and got to his feet. 'You'll send the completed profile and all additional information to every field office, right?'

'Sure, and I'll also pass everything to one of my Interpol contacts. She'll distribute it if there's any suspicion he's gone elsewhere besides Switzerland and Germany. The authorities in Zürich and Munich will receive a copy directly, so I'll ask one of the linguists in DC to translate it into German first.'

'Tell me what you know so far.' Mosley reached into the refrigerator for a bottle of water. 'What breed of loony tune is he?

'There's nothing in his childhood to suggest parental abuse or neglect is responsible and, in his identity as Konrad Kratz, he presented himself as a fully-functioning member of society. This leads me to believe he's psychopathic rather than sociopathic, and his sense of entitlement points to strong narcissistic traits,' Studdert said, feeling a flush of enthusiasm now he'd begun to share his expertise. 'His intelligence and attention to detail suggest he's an organised killer, meaning he either plans his kills or, if the opportunity or need to kill suddenly presents itself, he knows enough about police and forensic methodology to leave minimal evidence. This makes it less likely for the crime to be initially linked to him, at least in the beginning.'

'Do you think we'll ever catch him?'

Studdert smiled wryly, having heard this exact question more times than he cared to remember. 'Honestly? Yes, I think we will. The problem is what he'll do next to bring himself to our attention, or if he does nothing the trail could go cold, and for a long time.'

'So you're saying more people may end up dying before we're able to catch him?' Mosley asked. His face showed an uncharacteristically horrified expression. 'That's a mighty shit thing to know.'

'Yeah, that's the kind of stuff which keeps you awake at night,' Studdert replied. 'The knowledge that in some cases you probably won't catch your fugitive unless further victims are located.'

****

7.56pm MDT
Midvale, Utah

Hallberg beamed at his server and watched her set down a steaming burrito in front of him. The beer he'd sipped for the past twenty minutes had already begun to circulate a warming glow and now whispered its encouragement for a second round.

'Man, that's a beast. I'll be good for an hour or so after this bad boy.'

'Your good lady wouldn't approve,' Muñoz said tersely, still disgruntled he'd lost the toss over who was driving that evening, which meant forgoing an eagerly anticipated beer.

'What her eyes don't see, her heart won't grieve for – even if mine will,' Hallberg replied. He eyed Muñoz's Chinese chicken salad disdainfully. 'Were you a rabbit in a previous life?'

'I need some green stuff after all that rest stop trash that's blocking my arteries.'

'Our schedule doesn't allow for healthy eating,' Hallberg grumbled. He sliced into his all-time favourite meal and smothered it with soured cream and salsa. 'And we need to scarf this down so we can get back to the hotel and type up today's report.'

Muñoz's growling stomach reminded him they hadn't eaten properly since breakfast. 'The guy at the car lot was pretty helpful. I'll email the security footage back to Gibson so he can isolate a still for the board. Do you figure Kratz still looks the same?'

'He had a similar appearance in Zürich, but he's a smart guy so he'll probably work on the assumption we're only a few steps behind him. A new identity and a new appearance could stall us for longer.'

'Have you read that email from Joe Studdert yet?'

'Yeah,' Hallberg replied. A proud smile stretched across his reddened face. 'I tried making my own profile over the last few days. Nothing official, you know, just for practise.'

Muñoz raised his eyebrows. 'How did you do?'

'Pretty good for a beginner, apparently. I guess I learned something on that course.'

'Mosley's going to be relieved LAPD's bucks were put to good use.' Muñoz picked out a crispy wonton and snapped it in half. 'Do you think we'll glean much more information this week? I mean, I get the logic behind it, but we can't locate everyone Kratz may have encountered. The hotel staff recall very little about him, apart from him saying he'd left Vegas to join the church. Kept himself to himself and then took off two nights into the week-long stay he'd paid for.'

'Perhaps they assumed he'd seen the darkness and gone back to Sin City?'

Muñoz frowned. 'Or gone to collect whatever he kept stashed at his Colorado home.'

Hallberg swallowed a mouthful of spiced beef. 'Cash,' he stated with more confidence than he usually showed and then repeated the word. 'Or, stuff he could sell. Smaller valuable items are easier to transport and easier to conceal. Jewellery, that kind of thing. We'll take a good look around tomorrow afternoon. Golden PD assured me the place has stayed undisturbed since that forensics team went in.' He grinned, unable to resist making his next remark. 'So, we'll take advantage of this Golden opportunity.'

Chapter 23 – Thursday 13th August 2009

10.34am – MDT
Route 40, near Elk Springs, Colorado

The almost deserted road stretched ahead of them for miles; an asphalt ribbon tying together the sporadic gas stations and rural community stores offering brief respite to those passing through this remote area of Northwestern Colorado. In the passenger seat, Muñoz sighed and rested his aching head against the headrest. Rough yellow grassland blurred into the distance and small trees dotted an unrelenting landscape; the journey's monotony occasionally punctuated by other vehicles travelling in the opposite direction. The five hours of sleep he'd obtained between finishing the previous day's reports and his alarm clock sounding at 5.30am had barely sufficed; the long days officially beginning to take their toll.

Hallberg noticed his partner's eyelids struggling to remain open. 'Fifteen-minute stopover at the next place?' he suggested.

Muñoz nodded, the prospect of bitter gas station coffee more appealing than usual. 'So how much did we actually learn that we didn't know before?'

'He's changing his backstory, appearance and name to avoid detection.'

'We knew that already, so what's the point of following Route 666?'

'Wasn't that in Arizona, then they renamed it?' Hallberg asked. 'Yeah... I've also wondered whether this is a totally useful exercise. But, if we can find out his full range of aliases and disguises–'

'Surely he can't have an infinite repertoire?'

'Exactly!' Hallberg replied, pleased Muñoz appeared to follow his train of thought. 'There may come a time he has to recycle, and if the fake identity is in the system it'll flag up.'

'And then we catch the bastard,' Muñoz added. His stomach rumbled in protest at the time they'd eaten breakfast after leaving their Midvale hotel.

'In theory, yeah.'

Muñoz shifted position in his seat. 'No-one's certain he came this way. We've stopped at three gas stations already, and no one recalls the brown-haired version.'

'Folks on the run tend to think you're less likely to be stopped on roads like this, even if it's just a random check,' Hallberg said. 'We can't hang around for hours, so under the circumstances we've done all we can by leaving a photo and contact details in case the other workers recognise him.'

Muñoz stifled a yawn and adjusted the air conditioner's settings. 'How much longer before we arrive in this Golden place?'

'I'd guess five or six hours, taking into account any more stops. That's going to give us time to check into the hotel and relax for an hour before meeting that Agent Milne guy.'

'You think he'll be able to help?'

Hallberg nodded. 'It'll be useful to walk through Kratz's home, get a feel for the place. You can get an insight into a person from their home.'

'You figure?' Muñoz replied, wondering what insights could be gleaned from his recently redecorated Altadena apartment.

'Yeah, your home is an extension of your personality. How that's expressed reflects personal preferences and previous experiences.'

'And this applies to you?'

Hallberg's cheeks coloured. 'Probably, to an extent. People ask why I've chosen bland pastel shades for all the interior paintwork, but warm cream is what I grew up with. I had a happy childhood in a stable home, so you can theorise that's what I'm trying to bring to the home I've helped build for my own family.'

'What if he's styled his home straight from one of those magazines, for example?' Muñoz countered. 'That's not an accurate representation of an individual, apart from the stylist who put it together. And, even then I doubt many people intentionally choose to live in such a sterile environment.'

155

'Exactly, it gives little away,' Hallberg replied, nodding enthusiastically. 'From the photos Golden PD emailed, the place resembles a museum. It's beautifully decorated, has strategically placed ornaments... but there's absolutely nothing to offer an insight into the past or present life of its owner. It's like he wanted to leave the canvas blank and enable others to fill in their preferred version of him.'

'Has Studdert passed comment?'

'Not yet. The more information he gets, the more accurate he'll be in anticipating his next moves. There's little sense in making announcements to the public too early.'

'You should email your theory to him, see if he agrees.' Muñoz grinned at the second blush spreading across his teammate's cheeks. 'You said he was real positive last time. If you're on the right lines it could help when we visit Kratz's lair.'

'Paradise Hills. Kind of ironic, right?' Hallberg said, keen to deflect attention away from the theories he didn't feel entirely confident in sharing. 'I Googled the place. It's a small foothills community just off I-70, around a fifteen-minute drive from Golden. Ain't cheap, has nice views and is in the right area for decent schools. I'd live there.'

'Milne's meeting us at Kratz's house?'

'Yeah, at six. He's also reserved a table at some local restaurant for later in the evening.'

'I'm still amazed Mosley's been so amenable about the Feds being brought in. He usually complains they're like feral tomcats marking their territory.' Muñoz saw a puzzled expression flash across Hallberg's face and let out a snigger. 'They get defensive if cornered and leave a bad smell behind them.'

'For once I think he's grateful for their assistance. We've got cases piling up and Robbery-Homicide is pulling their collective hair out over those slayed prostitutes,' Hallberg said. 'Gibson mentioned there'd been another two yesterday, so there's no way they can take over this case. These latest victims bring the total to nineteen in a month.'

'Jeez, you can bet those guys have gotten less sleep than us.' Now more tired than ever, Muñoz registered a pang of guilt over his reluctance to get out of bed that morning. The car accelerated and the passing vegetation became a fuzzy line as his drooping eyelids lost their battle.

****

Steve Garner looked up from a thick pile of order sheets he'd filled in during a short lull in trade and pushed the papers to one side when he noticed a shadow fall across the bar.

'Welcome to the Edward II, sir. Would you like to place a food order?' he asked. The newcomer nodded and opened the menu he'd brought from a table nearby. His sharp blue eyes, black hair and lightly tanned skin drew an admiring glance from the woman beside him, to whom he seemed oblivious. Steve watched the man skim the choice of main courses and smile at the mention of one of his grandmother's specialities.

'Yeah, I'll try the steak and Guinness pie, and chips. Which beer do you recommend?'

Steve grinned. 'It'll have to be our signature brew, *Isabella's Revenge*. It's good stuff; the brewery's received requests from down south to supply pubs there and it's won a load of awards.' He raised his eyebrows in surprise. 'You've never heard of it?'

Konrad shook his head apologetically. 'Sorry, no. I've been out of the area for years.'

'So what brings you back into town?' Steve asked. He tapped the last of the food order into one of their computerised tills. 'You been away long?'

'A fair few years,' Konrad replied, turning his head to look at the main door. 'My family moved away when I was a kid because my dad's work relocated. I'm staying here for a couple of days for a job interview, and while I'm here thought I'd track down a couple of old friends I've not seen in years.'

Steve nodded and pulled back the pump to send foaming ale cascading into a pint glass, the pub's logo printed on its side in vivid scarlet letters. 'Sounds good; it's a shame to lose contact when you've been mates for ages.' He passed the drink across the bar. 'Your food shouldn't be too long, so just wave if you want me to pull you another pint.'

Konrad thanked Steve and returned to the small corner table he'd commandeered on arrival, its location offering unobstructed views of both the bar area and main door. He sipped the smooth malty liquid, enjoying the taste of authentic English ale. He'd always found that those bloody Yanks had no clue about decent ale.

Certain he hadn't been recognised, Konrad relaxed back into the leather armchair and surveyed the pub's décor. He noticed the crossed pokers above the bar, their tips painted flaming red, and a smile twitched around the corners of his mouth. He took a larger swallow of his pint and recalled Steve's penchant for joking around, before his thoughts turned to the man he'd discovered to be Steve's father-in-law.

That was rather a coincidence.

Roger Mortimer: the man sitting on his sizeable investment. He knew the old bugger would return it eventually, but time wasn't on Konrad's side and he needed financial stability for the next stage of his plan to disappear once and for all. He now knew where Roger lived, after following the old man to a neat detached 1930s property at the northern end of Blackpool. Based on the nature of some of Roger's business dealings, Konrad thought it likely there'd be a safe at the house, but whether significant sums of cash were kept there was unknown. The logistics of gaining access to check would need some careful consideration.

His musings jumped to those two Austrians. He hadn't actually wanted to kill them but, sensing the shit flying towards the fan, there'd been no other option. A split-second decision to obtain samples of their hair and plant them at both his homes might not throw the police off his tail for long, although it should buy him enough time to cover his tracks and disappear forever.

He'd found it easier than expected to fool Herman Schmidt and Jürgen Moser, the two men he'd met in Solvang. Konrad had fled to the town a couple of months earlier, in the days after he'd ignited a media furore by drunkenly slating the UK. His mind drifted back to that fateful evening he'd first picked up on their resemblance to himself, and to each other.

He'd soon engaged Schmidt in conversation at the bar and revealed himself to be half-German, leading to Andreas Baum being invited to join the friends at their table. The drinks flowed until the bar closed and the three men arranged to meet for another meal at the same time and place the next day, before parting with warm handshakes.

The following evening picked up where the previous left off. A steady supply of bottled beer complimented their meal and, now satisfied the alcohol had lowered their guard, Konrad ordered three more bottles and slipped a pair of small tablets into two of them. He returned to their table, where his companions drank eagerly. The Rohypnol rapidly took effect as the evening drew to a close; the original dye-free formulation he'd managed to obtain in New York ensuring the drug remained undetectable in their drinks.

From that point it became easier. Schmidt and Moser, by now beyond disorientated, readily accepted the offer of a lift back to their campsite. Minutes later, the rented Chevy edged through narrow lanes, its yellow headlights parting the darkness whilst Konrad searched for a place to pull over. He'd come to a halt on the inside of a bend, cut the engine and held his breath for nearly a minute. The slow inhalations and exhalations from the back seat confirmed both men had succumbed to the sedative, and that time was on his side.

Konrad carefully opened his door, walked to the trunk and propped a heavy wooden baseball bat against the car's bodywork. He eased open the rear door beside Schmidt, the man trapped in a chemically-induced stupor. Schmidt's eyes remained closed and a trickle of saliva seeped from one side of his mouth. Konrad pulled him from the back seat and let him slump onto the dry earth, then swung the bat against his right temple. He'd yanked out a handful of Schmidt's hair, pushed it into a small resealable plastic bag and repeated the procedure with Moser; the drugged man also powerless to resist his fate.

He pressed his fingers to their necks and realised they were both still alive, their pulses faint and thready as he considered his options. A Maglite's powerful beam sliced through the dense undergrowth covering the slope that descended away from the roadside. The area appeared suitably remote and he doubted many people used the lane, let alone went hacking their way into the vegetation.

Konrad dragged each unconscious man to the road's edge and listened to the snap of twigs as they rolled downwards. Certain that nobody was going to emerge from the pitch blackness smothering the area, he'd grabbed a shovel from the trunk and climbed down to the flattened area where Schmidt and Moser landed. Now he'd realised the bone dry soil made burial an impossible option, the flattened blade sent a succession of dull thuds into *the air, unable to drown the crack of fragmenting skulls. After rearranging a patch of nearby foliage to cover the bodies, Konrad climbed back to the road and slumped into the driver's seat, exhausted by his endeavours.*

He drove cautiously along the deserted narrow road and further away from the small former Danish colony until certain the second site he'd chosen wouldn't be linked to the first. The shovel glinted in the pale moonlight as it disappeared into a thicket with a resounding thud, interrupting the nocturnal chirrups of thousands of cicadas. Fifteen minutes later Konrad let himself into his hotel room, where he'd stood beneath the shower for longer than he'd usually tolerate, allowing the too-hot soapy water to obliterate any residual evidence.

Within his daydream, an invincible Konrad grinned. Nobody would prevent him from accomplishing whatever he'd set his mind to, not even–

'Your food, sir.'

The clatter of a large plate being lowered onto the table startled Konrad back to the present. Wisps of steam carried its delicious smell upwards and he smiled apologetically at his former acquaintance.

You couldn't really have ever called him a friend, isn't that right... Peter?

'Sorry mate, must have drifted off into la la land.'

'Rehearsing your interview technique?'

'Yeah,' Konrad replied and wrinkled his nose. 'Something along those lines.'

Steve nodded at the almost empty pint glass. 'Do you want another?'

Konrad tilted his head and considered the offer. 'Why not?' he replied, forcing joviality into his tone. 'It's not like I have to drive home.'

The knife carved through the pie's thick pastry, releasing an avalanche of meat and a rich savoury aroma. His stomach contracted as his fork stabbed a trio of chips and dipped them into the gravy seeping across the plate. Steve had certainly done well for himself, Konrad decided. He looked around the pub and blew onto the gravy-coated chip he'd raised to his mouth. Office workers in sharp suits sipped their drinks at the bar, a young couple out for a romantic pre-cinema meal gazed into each other's eyes and five sixty-something women cackled at the adjacent table now they'd decided to order two more bottles of wine.

Konrad devoured the meal as quickly as its temperature permitted and continued to keep an eye on the door in case Roger Mortimer put in an appearance. A lunchtime conversation with a disgruntled bar owner at the opposite end of Friargate revealed his quarry often popped into the Edward II early in the evening if he passed through Preston – *'to see the other pubs sliding into the shit',* according to Gerald Stephens.

Minutes later he sighed contentedly, drained his second pint of beer and decided to give Roger another five minutes. It wouldn't take more than a fleeting moment of eye contact to spook the old bastard and make him realise Oliver Stamford didn't let things drop so easily. Once he'd achieved that small objective he could get on with his main plan for that summer's evening and rectify a different kind of itch he'd recently felt an increasing urge to scratch.

Steve returned to the table and picked up the empty plate. 'Was that okay for you?'

Konrad patted his stomach and gave an emphatic nod. 'Bloody amazing, thanks.'

'What about some pudding?' Steve pointed to the nearby specials board. 'Can I get you a portion of either of those two beauties? Our sticky toffee pud is legendary in this area.'

Konrad glanced at the clock and wondered whether to buy himself more time in the pub, the decision made seconds later by the short, portly figure pulling open the main doors.

'I'd love dessert; I just haven't got the room.'

'Another beer?' Steve picked up the empty glass, pleased to see foamy rings still clung to its interior.

Konrad gave a reluctant shake of his head and held out £15. 'Better not, got to be up early in the morning,' he replied. 'Need my wits about me. This should more than cover the bill.'

'The interview?'

'Yeah, amongst other things.'

'All the best,' Steve said. He reached for the banknotes and smiled at Konrad. 'Thanks, and feel free to come in again if you're ever passing. We like seeing locals return from exile.'

Konrad shook Steve's hand and watched Roger adjust to the lower light intensity inside the building. 'Best pie I've tasted in ages,' he said, closing the distance between himself and Roger. Their paths converged seconds later and the older man's face and eyebrows quivered when *Oliver Stamford* paused and whispered something only audible to him.

Steve regarded his father-in-law with a puzzled expression.

'What's the matter, Roger? You look like you've seen a ghost.'

Roger regained his composure and pointed at the door. 'What did that bloody septic want?'

'Septic?' Steve echoed.

'Tank... as in Yank.'

'As in American?'

'Yeah, bloody idiots the lot of them. Why was he here?'

'He's not American,' a confused Steve replied. 'He said he's from here originally and moved away when he was a little kid. He certainly sounded like he's from round here.'

'You taking the piss?' Roger exclaimed, his nerves shrieking for a pint of *Isabella's Revenge* before he returned home.

Steve shrugged and made a mental note to mention her father's strange behaviour to Charlotte. 'No, he said he's in town for a couple of days for a job interview and wants to catch up with a couple of old friends he's not seen in a while. Came across like a decent enough bloke.' He eyed Roger suspiciously. 'Why did you automatically assume he's American? Do you know him?'

'No, no...' Roger blustered. 'He does look rather like a guy from Nevada I knew a few years back. Must be the senility creeping in already, eh?'

Steve cleared the table Konrad had vacated. 'Have a seat, you seem stressed. Are you all right?' he asked, before beginning to wipe down the table's surface.

'Yeah,' Roger said quietly and bit his lip whilst easing himself into a chair. 'Just a bit on edge since a little visit I received yesterday.'

Steve placed the dirty plate and glass on an adjacent table 'Who from?'

Roger waited for his son-in-law to drop into the opposite chair. 'A disgruntled tenant arrived at my house and started hurling obscenities,' he replied. 'The fellow who jointly owns the property wants his share of the bounty, so I've got to sell the place.'

'The American guy?' Steve frowned and turned to the door.

'Doesn't matter.'

Steve motioned for Mikey to pull them a couple of pints and turned his attention back to the pale man sitting opposite him. 'What happened?'

'Bloody knuckle dragger turned up on my doorstep shouting and bawling,' Roger replied, still embarrassed by the memory. 'Neighbours were twitching their net curtains and everything. I explained again what I'd stated in the letter but he got proper pissed off. If Stuart hadn't been mowing the grass next door, I reckon he'd have planted one on me. Big bugger, he is. I offered to set him up with a chap I know who rents properties further up the coast and he told me to shove it up my arse. Cheeky bastard.'

Mikey set down a pint in front of Roger. 'Looks like you need this tonight, old man,' he said before returning to the bar to pour a second for his older brother.

Steve saw Roger's trembling hand pick up the glass and endeavoured to hide his concern. 'Tell me if you have any more bother, although I'm sure it'll all settle down in a week or so.'

****

5.08pm – PDT
Route 395, near Reno, Nevada

Anna tore open the Twix's foil wrapper and pulled out a chocolate coated finger. 'It'll take a lot to make me part with half my stash,' she said, waving it under Sam's nose until he lifted one hand from the steering wheel.

'Don't even go there.' He narrowed his eyes in an unconvincing attempt at anger. 'You and the kids have done well enough out of me today. You drag me around the shops, make me pay for everything and carry all the bags – and then you deny me chocolate.'

'Can't believe how much hotter it is down here. Apparently it went down to forty degrees around Tahoe last night,' Anna commented, remembering the weather update they'd listened to on the drive north to Reno that morning. 'It was real cold getting out of bed. Those summer pyjamas don't cover nearly enough.'

'You make it sound like that's a bad thing,' Sam said. He opened his mouth to continue but was silenced by one finger of the chocolate bar.

'Sorry, comfort comes first,' she added, referring to the two bags of heavier weight nightclothes purchased that afternoon. 'If we're back in Golden soon, they'll come in useful this winter. I've wanted some new stuff for months and the kids go through clothes so fast.'

Sam removed the chocolate from his mouth. 'We should stop feeding them,' he said and a wide grin formed on his face. 'That'd slow down their growth.'

Anna playfully cuffed his arm. 'I'll bear that tactic in mind if you start getting porky over the Holidays.'

They fell silent to enjoy the chocolate's sweetness, both wishing they'd picked up an extra bar at a small news stand adjacent to the parking lot. Sam glanced at the Saab's rear-view mirror and his eyes swept across the asphalt behind them for the fifth time in under a minute.

Anna shifted in her seat. 'What's the matter?'

'Are the kids asleep?' he asked, his tone unexpectedly serious.

She nodded. 'I think it'd take a bomb to wake them. Why?'

'Don't turn round. Can you see that black car two cars behind?'

Anna squinted into the side mirror. 'The station wagon?' she asked, eliciting a curt nod from Sam. 'What about it?'

'It's been behind us literally since we pulled out of that parking lot in Reno.'

Anna swallowed. 'Who's in it?'

'Can't see, I think there's just a driver. It's hard to tell due to the distance they're keeping.'

'Are you sure?'

He detected the growing fear in her voice. 'Yeah. You remember what Milne said. We're to keep vigilant for anything suspicious. I'm not saying they're following us, but it's better to be safe than sorry.'

She peered into the side mirror again. 'What are you going to do?'

'There's a right turn soon, which goes to Lake Tahoe.' Sam pictured the map he'd been memorising since their arrival, ensuring he knew a selection of alternate routes with which to vary their journey each time. 'I'll turn down there without signalling and go the long way back.'

'What if they follow?'

'Take another right at Incline Village and go the long way back to Reno. In the unlikely event we need to go to the police, I'd rather do it there than near Tahoe and lead them to where we're staying. Hold on!'

Sam swerved into the exit lane and swung the steering wheel to the right. Anna grabbed the door handle whilst the vehicle made its sharp manoeuvre and then briskly accelerated towards a line of mountains in the near distance, their peaks jutting into the blue sky. He checked the rear-view mirror again and noticed the vehicles on the road they'd left becoming progressively smaller.

'Has it followed us?'

Sam shook his head. They reached an intersection and sped through its set of traffic lights, thankful they'd stayed green. 'Doesn't appear so. I want to prove that before we consider heading back to Kings–'

A sleepy voice from the back seat interrupted him. 'Daddy?'

'Are you okay, sweetheart? Did we wake you?'

'What happened, Daddy?'

'Uh... a deer ran out in front of the car and Daddy had to drive around her,' Anna said. She twisted her neck until she could see Angela in her car seat, the little girl now rubbing her eyes.

'Is she okay, Mommy?'

'Yes,' she replied, relieved to see John hadn't woken. 'You go back to sleep, we've still got a long way to go.'

Angela's eyelids drooped as Sam increased his speed and extended the distance between the family and Route 395. He and Anna maintained a contemplative silence, both periodically checking the looping road behind to confirm the black station wagon hadn't doubled back. Sam stared straight ahead whilst Anna's unfocussed gaze blurred the landscape flashing past, its desert scrub gradually merging into forestry.

They soon reached the intersection with Tahoe Boulevard, where Sam turned left and followed the lake's shoreline until he pulled into a parking area beside a small bay and came to a halt. He silenced the engine and rested his head in his hands, relieved to feel the adrenaline beginning to wear off. Tiredness gradually replaced the fear and he sensed Anna's hand on his knee.

'Hey, you okay?' she asked when his eyes stayed closed. 'That was some driving you did back there.'

Sam slowly exhaled, opened his eyes and turned to face her. 'How long are we going to be living like this?'

'They'll find him,' she replied, watching his jaw clench. 'As I said, despite his best efforts he's still leaving clues. They've tracked him to Germany and he appears to be living up to Joe Studdert's theory he's choosing locations he's familiar with.'

'He's one of the best,' Sam muttered. 'If anyone can locate Kratz, it'll be Studdert.' He fell silent, stared at the lake's surface shimmering in the afternoon sun and silently wondered how much longer that task would take.

****

8.22pm – MDT
Golden, Colorado

'Sleeping Beauty here's on chauffeur duty tomorrow,' a grinning Hallberg commented, after he'd thanked Colin Milne for passing a small jug of milk across the table.

Milne carefully stirred the contents of his coffee cup. 'It's a nice drive down to Cortez,' he said. 'I know your minds are on the case, but try to take time to enjoy the scenery. My wife and I own a cabin near Durango; we try to get there whenever we can.'

Muñoz smiled politely, finished his fourth cup of coffee since their arrival in Golden and hoped the additional caffeine wouldn't affect his chances of getting a decent night's sleep – and his ability to focus on driving the next day.

The detectives had arrived at Kratz's home near the top of Paradise Road two hours earlier to find Milne's SUV already occupying the driveway. The tall, grey-haired man alighted from the vehicle as Hallberg brought their rented station wagon to a halt and, after warm handshakes and enthusiastic greetings, the three men entered the house. Muñoz immediately felt a pall of unease descend over him and silently rebuked himself, attributing his edginess to the combined effects of sleep deprivation and too much coffee.

Hallberg pulled a small Dictaphone from his pocket and took the time to record his observations of each room. His keen eyes scanned their surroundings, where little evidence of the extensive forensic work carried out a few weeks earlier remained. A light covering of dust coated the polished mahogany surfaces and confirmed the house had lain undisturbed since the CSI team leader locked the front door for the last time.

They'd examined the entire property; its succession of sterile rooms offering precious little insight into the man who'd previously resided there. Despite the pleasant warmth of a Colorado summer's evening,

166

Hallberg shivered as they climbed the staircase to the second floor and walked along a narrow corridor. It widened at its furthest point and he saw that three doors led off from each side, those to the left quickly identified as the master bedroom, the study and a linen cupboard. What lay beyond the middle door produced the most interest: an old-fashioned safe, its heavy metal door ajar.

Hallberg's thoughts returned to the present. He smiled and thanked their server when the young man placed a large fresh fruit platter in front of him.

'You must be feeling ill,' Muñoz said, hoping his tiramisu lived up to its Italian translation.

'Guilt-free Holey Heaven for breakfast tomorrow.' Hallberg picked up a fork and admired the colourful selection. 'Looks pretty good, right?'

'How is it working alongside Joe Studdert?' Milne asked. He scanned the restaurant's modern interior in anticipation of his dessert's arrival. 'He's said to be one of the best.'

'We haven't actually met the guy yet,' Muñoz replied. He picked up his spoon and met Milne's gaze. 'We've Skyped a couple of times from our hotels. Mosley has finally gotten himself set up at home while Studdert stays at his place this week. Do you know him well?'

'We've been in regular contact over the past year. One of my agents also co-ordinates the New York unit Studdert belongs to'

Hallberg nodded at Milne. 'Sam Bury's CSRU?'

'You met Sam when he was in LA?' Milne asked.

'Yeah, he's a good guy. Consulted directly on the Kratz case,' Hallberg said.

Milne adjusted the napkin on his lap. 'You're also aware of how Kratz targeted Sam?'

The two men nodded and an uncomfortable silence descended. 'Yeah, last summer, right?' Hallberg eventually commented. 'Sam said he'd worked with Kratz periodically on *H.O.S.T.A.G.E.*, so he assumed Kratz suddenly thought he'd been recognised and decided to remove the chance of a positive identification.'

'Sam hasn't said a huge amount since,' Milne continued. 'However, he recently disclosed that Kratz made him feel uneasy for months before the MVA, but couldn't pinpoint why.'

'Sam mentioned the scumbag always seemed too good to be true,' Muñoz said.

'Kratz is manipulative and able to conceal his identity.' Hallberg picked up his fork and speared a chunk of watermelon. 'He's done this by assuming a succession of aliases, changing his appearance and accent–'

'And fleeing the country,' Muñoz interrupted as a burst of enthusiasm replaced the exhaustion he'd endured since that morning. 'All of which costs money. You can obtain fake ID if you know who to ask and can cross their palm with the green stuff. Last minute flights can be expensive.'

'The safe at Kratz's home was almost empty,' Milne said, his tone thoughtful as he mentally walked through the house from room to room. 'CSI said they found no items of value inside when they processed the place. Apparently he left a couple of legal documents – and nothing to indicate an escape route or hideout.'

'What about hidden finances?' Muñoz asked. 'Like keeping another bank account under an unknown alias.'

'Again, there's nothing to indicate this. However, that the safe was open suggests there *had* been something useful in there and he was rushing to get away.' Milne leaned back in his chair. 'Maybe cash, or valuable items he'll sell to generate it.'

'I'd build up an escape fund gradually over the years, in case I needed to run.' Hallberg suggested. 'You can't tell me he wasn't aware his cover could be blown at any time?'

Muñoz frowned and wondered what he'd do if he ever found himself in Kratz's situation. 'What if he hadn't been able to return home? Say if the cops were waiting for him here.'

Hallberg lowered his voice. 'He has another stash somewhere else.'

'We didn't find anything obvious at Brockmont,' Muñoz said. He frowned at his returning memories of the tedious stake out and his fake marriage to a Glendale PD officer.

'Does he own any other homes?' Milne asked.

Muñoz shook his head. 'Not that we've discovered.'

'So if there is another, it'll be under an alias.'

'That figures,' Muñoz agreed after he'd digested Milne's last statement. 'Maintaining a bolt hole for if he ever needed to go off the grid makes a lot of sense. He regularly moves from place to place to throw us off the scent.

If we work on the assumption he's aiming to return to the US, we need to narrow down potential locations.'

'It'd be somewhere he has no apparent connection to. Even Kratz isn't arrogant enough to attempt to hide in plain sight,' Hallberg added. 'His face has been too familiar for years, so you can bet your ass folk in Denver and Glendale will be keeping an eye open.'

Milne nodded sagely. 'They will be when news of a fifty thousand dollar reward goes public tomorrow.'

'What time is tomorrow's press conference?' Muñoz asked, his voice muffled by the hand stifling a yawn.

'Around two.' Milne signalled to their server for additional coffee. 'Joe Studdert is doing the honours.'

'This is going down like a turd on the Walk of Fame,' Muñoz added, thinking back to an entertainment bulletin they'd viewed during lunch a couple of days earlier. 'And, it's rumoured he was due to get one of *those* stars next spring.'

'Has Studdert considered the possibility of an unknown residence?'

'He hasn't mentioned anything,' Hallberg said. 'I'll email the suggestion to him later.'

Milne swallowed the last of his water. 'I can ask Niall Demaine to research it.'

'Man, he might be one of the best, but that's one hell of a big undertaking.' Hallberg massaged his temples and sniffed loudly. 'Assuming Kratz has one and it's in this country, that's fifty states to plough through.'

Milne extracted a small spiral-bound notepad and a pen from his jacket's inside pocket. 'Let's assume it exists and it's in a different state to either of his currently known homes. That potentially excludes Colorado and California.'

Hallberg frowned. 'California's a big place… let's say we just rule out the southern half?'

Milne nodded and jotted down a succession of bullet points to go pass on to Demaine the following morning. 'So, what kind of location?'

'Cities lend themselves to feelings of anonymity, but contain more people to potentially recognise you. Small towns or villages usually have more of a community feel, increasing the likelihood of being recognised as an incomer. New folk in small towns are often viewed with suspicion until

169

enough is learned about them... unless newcomers or a constant turnover of residents are a regular part of local life.'

Milne stopped writing and raised an eyebrow at Hallberg. 'A small place with a transient population?'

'Or one that's popular with vacationers,' Muñoz suggested, his mind racing through new possibilities.

'Somewhere there's lots of holiday homes, which the owners may only visit a couple of times a year,' Hallberg said.

'I can think of numerous places fitting that description. Are you familiar with Breckenridge?' Milne watched them both shake their heads. 'It's a pretty little ski town just over an hour from here. Breck also caters for the summer tourist market and city dwellers keen to own their little patch of serenity in the form of a forest cabin.'

Hallberg failed to hide his surprise. 'You think he'd go that close?'

Milne shook his head. 'No, although it's the type of area where he wouldn't come under excessive scrutiny. If he owns a place he only occupies periodically and plenty of other local properties are also second homes, he wouldn't be an anomaly. You do realise this research would be in addition to Demaine's regular workload?' he added, concerned the two detectives were building up false hope. 'And, there's no guarantee we're on the right lines.'

'So how can we narrow down the search area?' Muñoz pressed on, reluctant to discard their latest lead, however tenuous.

'That's for Demaine to decide. I'd guess he'll identify towns fitting the criteria and then try to link vacation homes to their owners' permanent homes. Those which don't tie into a permanent address are subjected to further investigation.'

'At one state per day, you're still talking a minimum of seven or eight weeks,' Hallberg said. 'Let's say we start by focussing on the northern half of California and the states neighbouring Colorado,' he continued, a hopeful expression appearing on his freckled face.

Milne sighed and hoped he wasn't about to pour cold water on their ideas. 'Our problem is it's only a theory, and a pretty far-fetched one at that. I'll brief Demaine tomorrow morning but, even if something does reveal itself, I can't see it being immediate.'

Muñoz nodded and stared into the darkness beyond a row of nearby windows. 'Me neither.'

Chapter 24 – Friday 14th August 2009

3.49pm – BST
Preston, England

Little more than a stone's throw from West Side FC's stadium, Sainsbury's occupied a large site across the four-lane road traversing the town in an east-west direction. As was usual on any Friday, its car park began to fill by mid-afternoon; a tinderbox of those who preferred to detour via the supermarket on the way home from the last school run of the week.

Konrad parked the Astra in one of the spaces furthest away from the store, keen to avoid any human interaction and the possibility of an out of control trolley denting his hire car. He weaved through rows of parked cars to a line of concertinaed trolleys, freed the one nearest to him from its neighbour and made his way into the store. The brightly lit interior differed from the memories of his last visit over nineteen years earlier, a couple of days prior to the Umpleby family leaving England for good.

Time flies when you're having fun.

He retrieved a hastily written list from the back pocket of his jeans and attempted to memorise its combination of edible provisions and *other stuff*. Despite having no intention of staying in the country for more than another week, there were things he needed to take care of. Hopefully a conversation would be enough, but thorough preparation was vital – in case Roger needed to be permanently silenced.

Konrad contemplated his apparent recent change of heart that had seemingly manifested itself in a sudden reluctance to kill people. Previously he'd given the act no second thought and, if someone needed dispatching in order for him to achieve his goal, so be it. These days he preferred to settle the matter without murder. He considered his motives, or lack of them, as he pushed the trolley into an aisle where a colourful display of generic kitchen goods reached up towards the ceiling's fireproof tiles. The act of killing obviously generated its own special brand of attention from the police, media and general public: the type of attention he didn't want focussed on him. To achieve his objectives with no loss of life would, in theory, enable him to remain under the law's radar indefinitely.

However, if *dead* was required then *dead* it would have to be.

He stopped beside a row of kitchen knives and admired how their highly polished blades reflected harsh light from the fluorescent tubes overhead. Konrad picked up the nearest one, fingered its sharp edge and imagined the damage it was capable of inflicting. He placed the carving knife in the trolley, a welcome addition to the twine bought from the gardening section of a DIY store on North Road which he'd visited within minutes of leaving the hotel.

Over that morning's breakfast he'd considered the most effective method of killing Roger Mortimer, should such an outcome be unavoidable. Konrad glanced up and down the aisle, relieved to see a teenage assistant ignoring him. She seemed content to arrange a selection of garish mugs on a nearby shelf, her curtain of scarlet hair flopping over her eyes as she swayed in time to the tune reverberating inside her head.

Or maybe it's just an effect of the lead pipes around here?

He moved on and located the cling film amongst a wide selection of food storage products in the neighbouring aisle. None of that cheap economy stuff, he wanted the *extra thick* version.

****

8.56am – MDT
Route 285, near Jefferson, Colorado

Hallberg whistled from the passenger seat as they swept around a corner and the South Park basin came into view. A surprisingly emerald shade of green ringed by distant mountains spread out ahead of them, the bare rock above the tree line speckled by residual snow from the previous winter. 'Even the sky's bigger here,' he said, staring into an infinite expanse of blue above the grey summits. 'And that cloud over there looks like Mosley.'

Muñoz laughed. 'Didn't I say the old bastard always finds a way to keep an eye on us?'

Hallberg's head darted from side to side in an exaggerated manner. 'In that case there'll be another one nearby that looks like my wife.'

'Milne got it right about the scenery, Katharine sure would love this,' Muñoz commented when the car rounded another bend on the highway. 'Assuming this case wraps before I retire, this'll be the next vacation we take. A Rocky Mountain road trip: ten days of fresh mountain air, and no Konrad Kratz.' He watched the wipers clear a film of dust from the windshield. 'I agree it's kind of pointless stopping to make enquiries today; he could have gone any number of ways beside this. We need to check out if there's anywhere in Cortez he kept cash or other valuables. And it's not a million miles from Denver, so it wouldn't make maintaining a vacation home impossible.'

'In the same state?' A dubious Hallberg processed Muñoz's statement. 'I thought we said he won't be hiding so close to home.'

'I guess so, although it's hardly on Denver's doorstep.' Muñoz frowned as he raked over various scenarios. 'We suspect he hid valuables in Paradise Hills, and to put all your eggs in one basket carries a huge risk. If that's his only stash and he couldn't gain access to retrieve it, he'd be up shit creek. I'd hazard a guess he'd have a back-up location known only to him. Maybe a safe deposit box at a bank?'

Hallberg nodded. 'We go to Cortez's banks, find out who accessed these boxes during the days Kratz came to town and Mosley can get someone to run background checks on any names.'

Muñoz raised his eyebrows. 'They think he's left Europe?'

'The cops are tracking him over there and that Studdert guy suggested he may try to return to America, especially if he has hidden finances here. Even Kratz can't survive on thin air.'

'Could he have made financial provision in Europe? Gibson mentioned the guy has family connections to Bavaria and Switzerland.'

'There's no record of him having left the country, using either the Kratz or Umpleby name, since he arrived in 1990,' Hallberg said. He reached for a bag of Jolly Ranchers and offered them to Muñoz. 'Who knows what other aliases he's used over the years, and if he used them to go abroad.'

'So unless new evidence suggests otherwise, we work on the assumption he didn't leave until recently and made financial provision in the US.'

'You sound very sure he'd do that.'

Muñoz cast his eyes to the right and winked. 'Wouldn't you?'

'Wouldn't I what?' Hallberg looked up from the directions he'd printed that morning, his voice muffled as he used his teeth to twist the brightly-coloured candy free from its wrapper.

'Have something to fall back on.' A grin spread across Muñoz's face. 'If I went on the lam, I'd make sure I had monetary reserves.' He pushed a Jolly Rancher into his mouth and immediately grimaced. 'Can't believe you gave me cherry, you asshole. You know everyone hates cherry.'

Hallberg laughed as he detected the less offensive flavour of artificial watermelon. 'But, say he doesn't have reserves to fall back on,' he countered, noticing an RV ahead of them slow before it turned onto a side road. 'It's unlikely, based on what we already suspect is his motive for returning to the Colorado home. And, what if he's so arrogant he thinks he can stay under the radar forever?'

'Working for cash,' Muñoz replied. He accelerated now the road ahead was clear. 'Maybe posing as a migrant worker, never stopping in one place for long.'

'Too risky, only mere mortals may get away with that. Kratz...' Hallberg stifled a yawn and then continued. 'He's world famous. If he hung out with the same folk all the time, he'd most likely be recognised. And, many migrant workers tend to be Hispanic, so he'd stand out big time. He'll want to isolate himself, keep a low profile. And he *had* the financial means to squirrel it away.'

Muñoz raised a half-full bottle of water to his lips and took a couple of gulps. 'Speaking of profiles, what's Studdert said?'

Hallberg smiled proudly. 'I took your advice and emailed him last night to share my ideas. He sounded interested and said he could use some of it. He also said not to rule out more rural parts of Colorado and California's southern half.'

'Atta boy!' Muñoz wedged the bottle between his knees and aimed a punch into the other man's bicep.

'Yeah, but he'd probably already thought of it.'

'In that case you did good.'

'You think so?' Hallberg shook his head. 'Doesn't change the fact the scumbag's still out there, does it?'

****

2.34pm – PDT
San Fernando Road, Los Angeles, California

Normality soon resumed after an unusually cloudy start to the day and, by mid-afternoon, the City of Angels found itself bathed in the Californian summer sun's relentless glare. Intrigued members of the public joined the local and national media gathered outside the precinct, where a cordon of police officers amplified the expectant yet uncertain tension hanging in the air.

Inside the building, Joe Studdert and Ronnie Mosley huddled over a solitary sheet of paper to finalise the statement due to be delivered ten minutes later; a statement set to reveal Kratz's suspected involvement in Starr Mountain's death and bring their hunt for the fugitive further into the public eye. A large crowd occupied the small parking area to the station's frontage, and camera crews and newspaper photographers now jockeyed for the coveted spots closest to a recently erected small podium.

Mosley patted Studdert on the shoulder. 'You're happy to do this?'

He nodded. 'Sure am. If this means we find the creep faster, it means everyone's lives can return to some semblance of normality. Your team gets to sleep, I go home to my wife and Sam brings his family home safely.'

'You think we're giving them enough information?' Mosley picked up his empty coffee cup and huffed his disappointment. 'What about the other homicides?'

'Starr Mountain was a popular guy and you must remember the media frenzy generated by his disappearance and confirmed death. If they're given any excuse, the media always resurrects that case,' Studdert replied. 'Bring the disgraced Kratz into the equation and double the public outrage. We give people the facts, new leads come in and hopefully we're able to verify them against pre-existing evidence or theories.'

'So you're not giving them a profile?'

'Not just yet. I still have some things I want to refine, although Dave Hallberg has been assisting.' Studdert acknowledged the pride on Mosley's face. 'He's got ability, and he's completed some additional study to compliment the classes he attended. I'll only mention a little about the type of person Kratz is because I think revealing every detail of where he's been and exactly what he's done will induce panic.'

'And saying that his whereabouts are unknown won't?' Mosley replied.

'Like you said, this is a big ol' country.' Studdert paused to swig from a bottle of water. 'We say we need to narrow down his location, and there's a big, fat reward. That's millions of eyes scanning every man they see in the hope of claiming the bounty.'

'How far did you get?'

'Demaine's provided a pretty comprehensive family tree stretching back four or five generations. Dad's side is English, predominantly from North Yorkshire and not a million miles from where my old dad emigrated when he was a small child. Mom's side is Bavarian, and her maternal grandparents relocated to Augsburg from the Zürich area.'

Mosley nodded thoughtfully. 'Swiss?'

'Yeah. Explains why he flew to Zürich and then travelled to Munich,' Studdert replied, diverting his attention to the small wall-mounted television tuned to a local news channel.

'He then went to Augsburg. Isn't that near Munich?' Mosley saw Studdert nod. 'And did you find the name Baum in the tree?'

Studdert raised his eyebrows. 'Yeah, how'd you know?'

'You said something a few days ago about him possibly using old family names. His mother's maiden name was Kratz, and I assume Konrad occurs somewhere in the family?'

'Peter Umpleby's middle name was Konrad, possibly in tribute to his mother's father's father. The Andreas comes from his grandfather Andreas Kratz, born in Augsburg in 1916,' Studdert explained, having memorised the family tree's first four generations. 'Bear in mind he appears to change the alias or aliases he's been using, depending on the country's language. There's a strong link between Andreas Baum and André Wood. Baum translates from the German word for tree, and I don't really need to explain Andreas and André.'

'Yeah, I'd worked out the first names,' Mosley said. 'My grandmother was Austrian, but my knowledge of German is pretty much zero. The only language options at my high school were French and Spanish, and I was way beyond shit at both.' He cracked his knuckles and grinned at the

176

thought of Señora Lopez's melodramatic displays of despair whenever she graded his test papers. 'Have you discovered any other aliases he's used in the past?'

'Not yet,' Studdert replied. 'I've been generating English, German and French versions, and randomly combining them.'

'For Demaine to put through the system?' Mosley asked. He glanced at the wall clock. 'Are you ready to face the lions?'

Studdert nodded. 'It'll help, *if* we can narrow down his location.'

A young female officer opened the incident room's door. 'Agent Studdert?'

'That's the guy over there.' Mosley nodded in the other man's direction and lifted a prompt sheet from the desk. 'Guess it's time for you to go wow your public.'

****

4.29pm – MDT
Denver, Colorado

A light knock startled Milne, rousing him from the paperwork he'd been engrossed in for the previous forty minutes. He blinked to remove a gritty feeling from his eyes and looked over to where Demaine waited in the office's doorway.

Milne reclined and laced long fingers behind his head. 'You've found him already?'

Demaine mirrored Milne's tense smile and shook his head. 'It's like seeking a very fine needle in a Texan-sized haystack.'

'Do you have a method?'

'Kind of, I guess,' he replied. 'First I ruled out the obvious, like all Kratz's known aliases. All homes and businesses registered under these names were cross referenced and linked to law-abiding citizens.'

Milne frowned and narrowed his eyes. 'I suppose I should have realised that's too easy. What's Plan B?'

'Studdert emailed a preliminary profile suggesting Kratz may have an unknown hideout registered under a one-time alias. One of the LAPD detectives theorised Kratz will avoid the two states he has obvious ties to, namely Colorado and California. However, Studdert said I should include

177

southern and central Colorado, and shouldn't rule out the northern half of California and the more rural areas in its southern half.'

Milne pointed at a map on the opposite wall. 'You can certainly drive from LA to San Francisco in a day.'

'Exactly!' Demaine exclaimed. 'Studdert said a hideout, if it exists, will be inside a day's drive of either home. Longer distances involve overnight hotel stays or commercial flights and increases the risk of being recognised. I've identified two areas to focus our search on, each one covering a ten-hour drive from either Golden or Glendale.'

'Surely that's a huge area?' Milne countered. He slowly rose from his seat and crossed to the window, from where he watched a fork of lightning flicker and strike the distant Rockies.

'There's a central overlapping area in Utah around Salt Lake City and down to Richfield.' Demaine tapped his nose conspiratorially. 'Studdert said he'd expect Kratz to choose somewhere fairly equidistant from both houses and at least two hours away from them. Don't crap on your own doorstep, right?'

Milne's expression lightened and the merest hint of a smile twitched at the corners of his mouth as he poured water into a pair of crystal tumblers. 'Sorry it's nothing stronger,' he said as he handed one to Demaine. 'Inside that area of overlap you've identified, do any towns fit Studdert's idea of where Kratz might choose to lay low?' he asked, attempting to remember details of a visit to the area nearly a decade earlier when he'd collaborated with their Utah counterparts to solve a kidnapping case.

Demaine sipped his drink and relaxed against the chair's smooth leather. 'That's what I'm working on. Utah has plenty of cute little places up in the mountains to the east of Salt Lake City that are popular with vacationers, plus there's the city types wanting to own a little piece of paradise away from the daily grind. I'm circling all the possibilities on a map, before doing a more in-depth analysis.'

'Perhaps you should focus your efforts on the Californian side. Kratz spends more time in Glendale than in Denver so he's more likely to need to get away from there, right?'

'Yeah, there's an obscene number of places inside a half day drive of La La Land,' Demaine replied. He rubbed his eyes, red and sore thanks to six hours of staring at a trio of computer screens and the maps he'd generated. 'This is pretty much an infinite task and we're talking thousands of square miles just in the southern half of California. I can identify places where there's a high proportion of vacation homes owned by Angelenos, but is Kratz really going to follow the herd?'

'This is the problem we're facing.' Milne stifled a yawn, his recent longer than usual hours showing their effect. 'The variables are too diverse. Unless something more specific comes to light, the odds of discovering him – if he's actually there to discover – are millions to one. We don't have the time or resources to investigate this to the degree it requires.'

Demaine shrugged his shoulders. 'If he owned somewhere further afield he could claim he's vacationing from a different city. San Francisco, or maybe Vegas?'

Milne rested his elbows against the heavy oak desk and closed his eyes. 'This is a monumental undertaking which has the potential to consume all your working hours.' He shook his head and resumed eye contact. 'Your priority is whatever comes into this field office. Sam and his family are safe where they are and, however harsh this sounds, we don't need to find Kratz by tomorrow.'

He watched Demaine back out of the office, then balled a fist and rested his chin against it. Was Kratz still in Europe, or would he be brazen enough to return to the States? He thought back to Studdert's chess analogy of planning a strategy before your opponent made one of their many possible moves, to pre-empt their tactics in order to close them down and ultimately defeat them.

Meanwhile, in a small office on the floor below, Demaine assumed an almost identical pose. His gaze blurred the maps he'd printed and pinned to a notice board, turning them into a swirling torrent of colours. Was the answer hidden within them, or would their question remain unanswered forever? He closed his eyes and swallowed, allowed himself a minute of empty thought, then calmly resumed his duties.

****

Hallberg and Muñoz wasted little time in beginning their tour of the area's banks after arriving in Montezuma County five hours earlier. They'd immediately ruled out those in Mancos and Delores, thanks to a lack of unusual transactions occurring in the time frame spanning Kratz's visit to the area. From Delores they'd driven the short distance to Cortez, where the town's main drag took them past a patchwork of gas stations, hotels, food outlets and most of the remaining banks on their list. Much to their relief, each manager readily complied in providing the names of a handful of customers who'd requested access to their safe deposit boxes; the details already forwarded to Mosley and Demaine.

The detectives' station wagon pulled up outside its final destination of the day later than they'd expected. Muñoz surveyed their motel's fifties style light blue frontage and a nearby carpeted external stairway, and frowned at Hallberg. 'Looks kind of old-fashioned,' he said in a dubious tone.

'Perhaps it's good we're only staying one night?' Hallberg replied. 'Although I Googled the place; it's gotten lots of good reviews.' He hoisted his trolley case from the trunk and lowered it to the ground. 'What do you say to grabbing a couple of beers to chill for later?'

Muñoz pulled on his own case. 'If writing today's report doesn't send me to sleep first.'

Hallberg pointed the remote key at the car and activated its central locking. 'Have you heard if there's been any progress back home?'

'Nothing significant, or we'd have heard from Mosley.' Muñoz gave Hallberg a baleful stare. 'Do you still really think this is a worthwhile exercise?'

'I guess Mosley hopes we'll find someone he's spoken to.'

'That's kind of a tall order. You really think he'd let something slip?'

'He gets drunk, or maybe gets lucky…' Hallberg winked when Muñoz's eyebrows rose and fell. 'I'm sure even Kratz's tongue can be loosened.'

'Says the voice of experience,' Muñoz replied, shaking his head in amusement. 'Can't see him hanging out in bars. He'd need to keep his wits about him in case he needed to escape. Getting pulled for DUI ain't going to do him any favours.'

Hallberg slowed to negotiate the case's wheels over the kerb. 'We can't stop every woman on the street, hold up a photo and say *'Did you hit a home run with this guy?'*, can we?'

Muñoz laughed at the imaginary picture being wafted in his face. 'Studdert made a statement this afternoon and it's going to be broadcast across the country. Assuming it wasn't dark the whole time, some unlucky lady out there might recognise him.'

'Say she *does* exist and can't come forward? That–' Hallberg hushed when he noticed a young woman a few feet away pull her door shut, pick up a pair of plastic buckets and make a beeline for an ice machine on the other side of the parking lot. 'That's suicide if she's in a relationship, or worried about damaging her personal or professional reputation.'

Muñoz adjusted his backpack, uncomfortably aware of how its strap now cut into his shoulder. 'She'd need to have one hell of a lot at stake if she passes up on the current bounty on his head. I guess plenty of folks consider twenty thousand a handsome sum.'

'You haven't heard?' Hallberg said, grinning at Muñoz. 'Since lunchtime the suits have opened their wallets considerably wider. Try nearly trebling it.'

****

11.18pm – PDT
Glendale, California

As the sitting room's large grandfather clock stuck eleven, Tony and Susie politely declined the offer of a nightcap and bid her parents goodnight. They climbed the curved staircase and stopped at the first bedroom, sharing a smile when they saw the halo of light brown hair on Daniel's pillow. Satisfied their son was soundly asleep, they padded along the landing to their room and took turns to shower away the day's grime from their tired bodies.

Susie plumped up her pillow and watched Tony emerged from the adjacent bathroom, a cornflower-coloured towel wrapped around his waist. He flashed a smile at her and lifted a smaller matching towel, which he used to rub the excess water from his dark hair.

'Is there no other option?' she asked, unable to keep the concern from her voice now her thoughts had advanced twenty-four hours into the future.

'There'll be a posse of hairy-arsed cops with fully loaded guns watching my every move,' Tony replied. He let the small towel drop to the floor and ignored her reproachful stare, unsure whether she objected to his apparently blasé attitude or the dampness seeping into the carpet. 'I'll be perfectly safe,' he added. 'Honestly, they won't let me come to any harm.'

She sighed and dragged her hairbrush through a stubborn tangle. 'How can you be sure?'

'Listen, love; it'd sound bloody stupid if an American asked for a UK passport.' Tony forced a chuckle whilst he rummaged through the middle of three drawers. 'To quote Mosley, his team needs a *goddamn Limey.*'

'I'm worried about you. It's not like we usually deal with this kind of stuff,' Susie retorted. She climbed into bed and pulled the covers up to her neck. 'Lab rats like to stay safe in their cages, that's what you always say to me.'

'It'll be interesting,' he replied, adjusting the waist tie on an oversized pair of West Side FC shorts. 'You know, see how the other half does it.'

'Dead bodies and blood spatter don't threaten to pull a gun on you.'

'I'll be fine!' He aimed a swift kick at the towels to send them sliding onto the bathroom's tiled floor. 'I understand you're worried, but we'll be back home on Sunday.'

Susie reached across her nightstand to turn off the lamp. 'Yeah, can't believe I'm actually looking forward to work on Monday morning,' she replied.

Tony joined her under the covers after hanging the towels on their rail. He draped an arm over her waist and kissed her. 'Your mom and dad have been great, letting us stay all this–'

Susie ran a hesitant finger over his chest. 'Urgh, you're still damp,' she hissed. 'Yeah, they've sure enjoyed spoiling Daniel,' she added, her grin undetectable in the low light. 'Are the cops keeping you updated once we get home?'

'Gibson said he'd share any significant developments. I did say I'd come back if they need a *goddamn Limey* again. They don't think they will.'

'Is Walt gonna stand for that?' she asked, referring to their cantankerous temporary boss. 'Mike said he'd been bitching and whining.'

'I'll cross that bridge if we come to it; I'd like to see him take on Ronnie Mosley though. Anyway, the new guy starts soon and he can't be any more of a tool.'

Susie shifted position under Tony's arm, snuggled closer and felt him kiss the top of her head. 'We've gotten old. It's not that late and we're falling asleep,' she said, a yawn muffling her words. 'Who knew retail therapy and lunch with the girls could be so exhausting?'

'How much did Deanna and Lucy *make* you drink?' he asked, nudging her in the ribs. 'Don't deny it.'

She laughed and attempted to tally up the succession of cocktails they'd ordered that afternoon. 'It would have been rude not to. We hadn't gotten together in such a long time before today.'

'I'm glad you had fun.'

'You won't say that when the credit card bill arrives.'

Chapter 25 – Saturday 15th August 2009

11.48am – PDT
Brockmont, Glendale, California

The Glendale PD cruiser received a number of surprised stares from slowing motorists as it negotiated Ridgeview Drive's narrow twists and turns. Mosley leaned his aching head against the passenger side window and admired the area's upmarket homes, knowing their varied architectural styles and pristine front yards commanded a sizeable real estate return for those choosing to sell their little patch of hillside paradise.

'Goddamn soccer moms and their shitty spatial awareness,' Glendale detective Paul Whitehead grumbled when a silver SUV cut the corner they'd been due to reach seconds later. 'These roads and those things ain't a good combination.' He checked his rear-view mirror, brought the cruiser to a halt and saw Mosley's gaze shift to the right. 'Yeah, it's quite a view.'

Mosley looked past the high-rise buildings of Glendale's downtown area to where distant skyscrapers formed LA's instantly recognisable skyline, dulled by a light haze now the heat of the day had set in. 'Wouldn't mind a piece of this myself, but on my salary it's all I can do to stay in Altadena these days,' he replied.

Whitehead removed his foot from the brake, made a left turn and continued their ascent without encountering any additional traffic. They cut through a steep section of sloping pale rock partially covered by wild vegetation and cautiously rounded a second left turn offering a more impressive panorama; the familiar urban sprawl unnaturally peaceful from their elevated position. Neatly tended lawns, garden plants and spruce replaced the rocky outcrops and Mosley observed a significant number of cars parked in the road, bolstering his hope that maybe enough people were home to make the admittedly short journey worthwhile.

One last turn brought the two men onto Rimcrest Drive and Whitehead slowed to pass its immaculately maintained homes. Mosley narrowed his eyes and thought back to early July, recalling the days spent surveilling Chateau – or should that be Schloβ? – Kratz from the empty property across the street.

'I missed the stake-out,' Whitehead commented after he'd parked the cruiser outside the sprawling property which technically still belonged to Kratz. 'My wife and I were on vacation in Florida. Humid as hell down there at this time of year.' He watched Mosley appraise the dead-end ahead, which had been widened into a circle to allow all but the largest vehicles to make a comfortable U-turn. 'Might have been my only chance to live in a place like this. You think they're going to build something there?' he added, gesturing towards an empty patch of rough ground visible beyond two layers of chain-link fencing.

'I guess if you have enough green in the bank anything's possible.' Mosley opened the passenger door and flinched at the blast of heat flooding the car. 'Place had an awesome pool,' he continued and pointed at the recently occupied house from where they'd mounted the stake-out. 'Not sure we should have used it; Muñoz and Menendez agreed it added to their illusion of being a married couple.'

'Menendez?' Whitehead echoed. 'That's one ambitious lady.' He fell silent and popped a mint into his mouth, hoping to allay the sudden nicotine craving putting him on edge.

Mosley turned through 360 degrees to survey the street again. 'Bet these folks are going to be ecstatic to see us again. They sure as hell complained about being questioned last time. Anyone would think they liked being neighbours with a total psycho.'

'Guess it's the media presence more than anything,' Whitehead replied, loosening his tie to alleviate the dampness beneath his collar. 'We got called out a couple of times when some of the more unscrupulous publications had gotten a little too demanding. And remember, it's not like they know he's a *prolific* serial killer.'

'Perhaps now they've heard of his suspected involvement in the Starr Mountain case, they'll be more willing to assist. That little snippet went global inside an hour and the world's media is going nuts.' Mosley grinned at the memory of a local reporter hollering questions through a megaphone at police officers driving out of the parking lot the previous evening.

Whitehead set off towards a large house to the left of Kratz's. Its tall iron gates formed an imposing barrier between the men and a sweeping herringbone brick driveway that offered parking for at least five cars. 'So you've gotten some new evidence, and that's why you wanted to come up here and speak to these folks again?'

Mosley fell into step beside the Glendale detective. 'Not really. There's this FBI profiling dude working with us for a couple of days.'

'The Feds are in on the case?'

'Yeah, Agent Studdert's actually a decent kind of guy,' Mosley replied. He smiled at Whitehead's surprised expression. 'He's delivered this theory Kratz has a secret hideout less than a day's drive away from here. Kratz owns a vacation home near Denver and he's never made any great secret of that, so Studdert figures there's a chance Kratz may have inadvertently mentioned something to his neighbours. Apparently he's a sociable guy and regularly hung out with these people, so who knows what he let slip after a couple of beers?'

Whitehead's finger hovered over the intercom button beside the gates. 'Kind of strange why a big TV star chose to live here and not closer to Hollywood.'

'He said in some interview he preferred the hills, that they reminded him of Colorado,' Mosley replied, his eyes rolling behind their dark lenses. 'Studdert thinks Kratz deliberately chose Brockmont to make him appear more down to earth than other Hollywood types. It's an upmarket area, but there's still a range of houses and backgrounds here and it would humanise him to live among the general public.'

They were interrupted by a crackle of static from the intercom unit. 'Yeah, we don't want no more religious calls on the weekend. When will you–'

Mosley cut in and drowned out the irate teenage voice. 'Save it, son. We're from the Glendale and Los Angeles Police Departments. Is your mom or dad home?'

They waited for a reply and Whitehead tutted now silence reigned across the street. 'Hey, kid! You still there?' he said, his voice low and brusque. 'Some of us want to get home before nightfall.'

'Uh, yeah. Just hold on a sec, uh, sir.' The stuttering teenager found his voice at the same moment Mosley's foot began to tap out an irritated beat. 'My mom's in the kitchen fixing lunch, I'll go get her.'

Whitehead rubbed his belly. 'You think there's a sandwich in it for us?' he whispered.

The static interrupted them for a second time. 'Police, you say?'

'Yes, ma'am,' Whitehead replied, hoping he'd injected sufficient politeness and patience into his tone. 'Can we speak with you?'

'Is there a problem in the neighbourhood?'

'Perhaps we can discuss this inside? We promise we'll take up as little of your time as possible.'

There was another pause. 'Hold up one of your badges to the screen.'

'Detective Paul Whitehead, Glendale PD,' he said. Sweat started to trickle down his back. 'If it reassures you, we can wait in the car until you confirm my identity with the precinct.'

A loud buzz filled the air, followed almost immediately by a click as the gates swung open to allow the two men access. They approached the house and waited beside a row of tall trees offering meagre respite from the relentless sun whilst they scanned the building's front elevation. It took seconds for a smooth oak front door inlayed with Tiffany-style glass to open, revealing a petite woman whom Mosley judged to be in her late thirties – although experience told him she was probably anything up to a decade older.

She lowered an expensive pair of designer sunglasses and held out a slender manicured hand. 'Yelena di Marco,' she said, a trace of an Eastern European accent audible. 'Please forgive my son's lack of manners.' Yelena turned back to the open doorway and beckoned to a tall skinny boy Mosley estimated to be around sixteen years of age. 'Mikhail, you come apologise to these detectives.'

He slowly approached the trio of adults and squinted from face to face. 'Sorry, guys. Guess I assumed you were someone else.'

'No worries, kid,' Mosley said. He returned his attention to Yelena. 'You're having problems, ma'am?'

'We've gotten a lot of trouble recently from religious callers. Keep pressing the buzzer and won't go until someone comes out. The neighbours are also getting pissed off. The guy across the street thinks they're reporters trying to dig up dirt on Konrad Kratz.' She saw Mosley and Whitehead exchange a knowing glance. 'That's why you're here, right?'

Whitehead nodded and followed Yelena into the house. 'Yes, ma'am,' he replied. 'We'd be grateful if you'd answer some questions.'

'I told your undercover cops everything I know,' she said. 'Come on, guys. Kratz disappears, newlyweds move into the house opposite, lots of comings and goings.' Yelena's wide smile exposed an array of expensive dental work. 'And then they moved out in under a month. Either they had the marriage from hell, or they were cops.' She closed the door and led them across a huge marble-floored entrance hall. 'Anyway, you must be thirsty. I will get you iced coffee if you wish, or I can make it hot?'

'Iced sounds great,' Whitehead replied. 'It's hotter than Hades out there.'

Mosley nodded his agreement and exhaled loudly as they entered a kitchen straight out of an upmarket interior design magazine. 'You have a beautiful home,' he added, staring through an expansive glass sliding door to a large swimming pool and hot tub, beyond which the hillside dropped away to offer the same view they'd admired minutes earlier.

'It's a good area for raising the kids.' Yelena retrieved a huge jug of dark liquid from an oversized refrigerator and lifted three glasses from a wall cupboard, then eased herself into a tall seat behind the adjacent granite countertop. 'So, you guys are hungry? I have homemade muffins in that tub. Slide it over please, Mikhail,' she said, reaching over to intercept the large red container.

The two men smiled their appreciation. 'That's very kind of you, Mrs di Marco,' Mosley said, scanning the room. 'This is purely the start of another round of informal visits to your neighbourhood; we figured recent developments may have triggered things you'd previously forgotten. We really don't want to keep you longer than necessary, so we'll start.'

A chunk of ice clunked against the tumbler's thick glass when Yelena raised it to her lips. 'Go ahead.'

'Firstly, how well did you know Kratz?' Mosley asked. He picked up his own glass and sipped the drink.

'He moved onto Rimcrest a little over two years ago,' she said. 'We recognised him straight away. To be honest, we were surprised to see such a big star move in. Our preconceived ideas were soon changed.' Her eyes darted between them and Mosley's nod encouraged her to continue.

188

'He was a cool guy, you know? Threw pool parties for the neighbours, accepted reciprocal invites, he gave autographs to the kids and arranged a guided tour of the *H.O.S.T.A.G.E.* set for us during a family vacation in New York.'

'You ever spend time together on a one-to-one basis?'

She looked at him sharply. 'Meaning?'

'Like this… coffee and muffins. Or maybe he got together with your husband for a few beers and a game of pool?' Mosley pointed to the games room visible beyond a large curved archway.

'Not really,' she replied. 'Bruno isn't home much; he's a defence lawyer in the city and works long hours. I can ask him to give you a call.'

'I'd appreciate it. So, you'd consider yourself and Kratz to be friends?'

'I guess you could say that. I mean, he wasn't here often because of filming commitments. We'd get together and catch up from time to time. Maybe once a month, on average.'

Whitehead drained the contents of his glass. 'Did he discuss vacations?'

'Vacations?' she echoed.

'Yeah. Places, activities.'

'Over the past couple of years he's spent much of the time in New York filming *H.O.S.T.A.G.E.* He comes back during filming season for the occasional short break, but I know he has a place in Denver too.'

'Any other vacation homes?'

'In addition to Denver?' She shrugged and raised an eyebrow. 'None he ever mentioned.'

'And when the show's on its summer hiatus?' Mosley asked. 'Does he stay here until it's time for him to return to New York?'

'He does spend time here, although not always on weekends.'

He nodded. 'What happens on weekends?'

'Not every weekend, say every other weekend. He'd drive away on the Friday morning and not return until late Sunday night.'

'Did you ask where he went?'

'Kind of. He just grinned and said it's good to unwind. I assumed he'd gotten himself some lady friend in another part of town.'

'And he was driving the Beemer?'

She frowned and searched for a specific memory. 'No, I thought it was strange. He'd leave in a Honda sedan. Don't ask me the type, I know little about cars. That's man's stuff, right? Anyway, I guess I thought he was trying to avoid being noticed. Perhaps he was having a fling with a married woman and sneaking her off someplace else?'

'There's a Honda in the garage,' Whitehead commented, his interest piqued. 'We just assumed it's a decoy car for blending in and avoiding the paparazzi.'

'You've been a great help, Mrs di Marco. If your husband remembers anything relevant we'd be grateful if he'd call us,' Mosley said and reached into his wallet. He hesitated and glanced at a nearby window ledge before handing his business card to her. 'You said *the kids*. How many do you have?'

'Besides Mikhail?' she said, eyeing the small rectangular piece of card. 'Galina just turned twenty-one and has taken a year away from college. Why?'

'I just wondered whether other members of the family may be able to assist.' He ignored Whitehead's quizzical expression. 'Why did she take a year out?'

Yelena picked up a framed photograph from the window ledge. 'This is her daughter, Anya,' she said and gazed lovingly at the image of a plump baby girl, her blonde curls complimented by a pink floral dress. 'I never thought I'd be a Babushka so young. Galina does well. She looks after the child and gets up every night. Insists on doing it all herself.'

Whitehead harboured an inkling of the latest idea to take root in Mosley's mind. 'She isn't with the father?' he asked.

'Father? Whoever the hell that piece of shit is,' she spat. Her son's eyes widened and he shrank back. 'Claims she met him at a party, and said she was so drunk she doesn't remember who he is.'

'Claims?' Mosley repeated innocently, now he realised Whitehead followed the same train of thought.

'She's my only daughter, but really she isn't that kind of girl,' Yelena said, fully aware she sounded like a mother in denial. A frown played around her forehead and she stared pointedly at Mosley. 'She dreams of following her father's footsteps in the legal profession and she always worked so hard at school. Homework took priority over socialising. She said she'd shared a few kisses with boys from school, but she's no whore who gets drunk and has casual sex at parties.'

Mosley glanced at the photo again. 'You think she's protecting Anya's father?'

'From my husband?' Her forced smile became brittle, as if her composure would shatter at any second. 'Maybe. Bruno said he'd do time if he ever catches the *sperm donor*.'

'Have you any idea who he is?' Whitehead asked as she shook her head and a solitary tear traced its way down one cheek.

Mosley leaned across the counter and patted her arm. 'How well did your kids know Kratz?'

She swallowed heavily and looked at her son. 'Mikhail?'

'He seemed a nice enough guy,' he said, a trace of nervousness audible. 'Always took time to sign autographs for people.'

'What about Galina?'

'I can ask her to give you a call.' A manicured finger stroked the edge of Mosley's business card. 'She's gone to the Galleria with her cousin to spend all the money she received for her birthday on the baby.'

'Must be tough on a young girl, being a single mom so young?'

Yelena smiled weakly. 'We manage.'

Mosley extended his hand and rose to his feet. 'Many thanks for your time ma'am, we won't keep you any longer.'

'Any time,' she replied. She escorted them back to the front door and offered another sad smile. 'You guys have a safe journey.'

Whitehead echoed his companion's thanks and inwardly groaned when the warm air enveloped him on their return to the cruiser. He opened its doors to dispel the build-up of heat inside and frowned at Mosley across the vehicle's roof whilst they waited for the air conditioning to work its magic.

'Why the sudden interest in her daughter?'

'Because I'd have reacted in the same way if it was my daughter,' Mosley replied. He knew exactly how ecstatic Kim had been to be offered a place to study medicine at UCLA, after years of dedicated study reaped their reward. 'She's not that kind of girl either.' He saw a middle aged woman unlocking a Mercedes on a nearby driveway cast a swift look in their direction. 'Did you get a look at the kid's photo?' he whispered.

'Yeah, pretty little thing and a cute smile,' Whitehead said. He frowned and psyched himself up to brave the car's overheated interior. 'It's weird how she's a little blondie and the rest of the family's dark.'

'These things can skip generations.' Mosley shook his head and wondered if his instincts were correct this time. 'Kratz moves in a couple of years ago, and Saint Galina gets herself knocked up.'

Whitehead nodded. 'You think Kratz is the baby daddy?' He watched Mosley shrug and then continued. 'We haven't enough evidence to demand a DNA sample to compare to the one that's almost certainly Kratz's.'

'If the kid *is* Kratz's do you figure he knows?'

'Why stay quiet if it's his?' Whitehead laughed and assumed a falsetto voice. *'Cough up the Benjamins or I'll rat you out to the press.'*

Mosley twisted the top off a bottle of tepid water. 'Either she's blackmailing him.'

'Or he's buying her silence.'

'Say that's true, where's the money?'

'Galina's bank account?' Whitehead suggested, waiting for a delivery truck to pass before he pulled away from the kerb.

'I'd suggest they opened an account for Anya,' Mosley countered. He retightened the bottle top. 'Open it in her name and pay in cash.'

'Has the FBI checked Kratz's accounts?'

'I'd guess so,' Mosley replied. 'They'd need to check for big cash withdrawals. Based on this idea of a secret bolthole, we thought he might periodically withdraw a nice little stash to squirrel away. If it's increased in the past few months that could signify additional financial commitments.'

Whitehead swung the cruiser around to the right and commenced their descent. 'And babies are pretty demanding on the old wallet, right?'

'Right,' Mosley agreed. The approaching road surface blurred as their speed increased. 'I'll mention it to Studdert, see what he can dig up.'

****

8.45pm – BST
Blackpool, England

By the time Roger Mortimer emerged from the Co-op on Layton Road, the evening sun had begun its descent into a darkened sea; its fading light adding to his unease. Since the altercation with Clive Porter three days earlier he'd been decidedly on edge, especially after the man's rage dissolved into threats of what he'd do to Roger and his wife if the Porter family found themselves homeless in October.

He looked up and down the road and eyed the cars parked on either side of the street; anonymous vehicles blending into their equally innocuous surroundings. A loud cackle startled him and he spun around until he spotted a group of young women, probably in their late teens – *though you could never be sure these days* – swaying towards a nearby bus stop. He assumed they planned to go into town, where the bright lights and offers of cheap booze from competing bars and nightclubs made the place a magnet for the party crowd.

The skin on the back of Roger's neck prickled when he attempted to look inside the nearest car. Dusk and a faulty streetlight combined forces and the interior's impenetrable darkness intensified the feeling he was being watched. Oblivious to the weight of two wine bottles and seven tins of cat food, he gripped the plastic bag's handles more tightly and scuttled past a tanning salon to where he'd parked the Jaguar.

Roger passed the bag to his other hand, enabling him to dig into the depths of his trouser pocket. The smooth remote key felt reassuringly heavy in his damp palm as he pointed it at the vehicle to deactivate the central locking. He glanced to each side and pulled open the driver's door, eased himself into the comfortable leather upholstery and inserted the ignition key.

A quick flick of his head told Roger the road remained clear and he moved the shift into *drive*, eased his foot off the brake and accelerated away, eagerly anticipating the crime thriller scheduled to start fifteen minutes later on BBC1. The traffic lights immediately ahead turned to green and he emitted a sigh of relief, unsure whether or not to be amused by his – could he go so far to call it paranoia? All he needed to do was follow a diversion to avoid those bloody roadworks on Westcliff Drive and he'd still be home in a matter of minutes.

Roger wasn't sure when he'd become aware of the twin points of light in his rear-view mirror. Their size increased when the car – he assumed from the level of the headlamps that they belonged to a car – continued to gain ground. He expected it to continue its rapid acceleration and overtake on the empty stretch of road ahead, yet it remained behind him. Roger sighed and cursed the town's younger motorists who seemed to think the speed limits should be increased by an additional fifty percent. He decided to drive along a narrow terraced street to cut the corner, working on an assumption the little git would barrel across the approaching junction and head for the seafront.

To his surprise the car, most likely a dark hatchback if his eyes weren't playing tricks on him, copied the move seconds later and kept a constant distance from his rear bumper. Icy fingers of fear tightened their grip and spurred Roger to turn left onto a side street, taking him further away from home.

The town's famous tower appeared in the distance and, without indicating this time, Roger yanked the steering wheel, squealed around a corner and accelerated down a long, straight stretch of road. The pursuing vehicle edged closer and closer, sending the contents of his shopping bag rolling around the passenger footwell where he'd placed it minutes earlier. No longer in any doubt that some bastard was following him, sweat trickled down Roger's forehead. He swung through a sharp right onto Palatine Road, passed the college and sped closer to the town centre, its low-end shops and amusement arcades becoming little more than a blur.

The headlights from behind filled the rear-view mirror, his mouth parched now the speedometer approached 50mph, his sole focus to reach the police building beyond the next junction. The approaching traffic lights turned to amber and Roger slammed his foot to the floor to activate the Jaguar's powerful kick down. His pursuer followed, the manoeuvre audibly angering the driver of a Renault Clio waiting perpendicular to the junction.

The police station's brightly lit frontage came into view, along with two patrol cars parked outside. Roger careered into the car park, screeched to a halt and, with a burst of speed that belied his age, leaped out onto the uneven tarmac. A Vauxhall Astra rolled past, its rapid deceleration affording him closer scrutiny.

The dark-coloured hatchback looked familiar, although its exact shade proved difficult to establish in the sickly yellow light provided by a row of streetlamps. He was sure he'd seen a similar vehicle in the past few days, and an oval sticker in the bottom right corner of its windscreen triggered vague memories. He could see the silhouette of a man behind the wheel, his face in partial shadow when the car braked and then moved slowly into the distance.

Roger watched the red tail lights fade and finally disappear around a bend leading to the seafront. He exhaled loudly and leaned against the Jaguar's paintwork, now jaundiced by the sodium glow. His heart continued pounding against his ribs and he wondered if this was it: was he having a coronary to match the one that ended his father's life?

What the hell was all that car chase nonsense about?

A rectangular POLICE sign above the doorway recaptured his attention. Roger stared at it and wondered whether to report the incident.

Don't be so bloody daft. What are you going to tell them – that some dickhead was following you? Like they'll take it seriously when people are getting battered half to death on that sink estate down the road every night.

Roger focussed on controlling his breathing, aware his heart rate had started to slow. A passing van blew a light breeze over his arms, the exposed flesh damp with perspiration. The squeal of brakes startled him and he shuddered at the sudden chill climbing his spine.

Get a grip, you bloody woman!

Now satisfied the hatchback had left the vicinity, Roger collapsed into the driver's seat and sat there for an indeterminate length of time. He sighed again and decided to head home via a longer route. Maybe he'd make a couple of detours through well-lit areas, just in case the other vehicle suddenly reappeared.

Wouldn't that suggest you're being deliberately targeted?

Still entertaining that idea, he restarted the engine and waited for a line of cars to pass. Might someone be actively singling him out? Trying to put the frighteners on him, or even instigate a fatal crash? Roger shook his head and marvelled at the absurdity of the situation, then joined the end of the procession and gently depressed the accelerator.

The streetlamps had reached maximum output, providing enough energy to flood the roads and cautiously seep into doorways and alleyways. The number of vehicles on the roads had decreased since he'd driven to the Co-op, and Roger wondered whether he should be reassured or perturbed by this. His thoughts returned to why someone wanted to follow his car, assuming it wasn't some bloody scumbag from one of those shitty estates the council kept building.

Who've you pissed off recently?

He thought back through his recent interactions. Clive Porter: he'd been one mard-arsed bastard – storming round to Roger's home and hurling threats in front of the neighbours. Maybe this was Porter trying to put the frighteners on him in order to make him take the property off the market?

Roger glanced at the empty road in the rear-view mirror and, without indicating, turned left. The only other guy he could think of was Oliver Stamford, the American businessman who'd demanded a swift return on his investment. Stamford appeared angry, desperate even, but he didn't come across like a raging nutter.

Unlike Porter.

The ten-minute drive back to Keys Drive, the quiet residential street where he'd lived for the past forty years, passed uneventfully and Roger's pulse rate and breathing returned to normal long before the Jaguar eased onto the driveway. He found the house in darkness, the absence of a VW Polo in front of the garage confirmation that *the wife* had yet to return home from her weekly bingo night. Despite his guilt over being pleased to return to an empty house, Roger made a beeline for the drinks cabinet and poured himself a large Courvoisier – once he'd carefully removed his shoes and arranged them neatly on the mat.

He wearily climbed the stairs, holding a glass in one hand and the curved bottle in the other. The brandy's warmth radiated through his stomach and soothed him as he peered up and down the road from behind the master bedroom's wide bay window. At least Keys Drive was always tranquil in an evening. The last glimmer of an impressive orange sunset faded above the rooftops of two Dormer bungalows further down the street as the breeze animated a beech tree in the front garden. Even though the alcohol had now begun to diffuse into his bloodstream, Roger maintained his conviction the dark hatchback would drive past his home at any minute; its owner's malevolent eyes boring through the bedroom's leaded glass window.

Roger frowned and swallowed another mouthful of brandy. The recent memories of a similar car continued to flicker through his brain, infuriatingly vague when he tried to recollect the images in more detail. He knew this type of car was hardly a rarity in this neck of the woods, but something wasn't sitting quite right.

He sighed, picked up the bottle and poured another generous measure into his glass.

****

3.30pm – PST
Phoenix, Arizona

An uneventful drive from Cortez to Phoenix, coupled with surprisingly low levels of traffic on the more rural roads, ensured Muñoz and Hallberg's arrival nearly an hour earlier than anticipated. They'd followed I-17 southwards and exited the freeway closest to Phoenix's main police building, where detective Manuel Jimenez, a tall, muscular man in his late forties, arrived in the lobby to greet them with bottles of chilled water. The three men exchanged warm handshakes, then retreated to Jimenez's fiercely air-conditioned office to follow the movements of their fugitive's green Ford Taurus during his time in the city.

Thanks to a complex city-wide network of surveillance cameras, a rookie officer assigned to the task of locating the vehicle had quickly spotted the Taurus on the town's north side. She'd built up a comprehensive catalogue of movements before the anonymous man covered the short distance east to Scottsdale a week later, a journey Muñoz and Hallberg intended to take the following day.

Two days into Lucia Castro's retrospective surveillance task, she'd followed the Ford from Peoria to near an upmarket Biltmore shopping village and watched its driver park on a side street, extract a briefcase from the trunk and cover the short distance to the retail complex on foot. The man entered a high class jewellery store and emerged onto the sidewalk around ten minutes later with no discernible difference to his appearance or demeanour, from where he'd hailed a cab.

The cab company's records revealed Sky Harbor Airport to be their passenger's destination, and an hour spent with airport security allowed Castro to follow her quarry's movements around the arrivals area. From numerous angles, thanks to another dense network of surveillance cameras, she'd watched him enjoy a chilled drink in Starbucks and visit the restroom. Kratz's frequent glances at the silver-coloured watch adorning his right wrist also led Brady to surmise the man either had a later obligation at a specific time, or that the item was a recent purchase.

Additional footage showed Kratz hailing another cab that this time returned him to a block away from where he'd parked. He'd covered the twenty-minute drive back to his hotel without incident; the following five days equally unremarkable. Until his relocation to Scottsdale, Kratz left the hotel on a daily basis to buy provisions and did very little else to draw attention to himself. Jimenez ran through the condensed and accelerated footage whilst Hallberg and Muñoz made notes, his pride obvious when he explained how Castro had already arranged for them to interview the jewellery store's owner, Michael Auden, the following morning.

'Who *is* this guy?' Jimenez asked after he'd paused one of the images flickering on the screen. 'He must have done something real bad to demand this level of investigation.'

Muñoz nodded. 'You could say that.'

'Big confidential case?' Jimenez's hazel eyes widened. 'I understand.'

'Yeah. Sorry, man.'

Jimenez raised his greying brows. 'Why's he in Phoenix?'

'Good question,' Hallberg replied. 'We tracked him here using one of his aliases and we figured he chose Phoenix because he has no apparent link to the city. According to the hotel manager in Peoria, he said he was a businessman from Provo, Utah.'

'Castro did a good job, right?' Jimenez said. He opened the office door and accepted three large cups of iced coffee from a young female officer. 'That's awesome, Juanita. You know you'll always own my soul?'

'She sure did,' Hallberg replied, grateful for something both cold and caffeinated. 'This has given us a lot to go on. He must have visited the jewellers for a reason.'

Jimenez narrowed his eyes and sipped his drink. 'I'd say he's converting cash into something less obvious? You know, buy something expensive and wear it.'

'I guess that question may be answered tomorrow morning,' Muñoz said. 'We'll let you know what we learn from this Auden guy, and if we need further assistance we'll be back in touch.'

****

Unusually for the time and the day, the homicide incident room radiated an air of expectation now the evening's covert operation would soon get underway. Two uniformed officers, a young man and woman who would later pose as a couple out for an evening of drinking and dancing, listened intently to Mosley conclude the briefing he'd begun five minutes earlier. At the group's centre, Tony felt a prickle spread across his shoulders and neck, the result of him starring as the now-reluctant centrepiece of the sting.

'Harry Lee is the one you want to approach,' Mosley continued, the trip to Brockmont and an afternoon spent fine-tuning the operation apparently doing nothing to dent his resolve. 'Get him to admit what he does and to accept your cash and a photo, then walk away. We'll tail him to his home and swoop. We've already briefed the arrest team, and assuming we get the evidence on tape there'll be no problem executing our warrant to search his place.'

Tony gave a dubious frown. 'Won't he suspect I'm wearing a wire?'

Mosley shook his head. 'Not if you act normal.'

'What if he asks how I heard of him?' Tony's tone was sharper than intended and hinted at his growing reluctance to participate. 'It's not like something you hear by the chiller cabinet at Trader Joe's, is it?'

'You asked around and heard whispers he's the best.' Mosley grinned and slapped Gibson across the upper back. 'Pander to his ego and he'll want to prove you right. Always works on this guy here.'

Tony's expression softened and he failed to hide his amusement when Gibson flipped a middle finger. 'And assuming you trap him?'

'If all goes to plan he'll fess up, back up the old man's theory and we'll offer him a deal,' Gibson said, interrupting before Mosley could reply.

'Will you show him a photo of Kratz?' Gibson asked. 'You know, to get him to confirm he supplied a fake passport to the guy.

'No, in case he makes up a load of bullshit because he thinks it'll get him off,' Mosley replied, shaking his head. 'Tony's going to ask Lee about *Thomas Moulson* and give a general description. Kratz's appearance must be similar to around the time he departed from LAX, because if he'd looked significantly different it would raise red flags at check-in.' He glanced around the room and his gaze eventually settled upon a worried-looking Tony. 'You'll be fine,' he added. 'Our couple will be armed and dangerous if necessary and, because the capture will take place away from the premises, the owner is happy to let us in through the back. This means any security on the door won't discover their firearms.'

'Are they any closer to catching him?' Tony saw the others collectively raise their eyebrows. 'You know, in Europe?'

Mosley shook his head. 'The police in Munich managed to trace the hotel where Kratz stayed, and he did his trick of paying for a full week and leaving after three nights. He also claimed to be the British-born son of German parents and made a point of apologising for his rusty German, even though the owner said he was perfectly easy to understand. Kratz didn't indicate his destination but, based on Studdert's suggestion, we've requested they investigate Augsburg first.'

'What if he's ditched the Andreas Baum alias?' Tony asked.

'Yeah, it's been considered,' Studdert replied from the back of the room. 'Hotel owners will be asked if an Andreas Baum checked in on the date he left Munich. If there's no one of that name in their records, then whether a man giving it the Anglo-German cover story or similar description checked in, paid cash, and took off part way through his stay.'

'And if they get a dead end?' Tony continued.

'We'll face that if it happens,' Mosley replied. He clapped his hands to regain the others' attention. 'Tonight you'll enter the bar after our blissfully happy couple lose the uniforms and locate our target.' He grinned at the petite blonde officer and her male counterpart. 'Tony's going to buy himself a whisky and then he'll approach our guy.' He turned to Tony and addressed him directly. 'Offer to buy him another of whatever he's drinking, order the same for yourself, explain who you are, then surreptitiously show him the cash. We can't pounce until he's admitted what he does for a living and you've gotten him away from the premises.'

Tony nodded. 'I could say I do business with the fake Thomas Moulson and that's where the recommendation came from.'

'Sounds plausible,' Mosley agreed. 'Just keep it vague and mention imports and exports if asked. Say as little as possible.'

Tony glanced at his reflection in the computer's screen. 'Paul Kelly,' he murmured, repeating the undercover name he'd been given an hour earlier. 'The latest weapon against Konrad Kratz.'

Chapter 26 – Sunday 16th August 2009

9.18am – PDT
San Fernando Road, Los Angeles, California

Over twenty-four hours since leaving the warmth of his bed, Mosley's patience had worn paper thin and the tension in the interview room was detectable to all nearby. 'It's been a long night and I'm oh-so-tired, Harry. Why don't we dispense with all the bullshit, you tell us what we need to know and I can finally go home and catch up on my beauty sleep? What do you say, Harry? C'mon...' he wheedled, his head leaning to one side in a pleading manner.

The skinny Oriental man crossed his arms in defiance and narrowed his eyes at Mosley and Studdert. 'You guys don't know shit,' he spat.

Mosley's demeanour changed in a shot and Harry Lee swallowed when his subconscious registered the angry detective mirroring his body language. 'We know you're in the business of supplying fake passports. We know you were at the Coconut Club last night hoping to score some business. We know Thomas Moulson ain't really Thomas Moulson.'

Lee re-crossed his thin arms. 'That creep?'

'Jeez, he must have been king of the creeps if that's what a piece of shit like you thinks. Cut the crap, Harry. We *know* what you've been doing, and supplying a fake passport to a wanted serial killer to help him escape ain't really going to cut you a deal in court.'

Lee's almond-shaped eyes widened. 'That Moulson guy's a serial killer?'

'You have nothing, and I mean *nothing*, to prove my client is responsible for this!' Lee's public defender said, her voice louder than expected. 'This Thomas Moulson guy could be the man you're looking for.'

'No he ain't,' Studdert added. He glared at the young woman he wasn't sure looked old enough to graduate high school, let alone law school. 'Thomas Moulson is a respectable, law-abiding Brit whose identity you just happened to steal, Harry. The guy you gave a *fake* passport to in the *name* of Thomas Moulson is responsible for a body count that's now too far into double figures and set to rise. And it's all down to *you*.'

Rani Shah straightened a crease in her tailored skirt. 'And you have evidence to prove this?' she demanded, infuriated by how the two men continued to undermine her.

'You want that on your conscience, Harry?' Mosley added, without missing a beat.

'How the fuck was I meant to know?' Lee bellowed, all traces of bravado gone.

'Chances are people who want a fake passport ain't the epitome of sainthood,' Studdert replied in a low voice, his carefully maintained calmness having the opposite effect on the man seated across the table from him. 'He's a goddamn psycho who you helped get away.'

Mosley reclined and laced his hands behind his head. 'You're looking at a lengthy stretch for this, Harry.'

Studdert nodded his agreement. 'You didn't just supply the Moulson passport. Our source informed us you made fat stacks out of our guy. Supplied him with enough fake passports to last a lifetime.'

'You know more about this guy than you're letting on,' Mosley said, his voice barely audible.

'We're cops, Harry,' Studdert continued. 'We get paid to find out what backstreet criminals like you are up to.'

Mosley lunged forward, the speed of his movement startling the worried man. 'So, how many more passports did you supply, Harry?'

'Jeez, don't you idiots listen?' Lee sighed, realising the two men wouldn't release him unless they obtained the information they apparently knew he'd withheld from them. 'This is the truth, man. It was just the one for this guy.'

'Our guy would have more than one fake ID. Police Academy 101 tells us that.'

Lee narrowed his eyes at Mosley. 'You think I'm the only guy in town? Go to any big city. If you have enough cash you can buy anything.'

Studdert nodded. 'So Harry, who's your main rival?'

'I ain't no grass.'

'C'mon, Harry, you're good at what you do,' Studdert said, resuming the tried and tested *Good Cop* role. 'It ain't legal, but we recognise the quality of your product. Don't you want to send down your competitors?'

'Don't matter,' Lee snapped. 'You douchebags said you're going to send *me* down.'

Studdert's smile oozed faux sympathy. 'If you give us the names, you'll get a much lighter sentence. We clean up the trash for you and, when you get out a good few years before they do, it gives you time to re-establish yourself.'

'Legally, of course,' Mosley interjected.

Studdert nodded and smiled. 'Maybe in a new city.'

Lee turned to Shah, who shrugged in reply. 'Give me a pen and paper,' he whispered to her.

Mosley beckoned for Studdert to follow him out of the room. They joined Gibson behind the one-way glass and saw Lee scrunch his face in concentration, pick up the pen he'd been given and began to write.

'If we let him go we'll need to check out any names first.' Mosley stroked the stubble on his cheeks. 'We can only hold him for another few hours unless we charge him.'

'I'll get on it,' Gibson offered. 'Give me the list and any additional details. I'll put the info through the database and see what we pull up.' He hesitated and looked at the two older men. 'You think he's telling the truth?'

'Yeah, I think he is,' Mosley replied, reassured by Studdert's nod. 'Either way he's up to his scrawny neck in the shit. If it buys him a shorter time inside it's in his best interests to confess.'

Gibson stopped in the doorway. 'You think he knew he was selling to Kratz?'

Mosley narrowed his eyes and noticed Lee lowering the pencil. 'I'm not so sure. If he had any idea what Kratz has done, you'd think he'd identify the piece of shit in the hope of appearing co-operative and reducing his sentence further. You've got to have been in a coma not to have heard what our buddy Konrad has been up to.'

Gibson watched Studdert re-enter the room to retrieve the sheet of paper. 'Anything new on the son of a bitch?' he asked, turning to Mosley.

'Yeah, just before Lee's sorry ass got dragged in. Police in Augsburg traced Kratz, or should that be Andreas Baum, to a hotel in the city – but he disappeared days ago, part way through the week he'd paid for.'

'Sounds familiar,' Gibson commented. 'Any leads on where he went?'

Mosley shook his head. 'That's why I want this asshole to confess to any additional passports he supplied to Kratz. Failing that, I want the names of any rival producers so we can question them. That slippery bastard needs taking out, once and for all.'

****

10.34pm – PST
Biltmore, Phoenix, Arizona

Refreshed by a hearty breakfast and a later than usual start, Hallberg and Muñoz loaded their luggage into the station wagon before checking out of their Peoria hotel. They'd exchanged light conversation during the forty-minute drive across town; half-listening to the satnav Muñoz had programmed in case of unexpected diversions.

After parking in a quiet corner of Biltmore's customer lot, they reluctantly left the car's cool interior and crossed the baked ground to where the first of many high-end stores and restaurants vied for custom. A walkway between the buildings provided a shady cover until it opened out onto a grassy area, where an ornamental fountain and ample seating offered the opportunity for weary shoppers to recharge their batteries against the intense Sonoran heat.

'My wife would love this place,' Muñoz said, grateful his wallet remained wedged firmly in his pocket. 'Perhaps we should buy them a little something to make up for this trip?'

Hallberg shook his head and lifted a reddened arm to mop sweat from his brow. 'Dry heat, my ass,' he grumbled. 'Studdert warned us, but this is unbearable.'

'Phoenix is his hometown?'

'Yeah, can you believe the crazy bastard says this is preferable to summer in New York?'

Muñoz thought back to his one and only visit to the Big Apple. 'It's humid as hell up there at this time of year,' Muñoz replied. He spotted the jewellers further down the block and nudged Hallberg. 'That's the place.'

They made a beeline for the store, its interior providing a welcome refuge from the triple digit temperatures outside. A slim man in his early fifties peered over the top of a pair of reading glasses at the two strangers and offered them a stilted smile.

'And how may I be of assistance today?' he enquired as they approached the counter. His expression changed when Muñoz pulled open his jacket to reveal an LAPD detective shield. 'Ah, you're the detectives from California? I may have some information for you.'

Hallberg extended one hand to Michael Auden and pointed to his companion with the other. 'I'm Dave Hallberg and this is Emilio Muñoz. We sure do appreciate your time.'

'Not at all,' Auden replied. 'It was amazingly quick and easy, all things considered. Only five customers entered the store that afternoon, and all our security footage is stored digitally. We find the latest technology to be a worthwhile investment.' He gestured to a number of locked glass cases containing an assortment of glistening jewellery probably worth more than the combined value of their homes. 'Based on the photograph provided by the Phoenix Police Department, I identified the customer you wish to trace as a Mr Anthony Chamberlain.'

Hallberg winked at Muñoz. 'That's another to run through the system. What was the purpose of his visit?'

'He claimed he'd won an international contract for his company that resulted in a sizeable personal bonus,' Auden replied. 'Even after negotiating a sizeable discount for cash, he parted with $120,000 for a Rolex.' He smiled at Hallberg's whistle of astonishment. 'I've copied the documentation for you. There's a serial number and the address he provided–'

'Did his insistence on paying cash not arouse any suspicion?' Hallberg interrupted.

Auden's expression remained neutral. 'If the bills aren't counterfeit, it's not my place to judge a person's method of payment.'

Hallberg inspected the documentation. 'These papers are necessary to sell on the watch?'

'To a reputable dealer or buyer, yes. There's also the watch's unique serial number. If anyone sends it for a service, we can arrange for it to flag up as being of police interest, much like Rolex do for any of their watches which have been reported stolen.'

'How does it work for the black market?'

'Checking the serial number is all that's needed to reveal the watch's origins. He could sell it without the box or documentation, but he'd have to be prepared to make a serious loss.'

Muñoz stroked his chin and noticed Auden's sleek gold cufflinks. 'What if he returned to you for a refund? Would you comply?'

Auden pondered the question. 'Only if the item developed a fault. We do sell customers' pre-owned jewellery and watches but, as I said, returning an item in perfect working order would incur a sizeable financial loss for the customer.'

Hallberg nodded. 'And if that occurred, you'd inform us?'

'Of course, it's part of my public duty to assist the police in apprehending a wanted felon.'

'In that case, I'll leave you both our cards,' Hallberg replied. 'Many thanks for your assistance and your time.'

Auden smiled and shook each man's hand in turn. The detectives nodded their acknowledgment of a woman who'd entered the shop seconds earlier, her attention quickly focussing on a display of diamond necklaces she'd spotted upon arrival.

They left the store's cool confines and trudged back towards the parking lot, until Muñoz stopped and checked a map of the retail area. 'You do realise there's a Cheesecake Factory right around that corner?' he said. 'We don't need to be at the precinct for over an hour. What do you say we make a start on today's report?'

Hallberg finished the water in his plastic bottle, crushed it and replaced the lid. 'There's always room for coffee.'

'And the rest,' Muñoz added as they picked up their pace. 'At least we'll be home tomorrow afternoon. I checked out some online reviews and the Scottsdale hotel looks a cut above the others. Seems popular with business types.'

Hallberg grinned and held open the door. 'I'm going to sleep like the dead tonight.'

The restaurant's cavernous interior was quieter than expected, the interstitial time between breakfast and lunch meaning they were immediately directed to a table and left to peruse the vast menu. Muñoz set down the ring-bound booklet and caught Hallberg's eye.

'Haven't you wondered why Kratz went road tripping, rather than lying low at this theorised unknown location? What if this hidey-hole place of his don't exist and we've been on a wild goose chase for over a week?'

'He's playing a game by leading us to a series of random destinations to throw us off the scent,' Hallberg replied. 'I still say the best bet for him lying low is to return to US soil. We locate where he's made provision for this, and then we find him.'

'You figure?'

Hallberg watched a young woman wipe down a nearby section of tables. 'My best guess is Kratz knew his real life persona had been plastered all over the news. If his alias turned up somewhere at the exact same time someone may make the link, identify him and turn him in to the cops.'

Muñoz nodded. 'You think this trip has actually made much difference?'

'Sure,' Hallberg replied with more enthusiasm than he'd presently mustered. 'What we've just learned about the Rolex is something we can investigate. What's the point of having a top-of-the-line watch when you're on the lam? A cheap one would do the job equally well. He won't keep it forever. Sell it on and use the cash.'

'And that'll flag up?' Muñoz asked. 'What if he sells it on the black market?'

'He'd lose too much money,' Hallberg said. 'The watch is going to flag up if we register its serial number on all the relevant databases. He won't sell it too far from wherever he hides out. Not more than a day's drive away.'

Muñoz raised an eyebrow at the approaching server. 'How'd you figure that out?'

'No flights, no hotel stops and no sleeping in your car overnight with either a six figure Rolex on your wrist or a pile of cash in the trunk.' Hallberg allowed Muñoz enough time to consider his words. 'Car might get jacked, right? He thinks he's smarter than us, and that he'll evade us forever. Sometimes the littlest things lead to your downfall.'

****

Sam undid the top button on his shorts and stifled a belch. 'That was one hell of a meal. Whoever said the way to a man's heart is through his stomach definitely knew what they were talking about,' he said, stuffed to bursting from Anna's version of the Kobe burger and sweet potato fries meal they occasionally enjoyed at a small grill house in Winter Park.

Anna carried their stacked plates to the dishwasher and nodded. 'You've rediscovered your appetite?'

'Yeah, I haven't really fancied anything substantial over the past week,' he replied. 'Finding out you may be the target of a psychopath isn't conducive to food sitting comfortably.'

'You want another beer?'

'Why the hell not?' Sam draped his arm over his stomach. 'I'm too full to move, so you'll have to get it. Anyway, you're closer to the fridge.'

She shot a pointed stare in his direction. 'You'll be wearing it at this rate, smart ass. Anyway, just one more bottle for you. Can't have you arriving at your new job in the morning nursing a hangover.'

Sam nodded. 'Yeah, I suppose.'

Anna returned to her seat and pushed a chilled bottle of Nevada Silver Label Ale across the table. 'You okay?'

'Believe it or not, I'm more nervous about this than my first day at the Denver field office.' Sam picked at the smaller label on the bottle's neck. 'What if I stuff things up?'

She stared at him and noticed how the dim light radiating from below the wall cupboards cast long shadows across his face. 'You won't.'

'You can't say that,' he continued. 'What if the other agents let something slip? I'm worried my cover's going to end up being blown.'

Anna reached across the table and linked her fingers between Sam's. 'You'll be fine tomorrow.' She saw him reciprocate her smile. 'You know I have every faith in you.'

'That also scares me. I don't want to let down you or the kids.'

'You won't let us down.' She walked to the balcony, its smooth wood bathed in the pale moonlight seeping through narrow gaps in the clouds. 'Come on, let's go sit out until it gets too cold.'

Chapter 27 – Monday 17th August 2009

8.27am – PDT
FBI Resident Agency, Stateline, Nevada

Anna pulled into a parking bay and turned off the SUV's engine. 'Ready to roll?' she asked, fully aware of Sam's tension as he watched two women approach the building.

He nodded. 'I'll be fine, honestly. I'll text when I'm nearly ready to be picked up.'

'We could always lease a second car,' Anna suggested. She twisted her head in time to see John throw his favourite toy rabbit at Angela. 'Hey, little guy, quit annoying your sister,' she added in a faux-stern tone, then smiled at his delighted squeal.

'Mommy, tell him to stop,' Angela whined. She squirmed in her car seat, impatient to return to the sandy beach they'd visited most mornings.

'I'll bike it,' Sam said. 'I'd prefer not to join a gym and I need to do something to maintain my fitness.'

Anna wrinkled her nose. 'You'd be sweaty all day. I could drop you off in the morning and you cycle back later?'

Sam considered the idea and nodded again. 'Yeah, that sounds okay. I'll use the mountain bike I found in the garage 'til we can go shopping for a better one.' He kissed Anna's cheek and got out of the car. 'Anyway, I'd better go.'

'Have a good day!' she called. 'You hear me?'

He opened the rear passenger door and ducked his head inside. 'Listen to me, you little monsters,' he said, smiling at Angela's bared teeth. 'You two are going to be so good today that Mommy thinks the behaviour fairy came down in the night and cast a spell on you both.' Sam kissed a giggling Angela on a flushed cheek. 'Got that?'

Eager not to be forgotten, John squealed again as Sam leaned in further and tickled his ribs. 'You do the nasty stuff for Mommy before I get home. Do you understand me, Buster?'

Anna cleared her throat. 'I heard that,' she muttered and rolled her eyes at Sam's laughter. 'Be safe,' she mouthed when he turned to wave at them from the entrance, only partly reassured by his thumbs up.

****

4.35pm – MDT
FBI Field Office, Denver, Colorado

Niall Demaine stretched and cast an affectionate glance at the computer he'd nicknamed Marilyn; a powerful machine linked to the bank of monitors filling the small room's entire back wall. Milne's latest orders were relatively straightforward: go over Kratz's known bank accounts with a fine toothcomb and identify any patterns missed by LAPD, which may indicate where the hell the elusive piece of shit was hiding.

Demaine also hoped to identify any recent changes in Kratz's financial obligations, thanks to a joint prediction from LAPD detective Ronnie Mosley and his Glendale counterpart Paul Whitehead. Much to his disappointment, there'd been no regular payments to any other named account, leaving nothing definitive to suggest a hideout in the hills – or that Kratz had indeed fathered Galina di Marco's baby daughter, Anya.

In spite of this, one detail piqued Demaine's interest. Six months earlier, a semi-regular cash withdrawal had taken on a monthly schedule and almost doubled its magnitude. Demaine clicked back through the years to reveal numerous four-figure withdrawals in both the Los Angeles area and Golden since 2002. He raised an eyebrow, surprised to find no recent record of these flagging up for further scrutiny, and resolved to delve further into the transactions later – already assuming they were linked to the nest egg Kratz was thought to have squirrelled away for a proverbial rainy day.

The shit was certainly raining down on the bastard these days.

His thoughts returned to Galina di Marco's checking and saving accounts. The subpoena required to gain access had induced a considerable headache further up the federal food chain and stretched

Milne's powers of persuasion to their limit. A ray of hope replaced Demaine's disappointment at the absence of cash deposits mirroring Kratz's withdrawal pattern, now he'd noticed a standing order set up six months earlier.

A modest monthly sum of one hundred dollars arriving from an account in the name of Anya di Marco sent a prickle up the back of his neck, a familiar feeling that told him his instincts were likely to be correct. He picked up a pen and scribbled a reminder to ask Milne to subpoena the baby's account details, in addition to security footage from the Wells Fargo Bank on North Brand Boulevard, for all the relevant dates.

The action of writing down the date caused Demaine to glance at the adjacent screen, where Kratz's seven-figure bank balance still maintained its impressive impact. Demaine stopped to wonder what it would be like to never worry about paying the bills or taking his beat-up old car to the shop for a routine check. He scrolled back six months and scanned February's statement, when the regular $8,000 cash withdrawals had commenced.

Coincidence? Although the first $8,000 withdrawal occurred soon after Anya's birth, there was no immediate way to tell whether the transaction was destined for the baby's account, but he'd have wagered a year's salary on it. There was then the issue of getting another rapid out-of-state subpoena, something unlikely to endear him to Milne or Pearson.

Demaine jabbed a series of numbers into the telephone's keypad and lifted it to his ear.

****

4.05pm – PDT
San Fernando Road, Los Angeles, California

No perceptible changes, let alone improvements, had occurred in the homicide incident room over the previous week. The place was still too cramped, waste baskets overflowed by mid-afternoon and its coffee machine brewed something probably able to strip paint if the need ever arose.

Mosley glanced up from the report he'd been typing and his characteristic scowl melted away when he registered Hallberg and Muñoz's arrival. 'You're glad to be back, I take it?'

Muñoz grinned happily. 'Never thought I'd say it, boss... but, yeah.'

'Email any outstanding reports to me and get the hell out of here, I'll see you both Wednesday afternoon.'

Hallberg winked and shook Mosley's hand. 'Has anything new come in today?' he asked, pulling his laptop from its bag.

'Yeah, Gibson's on it right now. And, a couple of hours ago, I picked up the Austrians' tox screen on the way back from dropping Studdert at the airport.' Mosley handed a copy of the report to Muñoz. 'It makes for interesting reading.'

'Roofies?' Muñoz's eyebrows lifted as Mosley nodded. 'How come they didn't notice? The new version colours your drink.'

'This may have been an old batch. The crime lab told us its original formulation is still out there for those who have the cash and the contacts,' Mosley replied. 'I don't know if it loses its effect over time, but from the amount in their bodies he wasn't concerned about them making a full recovery. He dosed them up big time.'

Muñoz frowned, a combination of tiredness and hunger making it difficult to generate any enthusiasm for this latest development. 'I wonder how he got a hold of the old stuff?'

'He's rolling in cash, can change his appearance and knows how to act,' Hallberg said. Excitement crept into his tone and overrode the urge to return home and enjoy a couple of relaxed family evenings. 'I'll contact Higgins and his guys at the DEA. They'll be aware of any other cases around here and they could also contact their counterparts in Denver and New York to see if anything similar has occurred in either of their cities. We–'

Hallberg stopped his monologue and visibly deflated now Mosley's scowl had returned. The senior detective jabbed an index finger at the door, ordering Hallberg and Muñoz to pick up their belongings and walk into two days of freedom.

****

7.25pm – PDT
Wilshire Boulevard, Los Angeles, California

Special Agent Mark Baxter stared at the screen directly in front of him and then grinned, amused that a six-month-old baby girl boasted a bank balance larger than many people who'd worked for their entire adult life. The $4,000 used to open the child's account was regularly supplemented by a tidy cash sum of $2,000, paid in every four to five weeks. He noted the transactions had flagged up for additional scrutiny, yet were deemed innocuous enough not to require an investigation.

The perks of coming from a wealthy family?

It took Baxter a matter of minutes to cross-reference these deposits against Kratz's bank-based activity. Without fail, whilst in Los Angeles during breaks from filming *H.O.S.T.A.G.E.*, Kratz made a cash withdrawal on either the same day or the day before Anya's account was credited, adding credibility to LAPD's *baby daddy* theory. From what Baxter knew of the man, he hardly seemed the type to care for the welfare of anyone other than himself, so either blackmail from Galina or his own desperation to keep the development out of the media was the most likely explanation.

DNA from Galina and her daughter could confirm beyond doubt that Kratz was the baby's father *and* the third hair sample at each of his homes belonged to him. Baxter rubbed his aching forehead. He knew the evidence he'd gleaned would still not be enough to go straight for the DNA request jugular. It was urgent they obtain the security footage Demaine suggested earlier, and keep their fingers crossed that at least one sequence placed Kratz and Galina either inside or close to the bank at the same time. He took a deep breath and reached for the phone again.

****

7.37pm – PDT
Kingsbury, Nevada

Sam closed his eyes and stepped into the shower. Sharp jets stung his face and leached hours of tension from his body, which slowly swirled around the plughole and into oblivion. He continued to hold his breath and enjoy the sensation, until familiar feelings of guilt put in a swift reappearance.

Sam thought back over the hell endured by his family for the past year and, more specifically, the past ten days. Anna had never once complained about their situation, although the extra special dinner she'd promised that night was no doubt in case his first day hadn't gone as expected.

Sam rinsed the shampoo from his hair and stayed beneath the warm water for another minute, then reluctantly reached for a nearby towel to wrap around his waist. He paused in front of the partially fogged mirror and decided the face returning his stare looked older than he'd expected. It matched the physical weariness he'd experienced more often since last summer; something he suspected to be a permanent effect of the accident which nearly ended his life. A droplet of water freed itself from Sam's hair and trickled down the side of his face. He couldn't put his finger upon why, but the feeling was disconcerting in its familiarity.

He pulled a smaller towel from the rail and rubbed it over his head on his way into the main bedroom. A light breeze gained access through the open window and cooled his damp skin, swiftly reminding him how quickly the evening temperature fell in this area and that fall would soon dominate. Perhaps it was time to break out the sweatpants and give in to the climatic differences of their new surroundings?

Minutes later, Sam – wearing the pair of shorts and a t-shirt he'd plucked from the back of a chair – climbed the stairs leading up from the cabin's lower floor. 'Smells delicious,' he called, smiling to himself as he sank into the sofa and spotted a generous tumbler of whisky on the nearby coffee table.

'Ten minutes, so don't even think about falling asleep,' Anna replied, her raised voice barely audible above the extractor fan's low hum.

Sam brought the glass to his lips and surveyed the room through an amber-hued distortion. Smooth liquid glided down his throat and spread its warmth throughout his stomach. He closed his eyes, relaxed against the cushions and inhaled appetising aromas of garlic and tomato. Anna's deviation from the traditional English food she tended to cook whenever she suspected he'd had a bad day was a surprise, albeit a pleasant one, and a loud gurgle from his stomach reminded him lunch had been a small, hurried affair. His thoughts drifted in random directions, never settling on anything for long enough to give it proper consideration. A light tap on his forearm soon progressed to more insistent shaking and he recognised Anna's voice.

'I knew you'd fall asleep!' Her smiling face came into focus when he opened his eyes. 'You have ten seconds to wake up and haul your ass to the table.'

Embarrassed, he pushed himself upright. 'Christ, I'm sorry. One minute I was enjoying that little aperitif you'd left for me, the next...'

'Snoring like a bear with a sore throat,' she continued and pointed to the drink he'd been fortunate to set down before sleep had taken over. 'Doesn't look like you'll need any sleeping pills tonight.'

The fog dispersed from his mind as Sam plodded across to the room's dining area. The table's settings would not have been out of place in a restaurant, its placemats and napkins arranged in a manner suggesting Anna had given a lot of thought to the evening. He smiled again, placed his almost empty glass on a coaster and relaxed into his seat.

'What did you make?' he asked at the sight of Anna carrying two plates in oven-gloved hands. 'It smells wonderful.'

She set down the larger portion in front of him. 'It's Gnocchi alla Castello Bury.'

Sam reached for the parmesan. 'It looks uncannily like Gnocchi alla Castello Bouvier. I hope it tastes as good as that one; you do realise it's one of my favourites?'

'Yeah, it's my mom's recipe.' She took a seeded bread roll from a basket in the middle of the table. 'Seriously, how did you find everything today?'

'Better than I thought,' he replied. 'This sounds really terrible but, apart from Masters, I don't have much to do with the other agents. I just do my CSRU work from an office at the back of the building.' Sam positioned a chilled bottle of Pinot Grigio to one side of him and reached for a corkscrew. 'They seem like a friendly bunch though. Most of them were out today near the Nevada shoreline, a bit further north from here where they've had reports of a community camping in the forest. Intelligence suggests it's probably some sort of religious cult. The taskforce assigned to the investigation know next to nothing about their alleged beliefs though.'

Concern appeared on Anna's face. 'Will you be involved in that investigation?'

He shook his head. 'Not really. I'm holed up in a little cave that makes Demaine's *Den of Iniquity* look like the White House,' he said, his disappointment evident. 'I've been in email contact with Milne. He sends his best wishes.'

Sam saw her smile fail to reach her eyes. 'Anything new on Kratz?' she asked.

'Nothing relating to his current location,' he replied. 'They're trying to find out if he's still in Europe. The world's a bloody big place; he could be anywhere.'

Anna reached across the table and patted his hand. 'They'll get him.'

They ate without urgency, enjoying the food and each other's company. Sam listened intently to the details of Anna's day, starting with taking the children to Kiva Beach after dropping him off at the resident agency. By early afternoon they'd visited Safeway and returned to the cabin where, after a light lunch, Angela helped entertain her baby brother, which in turn enabled Anna to tidy the living area and make a start on the evening meal.

A second glass of wine continued to numb a week of edginess and its effects became more noticeable when Sam rose to his feet to stack their plates. He followed Anna into the kitchen and carefully set down the plates on the countertop. 'What's for dessert?'

She opened the refrigerator. 'I bought it,' she replied apologetically. 'There was logic involved too.'

He tutted loudly. 'Real men need real food.'

'So mass produced will suit you fine,' Anna retorted. 'Baked cheesecake good enough?'

'I suppose it'll do.' He noticed part of its smooth surface was missing. 'Angela?'

'I put it in the cart and she was *so* excited!' Anna cut two generous portions and laughed at the memory. 'I had to use something to bribe her to go to bed a half hour earlier.'

Sam raised an eyebrow as Anna returned to the table and set down a pair of dessert plates. 'I'd been wondering why she didn't argue.'

'And I promised we'd save her another piece.' She lifted the spoon to her mouth. 'So, fill me in on your day.'

'Masters met me and introduced me to the other agents over coffee.' Sam chewed a piece of cookie crust and smiled his approval. 'I spent the rest of the morning holed up in the bat cave catching up on the CSRU work I'm way behind on. That'll keep me busy for a couple of weeks, I reckon.

Went for a walk at lunchtime, bought a sandwich, looked over that cult stuff for Masters and then you picked me up. Hardly exciting, but at least it means we're safe.'

Anna couldn't hide her surprise. 'I thought you wouldn't be working that case?'

'No, he just wanted fresh eyes. You know, see if I dredged up any earth-shattering revelations.'

She swallowed a mouthful of cheesecake. 'Did you?'

'Not really. They haven't got much to go on at the moment.'

'So it's more of the same tomorrow?'

He shrugged. 'I suppose so.'

They ate more quickly this time. Sam was first to set down his spoon and he chuckled at Anna's determined effort to finish the last of her dessert. 'Eyes bigger than your belly, that's what my grandfather used to say.'

She frowned at the sudden intensity of his gaze. 'What's the matter?'

'It's not just the scenery round here that's amazing.' Sam reached across the table and gently stroked the wedding band on her finger. 'I'm a really lucky guy.'

'Smooth...' she replied, giving his hand a reciprocal squeeze after they got up. 'I've been busy all day and barely had time to shower before I drove down to the agency. I'm hardly dressed for a romantic dinner.'

They stood in front of the sliding glass doors which opened onto the balcony. Sam watched the distant pink sunset begin to fade and felt Anna rest her head against his chest. 'I'm just grateful you're here at all,' he whispered.

Chapter 28 – Tuesday 18th August 2009

Andy Parker cast an eye over the printed menu and smiled at Franco Volonte. 'Seems like a good selection,' he said. 'I'll have to run it past the vice-Chairman, but can't see any problems there. Latham's usually quite agreeable, so I'll bell you in the next day or so.'

Franco nodded and placed two pints of *Isabella's Revenge* on the table occupied by Steve and Andy since opening time. They'd first met nearly three decades earlier on their first day at Crettington Primary School, where the trio and another three boys had found themselves seated around the same table. Five of them had maintained a close friendship over the years, despite Sam and Tony relocating across the Atlantic for study and then work.

The sixth boy was a different matter. Peter Umpleby had quickly slipped from their memories after his now-deceased father's job relocated to Colorado in 1990. Since then, their lives had all diverged, yet they'd always managed to maintain contact – whilst rarely affording Peter a second thought.

Until a media circus went global twenty-four hours earlier.

If the FBI wanting Konrad Kratz for a series of murders wasn't enough, there then came the revelation that Konrad Kratz wasn't really Konrad Kratz. Preston's dubious honour of being the epicentre of this unwanted attention meant an avalanche of international media outlets immediately descended upon the usually anonymous town to demand answers – and irritate the locals – in their desperation to obtain any kind of scoop.

Steve considered the time difference and decided to wait before attempting to contact Sam and Tony, much to the dismay of his younger brother Mikey – who'd been glued to the BBC's news channel since the story broke. A dog-eared copy of the *Preston Evening Chronicle* on the bar grabbed Steve's attention and he leafed through it for a second time, incredulous that a *H.O.S.T.A.G.E.* promotional photo covered most of the front page. He glanced over to Andy Parker, who appeared to be consuming his beer at a similar pace, and returned his attention to the newspaper.

Mikey set down the small knife he'd used to chop a quintet of lemons and lifted a couple of pint glasses from a shelf above the bar. 'Two more pints?' he asked, surprised to see them both nod. 'Things can't be that bad. Have you heard something new?'

'Roger's just phoned,' Franco replied. 'He said he's nearly out of that traffic jam round the corner and he'll be here in a couple of minutes.'

Andy arched an eyebrow. 'To what do we owe the pleasure of the old man's company?'

'He wants to cast a beady eye over the menu I planned for the West Side chairman's birthday event and see if he can make any other suggestions.' Franco reached for a packet of Scampi Fries. 'The old sod's hoping for some good publicity in the local press from Latham's do, so he wants perfection.'

'Fair enough,' Andy said, his gaze drawn to the silent news bulletin on a plasma screen television Steve usually only switched on for football matches. 'I take it you've already heard the big news?'

'Mental, isn't it?' Franco exclaimed. 'Konrad Kratz isn't just Peter Umpleby – he's a bloody serial killer too! You couldn't make it up.'

Steve nodded. 'I always knew Umpleby wasn't normal.'

'Same goes for Kratz,' Andy said. 'I'd still punch his lights out for the way he treated Vicky on set.'

'Have you heard from your sister?' Steve picked up his glass and took a welcome sip. 'She must've heard something?'

'Yeah, she phoned late last night after the story really broke. She's been told by the network not to say anything, so don't repeat this as–'

Roger pushed open the main door and limped over to the table. 'Jesus H. Christ, those bloody bus drivers need to learn how to drive these days,' he grumbled.

Steve offered Roger a sympathetic smile. 'What happened, Pops?'

'Pillock crashed into a bus shelter and hit two of his would-be passengers. Told you public transport's bad for your health.' He pointed at the only full pint on the table. 'That for me?'

Steve pushed it over to him. 'Fill your boots, old man. You want to take a gander at the menu Franco's come up with?'

'Aye, maybe later,' Roger said. He took a large gulp of the malty liquid and felt the tension seep from his back and shoulders. 'Let me focus on the important things.'

'You feeling okay, Roger?' Steve held his palm against the man's forehead. 'Sun been getting to you?'

'Cheeky bugger,' Roger replied. He chuckled and slapped another copy of the *Preston Evening Chronicle* down on the table. 'Seen this?' The three younger men all nodded. 'Did you know him? You're the same age.'

Andy swallowed a mouthful of crisps. 'Yeah, we all went to the same school. He left when we were fourteen and he wasn't missed.'

'I was never arsed, but my missus liked that *H.O.S.T.A.G.E.* programme. She said he's a bloody good actor.'

'You're not wrong there, Roger,' Andy said. He crushed the empty crisp packet in his fist and dropped it into the bin.

'Can't believe the man's a serial killer, and that he's from here.'

Franco laughed at Roger's comment. 'The two things aren't mutually exclusive.'

'You heard anything? Like insider stuff.'

Andy shook his head at Roger. 'You know the same as I do.'

Roger stood up and winced. 'Better pay a visit, the wife reckons I'm turning into a bladder daddy. And, keep your grubby paws off my pint.'

'What did your sister have to say?' Steve asked, now his father-in-law was out of earshot.

'They were called in for an urgent meeting with Wolf's big knobs,' Andy replied. 'The network had no idea Kratz... Umpleby... whoever... was a first-class psycho when they cast him, and as far as they're concerned they've got a massive damage limitation exercise on their hands. The rest of the cast and crew have been warned not to speak to the press or even discuss it with friends and family at the moment, so I'm trusting you lot.' He watched them process the information and nod. 'They haven't got a clue where he is or what he's been up to since he disappeared the best part of two months ago. The FBI and Interpol are hunting him.'

'Interpol?' Franco echoed. 'Doesn't that suggest they think he's gone abroad?'

Andy shrugged. 'Maybe, though they may just be keeping their net wide open.'

'You say the Feds are involved, so has anyone heard from Sam?'

Steve shook his head at Franco. 'I tried ringing him a few days ago and got no answer, so I left a message and he's not returned the call.'

'You reckon he's okay?' Franco asked as he admired the rings of foam encircling the inside of his glass.

Steve frowned. 'Why shouldn't he be?'

Andy shook his head when Kratz's face filled the plasma screen. 'Sam's pretty good at keeping in touch. I wonder if he's contacted Tony?'

'I'll try phoning later,' Steve suggested. 'Anna or Susie wouldn't be best pleased if we woke them up now,' he added, imagining Charlotte's reaction to such an intrusion.

'I don't reckon it's medical,' Roger announced. 'A ruddy great pot of tea and too long in that traffic jam, that'll be it.'

Franco grinned. 'Age catches up with us all, Roger. My grandfather was just the same.'

'Shut up and pass us that menu over,' Roger snapped. He pulled a pair of glasses from his shirt pocket and read the information carefully. 'Aye, it's pretty good. Not as gormless as you look, lad.'

'Such flattery,' Franco replied. 'Not too fancy for you?'

Roger shook his head and picked up the newspaper he'd previously left on the table. 'Not had chance to have a proper gander.' He unfolded the newspaper and spread it across the desk. 'The shop next door just got another pile delivered and they're going like hotcakes. Saw some team from Sky News hanging round near the station too.'

Steve grimaced. 'Just what we need.'

'This the fellow? Handsome chap, eh? No wonder the wife likes watching.' He stared at Steve. 'Do you recognise him? I mean, does he look much different from your schooldays?'

'Well, suppose he's taller and he's put in a fair few hours at the gym. It's hard to remember in that much detail. It's been the best part of twenty years since we've seen him and we tried to avoid him at school.'

'Obviously he isn't going to look like that these days,' Roger said, his face scrunched in concentration. He took a pen from his pocket and started to shade in Kratz's hairline.

Franco and Andy exchanged a puzzled glance. 'What are you doing that for?' the latter asked.

'Just giving him a makeover, like those police sketch artists do.'

Steve frowned at the photo. 'What makes you think he'd have dark hair?'

'Opposite of blond,' Roger said, like he'd stated the most obvious of facts. 'And I reckon he'd comb it back instead of forward.'

'Who do you think you are? The next Cracker?'

'Now *that* was a good programme,' Roger replied. 'So much better than the so-called crime stuff on the box today.' He held up his handiwork, glad the others were unaware of the icy sensation travelling across his shoulders and down the back of each arm.

'Have you seen him, Roger?' Andy asked. He coughed in a feeble attempt to stifle his laughter. 'Has he been rollerblading down the Prom waving candyfloss in the air?'

'Not this week,' Roger replied. His appetite departed when Mikey approached the table and set down a plate of chips in front of him.

Mikey pulled up a chair from the empty table beside theirs. 'I much preferred him blond.' He took a gulp of the pear cider that had recently taken the town by storm and pretended to wipe away a stray tear. 'I'd love to know where he is. He could be anywhere. Maybe he's come back here, thinking folks won't guess he'd be so brazen. That's what I'd do.' He ran his fingers through his hair, a garish shade of orange for the past fortnight. 'This would definitely have to go,' he added in a sad tone. 'I'd go mousey brown and start dressing like Steve. I'd then go anywhere and everywhere, and nobody would have a bloody clue.'

Franco smirked at Steve. 'He's got a fair point there.'

Steve folded his arms and leaned against the smooth leather. 'I'm sure the cops have already thought of that one.'

Mikey and Franco nodded, both amused by Steve's indignant expression.

Steve carefully observed his father-in-law and sensed something else occupied his mind. 'You've gone very quiet, Roger. You okay?'

'Yeah, son. Proper champion.' He chewed on a chip for longer than necessary and forced himself to swallow it. 'Just got a spot of business to take care of later.'

****

8.53am – PDT
San Fernando Road, Los Angeles, California

Ronnie Mosley cleared his throat, signalling the need to get down to business as his teammates sipped their coffees, the drinks cooled all too soon by a nearby temporary air conditioning unit. They listened attentively to Niall Demaine's conveniently translated update from Augsburg's police, who'd eventually traced Andreas Baum to a city centre hotel. An infuriating malfunction of the city's surveillance camera network appeared to coincide with Kratz's departure from the city, and fruitless inquiries at local car rental agencies and an analysis of the limited footage obtained from the Hauptbahnhof failed to identify anyone bearing an obvious resemblance to their quarry.

'Where do we go from here?' Gibson asked.

'We focus on assisting Glendale with the Galina di Marco side of things.'

Muñoz launched his empty cup into a nearby trash can. 'Has she agreed to talk?'

'Not yet,' Gibson said. 'The FBI in Denver investigated Galina's and Kratz's bank accounts and found significant circumstantial evidence. Demaine contacted Agent Mark Baxter closer to home, who called in a favour to get a warrant for the baby's bank account. This uncovered additional evidence to suggest Kratz is the sperm donor. Whitehead said they'll invite Galina for interview in the next couple of days, and they're putting together a nice little presentation now the bank manager has agreed to release surveillance footage directly to Glendale.'

Muñoz folded his arms tightly across his chest. 'What if she declines?'

Mosley grinned in a reptilian manner. 'Trust me, she'll play ball. She's frantic to get her schooling back on course and follow in Daddy's footsteps by becoming some big hot-shot defence attorney. Can you imagine her career ending before it starts? Would *you* want to take to the stand

223

knowing the opposition is going to drag up your private life at any opportunity?'

'It would reduce her credibility and show she's easily influenced,' Hallberg agreed. 'And, there's the issue of the family's reputation. Daddy is one of the best in his field and Mommy jointly owns one of the most exclusive boutiques in Glendale. It's better the public think she had an accident with a mystery ex-boyfriend and then makes a success of her life, rather than forever being known as the girl who got herself knocked up by Konrad Kratz.'

'Exactly,' Mosley replied. 'We don't know the circumstances yet, but she's likely gotten drunk on something – be it his charm or a couple of cocktails. Mom implied the girl has never been a big one for partying, suggesting she's not used to male attention or the effects of alcohol. If Kratz picked up on that, he'd have easily exploited her.'

'Is anyone from this precinct going to be there?' Gibson asked, hopeful he'd be offered the opportunity after a week of being cooped up in the incident room.

'Oh yeah, there sure is.' Mosley's grin widened. 'Whitehead's reserved a front row seat for l'il ol' me.'

****

5.40pm – BST
Blackpool, England

Roger Mortimer washed down two aspirin with a large glass of whisky and hoped the tablets would eradicate the dazed feeling he'd brought home from his meeting at the pub. Thankful his wife and her two sisters had cleared off to York for the day, he'd intended to use the resulting solitude to decide how best to remedy the Oliver Stamford situation ...

...Or should that be the Konrad Kratz situation?

Whether it was the angle they'd taken the photo from, or the lighting, or even some type of neurological dysfunction, Roger was gobsmacked to recognise the American businessman currently giving him a Nevadan-sized headache.

Half a bottle of Bushmills later he'd become engaged in a one-sided staring match against the phone, before he finally picked up its cordless handset. His fist closed around Stamford's business card, almost certain the dark-coloured hatchback following him last week was driven by the same fellow. Since then, he'd also recalled a similar vehicle parked near the pub they'd held their first meeting in ten days earlier.

Gotcha, you piece of conniving shit.

Roger entered a series of digits into the handset, carefully read the number back to himself and allowed the phone to dial. An uncomfortable feeling spread through his chest and into his throat, leaving Roger unsure whether nerves or alcohol were responsible. He heard a faint crackle and swallowed heavily.

'Hello?'

'Mr Stamford? It's Roger Mortimer here.'

'Gee Roger! You sure know how to make a man jump out of his skin.'

'You enjoyed your meal last Thursday?'

'Yeah man, awesome.'

'I'll cut to the chase. I know exactly who you are.'

'Tell me more.'

'It's like this, Konrad. You need to bugger off back to the States and whatever little scheme you've got running over there.'

The three second silence felt like an eternity to Roger.

'And what incentive do I have?'

'This is the best bit and it's an absolute piece of piss. You forget about your investment, and I'll forget I recognised you.' Roger flopped back against the leather sofa and sniffed the last of the whisky at the bottom of his glass. 'Come on, Konrad. You must be a clever sod to pull off this double life for so long. Let's call it mutual backscratching.'

'I suppose you may have a point.'

'Get your backside out of the country by this weekend and my ageing memory will fail.'

'You're a very fair man, Roger. But how will you know I've gone?'

'Because if I don't get a postcard from Reno by the middle of September, the plod are going to be so far up your arse they'll be able to clean your teeth *and* smell your breath.'

****

Icy fear immediately replaced Sam's surprise at finding an empty driveway upon arriving back at the cabin. Blood pulsated inside his ears as he unlocked the front door, drowning out the silence that greeted him. He'd eventually spotted Anna's note on the kitchen table, her hasty scribble clarifying that John needed more teething gel and they'd be home soon.

The prospect of a long leisurely shower had proved quite the incentive during his homeward journey and, sweating heavily after a forty-minute ride from the resident agency, its high-pressure jets became impossible to ignore. He dropped his cycling clothes into the laundry basket, slid back the cubicle door and attempted to stretch his tightening muscles without overbalancing beneath the tepid water. His new exercise regime would take some getting used to, especially on a daily basis – but there was no way he could risk taking out a gym membership.

Conscious his family were likely to return within minutes, Sam turned off the water, hastily dried himself and pulled on the same shorts he'd worn the previous evening. The faint purr of an approaching engine carried through the bedroom window Anna insisted they leave open during the day, something he'd regularly warned her against since their move. He took the stairs two at a time and arrived at the top seconds before Anna steered the rented Saab onto the driveway.

She pushed open the front door and watched him pull a clean T-shirt over his head. 'Good day at the office?' she asked.

Sam frowned at the sound of John's loud cries from the back seat. He wrapped an arm around Anna's shoulders and pressed a kiss to her forehead. 'Are you okay?'

'Yeah, his gums are bright red and he's chewing his fist like it's gourmet steak.' She unclipped their son and narrowed her eyes. 'And, it looks like he's hungry.'

Angela folded her arms and followed her mother and the screaming baby through the door. 'He's always hungry.'

'That's because he's growing very quickly.' Sam ruffled her hair. 'You used to be just the same.'

She shook her head. 'Not me, Daddy.'

'Oh yes you were,' he said. 'And you were extra loud if we bought vanilla pudding. You always recognised the label.'

She winced when John's cries continued inside the house. 'Can we go for a walk?'

He nodded. 'Maybe just a short distance. Daddy's legs are aching.'

'Why?' Angela folded her arms again and tilted her head. 'Did you go running?'

'I rode my bike home earlier and pedalled too hard going up the hill.'

They walked along the faded asphalt until Angela pulled on Sam's hand. He scanned the road ahead, his prediction confirmed by the sight of a large ginger cat sniffing the sparse vegetation beside an adjacent cabin's driveway.

'Can we get a cat, Daddy?' Angela asked. She crouched around ten feet away from the animal and giggled as it ran up to her, its fluffy tail quivering with excitement.

Sam heard the cat's owner open his front door and start to shake a box of kibbles. 'Maybe when John's old enough to understand how to care for one,' he replied, unsure whether Anna would welcome a furry addition to the household.

The elderly man walked down the driveway and broke into a toothy grin. 'You hangin' with your new little friend again, Monty?' He winked at Angela and noticed the intense concentration on her face whilst she stroked the cat's back.

Sam raised his eyebrows. 'You okay, Mal?'

'Never better since I escaped from the city and retired here. You hit the wrong side of sixty and you realise if you don't make the change, you never will.'

'Looks like the change suits you.'

'Hell yeah!' he replied and grinned at Monty rolling in the dust. 'And, it looks like you and the family have settled in well. How much longer before you return to Washington?'

'Not sure yet, it's an open-ended contract.' Sam shrugged and recalled the cover story he and Anna recently devised between them. 'Could be two months, could be two years.'

Mal pointed at the dramatic views from their vantage point. 'This is a much nicer place to raise those kiddies than in the city.'

'You're not wrong.' Sam considered what else to add to their background. 'We've got used to it, but for us this is remote. I'm not sure if I can manage cycling back from the office every day.'

'A young man like you?' Mal punched his shoulder. 'Get out of here!'

Sam grinned and flexed his left ankle to release some of the tension that maintained its tendency to build since the accident. 'We're going to lease another car, especially for when the weather turns. Don't fancy cycling in the snow and ice.'

'You Brits are always thinking about the weather.' He tilted his head back. 'Barely a cloud in the sky.'

'You sound like my wife.'

'Where is the lovely lady?'

'The baby's teething and hungry; it's a dangerous combination.' Sam glanced back at the cabin. 'I'd better go and see if her eardrums are still intact, but maybe in a couple more minutes.'

Mal chuckled at Angela's obvious delight whenever the purring cat rubbed its face against her hand. 'The little lady seems quite taken with Monty.'

'She wants one of her own. I said we'd consider it after John gets a bit older and we know where we're going to be living permanently.'

Mal remembered his disrupted sleep the previous night. 'If he barfs up another furball at four in the morning, you can have that one,' he muttered. 'Anyway, I'll let you get back to family matters.' He gave the kibble inside the box a stronger shake. 'Monty, you get yourself inside or Daddy won't be givin' you no dinner.'

The cat watched Angela stand up and stretch her feet one at a time. 'Go get your dinner, Monty-cat,' she said seriously, her gaze never deviating as she watched him saunter up the driveway and into Mal's cabin.

'Speaking of dinner, isn't it high time you and your daddy tucked in?'

Angela rubbed her stomach. 'Mommy said we got pasta.'

'Sounds mighty fine to me, so you make sure you eat it all up. There's a nice pot roast nearly ready in there.' He slapped Sam on the back and followed Monty's lead. 'See you around, Sam. Come on over for a beer any time, our local stuff's way better than that swill you'll have gotten when you lived in DC.'

'You're on,' Sam replied. He saw Angela's puzzled stare flit between them and quickly fixed his smile. 'Right then, cheeky monkey. Let's fill that tummy of yours.'

'Daddy?' she said, her tone enquiring.

Sam's throat constricted, almost certain what she'd say next. 'Yes, sweetheart?'

'You said we lived in Golden.'

He knelt in front of her and took her hands. 'We di... we do,' he said and nodded to emphasise his point.

Angela shook her head, puzzled. 'So why did Monty-cat's daddy say we lived in DC?'

'I told him we lived near Denver because it's a big city he may have heard of,' Sam replied.

'Where the zoo is?'

He nodded and made her listen carefully to him repeat the two names. 'They sound alike, don't they?'

She shrugged. 'A little.'

'Mal and I haven't known each other for very long. I think he just mixed up the names and I promise it's nothing for you to worry about.'

She nodded and turned to the window where Anna bounced a pacified John up and down in her arms, the baby now happily chewing a finger of buttered bread.

Angela placed her hands over her ears. 'Is John better?'

'Until he grows another tooth,' Sam replied. He crouched down to kiss her cheek and smiled at his wife and son. 'Come on, let's go inside and get something nice to eat.'

Chapter 29 – Wednesday 19th August 2009

10.15am – PDT
Wolf Studios, Los Angeles, California

H.O.S.T.A.G.E. director Dev Vermúdez ran a deeply tanned hand through the tangle of black frizz he'd forgotten to brush that morning and stepped back from the water cooler. The day had promised to be a scorcher from the moment dawn cracked Hollywood's horizon, and Dev all but prayed the five big-name actors he'd invited to audition for Mick Senogles' replacement also radiated the same amount of heat.

If he had to be honest, Dev viewed auditions as a pain in the ass, especially at this stage of the summer. Weeks of uncertainty over Kratz's whereabouts resulted in his firing in absentia and immediately triggered a massive casting headache. If that wasn't enough, the production of season three was three weeks behind schedule; another thing promising to increase his hours at work *and* his stress levels.

Dev, the show runner and a quintet of writers eventually reconvened to devise a replacement character, modifying their existing scripts to coincide Senogles' off-screen fatal mission and the arrival of a new team leader. During a frantic yet productive weekend at Dev's isolated cabin near Big Bear, the unanimous decision to delay revealing too much about the new agent until later that season meant Ben O'Hara's in-depth character development would occur when the pressure of making up for lost time eased.

An urgent casting call issued a week earlier produced a torrent of interested high-profile actors, and scripts were hastily couriered to five fitting Ben O'Hara's general age and description. To Dev's relief, the recording schedule's reordering to only film the scenes lacking O'Hara had already reduced their production time deficit by nearly two weeks.

'Wakey, wakey!'

He opened his eyes and saw set designer Vicky Parker filling a plastic cup at a nearby water cooler.

'Jeez, woman. You trying to finish me off?'

She laughed and handed the cup to him. 'Penny for them.'

Dev raised one hand to massage the back of his neck. 'Man, I'll be glad when all this shit gets sorted and we're back on schedule. Wish I'd fired the prick when he didn't rock up the first day back on set.'

'Dropped him off the top of the Empire State, more like,' Vicky replied, scrutinising the water in a second cup she'd grabbed for herself. 'Don't these things give you Legionnaires' disease?'

'At least I'd get a rest from this place.' He raised the drink to his lips. 'A couple of weeks in the hospital would be awesome.'

Vicky took a gulp of her own water. 'Who do you reckon it's going to be?' she asked. 'I'm surprised to see Martin Crophill's put in for the role, especially after what happened to him last time he showed an interest.'

Dev nodded. The police had told him the young man spent nearly a year in the hospital, with around one-third of that time in a coma, after Kratz broke into his flat and pushed him off the balcony. Crophill was now lauded as a walking miracle; a succession of surgeries and months of physical therapy allowing his return to work with minimal physical restrictions.

'Yeah, Mr Miracle's ability to walk on water would save on special effects,' he replied.

'I thought you rated him?'

'I do, and it'll be one in the eye for Kratz if Crophill gets the role. That's if the piece of shit watches.'

'He'll watch,' she cut in. 'An egomaniacal bastard like him will want to assure himself his replacement isn't half as good as he was.'

'Get you,' he replied, unable to keep the admiration from his tone.

Vicky smiled and tapped her nose. 'I know my nutjobs.'

Dev let out a loud chuckle. 'I'll bet you say that to all the boys.'

****

Sam watched the computer's screen fade to black, then rubbed his eyes and yawned. His new cycling regime had proved more challenging as the week progressed, especially once he turned off Kingsbury Grade Road. The steep gradient and its series of sharp turns left him thankful that three months earlier he'd received the all-clear from his Denver-based physical therapist to resume regular rides up Golden's Lookout Mountain. At least he hadn't been thrown in cold here.

A flash of movement drew his attention to the office door, where a shadowy figure lurked behind its frosted glass. Jed Masters, the resident agency's lead agent, turned the handle with a faint squeak and smiled at Sam. A short, muscular man in his early fifties, Masters' tanned face and casual dress were fitting of a man who chose to spend most of his leisure time during the summer months hiking in the Sierra Nevada.

'Another long day over?' Shrewd hazel eyes flitted between Sam and the computer's blank screen. 'Do you have a minute before you head off?'

Sam nodded and pushed his chair back. 'Yeah, no problem. Is everything okay?'

'I just wanted to say how well you've settled in.' He held up his hand when Sam went to interrupt. 'Listen, it suits me fine having another brain and pair of eyes around the place, so don't you go feeling like you're any kind of trouble.'

Sam stared at the faded wooden floor. 'I'm really sorry you got all this dumped on you.'

'Hey, we all stick together. When my old buddy Colin Milne phoned out of the blue, I was only too pleased to repay the favours he's granted over the years. How's your family settling in at the cabin?'

'Okay, I suppose,' Sam replied. 'My wife would rather be back in Colorado. Deep down, I know she's unhappy.'

'Maybe, but she's still here.' He patted Sam's shoulder. 'What does that tell you?'

Sam shrugged and managed a grin. 'I reckon I'm a very lucky guy.'

Masters' expression hardened. 'Damn right you are. My ex-wife would've gotten out of there faster than the eye can blink,' he said. 'Listen, the guys want to take you out. Nothing exotic, just a burger and a couple of beers. You mentioned having family plans on Saturday already, so I suggested Sunday evening. Are you up for it?'

'That's really thoughtful,' Sam replied, genuinely pleased by the invitation. 'I haven't seen much of them since you introduced me on Monday, so yeah, thanks.'

Masters scowled and thought back over his day. 'On top of the usual stuff, that goddamn cult or whatever the hell they are is keeping us on our toes. Unless they cause big problems before the week is out, we'll work out a time for Sunday in the next couple of days.' He massaged the bridge of his nose. 'I'll be driving into town from Minden so I can give you a ride. It seems wrong if you can't have a couple of cold ones at your welcome meal.'

Sam untied his laces and slipped off his shoes. 'What about you?' he asked.

'Listen to me and listen good, kid.' Masters patted his stomach. 'When you're an old bastard, beer travels straight from your mouth to your gut. You'll be doing me a favour.'

Sam smiled and reached under the desk to retrieve his cycling kit bag. 'Thanks, although the first round's on me.' He saw Masters open his mouth and assumed he was about to disagree. 'No arguments; I owe you big time. Let's leave it at that.'

****

6.01pm – PDT
San Fernando Road, Los Angeles, California

Mosley closed the lid on his laptop and watched the others exchange high-fives, their spirits lifted after he'd relayed Glendale PD's latest update. 'Right guys, unless mass murder is committed overnight, I don't want to see your sorry asses in this incident room before ten tomorrow morning. You got me?'

'Sounds like things are looking up across the Valley,' Muñoz said at the sight of Mosley's wide smile.

He let out a low chuckle. 'Yeah, you could say so. Now it's been confirmed Galina di Marco and a man fitting Kratz's height and build carried out the transactions we've gotten ourselves a shitload more leverage.'

'They're going to interview Galina, right?' Hallberg asked. He threw his jacket over his arm, even though he knew it would undoubtedly remain too hot to wear the garment.

'Whitehead already made the call and arranged a warrant, in case she refuses to provide samples of both hers and the baby's DNA. Her old man's a hotshot lawyer in town and has a reputation for being difficult.'

Gibson nodded. 'Imagine if this gets out. What's it going to do to the di Marco family's precious reputation?'

Mosley winked and adjusted his tie. 'That's the angle Whitehead and Menendez are going for.' He pictured the woman who'd masqueraded as Muñoz's wife earlier that summer when both police departments combined forces to stake out Kratz's Brockmont home.

'Menendez?' Muñoz visibly paled at the recollection of Glendale's wannabe detective, whose attitude rivalled the size of the average C-lister's. 'As in Dana Menendez?'

'Yeah,' Mosley replied. 'If you want to accompany Whitehead this evening, you'll be able to get reacquainted with the lovely lady.'

Chapter 30 – Thursday 20th August 2009

4.04am – PDT
Kingsbury, Nevada

Night's swift descent cloaked the car in a stifling blanket and enhanced the threat of the unknown. Roadside scenery blurred until he was unable to separate the images and his unease built rapidly, a primitive response to the sinister entity waiting to emerge from the shadows. He glanced into the rear-view mirror, terrified to see the darkness maintaining its pursuit and threatening to smother the vehicle before he could reach safety.

The car slowed to negotiate a bend, this sudden change in velocity beyond his control. His foot slammed the accelerator to the floor and panic spread throughout his chest when the car continued to decelerate. A faint green light hovered in mid-air and the faint voice beyond it repeated his name; the sound burrowing deeper and deeper into his head. He squeezed his eyes closed and thumped the steering wheel, determined to secure his release from the invisible force pulling him back and reach the safety he knew lay beyond the green sphere.

He lurched forward and the voice grew louder and more insistent. It shouted his name as the SUV – yes, he now recognised it to be a government-issued SUV – roared closer to the green light and the protection it promised, a matter of seconds away. A scream ripped through his throat when the green flipped to red, morphing into a dying star that filled the windshield. His foot smashed the brake pedal to the floor and the resulting panic suffocated him as he ploughed straight into the widening orb. Something grabbed him. It shook his arm and touched his face. He needed...

'Sam!'

...to escape. Jagged shards of bloodied bone protruded from his arm when he tried to grab the steering wheel and Kratz's grinning face leered above...

'Sam! Wake up!'

...his surroundings, now a cocoon of dazzling white light as he loomed over him and brandished a syringe which swiftly arced through a downward trajectory.

'Please, Sam!'

Anna! He could hear her voice and the safety she promised. He needed to reach her, but something had grabbed his shoulders and was pushing him further and further...

'No, get off! Anna, help me!' Sam shouted, his eyes now open, staring wildly. He sat bolt upright and his manic gaze roved an uncoordinated path around the bedroom, illuminated by a lamp on Anna's nightstand. His heart pummelled against his ribs, adrenaline heightening his senses. Cool air met perspiration and Sam shivered against the chill spreading across his bare chest and back. The dim bedside light reflected from the sheen covering his face and he heard Anna's voice through the blood pounding in his ears, a faint yet soothing sound.

'It's only a dream, Sam. You need to calm down, you're safe,' Anna whispered. She watched his chest heave and gently stroked his upper arm.

Sam flinched at her touch. 'Where am I?' he gasped, the words ragged. Images from the dream flashed in and out of his mind and he stared at the doorway. 'He's come for me!'

'We're at the cabin, you're safe here,' she said. It sounded like she was speaking to him from a distance. 'Listen to me, Sam. I want you to lie down and take deep breaths.'

Sam was vaguely aware he'd nodded. 'I should check the road.'

'You're safe,' Anna repeated. 'Lie down and tell me what happened. What did you see?'

'I didn't.' Snapshots continued to bombard him and he gulped to stop the rising panic. 'I don't know what I saw.'

He felt Anna gently press a hand to his clammy shoulder and ease him back against the pillows. 'Take your time. Remember, you're safe and nobody can hurt you.'

'It was dark and I was in my SUV, the one I drive in New York.' Sam paused to take a deep breath and managed to regain control of the pictures rebounding inside his head. Anna nodded her encouragement and kissed his damp cheek. 'It slowed down but the lights were on green. I couldn't get away, then the lights turned red and it sped up and I couldn't stop. I was trapped in the car. My arm–'

'Your arm?' she echoed and squinted into the shadows where she knew two faded silver scars provided a perpetual reminder of the previous August.

His fingers subconsciously travelled to the same place and he closed his eyes and swallowed. 'I saw bone sticking through the skin. I tried to escape.'

She stroked Sam's hair back from where it was plastered against his forehead. 'Do you want me to go get you some water?'

The panic returned and Sam grabbed Anna's wrist. 'No, please stay.'

'I'm here.'

'Sorry,' he mumbled, suddenly embarrassed by his reaction.

Anna raised her eyebrows in surprise. 'Whatever for?'

'Waking you up. It's not like the kids will let you have a nap later.'

Anna carefully considered her next words. 'You haven't had a bad dream for months.' She squeezed his hand again, aware of how cool his fingers now were. 'Is there anything worrying you? You can tell me, right?'

'It's weird.' He shrugged, not willing to consider what lay behind the nightmare. 'I suppose it's just one of those things.'

Sam saw Anna turn onto her side to face him, closed his eyes and fell silent. The action of her hand stroking the hair away from his forehead soon took on a hypnotic quality and exhaustion overcame him as the adrenaline's effects wore off. He heard Anna's reassuring voice fade into the distance as his heart rate and breathing slowed to normal. Sleep crept closer; Sam only vaguely aware of her presence when she pulled the comforter over his chest.

Anna waited until she heard his deep regular breaths, then reached across to her bedside lamp and flicked the switch, mindful not to rouse Sam. Her eyes slowly adjusted to the insipid moonlight seeping through a crack in the drapes and she maintained her vigil, fully aware sleep would elude her until the following night.

****

10.22am – PDT
San Fernando Road, Los Angeles, California

Although a later start meant the three younger detectives arrived feeling refreshed, Mosley's timekeeping remained consistent, meaning he'd logged on to his computer and poured a second cup of coffee long before the clock reached eight. The local police bulletin appeared shorter than usual that morning, its main focus an incident involving a well-known local gang-banger. Mosley took a few seconds to marvel at the man's stupidity, and then diverted his attention to the six new emails in his inbox.

Four pertained to general police business: A husband and wife team responsible for a hold-up at a liquor store less than a mile from the police station were apprehended after a tip-off from their teenage son, aggrieved he hadn't been allowed to take some of the bounty to a friend's party. A pair of training courses, a request for information from the team investigating a homicide in Bakersfield – and two that especially captured his interest.

Mosley swallowed the last of his coffee and clicked on a reply from Martin Boothroyd, the detective leading the Preston-based cold case team eight time zones to the east. He skimmed its content, then re-read it more carefully and absorbed the details of Boothroyd's imminent visit to a recently located paternal uncle of Kratz's, his main objectives to obtain background information *and* a DNA sample.

The cursor hovered above the last email and Mosley considered the implications of the previous one he'd just closed. A familial DNA sample, coupled with another sample from Anya di Marco, should be enough to confirm the genetic profile obtained from Kratz's homes definitely belonged to the scumbag. He moved the mouse and clicked.

Mosley quickly read the short message, elated to learn that Glendale detective Paul Whitehead and officer Dana Menendez had corroborated his *baby daddy* theory during their visit to the di Marco family the previous evening. The young woman's tearful confession to her horrified parents that their once-illustrious neighbour had fathered their first grandchild generated angry scenes and, now they'd obtained mouth swabs from Galina and the baby, the detectives agreed to continue the conversation another time. This looked likely to be in Glendale PD's territory on Friday morning, assuming Bruno di Marco could rearrange a meeting with an anonymous celebrity client and accompany his distraught daughter.

Mosley returned to the present and saw an uncharacteristically bright-eyed Hallberg glance furtively at the others. He raised an eyebrow at Hallberg. 'What's eating you, man?'

'You heard the latest news from Tinseltown?'

Gibson gave an amused snort. 'Never thought you'd be the type to obsess over Hollywood gossip.'

Hallberg sipped his coffee and felt his cheeks colour. 'My wife heard it on the radio while she was fixing breakfast,' he mumbled.

'Yeah, yeah,' Mosley said. 'Come on, spill the news. I can see you're dying to.' He failed to keep the mirth from his voice.

'Do you remember Martin Crophill?'

Muñoz nodded. 'The bionic man? Goddamn miracle the guy's still alive, let alone that he returned to acting.'

'He's a nice guy too,' Mosley added. 'None of that Hollywood bullshit.'

Hallberg remembered the numerous unsuccessful hours they'd spent trying to solve the case two years earlier, and Crophill's later well-publicised appreciation of their efforts to find whoever attempted to kill him. 'Yeah, he's only gone and gotten himself cast as Kratz's replacement on *H.O.S.T.A.G.E.*'

****

11.47pm – BST
Blackpool, England

A half-moon revealed itself from behind a bank of clouds and made another feeble attempt at illuminating the Astra's sleepy surroundings. At this time of night there was no perceptible movement on Keys Drive; only the sound of two local tomcats shattering the tranquillity whilst they battled for the right to impregnate a dainty tortoiseshell queen.

Konrad sat behind the Astra's steering wheel and, from his roadside vantage point perpendicular to Keys Drive, watched the house's lights disappear one by one. He knew the old git was home alone, after following Roger from the town's main railway station where he'd dropped off his

239

wife earlier that evening. Konrad wondered where she'd gone with the large pink trolley case, and for how long. He'd driven back to the town's run-down centre and parked on a side street, away from the public car parks and police station. The Prom had barely changed in the past twenty years, its fresh air and perennial drunk tourists reminiscent of many a childhood day out – not to mention the traditional fish and chip supper he'd eagerly devoured. A fading blaze of reds and yellows on the horizon signalled the time had come to return to Roger's home, and Konrad couldn't help feeling grateful that thick clouds had returned to obscure the moon. He slunk through the garden gate and crouched behind a large bush, his ears straining for the entire time it took for his eyes to adjust.

Now he was sure the street slept soundly, Konrad retrieved a screwdriver and a pair of gloves from the inside pocket of his jacket, then merged into darkening shadows at the side of the house. The building's period features maintained their ability to instantly transport whoever opened them to the interwar years, sealing the deal when the newly-married Mr and Mrs Mortimer purchased their home in the late sixties. Konrad rummaged in his trouser pocket, the task made more difficult by the gloves' thin leather, and retrieved a small torch. He spotted the Yale branding above the keyhole and doubted the panelled wooden door was fitted with extra security locks. After all, it wasn't like Roger had chosen to live in Blackpool's equivalent of Beirut. The stained glass fractured with minimal sound and Konrad eased the fragmented shards from their frame and placed them beside the doorstep.

High-pitched yapping pierced the air, causing Konrad to startle and curse under his breath. The dog had presumably been let out to answer one last call of nature before its owners retired for the night and soon fell silent once again. He stared up at a large window above the door. Feeble light from the re-emerged moon reflected back at him, rather than an artificial yellow hue indicating Roger had awakened.

The hole in the glass was large enough to comfortably pass his arm through. Konrad took care not to snag his jacket on any residual sharp edges, twisted the lock and pushed. An unexpected calmness descended now the door's well-oiled hinges had permitted a silent entry and he looked around the kitchen, aided by the combined green glow of the oven and microwave's digital displays.

Home and dry...

The nearby *tick-tock* of a clock filled Konrad's head and he paused to centre in on the sound. He noticed a door to his left, walked across the slate floor tiles and cautiously reached for its handle. At least the old man seemed particular about his door hinges; the last thing Konrad needed was for squealing metal to announce his presence. The door opened into a wide hallway and he briefly flashed the torch at the floor to obtain a memory of the area's layout. A flight of stairs ascended ahead of him and he took their carpeted path to the first floor, testing each step in turn. Five doors confronted him at the top: four were closed, although the furthest had been left halfway open.

Konrad padded along the landing, pulled the handcuffs from his back pocket and listened to the regular low snores confirming that the house's master bedroom lay behind the furthest doorway. He slipped inside and groped the wall to find its main light switch.

'Where's the cash, you fucking prick?' he snarled, gripping the startled older man around the throat. Roger blinked repeatedly and desperately tried to fathom whether this was a nightmare or terrifying reality. His eyes attempted to open, but the harsh light streaming from the ceiling made the action impossible.

Konrad's palm made contact with a fleshy cheek. 'Wake your fat arse up! I haven't got time to piss about.'

Roger's eyes continued their battle against the sixty Watt bulb directly above. 'Who are you?' he choked out.

'You know full well who I am.'

'Oliver? Or should that be Konrad?' He managed to open one fluttering eye. 'Or Peter? Or whatever the bloody hell you're calling yourself this week?'

'Not as gormless as you look.'

'What do you want?' Roger tried to duck his head seconds before a second blow cracked his nose.

Konrad watched a pattern of red droplets spray across the duvet. 'My money.'

'Jesus H. Christ,' Roger groaned. He sniffed in a futile bid to extinguish the burning in his nostrils. 'I only had the houses put on the market yesterday and I've already told you that there's a bloody recession on. People aren't snapping up properties within hours of them being listed like what happened five or six years ago.'

Konrad swung his fist back. 'Where's the safe?'

Roger opened the other eye. 'Safe?' he echoed.

'You must have a safe here, surely?'

'No bloody chance, my missus would empty it within a week. She's worse than Imelda Marcos.' He noticed Konrad frown, the younger man obviously puzzled by the reference. 'She's already got more shoes than a Clarks factory. Feel free to check that damn cupboard over there.' He nodded across the room to a large wardrobe, his eyes widening when the grip on his throat tightened for a moment.

'I expected a return on my investment.'

Roger's bulging eyes glared pointedly at Konrad. 'I thought we'd made a deal after *recent revelations* on my part.' His voice carried a discernible wheeze. 'Don't you think you should've taken my advice and buggered off back to Yankland?'

'I never had you down as a xenophobe, Roger,' Konrad replied, the words barely audible. 'The thing is, I'm not a gambling man. If I was I'd have tried my hand in the casinos, there's the odd one or two in Nevada in case you didn't know. That philosophy also extends to my everyday life. I'm not a big risk-taker.'

'Which is relevant how?'

'I can't risk you not keeping your promise, Roger.' Konrad's grasp retightened around Roger's windpipe, this time ensuring he applied enough pressure to make breathing difficult. 'How do I know that the Feds won't be waiting for me on touch down in the States? They're pretty much falling over themselves to get their grubby little paws on me.'

'I'm a m-man of my w-word,' Roger stuttered, gasping for breath. Stars began to creep into his peripheral vision and perspiration formed on his brow. He saw Konrad reach into his pocket, unsure whether to emit a sigh of relief when a pair of fluffy leopard print handcuffs appeared and the pressure on his throat lessened.

'Don't worry, old man; I'm not into that kinky shit.' Konrad twirled the item round his head and laughed when he remembered the mortifying trip to Ann Summers earlier that week. 'But for all we know, *you* are.'

Roger realised his chances of escape were rapidly slipping away and a hopeless expression appeared on his reddened face. 'Listen, I've got an idea. Why don't you cuff me to the bed? My missus won't be back for another couple of days. Gives you time to disappear safe in the knowledge

I can't blab to the police, even if I wanted to. I'll tell her some kids broke in and did it for a prank.'

Konrad narrowed his eyes and appeared to consider the matter. 'I'd say that's a fair plan.' He nodded at Roger, who obligingly held his hands above his head and rested them against the wrought iron headboard. 'Hope I don't see any stirrings down below while I'm doing this, Roger. I have... had a sizeable gay following, and while I'm a pretty tolerant kind of guy it doesn't really float my boat.'

Roger swallowed down a wave of nausea and he glared at his captor. 'You're sick!' he spat.

'Yeah, you're probably right.'

'Aren't you going to leave me some water and a straw?' Roger asked. He wondered how he'd survive for three days until the wife returned home, not caring what she'd think about seeing him strung up like a pheasant in a butcher's window.

This time, the dark head shook. 'Again, can't take the risk.'

Roger's mouth flapping open and shut reminded Konrad of the stricken goldfish he'd removed from its bowl almost three decades earlier.

'But... but...'

'But nothing, Roger.' Konrad felt the hair on his arms rise, the excitement of seeing the man's terror too difficult to ignore. 'You won't be blabbing anything to the Old Bill. If anything, it'll be *you* they end up investigating.'

Roger's sudden expression of defiance momentarily unnerved Konrad. 'They'll never pin owt on me. The FBI will track you down and fry you on the chair, you bastard.'

'Local businessman found dead in kinky sex game gone wrong.' Konrad's smile took on a malevolent edge. 'I'm sure your missus would love that.'

'Dead?' Roger swallowed nervously. 'You don't have to.'

Konrad retrieved the cling film from where he'd dropped it on the floor and tore the cardboard case's perforated edge to reveal its shimmering contents. 'Auto-erotic asphyxiation,' he said. 'It's apparently a more common fetish than folks believe. Again, can't say it's particularly my thing. Believe it or not, I'm quite conventional when it comes to getting laid. As long as she's gorgeous and gagging for it I'm a happy man. But as for you, Roger, I reckon you've got your seedy side.'

Memories of his wedding night flashed before Roger's eyes and he shook his head. 'I've only been with one woman my whole life,' he said, his tone deflated. A lone tear welled in his right eye and he shook his head again. 'We were looking forward to growing old together and watching our daughter become a mother.'

'You said 'were', Roger. You seem resigned to your fate.' Konrad's smile widened and he pulled an arm span of transparent film from the roll.

Roger's eyes widened in horror. 'What are you going to do?'

'Surely you've worked it out now, Roger?' Konrad leaned closer and they locked gazes. 'You always came across as such a smart guy.'

'Please...' Roger whimpered, oblivious to the dark stain spreading across the front of his pyjama trousers. Konrad lunged towards him and wrapped the clingfilm around Roger's head. He bucked wildly, his features obscured when its additional layers metamorphosed into translucency and his head thrashed from side to side. Time became meaningless and Konrad stepped back; the hunter watching the hunted, his arms folded. Roger's movements weakened and diminished to nothing, his head lolling to one side as the life left his body.

Satisfied his work was now complete, Konrad inspected the room and checked his pockets. With a leering smile he grabbed the remaining clingfilm and flicked the wall switch to shroud the room in darkness, then slowly backed out of the door.

Chapter 31 – Friday 21st August 2009

10.21am – BST
Blackpool, England

Eric Dean pressed the doorbell for a second time and listened to his foot tapping out an impatient rhythm on the doorstep. Since finishing university for the summer and keen to bring in some much-needed cash, Eric had managed to secure two months work as a relief postman. To his surprise, he enjoyed his route – despite the frequent drizzle that had blighted much of the past two months – and plenty of beer money for his fast-approaching second year was already stacking up. He pressed his face to the glass and wondered if the Mortimers were on holiday. That would certainly explain the closed curtains downstairs. Eric had spoken to the old man two days earlier, hence his surprise there'd been no mention of an impending trip. He grinned and contemplated the possibility Roger and his missus were yet to emerge from their bed.

At his age? The randy old goat.

Eric had only met the man's wife once, after ringing the doorbell to deliver a package too large to fit through the letterbox. She'd also seemed nice enough, although from her demeanour Eric was pretty much sure the *Lady of the House* called all the shots. His foot began to tap more rapidly, signalling his reluctance to return the parcel to the sorting office until he remembered what Roger said the first time they'd engaged in conversation:

'Remember this, son. If summat big comes and we're out, just leave it in that unused coal bunker round the side. That'll stop the rain getting to it

and save us a trip to the sorting office too. Since the opening hours changed it's been a ruddy great pain in the arse to get there.'

Eric walked around the nearest side of the house and started searching for the bunker. Dampness filled the air, no doubt due to it receiving little direct sunlight during the day. He relived the five-a-side match he'd participated in the night before and theatrically swung his left foot to launch a fat clump of moss towards the back garden.

A sudden crunch stopped him in his tracks and he looked down and frowned. Why would they leave a pile of broken glass on the path? Eric's frown deepened and his dark brows merged when his gaze reached a jagged hole in the door's glass panel.

'Mr Mortimer!' he called, cupping his hands to project his voice into the house. 'Is everything okay?'

Silence.

'Mr Mortimer!' More urgency sounded in his tone this time. 'Are you in there?'

Deafening silence.

Eric became aware of his escalating pulse rate, dropped his postbag to the floor and pulled a mobile phone from his trouser pocket. He entered the same three digits on the keypad and paced back and forth until a crackle informed him the call had been connected, then released the breath he'd been holding and listened carefully.

'Emergency, which service?'

****

7.44pm – BST
Blackpool, England

Harry Irwin pushed himself out of the swivel chair he'd occupied for the past hour and stretched his torso to its full length. 'You don't reckon he's a pervert then?'

'I dunno, it's just all so contrived,' fellow detective Eddie Pell replied. He shook his head and watched a uniformed officer input information from a series of afternoon interviews with Keys Drive residents. 'It's far too convenient, if you ask me.'

Irwin patted the other man's shoulder in a rare display of gratitude. 'It's good of you to assist us on this case.'

Pell nodded. 'Well, you're short-staffed and Mortimer's got Preston connections. The Fat Controller thought I'd be useful back east if it's due to something that kicked off there first.'

Irwin grinned at Pell's reference to the unpopular Superintendent. 'So he's not ruling out murder?'

'On face value, it looks like a sex game gone wrong.' Pell shrugged his broad shoulders, unconvinced by his interpretation even after three decades in the Force. 'Mortimer doesn't have the reputation of a lady-killer and, like I said, it's too obvious. My gut feeling is the kinky stuff is a cover.'

'So, what do we have so far?' Irwin asked. He listened to his stomach remind him of their rushed lunch six hours earlier. 'I know I'm ready for some snap.'

Pell swiped a printed sheet from the desk he'd been allocated at the town's main police station, pushed a pair of wire-framed glasses further up his nose and read through the information. 'Postman tried to leave a parcel at the side of the house and noticed there'd been a break-in. He phoned 999 around half past ten and they dispatched a pair of local uniforms to the scene. Mortimer was found beaten, handcuffed to the bed and suffocated by...' Pell paused at the bottom paragraph. 'Five layers of clingfilm wrapped round his head.'

Irwin's eyes widened, still shocked by the cause of death. 'What sort of twisted bastard does that?'

'Exactly, it's just too much. That's why I think it's overkill.' Pell massaged the back of his neck to knead away the knots. 'From what I understand of these pervs who get off on choking each other, the idea is to come back from the edge before falling over it. He had no way of getting that stuff off his face. Without someone there willing to remove it, Mortimer's death was guaranteed. Don't know about you, but I like all the oxygen I can get.'

'At your age?' Irwin let out a snort of laughter. 'I hope you've got 999 on speed dial for when the coronary kicks in.'

'Cheeky sod,' Pell replied, failing to maintain his faux-serious expression. 'Anyway, forensics have been all over the place and it's just too clean. No third set of prints in the bedroom, suggesting whoever broke in wore gloves, and there's an absence of fibres on the glass left in the door. The blood in the room appears to be Mortimer's, so if he'd been shagging some tart behind his wife's back why stage a break-in?' He scratched the balding area at the top of his head. 'And, if he *was* having an affair he'd want to keep *everything* looking the same to not, pardon the pun, arouse suspicion.'

Irwin nodded and then turned away from Pell to thank a young uniformed officer who'd set down two mugs of coffee and a partially consumed packet of Rich Tea on the desk.

'Where's the wife?'

Pell grimaced. 'Near Stafford.'

'Stafford? We informed her hours ago, you'd think she'd be here by now.'

'She'd been in Northampton visiting her aunt in hospital,' Pell explained. 'Her cousin's driving her back. There's been a tanker fire on the M6 northbound and they're stuck in a nine-mile tailback.'

Irwin dunked the first of four biscuits into his drink. 'How much does she know?'

'Nothing, besides that he was found dead and the police are investigating.' Pell eased a biscuit from the packet and copied Irwin's actions, then dropped the sodden mixture into his mouth. 'To be honest, I hoped we'd work out the exact circumstances by the time she got back, even if we hadn't located a suspect.'

'Poor cow.' Irwin shook his head. 'Has Roger got any other family?'

'Just one married daughter who lives in Preston. Girl by the name of Charlotte Garner. Her husband Steve is a good friend of my son.'

'That your boy in the States?'

'That's the one,' Pell replied. 'He's now married with a kid and works in forensics in California.'

Irwin swallowed another biscuit. 'You must be a proud man.'

Pell nodded. 'That I am. He's been helping LAPD with the Kratz case. And, my grandson's a proper little smasher. Have we spoken to the daughter yet?'

'Hopefully within the hour.' Irwin looked at his watch. 'We've talked to her husband over the phone. He co-owns the Edward II, which Mortimer heavily invested in over the years.'

'Great place,' Pell said, patting his stomach. 'Steve always gives me mate's rates since I got him out of a couple of minor scrapes during his teenage years. So, Charlotte's actually coming here?'

'Yeah, poor girl. Steve said she offered so we wouldn't have to lose time by driving over to Preston,' Irwin replied. 'Her husband said she's in bits. She hasn't heard the details – I didn't think it right we tell her that stuff over the phone, but she knows her dad's dead.'

Pell scowled and pictured Charlotte's happy smile when she'd pulled a pint for him less than a week earlier. 'I'm not looking forward to this, not one little bit.'

****

11.23am – PDT
North Isabel Street, Glendale, California

Glendale's Police Department occupied a large modern pale brick building which bore no resemblance to LAPD Northeast Division's plain single-story construction. A surprisingly unenvious Mosley arrived shortly before eleven, acquired a visitor's pass and waited patiently in the lobby for a flustered Whitehead to arrive.

'Bad day at the office?' Mosley asked as Whitehead brusquely directed him to a sliding glass door and stifled a yawn.

'Bad couple of days is more accurate.'

A corridor with doorways on both sides and an elevator at its far end came into view. 'We've gotten ourselves a small bunch of kids who think they're badass gangsters and keep on trying to whip up a shitstorm in other neighbourhoods,' Whitehead explained. 'Four Armenians beat up on some Mexican kid walking home from a study session at the library. That's what started it all.'

'You expecting trouble this weekend?'

'We'll lay on extra patrols in the area and hope it scares them off,' Whitehead replied. He opened the vacant meeting room, made a mental note of the time and activated the air conditioning unit. 'The di Marcos should be here anytime soon.'

They exchanged small talk until the ringing telephone summoned Whitehead to meet the di Marcos in the lobby. Mosley observed his surroundings and decided the calm pale green décor and comfortable low chairs at one end were probably preferable to the starkness of a Northeast interview room. A Technivorm sat on top of a small kitchen unit at the room's furthest end and Mosley eyed the coffee maker with rampant newly-found envy, certain what it produced actually tasted like coffee – unlike the stuff he'd reluctantly developed a tolerance for back in his own domain.

Within a couple of minutes the door reopened and Mosley jumped to a standing position when a young woman and middle-aged man entered the room, their shared tension obvious. Neither appeared to have enjoyed a great deal of sleep over the past two nights, and shadows almost as dark as her hair swept around the hazel eyes Galina had obviously inherited from her father. Whitehead smiled at the di Marcos, pointed to a pair of adjacent chairs and proceeded to introduce Mosley and explain his role to date in the investigation.

Bruno narrowed his eyes. 'This is a great opportunity for you to pin something on my daughter.'

'We have no evidence Galina was aware of Kratz's activities,' Whitehead replied. 'Unless any suddenly appears to suggest otherwise, we'll treat her like another innocent victim.'

Mosley remained silent and observed Galina. She appeared younger than her twenty-one years, her tailored shift dress and jacket more appropriate for someone much older. Her hands balled in her lap and she hunched forward to stare at the floor, avoiding all eye contact.

Shame... or guilt?

Whitehead finished running through the various formalities, including that Galina had attended of her own free will and was permitted to leave the station at any time. A surveillance camera blinked steadily in its elevated location beside a double wall cupboard, from where it recorded both audio and visual footage.

Mosley distributed four glasses of water, took his seat and turned to Galina and Bruno. 'As you're aware, Detective Whitehead invited me here. Kratz is also responsible for a number of homicides within LAPD's jurisdiction, so anything you can tell us, no matter how small or insignificant it seems, could help my team to locate and apprehend him.'

Galina raised her gaze to meet Mosley's. 'I didn't know,' she whispered, her voice cracking on the final word. Fat tears rolled down her pallid cheeks and loud sobs filled the room as Bruno wrapped his arms around his daughter. Whitehead pushed a box of tissues across the low table and watched Galina take a handful. She wiped her eyes, then offered a weak smile of gratitude to the two detectives.

'Take your time and gather your thoughts,' Whitehead said. 'We want you to talk us through your interactions with Kratz. Start from the beginning and, if you need to stop at any point, take whatever time you need.'

Galina took a tentative sip of water and set down her glass. 'Okay, I'm ready.'

Whitehead smiled and cleared his throat. He confirmed that her family had resided on Rimcrest Drive since 1995; their move from Pasadena due to her father's need to be closer to his newly-created law firm's Los Angeles-based office. Galina and a number of neighbourhood kids had quickly made friends, although the call of college meant most had recently moved away. She'd chosen to stay close to home now she'd achieved an acceptance at UCLA's law school, which she hoped would assist with future legal networking in the city.

Galina saw Bruno's proud smile and grabbed another tissue. 'One day I'd hoped to be as successful as my dad,' she said, her voice wavering.

'You still can be, honey.' Bruno squeezed her hand and a fresh round of tears fell. 'Me and Mom will always help however we can.'

Whitehead nodded. 'I guess it's lonely for you, now so many of your friends have moved out of town?'

She sniffed and considered the suggestion. 'My cousins live nearby. We sometimes hang out together.'

He nodded again. 'Were you aware of Konrad Kratz's real identity?'

'As in being a movie star?' she queried, uncertain of the question's intended meaning. Whitehead nodded and her shoulders fell in relief. 'He's like, *king* of the A list but I never obsessed over him like some girls did. For the first year he lived there he didn't pay a whole lot of attention to me. We'd say *'hi'* if we saw each other out front or over the garden wall, and whenever he came home from New York he was always happy to sign autographs for my friends.'

Mosley had listened intently up to this point. 'When did things change?' he asked.

'It's hard to say,' Galina replied. She pursed her lips and stared up at the ceiling. 'Maybe after a year? Dad bought a car for me so I could come straight home from classes, study and have time to relax in the evening. We then finished for summer so, apart from some assignments and my reading list for the next semester, I had plenty of spare time while waiting to start work experience. I'd managed to arrange three weeks at a local law firm.'

Whitehead nodded and ran through the rest of the family's daily routine, which more often than not involved Bruno working late at the office. By all accounts, Yelena also put in long hours at the small exclusive boutique she co-owned in Glendale, apart from at the weekend when two assistants ran the store.

Galina went on to explain how she'd become friendlier with Kratz during her second semester at UCLA. Whenever possible she'd take full advantage of an empty house and study at home, before allowing herself time to relax in the pool. Kratz had been on a week's leave from *H.O.S.T.A.G.E.* and they'd started talking over the wall. She sighed heavily, the memories obviously adding to her discomfort. 'It was totally innocent and he didn't make a move on me. I was there for like an hour and then came home. He was a nice guy. He told me about the show and asked about my ambitions for the future.'

Whitehead set down his empty glass. 'How often did you and Kratz spend time together?'

'Maybe once a week at first. He'd sometimes come over to our house.'

'You never thought it strange this only happened if you were home alone?' He watched her shrug. 'And, when did the nature of your meetings change?'

'A few weeks later,' she replied. 'I went shopping with my cousin and I bought a new bikini. Konrad commented how nicely it showed off my figure. It was early evening and he asked what time my family would be home, so I said I didn't know and he asked if I'd eaten. I said I hadn't and he invited me for dinner.' She noticed the detectives exchange a glance. 'It wasn't anything special, just pizza and salad and a glass of wine.'

Bruno took a sharp intake of breath and cracked his knuckles. 'Son of a bitch!'

'Did he regularly offer you alcohol?' Whitehead asked.

'Sometimes. If I declined he never forced the issue.'

Mosley reclined in his chair. 'Had you developed feelings for him by then?'

Galina chewed her bottom lip. 'Looking back, I was flattered by the attention and that he paid me compliments. I assumed he was just being polite.'

'How did the, for want of a better word, *relationship* develop?' Whitehead asked. 'Did you sense he wanted more than what was then on offer?'

'In retrospect, yeah,' she whispered. 'I guess it was nice to have a… friend to talk to. I enjoyed hearing about the Hollywood side of things too. Konrad told me about movies and TV shows he'd been in, and showed me a couple of the awards he'd won. I thought hearing a little of how the industry worked from the inside may help my future career.'

Mosley narrowed his eyes. 'When did you start sleeping together, Galina?'

'If I ever get my hands on that bastard, I'll kill him,' Bruno interrupted, his eyes blazing.

'Galina?' Mosley repeated.

A crimson blush spread across her cheeks. 'It was one Friday evening. Dad was meeting one of his celebrity clients and Mom was out for dinner and a show with an old college friend. Mikhail was supposed to come home, then phoned around seven to say he'd be staying at Stevie's place.' She rolled her eyes. 'That's his *brother from another mother*'.

'Were you worried about spending the evening alone in the house?'

She shook her head at Whitehead. 'There's a top-of-the-line security system and, to be honest, I liked the idea of having a quiet night in doing what I wanted. It was getting dark when I woke from a nap and decided to hit the pool. I'd just placed my towel on the lounger when Konrad leaned over the wall and asked where the rest of the family was. I told him and he said he'd cooked up way too much pasta and I should come over, rather than eat alone.'

'Did he force you into anything you didn't feel comfortable with?'

She shook her head again, more emphatically this time. 'We shared a bottle of wine during the meal and I relaxed, like this was how women my age were supposed to spend a Friday night. I've devoted so much time to study and turned down dates with boys. I knew we weren't a couple, but it was nice. We carried our plates to the dishwasher and some cheesy song came on so we started dancing and Konrad grabbed my hand. I was laughing as I was getting real dizzy, I'm not used to having more than one glass of wine. I overbalanced, he caught me to stop me falling and then it was like some crappy rom-com. We stared into each other's eyes, and then we started kissing.'

'You didn't think to break it off?' Whitehead asked, struggling not to sound judgmental.

'I don't have a whole lot of experience,' Galina replied. She averted her eyes from his stare. 'He was a good kisser. We stayed in the kitchen for what was like forever, and then he asked if I wanted to go upstairs.'

'Is this the only time you and Kratz had sex?'

'No,' she said and dropped her head, her shame increasingly obvious. 'I thought he liked me, he'd tell me how beautiful I was and…' She resumed eye contact with Whitehead. 'My friends say how selfish their boyfriends are in bed, but Konrad wasn't. I put it down to him being older. It didn't bother me he'd had lots of girlfriends, he never made me feel inexperienced.'

'Did you consider pregnancy?'

'I've suffered from menstrual problems for years, so I take the pill,' she replied. 'We never used anything else. Then my period was late and I kept getting queasy. It didn't take a doctor to figure it out. I drove to Burbank because nobody knows me there and bought a pregnancy test. When I saw those two lines…'

'How long did it take you to decide to keep the baby?' Mosley asked, the question prompting Bruno to thump his chair's armrest.

She scowled at him. 'There was never a question that I wouldn't.'

'And when did you tell Kratz?'

'A couple of days later,' she replied. 'He said he'd provide financially if I kept his identity a secret. I needed to think of the baby's future, so I agreed he'd give me cash each month to pay into the baby's bank account.'

Galina eagerly gulped what little remained of her water before Whitehead resumed his questioning. The not-so-happy couple had generated their cover story within an hour on a sunny afternoon, the garden wall assuming a mediator's role. Galina recalled how she'd told people she attended a friend's party at an LA nightclub one Friday night and then stayed over at her place. 'It wasn't really my scene,' she said, concluding the tale. 'I didn't have to study and I thought I should be partying at my age. Konrad suggested I eventually tell my parents I got wasted on spirits and vaguely remembered sleeping with a guy, but not who he was.'

'I didn't believe it,' Bruno said in response to Whitehead's unspoken question. 'She ain't no whore.'

Mosley returned his gaze to Galina. 'Did you know that Kratz's identity was fake?'

'Konrad barely mentioned his childhood,' she said matter-of-factly.

'And you didn't know he's a serial killer?'

'Like it's something he'd tell her across the dinner table,' Bruno angrily interrupted.

Whitehead didn't allow Bruno the chance to continue. 'Has Kratz seen the baby?'

'Yeah, Konrad brought over a gift shortly after she was born. Anya was six weeks premature. She was a good weight and feeding fine so the hospital let us leave when she was five days old. He held her, but didn't really seem interested. It's sad. Even though she'll never go without what she needs, it would have been nice for her to know her daddy.'

Bruno pointed at a nearby wall clock. 'Are we done?'

'For now,' Whitehead replied. He reached into his jacket's uppermost pocket and handed a small business card to Galina. She traced a finger along its uppermost edge and listened to him thank for her cooperation, followed by the offer for her to call him anytime she needed.

****

8.39pm – BST
Blackpool, England

Steve Garner pressed a soft kiss against the top of his wife's bowed head. 'We can always leave this for tomorrow,' he whispered, wondering if he'd made an unwise decision to drive Charlotte to the police station, rather than accept the offer of a home visit.

Charlotte shook her head before dabbing her nose with a ragged tissue. 'I need to find out who did this to him, he deserves justice.'

He glanced at the large wooden doors which led inside the police station. 'I know, love.'

'I was going to tell him and Mum about the baby in a couple of weeks.' A fresh flood of tears streamed down Charlotte's mottled cheeks, her eyes puffy from hours of grief. 'He'd have been so happy; he always wanted to be a grandad.'

Steve sighed and kissed her head again, feeling helpless. 'Have you heard anything more from your mum?'

'Sid phoned a bit ago,' she replied and felt one of Steve's hands move to the small of her back. 'They've cleared the tanker and they've still got five miles to go 'til they get out of that bloody tailback.'

'Come on, let's go inside,' he suggested, keen to get Charlotte home as soon as possible.

He pushed the doors open, crossed to where Eddie Pell was standing beside the reception desk and nodded a greeting. Pell pushed himself away from the counter and shook Steve's hand, then cautiously put an arm around Charlotte's shoulders.

'We'll find out who did this,' he said. 'In spite of initial appearances, we're certain it was staged.'

Charlotte frowned whilst Pell led them to a small suite of interview rooms. 'Initial appearances?' she echoed.

'At first sight, things were contradictory to both the physical and verbal evidence we've recovered over the course of today,' Pell said. He held open the door to the family room where a child's wooden activity centre occupied one corner, its swirling metal loops festooned with brightly coloured beads providing an instant reminder of the grandchild Roger would never meet.

Charlotte slumped wearily into the nearest chair. 'You're saying his death appeared suspicious? Did some bastard kill my dad and try to frame him for something?'

Pell hesitated when Irwin entered the room and offered a strained smile to the couple. 'We think the killer tried to cover up *why* they murdered your father.'

She shook her head, as if trying to remove the memories of the past six hours, and her pained eyes looked straight at Pell. 'I don't understand,' she whispered.

'There's no way to sugar-coat this. We found your father handcuffed to the headboard. Now, however hard this is, I need you to hear me out.' Pell watched Steve's hand cover hers and squeeze tightly. Charlotte nodded at

Pell, the action barely perceptible. 'You're aware the postman raised the alarm?' She nodded again. 'A pair of uniformed officers gained entry and located your father in the largest bedroom at the front of the house. Like I previously said, your father had been cuffed to the bed–'

'How did that kill him?' Steve interrupted, worried about how hearing the uncompromising details of her father's death could affect Charlotte and their unborn child.

Pell took a deep breath. 'He suffocated when his airways were obstructed by multiple layers of clingfilm.'

Irwin leaned forward. 'There's no delicate way to put this. We think the killing was staged to imply your father was engaged in some sordid little affair, although the fact the property was broken into heavily contradicts this.'

Charlotte shook her head emphatically. 'Dad would never cheat on Mum. They'd been married forty years. They may have bickered over silly little things from time to time, but they adored each other.

'He was a great bloke,' Steve added. 'A real character.'

Irwin ran his hands through the greying hair at his temples. 'Can you think of anyone who'd want to tarnish his reputation *and* kill him?'

'There'd been a run-in with a tenant he'd served notice on.'

Pell raised his brows, his interest piqued. 'When was that?'

'A week or so ago,' Steve replied, taking a moment to replay their conversation in his head. 'He mentioned it in passing at the pub and hadn't said anything since.'

Irwin hurriedly wrote a trio of bullet points on a notepad, then returned his attention to Steve. 'Have you got any idea why he served notice on this tenant?'

'Said he needed to raise some capital.'

'Was he in financial difficulty?' Pell asked. His mind processed the various permutations this latest piece of information suggested. 'That's if he'd admit it.'

Steve shrugged. 'Nothing I'm aware of. He did mention an investor who'd suddenly appeared after years of no contact. Apparently he wanted a swift return on his investment.'

Irwin twirled the pen between his fingers. 'Do you know anything more about the investor?'

'Apart from that he's American, no.'

Pell shrugged at Irwin and pointed to his notepad. 'We need to focus on the disgruntled tenant for the time being. One neighbour mentioned a man visited Roger a week or so ago, shouted abuse and threatened him. Unless proved otherwise, we'll assume this is the tenant. Once he's named, send someone round with a photo and ask the neighbour to verify whether or not that was the guy.'

Irwin nodded. 'I'll get on the case this evening.' He turned to Charlotte and tried to soften his expression. 'Did your father keep property rental records?'

'I assume so,' she replied. 'They'd be at the house if he did. I don't really know much about Dad's businesses, he always made a point of keeping work and family separate.'

'We'll head over later and have a look,' Pell said. He broke into an awkward smile and patted Charlotte's hand. 'Listen to me, love. I don't give a flying fig about your dad's businesses or whether he had his fingers in a couple of extra pies. My objective here is to catch and jail the person who did this. I have your number, and victim support will contact you in the next day or so. If you think of anything else, here's my mobile number. Call me any time – day or night.'

Her hand shook when she accepted the business card. 'Thank you, Eddie.'

'What about your mother?' Irwin asked. He held the door open and watched the couple shuffle through. 'She shouldn't be left alone.'

Charlotte leaned against a wall in the corridor and suddenly realised how tired she felt. 'Mum's cousin Sid is driving her straight to the pub; we're not expecting them for a couple more hours.'

'Unless she insists, we'd prefer to leave interviewing her 'til tomorrow.' Pell jangled the car keys in his pocket, anticipating a swift return to Keys Drive. 'She'll be mentally and physically exhausted by the time she gets to your place. If you give us a ring, one of us will drive over to talk to her – if she's up to it.'

Steve shook Pell's and Irwin's hands. Charlotte stared at the main doors, the urge to return home now threatening to completely overwhelm her.

Pell nodded at Steve as he carefully guided Charlotte's hunched frame out of the building. 'Take care, both of you.'

Chapter 32 – Saturday 22nd August 2009

4.42am – PDT
Kingsbury, Nevada

Anna's view remained unchanged long after she'd opened her eyes. A total absence of light around the drapes increased the uncertainty surrounding why she'd woken and she held her breath, listening for Sam's low regular exhalations. Would the nightmares he'd endured in the months since the accident continue to resurface now they'd moved to Tahoe? The *tick-tock* of their back-up alarm clock filled the room and her hand cautiously reached out to discover cold rumpled sheets where he'd fallen asleep earlier. She frowned and debated whether she should find Sam, her dilemma heightened by the worry he'd assume she was deliberately checking up on him.

Especially today, of all days.

Anna pushed the comforter down the bed and winced when cool air collided with her skin; the immediate puckering confirmation that the time had definitely arrived to pack away her summer pyjamas. She lifted the fluffy robe she'd purchased in Reno from a hook behind the bedroom door and knotted its belt around her waist. Maybe she'd buy some slippers next time and succumb to the *old age* Sam sometimes teased her about, a reference to their two-year age gap that worked in his favour.

Beyond the bedroom door, a faint glow unexpectedly illuminated the corridor. Anna held her breath and listened to the heavy silence emanating from the children's rooms. She ascended the wooden staircase, her bare feet silent on its cold surface, then realised the light she'd seen originated from the kitchen. It bathed the lounge area, its warm rays diluted. She rounded the nearest couch and sighed in relief when she saw

Sam slumped against the cushions, his mouth gaping whilst he slept. Anna noticed an empty mug on the nearby coffee table and narrowed her eyes as she picked it up and sniffed the faint aroma of whisky.

Anna touched him on the arm. 'Sam,' she whispered. 'It's time to wake up.'

He stirred and attempted to withdraw from her touch.

'Are you okay?' She shook him again. 'You fell asleep on the couch.'

Now open, his eyes followed an uncoordinated path around the room. 'That's ironic. I came up here because I couldn't sleep.'

She nodded, surprised he seemed oblivious to the room's temperature through his t-shirt and lightweight sweatpants.

'What time was that?'

'Not sure,' Sam replied. He offered Anna a weak smile and blinked repeatedly as he glanced at the clock. 'I didn't want to wake you, so I thought I'd try the hot milk and whisky trick.' He looked at the empty mug. 'It obviously worked too well this time.'

She sat beside him and pulled her robe tighter against the chilly air. 'What kept you awake this time?'

'Nothing specific.' He shrugged and turned away. 'Typical it's happened at the weekend. You never know, the kids might've let us have a lie in for once.'

Anna reached for his hand. 'Sam, I know what date it is.'

'Date?' he echoed and stared at the shadows stretching across the smooth floor.

'A year ago.' She paused, unsure how to continue. 'It's been getting to you.'

'What do you mean?' The fragile timbre in his voice told Anna she was correct. 'I'm fine, honestly. Still getting used to our new surroundings, I suppose.'

She shook her head and squeezed his hand again, more firmly this time. 'You tense up whenever August 22nd is mentioned on TV or on the radio and you think you're doing a great job of keeping your expression neutral, but that kind of makes it more obvious. There's the dream you had a couple of nights ago...'

'I'll be fine with you and the kids today.' He swallowed to clear the lump lodged in his throat. 'Picnic in the forest, then–'

'You should have spoken to me,' she interrupted. 'You should have said how you feel.'

'You've been sucked into this mess through no fault of your own; I didn't want to burden you again.'

Anna's eyes widened and tears pricked her eyelids. 'You're not a burden. How can you even say that?'

'You reckon?' Sam muttered. He withdrew his hand from Anna's and clenched it into a tight fist.

'Sure I do. You've faced some horrific stuff over the past twelve months and yet here you are.' She stroked his shoulder, where tension threatened to burst through the T-shirt's thin fabric. 'With your family, doing a job you love.'

He squeezed his eyes shut. 'It's like he's won. Whatever the hell his objective's been all these years, he's finally achieved it.'

'He'll *never* win,' she said, the amount of venom lacing the three simple words surprising him.

'You know what one of the worst things was? Besides the way I treated you and the kids, that is.'

'Honestly, it wasn't so bad.' She linked her fingers between his. 'Go on, tell me.'

He sighed and heard the air shudder during its expulsion. 'Losing over a week of my life and not being able to remember pretty much anything from the ICU, apart from being in pain. It still really gets to me.'

Anna bit her lip. 'I told you everything I could.'

Sam recognised the hurt in her voice. 'It wasn't enough. I needed more so I went to the hospital.'

'In New York?' Anna sounded surprised. 'You never told me you'd been.'

'I arranged to visit Bellevue for an afternoon during the first week in July.' He paused to compose his thoughts. 'He stole part of my life, everything from that time was pretty much just a blank. I thought I didn't want to know, but I've been lying to myself.'

She thought back to a conversation they'd shared in Breckenridge three months earlier. 'Who did you speak with?'

'A paramedic who treated me in the ambulance, and doctors and nurses from the ICU. They were amazing. I think part of it was seeing me return physically healthy.' He forced a sad smile. 'I suppose that side of things must be nice for them.'

'You want to tell me?' Anna whispered. 'Fill in some of *my* blanks?'

Sam frowned. 'You remember it all.'

She shook her head. 'Not the parts I wasn't there for. Sure, they gave me background information, but very little before you arrived at the hospital.'

He swallowed to lubricate his dry throat. 'The paramedic responsible for most of my treatment at the scene is called Jane Walton. Her team arrived in the ten minutes following the crash and I was unconscious until the fire department pretty much finished cutting me out, then I came round for a short time. She said she'd been most worried about my breathing. I was struggling and getting weaker, then I asked for you.' Sam tilted his head back and blinked rapidly. 'She reckons I must've thought I was dying.'

Anna saw unshed tears glisten and put an arm around his waist, not knowing how else to offer comfort. 'Why did she say that?'

'I told her...' He paused to wipe his eyes. 'I told her to tell you that I loved you. Apparently she told me I'd have to do it myself.'

She kissed Sam on the cheek. 'It took some time, but you did eventually.'

'Did you know my parents came to see me?' He watched Anna nod. 'They flew in a couple of days later, but I was on a ventilator and too heavily sedated to respond to them at first. They pumped me full of drugs for days.' He sighed and chewed the inside of his cheek. 'I wish they hadn't, because that's why I can't remember.'

'They tried to rouse you in the unit after you'd been unconscious for three days,' Anna said. 'You became so agitated and tried to pull out your tubes more than once. The first day you woke up was horrific; you had flashbacks and dislodged an arterial line. They needed to sedate you for your own safety.'

'Were you there?'

Anna nodded again. 'I felt so helpless because I couldn't calm you. I had to step back and leave the medical team with you while you were so distressed.' She gripped his clammy hand. 'It was terrifying.'

'I'm so sorry I put you through that.'

'You've nothing to be sorry for.'

Sam picked at a bitten nail. 'I spoke to the main nurse responsible for my care. Do you remember Sandy?'

Anna pictured the petite Jamaican woman and nodded.

'She said it was so good to see the *real* me, even if she did give me a bear hug which nearly re-broke my ribs.'

'That'll be revenge,' Anna said, her smile conveying genuine amusement.

Sam raised his eyebrows, worried what he'd hear next. 'What do you mean?'

'She didn't share what happened the first time she persuaded you to eat some cereal?' Anna smiled, not sure whether to feel guilty when a flash of horror crossed his face. 'You *really* hated having that tube through your nose and begged them to take it out. They tried you on liquids and Jell-O and you were fine with those. The heavier stuff didn't sit well at first and Sandy learned the hard way.'

'Bless her, she left out that grim little detail,' he replied, wondering what else hadn't been mentioned to him. 'Why can't I remember that? It must've been a few days later.'

'By then the doctors were happier with your progress. There'd been big improvements in your breathing and they said you were unlikely to develop complications. You were still in a lot of discomfort from all the fractures and they'd given you some pretty heavy duty painkillers, so you were confused a lot of the time. Plus, you'd gotten one hell of a bang to the head; it wasn't unusual during the first week for you to forget things minutes after they'd happened.' She smiled as Sam processed the information. 'What else did you and Sandy speak about?'

'She showed me round the unit, explained which machines I'd been on and what they did. She also gave me the patient diary I'd refused to accept. They'd kept it on the advice of Joe Studdert, in case I changed my mind.'

'Perhaps you can show it to me?' Anna suggested, hoping he'd open up further.

'It's in my bottom drawer back in Denver. It's like looking at a different person...' Sam's voice tailed off.

'What's the matter?' she asked, shocked to see fresh tears fall down his cheeks.

His breath caught in his throat. 'In the nurse's office,' he replied in a shaky voice. 'I showed her my all scars: my arm, my ankle, the big one down my front, the one on my head. Even where they put in the chest tube and I tore out that arterial line.'

263

Anna traced her finger over the skin above his left wrist. 'They're barely visible now.'

'Sandy said I should be proud of them; that they show I'm a *survivor*.'

'She's right. You won.'

He shook his head. 'So why do I feel like I've failed? That a whole year later nothing's changed?'

'Don't you see that you've succeeded?' Anna replied. 'You suffered all those serious injuries and returned to a demanding job under stressful circumstances. Your baby son's face lights up whenever he sees you, and his big sister probably thinks you can walk across the surface of Lake Tahoe.' Her thumbs brushed away the last damp trails from his cheeks. 'And, your wife thinks she was the luckiest woman alive when she worked late on a case one evening and bumped into a certain federal agent on *that* corridor.'

Sam smiled. 'She must be one hell of a crazy woman.'

She ruffled his hair. 'Almost definitely, especially *this* early on a Saturday morning.'

****

5.56pm – BST
Hutton, Preston, England

Detective Dave Sanderson offered another round of effusive thanks as he shook hands in turn with Mandy Hall and Rob Armitage. 'We're grateful you gave up your time to come in,' he continued, holding open the door. 'I appreciate it's a long time ago, but the information you've supplied certainly suggests Umpleby could've been responsible for Grace Winterburn's death.'

Rob returned his smile. 'If we can be of assistance again, don't hesitate to let us know. And,' he added in a lowered voice, 'we know: Mum's the word.'

His companion nodded. 'The press won't hear anything from us.'

'Back to the grindstone soon is it, folks?' Sanderson enquired.

'Yeah, a week on Thursday,' Mandy replied, rolling her eyes. 'Never mind, only a couple more years to retirement and becoming a lady of leisure.'

'Sounds good,' Sanderson agreed as he passed their *Visitor* badges to the receptionist. 'Well, enjoy the rest of your holidays.'

Deep in thought after both teachers' unanimous and emphatic assurances they would do, Sanderson watched them walk across the car park towards a silver Honda Civic. From their conversation, he knew they'd commenced their teaching jobs at Crettington County Primary School on the same day in September 1977; both now entering the twilight of their careers at the same institution.

Sanderson glanced at the wall clock behind the receptionist's desk and wondered how long it would take to transcribe the interview. His stomach contracted when he entered the communal office, urging him to complete the task and get home in time for the hotpot his wife had promised to make, complete with the red cabbage she'd recently taken to pickling. 'Christ, have none of us got homes to go to?' he commented.

Phelan wrinkled her nose. 'Seems that way.'

'You still working on those park rapes?' he asked, knowing Phelan had chosen to work that weekend in lieu of taking a day's holiday for her sister's wedding the following week.

Phelan nodded and watched Sanderson disappear behind a partition wall. 'The lab reckons they'll be able to extract DNA profiles from semen samples recovered from the victims. Their descriptions of the guy match, and obviously if we could link DNA to the cases it'll make it easier for us to either eliminate or convict suspects.'

Sanderson reappeared and set down the last two slices of the Battenberg he'd brought in that morning. 'Let's just hope the bastard's in the database.'

'Indeed.' Phelan stretched out her aching shoulders. 'So, what did you glean from Armitage and Hall?'

'They confirmed Umpleby was, and I quote, *'An evil little shit'.'* Sanderson laughed as she gathered the empty mugs from their desks. 'They've also been told explicitly under no circumstances to discuss this with family or friends, let alone the media.'

Phelan sucked air through her teeth and scowled. 'They're like bloody vultures. My sister got accosted on Fishergate yesterday. Folks are being randomly stopped in the hope they'll reveal a juicy snippet.' She stopped to cover her mouth and concluded the yawn by forcing an exaggerated sound through the back of her nose. 'What else did those teachers say?'

Sanderson returned to the kitchenette and dropped a teabag into each mug. 'Let's start by saying they don't remember him for the right reasons, and he stood out for being different from day one. Mandy Hall recalled being quite freaked out by him on his first day. She couldn't explain why at the time.'

'What about Rob Armitage?'

'He taught him further up the school and said he was the same – but bigger.' Sanderson carefully poured boiling water into the cups and laughed nervously at thoughts of his own primary school experiences at the hands of a particularly unpleasant classmate. 'The other kids didn't like him. They'd try to stay away from him.'

Phelan nodded. 'Was he a bully?'

'Just generally unpleasant. According to Armitage he was a bit of a bastard to a kid called Sam Bury. The typical victim type – shy, quiet, hard worker.'

'He's been in the *Evening Chronicle* a fair bit over the years,' Phelan commented. 'He's some sort of brainiac who ended up studying in the States and now heads an elite FBI unit'.

'The boy done good,' Sanderson replied, his admiration obvious. 'Can't see him wanting to come back here in a hurry.'

Phelan frowned and noticed the faint beginnings of a headache. 'Why did Umpleby specifically target Sam Bury?'

'Easy pickings, I suppose. Umpleby wasn't thick, far from it. The then head teacher wondered if the kid had learning difficulties because he hadn't made much progress. An educational psychologist assessed him and found he wasn't far off Sam's ability levels. Perhaps he perceived Sam as a threat, although I can't see why. From what they said, Sam was a completely different type of boy.'

Phelan smiled and gratefully accepted her drink. 'Did they remember Grace Winterburn?'

Sanderson cupped his hands around the welcome warmth of his mug, a treasured Father's Day gift hand-painted by his young daughter. 'They remembered the woman and the circumstances leading to her being on supply cover for the best part of a term. Apparently she didn't like the kid and called him *creepy*.'

'Was there any animosity between Winterburn and Peter? Did they ever have any sort of run-in?'

'She apparently tried to help him with his writing. Peter had difficulties gripping his pen that affected his ability to write neatly and for long periods of time. From what Armitage remembered it wasn't a success, and he resisted all suggestions of change. Winterburn eventually gave up; said it wasn't worth waiting for him to blow a gasket at any moment.'

'Interesting,' Phelan replied. She massaged her neck to relieve the tension generated by an afternoon hunched at her computer, enjoying this all-too-brief respite from a never-ending avalanche of cold cases begging for closure. 'Did they remember her last day?'

'Nothing specific. Based on the usual way of bidding farewell to departing staff, they said they'd probably have had a little gathering in the staffroom at the end of school and then gone home. Next thing they heard was she'd been killed in a car crash.' Sanderson picked up a colourful piece of cake. 'I gave them my card and said if they remembered anything else to ring me immediately.'

'Good work. While we can't definitely say he's responsible, in his eyes the kid probably had motive. Why kill her though?'

'To see if he could. If he succeeded – bingo! In his eyes he'd never again need to tolerate people giving him shit. Have you seen the file we received from the States?' Sanderson leaned forward and offered a wry smile. 'So you realise if he's capable of cold-bloodedly killing his parents, he's more than capable of this.'

'He was seventeen when his parents died. This happened around his tenth birthday.'

'Same method, probably the same logic,' Sanderson continued, his tone devoid of emotion. 'What we're worried about, both here and stateside, is what he'll do to evade capture. We don't have a clue where he is or what he looks like, but if he feels like his cover is ready to be compromised you can bet the body count will rise.'

****

6.14pm – BST
Terminal 5, Heathrow Airport, England

The man's sharp gaze raked the departure lounge from behind thick-framed spectacles. A lightly tanned hand slid into a side pocket of the loose-fitting combat pants he'd chosen to wear for the flight and touched the penultimate US passport in his collection, offering its silent reassurance that his plans were still very much alive.

Two hours earlier, *Anthony Collins* managed to secure one of three remaining seats on a British Airways flight to New York's JFK airport. The quietly spoken American stated his need for an urgent return to Albany, where his father lay seriously ill in a hospital bed; his apparent sincerity meaning the young cashier accepted Collins' Bank of America credit card without question. He'd immediately checked in his battered silver trolley case and passed through security, ready to spend the last of his time in the UK sipping coffee and watching a steady succession of aeroplanes arrive and depart.

The gate number appeared on a blue information screen to his right and Konrad Kratz rose to his feet, swung a rucksack over his shoulder and prepared to board.

****

3.13pm – PDT
Sly Park, near Pollock Pines, California

Anna lay back on a large tartan rug spread out between two tall ponderosa pines and inhaled deeply. 'Smell that air,' she said, closing her eyes before she took another breath. 'You, sir, are a genius at finding these picnic spots. Tell me your secret.'

From his supine position beside her, Sam held John above his chest and listened to the baby's delighted giggles whilst he worked through a well-practised repertoire of comical facial expressions. 'Google,' he replied. 'The perfect tool for finding the kind of hike accessible to a three-year-old.'

Anna offered a thumbs-up to Angela's attempt to build a pyramid from discarded pine cones. 'She loves the outdoor life here, doesn't she?'

'I suppose it's similar in many ways to back home. In general, this move hasn't been too sharp a transition for her.'

Anna watched him lift John again. 'The little guy's quite content too.'

'The little guy doesn't feel particularly little at the moment,' Sam replied. He winced now the ache in his arm muscles had become too much to ignore. 'Have you been feeding him bricks again?'

'You know how much he loves mealtimes.' She laughed when Sam groaned and lowered John until he was seated between them. 'Someone's getting chunky these days.'

Sam arched an eyebrow. 'You'd better not be talking to the big guy.'

'I'll keep you guessing on that one.' They fell silent and smiled at how Angela paid close attention to her footing now she'd moved away from the paved footpath. 'Hey sweetie, did you win?' Anna asked.

Angela knelt between them and let John grab her hand. 'A little,' she said, eyeing a packet of Oreos poking out of the nearby chiller box.

'Only a little? Did something go wrong?'

She shrugged. 'They won't pile up if they get too high.'

'That's too bad. Will a cookie help, do you think?'

Angela nodded. 'Please.'

Anna reached for the packet. 'What are you looking at?' she asked.

'Daddy's foot has a line on it.' Angela tilted her head and stared intently at Sam's left ankle, where bare skin emerged from the canvas sneakers he'd recently bought. 'My foot doesn't have a line on it, so why does Daddy's?'

Anna's smile froze and she looked at Sam. 'Daddy's foot got badly hurt last year,' she said, keeping her tone light. 'He went to the hospital for some doctors to make it better.'

Angela pressed the faded silvery line. 'Does it hurt?'

'No, sweetie,' he replied, wondering whether she'd link it to the more obvious scars on his arm she'd asked about months earlier.

'Did you get it chasing a bad guy?'

Sam nodded and licked his lips. 'Yeah, I suppose I did.'

'You got better, Daddy.' She watched him nod. 'So you're stronger than the bad guy.'

'You reckon?'

'Yeah. My daddy's stronger than all the bad guys.'

Sam reached out and stroked her shoulder. 'I try my best, sweetheart. Really, I do.'

Angela jumped to her feet. 'I'm glad you're my daddy,' she said matter-of-factly and happily accepted the cookie from Anna. She returned to the small mound of pine cones and Sam turned to face where his daughter now played, unable to stop the dappled sunlight on the forest floor from blurring.

'Told you she thinks you're the best,' Anna whispered. 'And she's not the only one.'

'Today's been wonderful,' he replied, struggling to keep the emotion from his voice.

She smiled when he eventually turned to face her again. '*Today* isn't over. Later, I thought we'd head back by Kiva Beach, tire out the kids and eat dinner once they're asleep. I went to the store yesterday and bought something special.'

Sam nodded and closed his eyes against a soft breeze swirling between the gnarled tree trunks – and the vague unease which showed no signs of abating.

****

11.18pm – EDT
Brooklyn, New York

Maria Volonte enjoyed nothing more than having guests to stay at the modest Brooklyn brownstone she and her husband Vincenzo had shared for over forty years. This evening, the atmosphere in the house was reminiscent of when her two sons and one daughter lived there although, like in many families, college and employment opportunities meant all three had moved away from the city. She still missed them terribly over a decade later, even though they all made a concerted effort to return to their childhood home whenever possible.

An hour earlier, Maria and Vinnie had returned to the house after collecting Giuseppe Volonte and his fiancée Carmela from the airport. The eldest son of her husband's nephew had made the first visit to the city since his teens, following in the footsteps of his younger brother Franco, who attempted to visit on an annual basis. Maria viewed the younger members of their distant family in England almost as fondly her own children, and was always ecstatic to receive a telephone call asking whether a room would be available.

Maria's smile widened further when she heard a clink of glass and Vinnie's deep laugh resonating from the den next door. That's one of the first things I fell in love with,' she said, casting her mind back to the mid-sixties. 'Such a rich sound – and so soothing, like a good gelato.' She reached into a cupboard and beamed when she located the strictly rationed large bottle of olive oil purchased on the couple's last visit to Milan. 'And he had those puppy dog eyes and such a wicked smile. He still has them, you know. I think he always will.'

'So, he swept you right off your feet?' Carmela asked, a hint of a childhood spent in London still evident in her accent. 'Sounds like it's in the genes.'

Maria nodded and silently admired how Carmela's glossy chestnut hair reflected the light in the same way hers had done nearly half a century earlier. 'And how did you meet Giuseppe? Such a handsome boy, he reminds me of my Vincenzo at the same age.'

'We have mutual friends and we met at their wedding,' Carmela replied. She sipped the last of the wine in her glass. 'He was quite the charmer.'

'Yes, there's nothing like a wedding to inspire future love.' She patted Carmela on the arm and lowered her voice so it was barely above a whisper. 'Is this the honeymoon before the wedding?'

Carmela shook her head and grinned. 'Giuseppe wants our big day to be extra special. He knows it's always been a dream of mine to see New York, so where better to buy the perfect wedding dress?'

'Such a romantic boy,' Maria replied, her eyes twinkling. 'He must also buy something for himself to wear at your big day.'

'He said he'd sort out the suits back home; maybe go down to London with his friends one weekend.'

'Let him buy the ties here,' she suggested. 'Beautiful deep blue silk will bring out those stunning eyes of his.'

'Yeah, they're a gorgeous shade,' Carmela agreed. 'Quite unusual, they certainly caught *my* eye.' She giggled as she twirled the empty wine glass between her fingers.

Maria thought back to their trip to the airport and a flush of embarrassment travelled across her face. 'I nearly went to bear-hug a total stranger while we were waiting for you,' she said, blushing when she saw Carmela's dark eyebrows rise. 'This guy came through near the front of the arrivals line. Same height and build as Giuseppe, and with that lovely glossy black hair too.'

'So that's what Uncle Vinnie meant by you needing new glasses.'

'The silly old fool, he knows I only need them for reading,' Maria said. The obvious affection in her tone combined humour and exasperation. 'This guy had the exact same striking eyes, that's why I thought he was our boy. It's like I'd seen him somewhere already, and I just can't quite put my finger on it.'

Carmela finished arranging a large bowl of salad and added a handful of cherry tomatoes. 'Perhaps you *have* seen him before,' she suggested, wondering why Maria appeared so perturbed by a simple case of mistaken identity.

'Where would I recognise him from?' Maria asked, the idea she'd begun to develop the same senility as her eldest sister never far from her thoughts.

Carmela sprinkled fresh basil over the bubbling lasagne Maria had lifted from the oven. 'Well, one time I saw this guy in Manchester when I was in town shopping. He looked really familiar but I couldn't place him. It was only when I was round at my sister's place and she insisted on watching Coronation Street that I realised it was one of the show's actors.' Carmela picked up the salad bowl and placed it on the large wooden dining table. 'Perhaps you've seen him in town, or at the supermarket, or he just looks like someone famous,' she added, hoping to reassure Maria.

'I felt silly,' Maria replied, a hint of sadness audible. 'You get to my age and...' She gestured to the den to indicate it was time for the men to join them.

'There's no need to feel like that, Maria,' Carmela called across the room from the doorway. 'The answer will come to you when you least expect it. Now, let's get those two in here and then we can dish up.'

****

11.41pm – PDT
Kingsbury, Nevada

Shadows danced on the bedroom's walls as a flame fed by an almost spent tealight on the dresser repeatedly stretched to its maximum height and then dipped. Sam gazed around the room, its smooth plastered white walls intersected in places by wooden beams that gave a faint rustic air to the cabin's deceptively modern interior.

The continued sound of water from next door told of Anna's reluctance to tear herself away from the power shower's enjoyably sharp cascade. Sam smiled at her repeated requests he install the same model if they ever returned home to Golden. He considered joining her and his grin widened, knowing the large cubicle offered more than enough room for two.

The previous night's disrupted sleep and the more recent three bottles of beer during dinner meant a drowsy Sam soon closed his eyes and allowed his mind to drift. He replayed the day, only vaguely aware the shower had fallen silent; casting images onto the insides of his eyelids until Anna re-entered the room and pulled a towelling robe around her.

She vigorously rubbed a large towel over her hair to remove the excess moisture. 'I hope you're only entertaining nice thoughts,' she said. 'That smile could mean anything.'

He opened one eye and pulled the comforter over his chest. 'At present there's very little blood flowing to my brain, thanks to your insistence I eat half a cow two hours ago and then wash it down with half a brewery. I've got very little remaining capacity for any type of rational thought.'

She returned the towel to the shower room. 'That's a good thing.'

'Yeah, I suppose.' He listened to her open a drawer and pull out a new pair of three-quarter length dark blue pyjamas. 'Do you want me to set the heating to come on tomorrow morning?'

Anna let her robe fall to the floor and pulled on the pyjamas. 'Better not, else the place will be like an oven all day. It'll be okay once the kitchen warms upstairs during breakfast.' She twirled around and rubbed the soft cotton between her fingertips. 'You like?'

Sam raised his head. 'Mmmm, they do fit nicely. But, I've got to say I always prefer the look between you losing the robe and putting anything on.'

'Ass,' she said. 'Anyway, I'll bet you're wearing those Broncos shorts again.'

He turned onto his side and stifled a yawn. 'Who bought them for me?'

'Yeah, about that. At the time I didn't realise exactly how much I'd enjoy making you take them off.'

'Me neither,' he replied through a lazy grin.

She pulled back the comforter and rolled her eyes. 'I knew it.'

'I like wearing them, and I'm very comfortable right now.'

Anna climbed into bed and turned to face him. 'I prefer them on the floor.'

'It'll take a lot of persuasion for you to get rid of them tonight.'

She pulled on the tie running through his waistband. 'I can break hardened criminals, so you'll be a piece of cake.'

Sam closed his eyes again. 'We'll see.'

Anna's other hand moved to cradle his cheek, surprised to feel him turn his face away when her lips lightly brushed his. She moved her head away and looked at him in surprise. 'Sam?'

'I'm sorry,' he said, then rolled onto his back. 'It sometimes hits me at random times. I see a clock, calculate the time difference. You know, *this time exactly a year ago I was–*'

'You'd be coming out of surgery and I was struggling to hold it together while the flight prepared to take off. You're not the only one who's found today difficult.' She saw the raw hurt in his expression and shook her head. 'Oh Sam, I didn't mean it to sound like that.'

'I know.' He stared at the darkened ceiling and realised the tealight had burned itself out. 'I hate the way I forget you actually have to remember that day. I can't imagine what it's like to receive a phone call and then drop everything. Perhaps I shouldn't be bothered I remember nothing of the accident and little of what happened in ICU?'

'Of course it should, although it may have been beneficial in some ways,' Anna replied. She reached for his hand. 'You were in a lot of pain and unable to process what was happening. You were justifiably terrified so don't feel bad the staff made it easier for you.'

Sam nodded, pulling her closer. 'Thank you for today, for making it special.'

She draped an arm across Sam's waist and snuggled closer, knowing he'd relax and sleep would overwhelm them both within minutes. 'You don't need to thank me, Sam. For anything.'

Chapter 33 – Sunday 23rd August 2009

Although Konrad had gone a full day without sleep he felt invigorated; as if officially being on the run could activate energy stores he didn't realise he possessed. He'd left the bustling airport four hours earlier, disappearing into the thick humidity of a New York night to hail a cab to Manhattan...

Like any stereotypical tourist.

...before he merged into the unexpectedly large late-night Chinatown crowd. By chance, he'd spotted a dollar van ready to leave and bought himself a one-way ticket out of the city. The thirty-minute journey from Manhattan passed without incident, taking him to Sunset Park where he'd soon located a beat-up Honda Accord. Of course, as was now the norm, he'd no intention of using the car for any longer than he needed to, something its elderly owner might well have been grateful for.

If the old git had lived long enough after he'd been ambushed to learn of his beloved car's fate.

I-78 now curved around to the right, revealing an almost deserted stretch of highway ahead. Konrad's foot eased off the gas pedal and a sly smile crept across his face. His intention to permanently go off the grid lay somewhere over the darkened horizon and, if all went to plan, he'd reach his first destination a couple of hours before breakfast, dump the car and grab something to eat. The Honda eased past a solitary truck and his gaze blurred for a split second, converging the two lines of sickly yellow streetlamps into a central point in the distance.

The weight on his chest lifted as he sped towards freedom.

****

10.06am – BST
Blackpool, England

The town's main police station, a concrete island in the midst of a chip wrapper-infested ocean, was a depressing place to work and, regardless of which side of the law a person frequented, an even more depressing place to visit. Since Roger Mortimer's suspected murder, detective Eddie Pell's assignment to the case led to the long-serving detective dividing his time between Preston's police station and its coastal equivalent – something he wasn't overly enamoured by, especially whilst dodging a long line of wind-battered caravans on the M55.

Pell narrowed his eyes and glared across a scratched wooden table as Clive Porter's sausage-like fingers clenched into two fists.

'I know fuck all about Mortimer's death! I already told you pigs that last night when you came banging on my door. Don't really give a shit, mind you, but I can't claim any credit.'

Pell moved closer, rested his arms on the table and lowered his voice. 'So you didn't like the guy then?'

'What does it sound like?' Clive retorted, his face reddening.

'It sounds like you bore malice towards him, Mr Porter, and that you wished bad fortune upon him. You shouldn't speak ill of the dead, especially those who met a particularly unpleasant demise.'

Clive banged a calloused hand on the table, causing it to wobble in a disconcerting manner. 'He told me I had to get out of the house. I've got a wife and kids, you know.'

'What's the notice period?' Pell asked, already aware of the answer.

'You what?'

'How long were you given to find a new place?'

'Two months,' Clive grumbled. His voice returned to a more socially acceptable volume. 'Two poxy months.'

Pell ran a hand through his thinning grey hair. 'That's not unreasonable, especially when it's stated in bold print in your contract.'

'Contract?'

'The one you and your missus signed five years ago, a couple of weeks before moving in.'

276

Clive eyeballed the man opposite him and decided to steer the interview in a different direction. 'I didn't kill him.'

'You've got motive,' Pell countered. 'And, you're not acting like you're saddened by his family's loss.'

'I'm not, but I'm innocent.' He emitted a weary sigh and shook his head. 'I'd never have hurt him.'

'So why threaten him?'

'What the fuck are you going on about now?'

'You made a little house call to Chateau Mortimer on...' Pell checked the sheet of paper in front of him. 'The twelfth of August, and then a little over a week later he's dead.'

Clive narrowed his eyes, his posture tense. 'I've never been to his house.'

Pell watched a droplet of sweat trickle down Clive's left temple. 'You've been positively identified by two different neighbours.'

'That's bullshit.'

'That's evidence. Now, you can either cooperate with us in the hunt for whoever killed Roger, or we'll assume you're withholding information. Obviously, you realise this'll cause us to focus the spotlight firmly upon you. It's your choice.'

Clive glared across the table and Pell matched his expression. 'You must be really desperate to bump up your solved crime figures. It's almost the last week of the month – you pigs not met your targets yet?'

The feeble attempt at antagonism went ignored. 'You took a little trip to Mr Mortimer's house and threatened him. His son-in-law told us Mr Mortimer recently mentioned a house call from an angry soon-to-be ex-tenant, so we obtained his letting records and dug up some photos of all adult males living in the properties. Like I've already said, two of his neighbours positively identified you.'

'So that makes me a murderer?'

'Well, there *was* that kid you put in hospital. You surely must remember the eighteen-year-old who ended up in the Victoria for a week after you claimed he spilt your pint in that nightclub. It may have been over a decade ago, but old habits die hard, pardon the pun. Isn't that right, Clive?'

Clive banged the table again. 'Either charge me or release me,' he spat, his face an intense shade of scarlet.

'You're a person of interest in an on-going murder investigation,' Pell continued. 'Therefore you'll be released on bail. You'll need to attend this station every Sunday morning to sign the bail binder, 'til we either decide to charge you or release you.'

'Sunday's my only day off,' Clive replied, and his voice took on a whinging quality. 'I'm working six days a week to afford the rent increase at our new place.'

'You don't show and you'll find out what happens,' Pell said. He glanced at the doorway. 'I need to verify something with the Inspector, go through the full conditions of your bail and then I'll accompany you to your current home to remove your passport. It goes without saying you don't even think about trying to leave the country.'

Clive's mouth flapped open and shut like a goldfish's. 'We've booked a two-week holiday in Benidorm and we're flying out in exactly a fortnight.' His expression changed and Pell almost detected genuine sadness. 'We booked it months ago, after saving up for nearly a year. My boys are so excited.'

'You'd better hope your name gets cleared by then, hadn't you?' Pell replied. He pushed himself up off the chair, his interview with Clive Porter concluded.

****

7.45am – PDT
Kingsbury, Nevada

Anna turned onto her back and savoured the bed's warmth as she gradually became aware of the daylight brightening the bedroom. The previous day's emotional strain enhanced her reluctance to wake and there was also a lingering thought that, even after three years of motherhood, Sunday mornings should surely be devoted to lounging around in bed.

Now she knew sleep was unlikely to return, Anna opened her eyes to the minimum width required to read the electronic numbers on her alarm clock. It was later than she'd expected and she rolled onto her side, from where she watched a small bubble of saliva seep from one corner of Sam's mouth.

Her eyes widened at the sound of a faint voice and she quickly eased herself from the bed, pulling her robe around her shoulders on the short distance to the children's bedrooms.

'Mommy!' Angela mumbled, her voice thickened by sleep.

'What's the matter, sweetie?' Anna said, trying not to grin at the sight of her daughter sitting bolt upright in the middle of her bed. 'And, what *have* you done to your hair?'

Angela's small hands reached for the hand mirror her mother had picked up from a nearby shelf. 'I look funny,' she said, admiring the blonde frizz that stuck out at tangents. She placed the mirror on the nightstand and rubbed her eyes. 'Where's Daddy?'

'Daddy's fast asleep. We need to be quiet so he doesn't wake up.'

She frowned when a beam of sunlight penetrated the gap in the drapes. 'Why is he still asleep? It's daytime.'

'Daddy's new job is very busy, so he needs to rest today.'

'Is Daddy's new job forever?'

Anna hesitated. 'I don't know,' she replied. 'I guess we need to wait for him to finish working here. Don't you like living in this cabin?'

'Yeah, I get to play with Monty-cat every day,' Angela said brightly. When she spoke again her voice carried less cheer. 'There isn't a Monty-cat at the other house.'

'We can change that,' Anna replied, smiling at her daughter's puzzled expression. 'Daddy and I had a talk, and we think it would be nice to get our own family cat if we go back to our other house. You'd like that, right?'

'I get a Monty-cat?' Angela's face lit up, all traces of tiredness gone. 'Will it be mine?'

'I guess you can be its main care-giver,' Anna said, smiling at her daughter's happy expression. 'Now, what do you say to breakfast while the boys are still asleep?'

****

11.51am – PDT
San Fernando Road, Los Angeles, California

Five thousand miles separated Preston and Los Angeles, and considerably less separated the pair of interview rooms Clive Porter and Harry Lee occupied that day. Both were small, sparsely furnished spaces lacking any natural light; a door and a large one-way glass window providing the only breaks in their mud-coloured walls.

In the seven hours since Clive Porter reluctantly relinquished his passport, the interrogation of Harry Lee had got well underway. Mosley sensed Lee's resolve slipping and therefore insisted on conducting the interview, much to the other three detectives' relief. By taking on the *Good Cop* role, Mosley hoped Lee would interpret the interview to be nothing other than a polite, routine conversation. A lack of sleep, Lee's poor acting skills and the man's insistence he didn't know what the hell Mosley was talking about led to this resolution deserting him within minutes.

'Cut the crap, Harry,' Mosley snapped. His fist hit the table and he frowned heavily. 'You must have contacts in the illegal supply game. You do the passports and driver's licences, so who supplies the drugs?'

The forger licked his lips and stared at the one-way glass. 'How long you been a cop?'

Mosley snorted and shook his head in despair. 'How's the longevity of my career relevant here?'

'Do you have any idea how many drug dealers there are in LA?'

'I'm not talking about some meth-head douchebag on a street corner, Harry. I'm talking about the high-end niche, if I can call it that.'

'High-end?' Lee echoed. 'What do you mean by high-end?'

'Where cash doesn't just buy the product, it also buys confidentiality. There's plenty of people in this town who'd do anything to keep their drug habit out of the media. Do you have any idea how many are addicted to prescription painkillers? Money can't buy them from a doctor, but the dealers can get you anything for the right price.'

'Who's gonna buy that kind of shit? Most junkies just want the next high.'

'It's Tinseltown, you idiot. We have people here packing enough cash to wipe their asses with hundred dollar bills. Some dealers are fully aware of this and, for the right price, they'll provide the celebrity's drug of choice *and* keep their fat mouth shut.'

Lee shrugged. 'What's this got to do with me?'

'The guy we want to speak with is badly injured. He'd need strong painkillers and antibiotics at the very least.'

'He's a celeb?'

'You know he's a celeb,' Mosley countered, thoroughly exasperated by now. 'And assuming he didn't reveal that information, you damn well wondered where the endless fat stacks of Benjamins came from. Cash like that don't grow on trees.'

'So who is he? Some D-list wannabe movie star?'

Mosley paused to scribble on a note pad beside him and then slid it across the table.

Within seconds, Lee's defiant expression changed to one of confusion. 'Am I supposed to thank you for that?' he asked. 'What the fuck does *Jesus loves you!*' mean?'

'Consider it a polite warning, because you're looking at a long stretch in a correctional facility where that's not the kind of thing you want to hear.' Mosley narrowed his eyes and used the name's Spanish pronunciation when he repeated the phrase aloud. 'Of course, if you co-operate there's no reason I can't use my influence to arrange a shorter, marginally more humane prison experience for you.'

'You're offering me a deal?'

'I guess you could see it that way.'

Lee sighed. 'There's this guy,' he said, and within the next couple of minutes gave Mosley and his teammates behind the one-way glass a detailed list of Lennie Stringer's products. Gibson and Muñoz listened to Lee reveal the neighbourhoods in which Stringer resided and conducted his business, on the days he wasn't posing as a courier delivering fruit baskets in Beverley Hills.

'Now, that wasn't too difficult, right?' Mosley said in a jovial tone when Lee slumped against the chair.

'You're an asshole, you know! A walking, talking asshole!'

Mosley's indifferent nod registered in the apparently deserted area behind the viewing window. 'Take him back to the cells.'

****

4.09pm – PDT
I-15, near Victorville, California

Daniel Pell's obliviousness to the parched desert landscape meant he slept deeply, lulled by the purr of the Volvo's powerful engine. The car's temperature display rose to 111°F and a relieved Tony spotted a sign informing them a mere two miles separated them from their exit, knowing this also translated to being twenty minutes from home.

'Soon be back at the ranch,' he commented, grateful for Susie's offer to drive after the long hours he'd put in over the past five days. 'I can't say I'm sad to have arranged those two extra days off work.'

'Do you miss the city?' Susie asked. She glanced into the rear-view mirror at the highway they'd left behind, bleached by unrelenting sunlight.

'Do you?' Tony countered.

She thought for a moment and her gaze returned to the approaching off-ramp. 'It's fun to visit. Saying that, it's sure nice to get back to a quiet life.'

'I'll say.'

Susie flicked the turn signal and gently applied the brakes. 'It's kind of quiet out here. Maybe too quiet?'

'Most of the time I don't miss the city,' Tony replied. He fell silent and considered the matter. 'I suppose there's times it would be nice for Daniel to see more of your family. And, we'd probably be able to live closer to work.'

She chuckled. 'When it comes to LA, closer don't always mean faster. Anyway, Silver Lakes is such a nice place to raise Daniel.'

'True,' he agreed. 'Now Paco and my cousins are out of the game, it may be worth considering a move back in a couple of years.'

'You've been thinking about this?' Susie asked, unable to hide her surprise.

Tony reached for a bottle of water. 'Occasionally, though the past couple of weeks have influenced things.' He took a long swallow of the warm liquid. 'We don't have to go all the way back, there's always the Inland Empire. Take San Bernardino, for example. On a good run through it's just over an hour back to Glendale.'

'You're serious?'

He narrowed an eye. 'So you wouldn't be interested?'

'I guess one day; there's no rush for now. Build up some experience at work and enhance the résumés. Daniel seems happy, but he's getting older and I hope he'll want to go see the family more often. There's definitely more going on for kids in that area.'

'Perhaps we should start looking into it?'

The car came to a halt at an intersection and she giggled at his serious expression. 'Anyway, we'll need to be closer to my mom.'

'Why's that?'

'You think Daniel's going to be an only child forever?'

****

8.01pm – PDT
South Lake Tahoe, California

In defiance of it being a Sunday evening, the burger bar soon reached full capacity and large numbers of vacationers, attracted to the town and its stunning surroundings, mingled amongst the locals. Within the latter of these two groups, three men and two women of varying ages drew little attention as their easy conversation flowed across the table.

An earlier than planned arrival gave Sam enough time to sink a couple of cold beers before ordering something to soak up the alcohol. The apprehension he'd felt over an evening out soon faded and he scanned his surroundings more slowly this time. Apart from at work, he'd made a huge effort to lower his profile and avoid situations where he'd stand out. Thankfully, Tahoe's tourist hot-spot reputation meant few people appeared to notice another English accent, let alone pass comment on it.

He'd cautiously accepted the invite, knowing any refusal to attend may potentially alienate his new teammates and put him under the spotlight. Anna maintained her more positive outlook and she'd encouraged him to also enjoy the company of the people with whom he'd be working for the foreseeable future. Masters' offer had extended to all the agents who took it in turns to make the daily commute to Stateline from either Reno or Sacramento, although some of those living further afield reluctantly declined this time.

Masters had arrived at the cabin to pick up Sam thirty minutes prior to the agreed rendezvous time, leaving Anna to persuade an unwilling Angela to remain in bed. Much to the men's surprise, the two solid lines of westbound traffic on Lake Tahoe Boulevard moved faster than usual for that time on a Sunday evening. Sam carefully observed different groups of people strolling along the sidewalks and waiting at crosswalks; their happy faces and carefree demeanours the opposite of his ever-present tension.

Sam caught a glimpse of a large wooden clock above the bar and pulled out his wallet. He ignored Masters' stare and pointed at his companions' almost empty glasses. Memories of a similar evening in Denver nearly nine years earlier flooded back, causing Sam to wonder if he'd ever see his Colorado-based team again.

'I thought I'd warned you, Bury. Put that goddamn cash back in your pocket.'

'At the Academy, nobody mentioned thanking people for welcoming you to a new team constituted disobeying orders.' Sam noticed the slightest hint of a smile appearing around Masters' mouth and unconsciously copied the expression. 'And, if expressing my gratitude for what you've all done for me since my arrival will get me fired, at least give me enough time to enjoy another beer.'

Chapter 34 – Monday 24th August 2009

5.06am – EDT
Akron, Ohio

A faint glimmer of light appeared above the city and spread cautious fingers along nearby rooftops. It gained strength with every passing minute and pushed back the darkness, until only the hotel parking lot's furthest corners remained beyond its reach. Within the shadows, Konrad lifted his case and wrestled it into the trunk of a middle-aged Dodge Avenger. The area above his waist uttered a sharp complaint when he succeeded, a non-negotiable demand that he take time to rest, and he gently lowered the trunk's lid. This uncharacteristic concern was not borne out of consideration for sleeping guests; his thoughts purely centred on ensuring his exit from this industrial Midwestern city was as unremarkable as the vehicle enabling it.

An uneventful overnight drive from New York had brought Konrad to a dubious area of Akron's eastern fringes early the previous morning, where he'd dumped the stolen Honda a couple of blocks away from a used car lot. In an exchange reminiscent of the one earlier that summer in Utah, the lot owner's delight in selling one of the less desirable cars on the forecourt meant he'd readily offered to deduct one hundred dollars for a cash sale.

Satisfied the Dodge provided an adequate anonymity cloak, Konrad drove to the north side of town. He stopped to purchase a foot-long sub from a small neighbourhood deli and drop the Honda's keys into a storm drain, then continued to drive an aimless route past modest streets and strip malls; burning gas to kill time. A small motel's weather-beaten sign advertising vacancies for that night caught his attention and the persuasive qualities of an extra fifty bucks allowed him to check in early; the teenage receptionist apparently more bothered about her half-completed manicure than the family-run motel's clientele.

A shrill alarm call catapulted Konrad into wakefulness a little over twelve hours later and, refreshed by a combination of uninterrupted sleep and free coffee in the lobby, he'd soon hit the road. The prospect of another long drive and a one-sided battle amidst Chicago's traffic did little to dampen his mood, although the issue of the global media lingered. He couldn't turn on the radio without hearing of the Feds' search for his current location.

Surely he'd done enough to throw them off the scent once and for all?

Konrad lifted a hand from the steering wheel, scratched his head and decided the black hair and baseball cap definitely needed to go, now that they'd fulfilled their purpose. He paused at an intersection and carefully checked both ways for approaching vehicles. He couldn't afford to be involved in any kind of collision – and the fatal consequences it might lead to.

****

11.16am – BST
Nidd, North Yorkshire, England

Martin Boothroyd watched fat droplets of unexpected rain land on the windscreen and flicked a finger to activate the wipers' intermittent setting. High hedges rising to each side cocooned him in a dappled green tunnel, the tranquil illusion interrupted seconds later by a straggly branch batting the dark grey Vauxhall's side. He listened to a satnav device suctioned to the windscreen's interior announce the last stage of an uneventful ninety-minute journey from Preston then removed his foot from the accelerator to edge around a bend in the narrow road, mindful of farming vehicles being driven as if they were the only thing on the roads. The village appeared when trees gave way to low hedgerows and offered a fleeting view across rolling fields, before an assortment of houses blocked the panorama.

The monotonous voice barked its final instruction to make a left turn and the car came to a halt on a sweeping gravel driveway. Boothroyd pulled the key from the ignition and took a few seconds to admire Dennis Umpleby's detached stone property. At first, Kratz's uncle was suspicious of the telephone call he'd received the previous week, during which he'd been asked to provide a DNA sample for the transatlantic investigation into his estranged nephew's whereabouts. It had taken all Boothroyd's powers of persuasion to convince the man that he wasn't perpetrating a hoax.

Boothroyd opened the Vectra's boot and noticed the house's ornate wooden front door swing open. A man whom he guessed to be in his early sixties appeared in the porch, his slightly hunched shoulders hinting at either nervousness or irritation. Boothroyd used his free hand to slam the boot's lid closed and offered a smile.

'Dennis Umpleby?' he called, the words travelling above the sound of small pebbles crunching beneath his feet. 'I'm Martin Boothroyd from Preston Police. We spoke on the phone the other day.' He placed his briefcase on the ground and shook the other man's hand. 'Good to meet you.'

'I'd say it's nice to meet you,' Dennis replied as he led him into the house's dark interior. 'However, under the circumstances...'

Boothroyd nodded. 'It must have been quite a shock?'

'You could say that,' he replied. 'I'm only glad my late Mum joined Dad a couple of years ago. At least they'll never know what an evil little bastard their eldest grandson was.'

Boothroyd lowered himself into a dark red leather armchair. 'As a family, do you have any contact with Peter?'

Dennis shook his head. 'Not since the funeral. We flew out to Denver, got told it was a tragic accident and that Peter was lucky to survive. If only he'd been sitting in the front, things could've been so different.'

'You're married and have two adult children?' Boothroyd asked, smiling at a petite woman of a similar age to Dennis, who now waited with uncertainty near the doorway.

'This is my wife, Barbara,' he replied. 'Our son Michael and daughter Andrea are thirty and twenty-five respectively.'

Boothroyd stood to introduce himself and offer his apologies for the events prompting his visit. Barbara smiled sadly and welcomed him to what had been her parents-in-law's family home before the elderly couple moved into sheltered accommodation fifteen years earlier. Her offer of tea accepted, she left the room and he listened to her footfalls fade along the hallway's polished parquet flooring.

'You've got a beautiful home,' Boothroyd said, admiring the room's period features.

'Chris and I grew up in this house,' Dennis replied. 'He was eighteen months older than me. We used to share what became Michael's bedroom, and then I moved into Andrea's room when we got a bit older.'

'It's a lovely area to bring up a family,' Boothroyd added. 'Rural tranquillity, cracking scenery and you're not too far from Leeds if you want to go to the big city.'

'Chris loved it here, but there just wasn't the work. He got that printing job in Manchester, met Liesel and then they moved to Preston. They wanted to eventually move back closer to this area, but *things* don't always happen like you plan.'

Boothroyd's gaze settled on a framed black and white photo on the wall. 'You mean Peter?' he asked. A middle-aged couple and two young boys dressed in fifties attire returned his stare. 'Didn't they want children?'

'They were told they couldn't have any, and then they were given that one.'

'They must've thought he was a miracle?'

'Definitely,' Dennis replied tersely. 'They never deserved the grief he gave them.'

'You've said Peter was the longed-for only child, who your brother and his wife never thought they'd have. Did they spoil him?'

'Did they heck!' Dennis didn't attempt to hide his indignation. 'Chris was adamant about that. They tried for a second baby, but it didn't happen and when they realised he was the kid from hell they stopped. Didn't think they'd be able to cope if they ended up having another like him. It's a shame, they were good parents. Despite how he turned out, they'd done their best to turn him round.'

Their attention diverted to the door opening with a faint creak and Barbara pushed a large trolley into the room. A large pot of tea accompanied a milk jug, sugar bowl and a trio of brightly painted mugs, reminding Boothroyd he'd eaten breakfast over an hour earlier than usual that morning.

'Milk and sugar?'

Boothroyd repositioned the drink coaster closest to him. 'Both please,' he replied, watching her pour the hot amber liquid into a mug. 'And, those look delicious,' he added when he caught sight of a plate piled high with a selection of apparently homemade biscuits.

'Fresh out of the oven a couple of hours ago,' she confirmed. 'Most of them are my mother's recipes.'

For the next five minutes Boothroyd made a concerted effort to put the couple at their ease. Quiet small talk filled the room and he observed how they leaned into one another and occasionally finished each other's sentences, appearing not to notice their habit. He set down his empty teacup and smiled sympathetically at them.

'Were you aware of Konrad Kratz? I mean as an actor, not an alias of your nephew?'

Barbara gave an emphatic nod. 'Oh yes, Andrea's quite the fan of *H.O.S.T.A.G.E.* Got me watching it too. We never recognised him though. He doesn't look like how we remember Peter, and of course the accent threw us off. I suppose we just assumed he was an American.'

'Did you ever attempt to contact Peter?'

Dennis nodded. 'Around six months after the funeral. We never heard anything back.'

'You didn't try again?' Boothroyd asked, his eyebrows raised in surprise.

'Can't say we were too heartbroken,' Dennis replied. 'We'd tried, and assumed he wanted nothing more to do with us.'

'Did you see him regularly before the family emigrated?'

'Family occasions. That's it really. It was always nice to see Chris and Liesel, though we'd never fully relax if Peter came along.'

Boothroyd cleared his throat to dislodge a stubborn shortbread crumb. 'He disturbed you?' he eventually managed to ask, then whispered his thanks whilst Barbara refilled their mugs.

'He disturbed everyone,' he replied, the memories generating obvious anger. 'Michael wouldn't be alone in the same room. Peter was never blatantly nasty, but he really unsettled his cousins. Andrea was pretty scared of him.'

Barbara set down the empty teapot and nodded. 'She was too young to explain properly,' she said, a slight timidity present in her voice. 'She seemed very uneasy whenever they visited and became very clingy. She was really reluctant to be apart from either of us.'

Dennis reached for her hand. 'They then moved to the States and we didn't see the point in reminding her by asking her, so we eventually forgot how she'd been.'

'Were you sad to see them leave?'

'Very much so. But the new job was a great opportunity,' he replied. 'Can't blame Chris for taking it.'

'What about Peter?'

'Truthfully?' Dennis locked eyes with the detective. 'No. It meant he wouldn't be coming here to visit.'

An idea that the Umplebys knew more than they'd chosen to reveal flitted across Boothroyd's mind. 'Did he ever do anything specific to trigger alarm bells?'

'Not that I can remember. He just had this *aura* to him,' Dennis said. His gaze settled on the opposite wall, as if he was attempting to recall long-ago memories. 'The kid was unnerving, like you constantly had to watch your back. He put Chris and Liesel through hell.' He paused again and shook his head. 'Verbally abusive, staying out late, drinking, girls. Liesel phoned Barbara regularly and she'd often be distraught.'

'It must have been quite a shock to learn Kratz is actually your nephew?'

'You're not joking, son!' he replied and gave a half-hearted chuckle. 'I'm not into that Hollywood nonsense, but the wife and our daughter have followed the story. A handful of people locally know I'm his uncle, and you can bet your life if it gets out beyond the village some greedy bugger in Knaresborough will flog the story to one of the tabloids. Can't say I fancy having those parasites camped outside the gate.'

'We're hoping to keep details of your connection under wraps,' Boothroyd replied. 'However, there's no definite DNA profile for... I'm not sure whether to call him Konrad or Peter, you know.' He shrugged. 'Neither seems right. The FBI has obtained a probable DNA profile, and needs more DNA from a relative to confirm this.'

Dennis snorted derisively. 'I'd have thought the randy little sod would've left a trail of offspring in his wake.'

'He was fourteen when he went to Denver?' a surprised Boothroyd clarified, wondering what he'd hear next.

'It doesn't mean he wasn't into trying to get his end away. Chris had to contend with two irate families who said Peter tried to coerce their daughters into sexual activity.' He shook his head yet again. 'You're seriously telling me he's not got any kids?'

Boothroyd leaned forward and lowered his voice, hoping the couple would realise what he'd soon share was for their ears only. 'Between us, police in Los Angeles have located a baby they believe he fathered. Having your DNA profile would help confirm or deny this, in conjunction with the DNA sample taken from both his homes.'

Dennis broke the stunned silence and watched his wife process the revelation. 'I don't mind you having some of my cheek cells, but why spend all this time, effort and money if you already have Peter's DNA?'

'He used DNA from two other men to contaminate both his houses. Although he knew it wouldn't throw off the police forever, it's certainly done the trick in slowing the investigation and buying him some time and distance. If we can partially match your DNA to that from the baby whose mother swears blind Kratz fathered her daughter, and to one of the samples found at his homes, any suspect can be either ruled out or arrested based on the results.'

Dennis saw Boothroyd retrieve an A4-sized clear plastic package from his briefcase. He ran through the legalities and method used during the procedure, before permitting Dennis to fill in and sign the consent form. 'Once the investigation is over, your DNA profile will be destroyed,' he added. 'We don't add it to the National DNA Database.'

Boothroyd donned a pair of thin latex gloves and tore open a sealed packet containing what appeared to be an oversized serrated cotton bud. 'Open wide,' he said, flashing a hint of a grin as he swept the stick over the inside of Dennis' left cheek. 'One down, one to go,' he added, deftly snapped the end of the wand and let it drop into a sample pot, then repeated the procedure on the opposite side. 'We'll put a rush on this; the big bosses have agreed to pay extra for the priority service.'

Dennis nodded and ran his tongue around the inside of his mouth. 'You'll keep me updated?' he asked. 'Chris and I were pretty close growing up, and I still miss him. Justice needs to be served.'

****

'You're seriously telling me this piece of shit is a drug lord?' Gibson spluttered in disbelief. He loosened his tie and stared through to the interrogation room. 'He looks like he's been sleeping rough under a flyover for the past decade.'

'All part of the act,' Mosley replied, noticing a frantic Lennie Stringer and his attorney confer. 'Claims he's never supplied drugs to anybody before, even though I called in a little favour informing me otherwise.' He laughed at Gibson's puzzled expression. 'A certain middle-aged actor who did a stint in rehab for a painkiller addiction. He owed me big time.'

Gibson whistled when the sound of Stringer's fist bouncing off the table penetrated the one-way glass. 'Who?' he demanded.

'Dwayne Fortuna.'

'No shit? How the hell did *he* owe you a favour?'

'Dumb bastard claims to be happily married, but it turns out he's gay as they come,' Mosley replied, rolling his eyes. 'You know how narrow-minded it is in Tinseltown, even today. Do you remember that missing Atwater teenager pimping his own ass in Hollywood three summers ago?'

Gibson shook his head. 'Don't think I worked that case.'

'I caught Fortuna cruising for rent boys off Santa Monica Boulevard this one time I received a tip-off and went searching for the kid. Sent Mr Big Ass Movie Star away with a warning not to come back, else I'd call his wife and the papers. Couple of days later a letter arrived at the station. He thanked me for my discretion and offered his services as a Hollywood snitch.'

'So you called him?' Gibson struggled to hide his grin. 'You devious bastard.'

Mosley winked and patted the younger detective on the shoulder. 'Yeah, he confirmed Lennie Stringer used to supply him with Percocet. Harry Lee claims Stringer gave Kratz his name and number and, along with Fortuna's previous purchases, we've gotten ourselves a pretty good case. Lee said Kratz asked if he knew who could supply him with painkillers and strong antibiotics. Lee and Stringer know plenty about each other's businesses, so you can't tell me they didn't have a mutually beneficial business relationship. We now need to make him crack.'

'You've seen who his attorney is, right?' Gibson said and swallowed nervously. 'The guy's a shark – knows every loophole going. He ain't interested in keeping scumbags off the street, he just wants a fatter wallet.'

'So what do you suggest?' Mosley interrupted. 'Just let the bastard go?'

'No, but neither of us wants to deal with Saul Keaton. And, this involves drugs, so why not call in the DEA?'

Mosley pulled out his cell phone and chuckled. 'Good call. Let's see how he fares against James Higgins.'

****

2.01pm – PDT
Stateline, Nevada

Sam leaned back in his chair and, along with the other two agents who'd gathered in the conference room, contemplated an information board revealed by Jed Masters minutes earlier. At its centre, a multitude of colour-coded lines criss-crossed Lake Tahoe and its immediate surroundings, snaking between photos of the evidence they'd obtained so far.

'Okay,' Masters began, intending to bring the briefing to a close after he'd shared two recent developments in the case. 'This guy here...' he pointed at a photo of an overweight man, 'is almost certainly Dirk Tyler. We believe him to be the leader of this cult, for want of a better word.'

Colleen Dexter, an athletic woman in her early thirties assigned to Stateline's Resident Agency nearly three years earlier, frowned at Tyler's photo. 'Are they claiming any religious affiliation?' she asked.

'Nothing specific at present,' Masters confirmed. 'Background checks were run on Tyler, assuming it's him. He did a ten stretch in San Francisco for burglarising elderly people in neighbourhoods adjacent to his, so let's assume he targets vulnerable sections of the community.'

'And, who's more vulnerable than a person facing emotional or spiritual upheaval in their lives?' Dexter said, a quiver of anger audible. Her hand subconsciously travelled to the gold crucifix beneath her blouse and stroked the warm metal. 'Connect to them, offer what's missing from their lives... maybe acceptance and love, or a sense of belonging.' She saw

Masters raise his eyebrows. 'And then the isolation starts. If they have money, persuade them to donate it, or maybe demand payment in sexual terms. People abusing religion to further their own agenda makes me so mad.'

'What our guy's into is presently unknown,' Masters continued. 'In prison he appeared to have some kind of revelation, saw the light and all that bullshit. He'd preach sermons to anyone who wanted to listen, and many more who didn't.' His gaze fell on the team's newest member. 'Bury, see what else you can dig up on our good shepherd.'

Sam's attention drifted back to the case and he nodded. 'Consider it done,' he replied, trying to ignore the reawakened memories from two days earlier.

Matt Jessop cleared his throat and raised a hand. 'What about sending someone in?' he suggested in a rich Louisiana drawl. 'Someone lost and seeking salvation in a place they'll finally be loved, bathed in the light of whoever they're worshipping this week.'

'The thought crossed my mind already,' Masters admitted. 'Their total lack of direction makes me wonder whether it's really a cover for something way more sinister than a bunch of hippies waiting for the flying saucer carrying their god to land.'

Jessop, of Creole heritage on his mother's side, nodded his head of thick, dark curls. 'So if we don't do that, we risk playing a waiting game for months, or maybe years?'

Sam nodded. *Welcome to my world,* he thought bitterly and half-listened to Masters conclude the briefing.

Chapter 35 – Tuesday 25th August 2009

Detective Harry Irwin held the thick wooden door open and waited for Steve Garner to enter the police station's family liaison room. To one side, a small window's patterned glass permitted natural light to enter, yet maintained the privacy of those inside. Irwin pointed to a drinks machine perched on top of a small fridge. 'Coffee or tea?' he asked. 'Or there's bottled water in the fridge, if you'd prefer.'

Steve sunk into one of two recently re-upholstered armchairs. 'Coffee's great, thanks.'

'So, how are you coping?' Irwin asked as he programmed the machine.

'Me? I'm managing okay, I suppose. It's Charlotte I'm worried about. She's not dealing with this too well. She can't understand why anyone wanted to murder her dad and, because nothing was stolen, you've said it wasn't a burglary gone wrong.'

'To be honest, son, we're struggling,' Irwin replied. He watched a jet of muddy brown liquid fill the paper cup and cringed at the knowledge of how it would taste. 'Until we establish a motive, we can't start to narrow down any suspects – other than that Porter fellow who Roger gave notice to vacate.'

Steve thanked Irwin and sipped his drink. 'He didn't mention any new business ventures and, because the pub and restaurant are so successful, he didn't really have time,' he said, conscious not to wince when the bitter liquid coated his throat. 'He said he wanted to gradually wind down ready for retirement. Said he'd got too long in the tooth for it all.'

'Maybe there was a deal gone sour from back in the day?' Irwin suggested, even though they'd already considered such a possibility.

'Your guess is as good as mine.'

Steve's frown stirred Irwin's interest. 'You've thought of something?'

'Maybe,' Steve replied, although Irwin detected a lack of conviction. 'A few weeks ago, he said something about an American investor wanting his share back. Roger got pissed off because he couldn't lay his hands on the cash immediately and this guy kept putting pressure on him to pay up.'

'Were they in direct contact?'

'I've no idea,' he answered. 'Can't you check phone records? I've seen them do it on TV.'

Irwin smiled, having heard similar comments many times in recent years. 'It takes time.'

Steve recalled something else, opened his mouth to speak, and then hesitated. 'There was this weird incident, if you can call it that, in the pub recently,' he eventually said. 'Some English guy came in for a meal and said he'd come back to the area for a job interview. Roger turned up just as he left and asked who the American was.'

'You didn't think to ask him more?'

'Not really,' Steve replied. 'I just thought he'd misheard because of traffic noise from out front. Roger brushed it off, probably put it down to getting old like he usually does.' He shook his head. '*Did*. You reckon there's a link?'

Irwin's pencil flew in a frantic path over a reporter's style notepad he'd brought to the meeting. 'Roger grumbles some business deal from across the Pond went sour, a stranger turns up in the pub and Roger thinks he's American.' There was a light tap as he set down the pencil. 'Could be coincidence, could be someone faking their accent.'

'He sounded English to me. Maybe with a hint of southerner.'

'Some people are good mimics,' Irwin replied. He stretched out his cramping fingers and picked up the pencil again. 'Can you give me a description?'

'Around my age, quite tall, dark hair. He ordered pie and chips, if I recall correctly.'

'Do you keep till receipts?'

'We keep records of all financial transactions,' Steve said. 'That won't help if he paid cash though.'

'And you have CCTV?'

'Yeah, behind the bar and above the door. You want me to find his visit? It's a digital system, so we can store all footage from the previous month.'

'That'll be a great help.'

Steve stared Irwin squarely in the eye. 'You think there's something in this?'

'I bloody well hope so,' he replied, worried he may have inadvertently raised the family's hopes. 'Obviously we'll keep an open mind, but unless something else comes to light it's the best thing we've got.'

****

9.30am – PDT
San Fernando Road, Los Angeles, California

Emilio Muñoz leaned back in his chair and reached for a rapidly cooling cup of coffee. 'It's like looking for Bigfoot,' he grumbled, re-reading the email Mosley forwarded before he'd left to meet DEA Agent Higgins. 'The Feds' analysis of Kratz's movements was meant to narrow down search areas.'

'And did it?' a hopeful Gibson enquired.

Muñoz snorted derisively. 'Depends how you classify the whole US and half of Europe.'

'I see Stringer's still reluctant to talk,' Hallberg added, keen to deflect the conversation to something marginally less likely to raise their collective blood pressure.

'That may change,' Muñoz replied.

'Oh yeah, the Mosley and Higgins show,' Hallberg replied, referring to the pre-arranged interview due to commence soon. 'Poor guy, having to face those two.'

The others grinned, knowing Mosley's bark to be frequently worse than his bite – although the same couldn't always be said for Higgins. A fiery-haired and fiery-tempered Scotsman, his sharp brain and no-nonsense approach meant he'd ascended the ranks at the DEA's Los Angeles Division since arriving in the US nearly two decades earlier. Mosley's decision to bring in Higgins was based on years of experience, telling him the man now known to be a major player in the Hollywood celebrity drug supply circuit would reveal his secrets – if only to reduce the sizeable jail term he faced.

'Maybe Kratz bought his drugs from Stringer because he'd heard of him on the grapevine?' Gibson drank the last of his coffee. 'Do you think he gave him any information about where he intended to go?'

'That's if Stringer knew it was Kratz doing the buying,' Hallberg replied.

Muñoz raised an eyebrow. 'You think they made small talk during a drug deal?'

'Maybe he tried to convince Stringer he ain't law enforcement,' Hallberg countered, irritated by Muñoz's flippant tone.

The conversation died and they returned their attention to a pile of case files, the perpetrators behind a recent spate of late night carjackings still no closer to being caught. A heavy silence descended and hung in the air until Mosley burst into the room and headed straight for the coffee maker.

Gibson spoke first. 'Please tell me he fessed up.'

'We won't learn anything more about Kratz, but plenty of pissed off celebrities are going to be looking for a new dealer.'

'Did he know he was selling to Kratz?'

'He says not,' Mosley said, failing to hide his anger. 'Apparently it's well known Kratz didn't do drugs.'

Gibson nodded. 'That figures. You don't want to get caught for a drugs offence if you're a serial killer on the sly.'

'And living under an alias,' Hallberg added.

Muñoz dropped a sheaf of papers onto his desk. 'So we're back to square one?'

'Looks like it,' Mosley agreed and glanced at the doorway. 'But at least our *wee pal* through there seems to be having a totally awesome day.'

****

7.09pm – CDT
Bismarck, North Dakota

ABC News hadn't made for cheerful viewing that evening, especially when one of the main reports featured his disappearance and hinted at the extent of the resulting manhunt. Konrad sighed and dropped the TV's remote control onto the bed, the display of irritation solely for his benefit as he stretched out on its quilted comforter.

A monotonous eight-hour drive north-east from Minneapolis had done little to improve his mood. He'd paid scant attention to the feelings of isolation offered by this sparsely populated region, where wide expanses of grassland flanked I-94 before stretching into the distance. North Dakota was wasted on him, its desolate beauty beneath an expansive clear blue sky merely an alternative route on his journey west.

The recently constructed hotel occupied a clearly visible spot from the Interstate, its immaculate exterior and a total absence of trash blowing around the parking lot a cut above the lodgings he'd tolerated for the past two nights. The only problem with hotels of this standard was their insistence on seeing at least one form of identification. Thankfully, the last fake driver's licence in his current collection had led to a smooth check-in experience.

Konrad padded across to the window and watched a bloated orange sun swallow the last morsels of daylight before disappearing beneath the horizon. It certainly wouldn't hurt to get an early night when he faced another long day behind the wheel. He closed the drapes and marvelled at how easily he'd formulated his series of lies and disguises over the years, enabling him to evade the public's seemingly insatiable desire to follow his every move.

They'd never discovered exactly where he went on some of his weekends off.

****

10.13pm – PDT
Kingsbury, Nevada

'Can't believe it's only Tuesday,' Sam grumbled as he climbed into bed. 'Time passes so slowly here.'

Anna rolled over and draped an arm across his waist. 'Hey,' she said, lifting her head so she could kiss his shoulder. 'You know they'll find him, right?'

He turned off his bedside lamp and plunged the room into darkness. 'Yeah, and how long will that take?'

'I understand your frustration,' she whispered. 'Not knowing is what really pisses me off.'

Sam sighed. 'We may never be able to go home.'

'I keep telling you he'll slip up.'

'And I keep saying you can't really believe that.'

'He lives a double life for fifteen years and one incident unravels all those lies.'

'So, he'll be on his guard even more.'

'He'll be on edge, nervous and more likely to make another mistake,' Anna replied. She snuggled closer and stroked Sam's bare chest. 'And, since Milne mentioned that reward, people are going to be actively looking for him.'

'We don't know if he's in the country.'

'He fled to Europe, but unless he has money there he can't live on thin air. He's had ample opportunity to set up a bolt hole and stash some cash.' She wondered for a split-second if she was trying to convince herself, rather than Sam. 'He'll be back, you mark my words.'

'And that's when it ends,' Sam commented, surprising Anna with the darkness in his tone. He planted a kiss on her cheek and moved his mouth closer to hers. 'Once and for all.'

Chapter 36 – Wednesday 26ᵗʰ August 2009

9.45am – BST
Blackpool, England

The sheer volume of traffic in the town centre's concrete maze left Steve Garner unsure whether to be surprised or relieved he'd encountered little difficulty locating a space in the pay and display car park adjacent to the police station. Steve noted the building's deserted reception area, something he was sure wouldn't be the same twelve hours into the future, even mid-week. He'd exchanged pleasantries with the middle-aged receptionist at the front desk until Harry Irwin arrived to escort him up to a suite of sparsely furnished third floor offices, around half of which lacked any natural light.

Steve sipped a surprisingly decent cup of coffee and waited for the detective to access the pub's CCTV footage for the fortnight leading up to Roger's death. Irwin had decided to work back from the day preceding the discovery of Roger's lifeless body and scrolled through all footage recorded between five and eight in the evening, his methodical approach rewarded fifteen minutes later by Steve jabbing a finger at the screen.

'That's him!'

'You're sure?'

'Yeah. He comes in, sits down, reads the menu and comes up to the bar to place an order. Drinks his beer, eats his meal, pays as he declines pudding and then heads for the door.' He fell silent and watched the man say the briefest of words to Roger, walk calmly through the door and disappear onto Friargate.

Irwin tried to ignore the adrenaline coursing through his body. 'Have you remembered anything else Roger told you?' he pressed.

Steve shook his head. 'He brushed it off. Seemed embarrassed because I'd said the guy sounded English.' The unexpected intensity of his gaze startled Irwin. 'What happens next?'

'I'll isolate the clearest images and see if we can get facial recognition done,' Irwin replied. 'We also need to talk to this customer, if only to eliminate him from our inquiries,'

'How are you going to do that?'

'Put simply, we'll try to find him on CCTV and trace him back to a home or vehicle.'

'Do you think he's the killer?' Steve asked. 'I mean, who'd want to kill an old man?'

'He's the only suspect we have at the moment.' Irwin wondered if he'd offered Steve an excessive amount of false hope. 'I'll give Eddie a ring, see if he can get the ball rolling.'

****

5.31pm – PDT
Kiva Beach, South Lake Tahoe, California

Anna clapped and cheered her daughter's unsteady run through the fine sand grains towards a small blue and orange football. 'Go get it!' she called. 'And throw it back to Daddy. Let's see if he can catch it *this* time.'

Angela giggled loudly and dropped to her knees to pick up the ball. 'Silly Daddy!' she exclaimed when Sam held out his hands and pretended to look sad. Gently undulating water nearby momentarily distracted him from the family's picnic and his eyes followed the succession of tiny waves, temporarily rendering him oblivious to everything else. The ball landed beside Anna and she immediately jumped to her feet and threw the ball back to Angela, who squealed in delight for the entire time it took for her mother to run towards her and grab the ball from her fingers.

Sam smoothed away a wrinkle on the oversized beach rug and smiled at John's expert grab for a piece of buttered bread, which he immediately pushed into his mouth with a dexterity beyond his age. An unexpected sense of contentment diffused through Sam as he chewed a pair of cherry tomatoes and listened to his wife and daughter's carefree play, realising he'd developed more of an appetite than at any time in the past week. His smile faded when a buttery fist grabbed the clean t-shirt he'd changed into less than an hour earlier and his attention returned to the chuckling baby, who'd rolled on to his side in an attempt to reach the last ham sandwich.

'You're still hungry?' Sam tore some crust from the soft white bread and offered it to John, whose chubby hands clenched the small piece of food and lifted it to his mouth. The new texture elicited a frown and Sam cupped a hand ready to catch any rejected food. 'I don't know what your sister will say about you stealing her butties. You're lucky, you know,' Sam continued as John's wide blue-grey eyes stared at him, his voice low so Anna wouldn't hear. 'All this upheaval and you're happier than ever. Perhaps I should try harder to accept this may be our permanent home. Our family has stayed together this time, so does it really matter where we live?' He paused to think whilst John inspected a second piece of crust. 'At least it's a nice area and my new colleagues are decent enough.'

John appeared to be listening intently to Sam and fixed his father in an earnest gaze. 'But surely it's better to find Kratz, and then we can return to Colorado?' Sam added, the subject of his monologue inaudible to Anna, who took Angela's hand and led her into the cold water, where a succession of tiny waves lapped around their calves. He felt a sinking sensation and almost a minute passed before he spoke again. 'I realise you two would miss the beach, but I miss our real home and working in Denver. Mommy's family must surely miss us too.'

They watched Angela run towards the blanket, push her feet into the warm sand and wiggle them back and forth. 'It's so cold, Daddy!' she shouted. 'My toes turned to ice.'

'And so did mine,' Anna said. She wrinkled her nose at the sight of John squeezing the last of the sandwich until liquefied butter seeped through his fingers. 'Looks like you taught him how to make a mess.'

'It's a guy thing,' Sam replied. 'That's why I always forget to put the beer bottles out for recycling. He'll be the same when he's older.'

Angela flopped down beside him and stared at the greasy marks on Sam's t-shirt. 'My toes are okay now,' she announced. A middle-aged couple taking it in turns to throw a ball into the water for a pair of chocolate Labradors gained her attention and she gazed longingly at the dogs, wishing that one day she'd be allowed a pet of her own.

Sam ruffled her hair and smiled at Anna's attempts to wipe the grease from John's hands. 'I'm glad to hear that, sweetheart.' Satisfied his family was as safe as possible, he casually scanned the distant mountains ringing the tranquil lake and registered more of the tension he'd harboured since their relocation slipping away.

He'd protect them at all costs.

****

9.57pm – MDT
Idaho Falls, Idaho

A fine spray of warm water, perhaps a little too warm, rebounded from Konrad's face and chest as he leaned into the shower's pressurised spray. The latest part of his journey had taken him through another mind-numbing experience – excluding the scenic interlude through the northernmost part of Yellowstone National Park, carefully sandwiched between I-94 and I-90's unrelenting tedium. He'd stopped to stretch his legs at the geothermal terraces above Mammoth Hot Springs, close to where a three-night camping trip during his second summer in the country had allowed his parents to fulfil their dream of visiting the National Park. Today he hadn't stopped for long enough to let the incessant stench of sulphur permeate his clothing and hair; reluctant to join the crowds of tourists cooing in excitement every time the baked ground belched forth another cloud of steam.

Konrad reached for the last of the complimentary shower gel, worked the product into a thick lather and massaged his neck and shoulders. His hands moved down across his chest and abdomen, and a familiar tenderness he'd been less aware of for the past week demanded he wipe the soap from his eyes and inspect the area around the healed exit wound. Although it had faded to a less angry shade of red he noticed the increased tension in the surrounding musculature and frowned at the idea of developing late complications. Surely after this amount of time he could assign it to being hunched at a steering wheel and driving a couple of thousand miles in four days?

Reassured by this more rational explanation and the prospect of reaching his destination soon, Konrad stepped out of the shower and grabbed a towel.

Chapter 37 – Thursday 27th August 2009

3.32pm – BST
Blackpool Police Station, England

An out-of-breath Eddie Pell slumped into a chair and gave an exasperated shake of his head. 'Bloody woman's bus got back late from ASDA,' he eventually managed to offer by way of an explanation for his lateness. 'Silly cow made me wait while she put half a tonne of frozen shite into the freezer, then traffic was murder getting out of Preston because of those bastard roadworks on North Road. Anyone would think she didn't want that burglar caught.'

Harry Irwin narrowed his eyes. 'You weren't supping a brew and munching a cream bun?'

'Not bloody likely! You should've seen the state of the place,' a grimacing Pell replied. 'Even the E.coli in the kitchen were trying to make a bid for freedom.' He draped his jacket over the back of his chair. 'You making me a cuppa? I'm gasping here!'

Irwin nodded an affirmative and covered the short distance to a small kitchenette, where he grabbed two large mugs from the sink. 'Can't believe some lazy bastard didn't wash up again,' he grumbled. 'If I ever find out who keeps leaving their crap in the sink I'm going to throttle their lazy arse.'

'Wasn't me. Her indoors has me trained better than any circus bear,' came the immediate reply. 'Hence I jump whenever you order me over to this godforsaken wasteland.'

Pell's three decades of experience and high conviction rate made him the obvious choice to liaise between Blackpool and Preston during the hunt for Roger Mortimer's killer. The veteran detective had decided to make this his last high profile investigation, and wasted no time in informing the Superintendent of his intention to retire once the case was solved – a decision now driving him to find whoever committed Roger's murder as quickly as possible.

Irwin carefully lowered two steaming mugs of tea onto his desk. 'Mustn't forget the biccies,' he announced, pulling a packet of chocolate digestives from where he'd wedged it beneath his upper arm.

'Is that your idea of five-a-day?' Irwin asked, raising an eyebrow whilst Pell carefully arranged a stack beside his mug.

'Nothing has entered this belly since breakfast and I'm bloody starving,' Pell replied. 'Good job it's the missus' birthday and I've promised to take her out for a meal tonight.'

Irwin dunked his first biscuit into the beige liquid. 'Anywhere nice?' he asked.

Pell chuckled. 'She likes it at the Edward II, but she'd go ape if I took her there and started asking folk questions.'

'Yeah, don't want to make it your last anniversary, eh?' Irwin's gaze settled on Pell's battered brown leather briefcase. 'I hear you've made some progress tracing their mystery customer?'

'Yeah,' Pell replied, his voice muffled by the biscuit he'd forced whole into his mouth. He reached into the briefcase presented by his team when he'd clocked up twenty-five years of service and leafed through a cardboard file of images isolated by CCTV operators the previous day. 'Thursday 13th August, just after half seven on Friargate. Do you think that's the same man Steve Garner identified? The time stamps tally up.'

Irwin studied the image Pell handed to him. 'Yeah, he definitely looks like the Yank.'

'I've got all the footage on a hard drive.' Pell rummaged in the briefcase again and handed the device to Irwin. 'It gets better, you know,' he added, his eyes gleaming as a series of surprisingly crisp images played across the screen. 'He leaves the pub, crosses Friargate and walks up Great Shaw Street, from where he drives off in a dark Vauxhall Astra. We sent the enhanced plate to the DVLA for identification. Turns out it's a hire car from a branch of Avis in central London, and was rented to an Anthony Collins on Monday 3rd August.'

Irwin watched the car set off in the direction of Preston's inner ring road. 'Wonder if he's still driving it?'

'No he's not,' Pell replied. 'He dumped it in a long-stay car park at Heathrow Airport last Saturday. Staff became suspicious when it wasn't collected yesterday, so they impounded it.'

'Who's this Anthony Collins?'

Pell swallowed his third digestive biscuit. 'I've phoned Avis' head office and they're going to send me the car's tracking data. That should tell us if he's been anywhere near Mortimer's home, or anywhere else of personal significance to either him or Mortimer.'

Irwin placed the folder on the desk and gulped the last of his coffee. 'About bloody time we started making progress. Let's hope the bugger turns up quickly.'

****

3.27pm – PDT
Winnemucca, Nevada

Konrad blinked repeatedly and rubbed his eyes to lessen the dusty sting delivered by an unexpected gust of hot dry wind. An hour earlier, the sudden appearance of the Avenger's refuelling lamp forced him to leave I-80's anonymity for an enforced break in this sleepy desert town, where he'd also taken the opportunity to deaden the hollow feeling in his stomach. His smarting eyes took in the distant mountains to the north, dappled by scattered clouds loitering in a deep blue sky – a colour he'd missed during his time in England. He certainly wouldn't miss the endless summer rain on the other side of the Atlantic either.

The ominous whine of an ageing red Ford pick-up faded and Konrad scanned the town's wide main street, bordered on either side by small town businesses and parked cars. He reached the opposite sidewalk and inspected at his reflection in the glass frontage of a women's fashion store. The man who returned his stare mimicked a pronounced frown and stroked what remained of their hair. Admittedly he never recalled styling it so short, but wasn't his main objective to avoid recognition and evade capture?

With one last look in each direction, Konrad unlocked the Avenger, slid into the driver's seat and turned the ignition key. The engine came to life and he re-checked his hair in the rear-view mirror until a trio of vehicles passed. Maybe he'd make the style – if you could call it that – less obvious by returning to the mousey brown shade he'd favoured in the past. He'd need to cook up a plausible excuse for such a dramatic change now he no longer needed to wear the wig.

The neighbours would surely pass comment.

****

6.18pm – EDT
Port Authority Technical Center, Jersey City, New Jersey

An hour later than he'd usually leave work, detective Jim Meaker powered down his computer and tried to ignore the temptation of a slice of pizza from his favourite café across the street. His screen faded for the next fourteen hours and he felt a familiar light-hearted punch land on his upper arm. Marie Goldstein, a twenty-year veteran of the team Meaker was assigned to five years earlier, also lived in Hoboken and they regularly carpooled together.

Meaker grabbed his car keys and pointed at the door. 'Ready to roll?'

'As I'll ever be,' she replied. 'It's been one hell of a busy afternoon. At lunchtime, I picked up a request from some Hicksville police department in England who think their main suspect in a murder case fled the country. Some guy named Anthony Collins dumped a rental car at Heathrow Airport last Saturday and, according to the airport's flight records, boarded an airplane to JFK.'

'Five days ago?' he asked, unable to hide his incredulity. 'Don't they realise what a big country this is? This guy may be anywhere by now.'

Goldstein nodded. 'They're hoping we can point them in the right direction – literally.'

'Is he American?'

'Maybe,' she replied with a non-committal shrug.

'Maybe?' he echoed. They left the room and fell into step along a wide door-lined corridor, where harsh artificial lighting loaned a sallow tint to both their complexions.

'One witness says he sounds English; however, the old man who ended up suffocated in...' she articulated the words carefully, '*cling film* referred to him as a *bloody Yank*.'

Meaker gave an amused snort. 'This *bloody Yank* don't know what the hell *cling film* is.'

'It's like Saran Wrap.'

'How'd you know that?'

She winked. 'Google.'

Meaker nodded. 'So you're on it?'

Goldstein pressed the button to summon the elevator. 'We are.'

'We?'

They heard a sharp ping and the polished metal doors slid back to reveal an empty elevator. 'That's right,' Goldstein shot back. 'If the surveillance footage I've asked for doesn't arrive by tomorrow morning, how does a little date out at the airport grab you?'

****

6.54pm – PDT

Kingsbury Grade Road, Kingsbury, Nevada

Sam pedalled frantically, ignoring the blood that pounded through his head and the burning protest of every muscle fibre in his legs. The steady pace of previous evenings was forgotten, displaced by an angry tornado of thoughts.

Will it ever really be home here? Or will we have to flee – again?

Colin Milne's email got straight to the point before the words blurred, its facts stated with clinical coldness: their European sleuthing had finally reaped results.

Konrad Kratz, using the alias Andreas Baum, had been traced from Augsburg to London via Paris. Sam, already wearing his cycling attire, pushed back his chair and pressed the computer off at the main button. He'd slung his backpack over his shoulders and barrelled past a surprised Jed Masters, bidding him a strangulated farewell once through the door.

Cars whizzed past Sam on his ascent and, not for the first time, he noticed how many drivers favoured the sturdy four-wheel drive vehicles better suited to Tahoe's winter snowfalls. Would the family experience a Kingsbury Christmas, or celebrate (or not) elsewhere? His thoughts returned to Kratz's return to England: was he there to rake in past debts or locate a hidden stash of cash, and then traverse international borders again? Or, maybe he'd viewed his homeland as a stepping stone on his way back to America?

Will that piece of shit ever get caught?

Sam steered around two snaking bends, oblivious to how his breath now came in ragged gasps. Until that moment, whenever he contemplated his family's future he'd always hoped they'd return to Golden. Could they really ever go back to exactly how it was one year and one week ago? That one day in the future they'd retrospectively view this time in their lives as if they'd been in some bad TV movie?

He doubted it immensely.

Additional doubts over his future at the Critical Situation Research Unit had also increased over the past six weeks. A life with his family always ranked as more important than climbing the greasy pole in the Big Apple, cementing his plan that if they ever apprehended Kratz he'd quit, devote himself to the Denver Field Office and go home every night – instead of spending four or sometimes five nights out of fourteen in a Manhattan hotel.

To compound the matter, what should have been quiet, family-oriented weekends had become increasingly difficult since his post-accident return to the CSRU position. One weekend he'd return to Golden, exhausted from the intensive hours required whilst in New York. The next weekend, only marginally rejuvenated by more regular hours in Denver, the knowledge he'd soon have to head east descended like an ever-thickening fog.

He knew it was only so long before he'd snap.

The last stretch up North Benjamin Drive to the cabin pushed Sam to his limits. He paused on its driveway to catch his breath and stared through the sweetly scented pines to Lake Tahoe's distant mirror-like deep blue waters, its tranquillity juxtaposed against his own feelings.

A shaking hand inserted a key into the lock.

The other balled into a fist.

Epilogue – Friday 28th August 2009

8.54am – PDT
Mattole Road, near South Lake Tahoe, California

Dale Hargreaves emitted a heavy sigh and watched his mental list of *things to do* commence its mocking scroll against his closed eyelids. To compound matters, a late arrival at the cabin only hours earlier meant he'd neglected to program the central heating to kick in around the time the sun rose above the Sierra Nevada's rugged expanse. Chilly mornings were a definite disadvantage of being over six thousand feet above sea level, even during the summer months; a fact confirmed when a reluctant foot emerged from its warm cocoon.

He opened his eyes, threw back the blanket and groaned. Cold air wrapped itself around his toned physique as he padded to the small, Nordic-style bathroom and a succession of profanities followed, now he realised there'd be no hot water for at least another thirty minutes. A man in his mid-thirties stared back at him from the mirror, a successful business analyst and writer from San Francisco – according to the owners of the nearest cabin, located past a row of tall spruce. He rolled his eyes and reached for a pair of glasses, convinced their brown rectangular metallic frames made him resemble a high school physics teacher.

It had been a while since he'd visited the cabin and it would take a couple of days to make the place comfortable, especially as he'd be *working* from there for the next few weeks. He glared at his reflection again and shook his head at the thought of the previous afternoon when he'd asked the barber for a more manageable style, only to learn of their differing opinions once most of his hair lay on the barbershop's floor.

Goddamn redneck.

Once he'd relieved the dull throb of a full bladder, Konrad Kratz reached into the Walgreens bag he'd dumped behind the bathroom door and carefully placed a small box of hair dye on a narrow glass shelf above the sink. Maybe later he'd be able to take a trip into town, safe in the knowledge he'd seamlessly blend into the mix of residents and tourists enjoying summer in the mountains.

Printed in Poland
by Amazon Fulfillment
Poland Sp. z o.o., Wrocław